SEVEN AGAINST MARS

SEVEN AGAINST MARS

MARTIN BERMAN-GORVINE

WILDSIDE PRESS

This one's for Daniel and Jonathan, my first readers this time. And in memory of Dr. Elsie Wiedner, who introduced me to the world of Mark Twain, and Ray Bradbury, magician of Mars.

Published by Wildside Press LLC.
www.wildsidebooks.com

BOOK ONE

MORNING STAR

Jack pushed his way cautiously
through the grayish-green Venusian
foliage. An Earthling would have found
the day overcast and broiling hot,
but to Jack it was on the cool side,
with a tang in the air that hinted at
the approach of the feared Venusian
monsoon. However, the storm was at
least an Earth-day away, and was the
least of his concerns at the moment,
for his beloved Anya, the girl with
the flame-colored hair who had captured
his heart, was trapped in the coils of
the dreaded Greater Venusian Medusa,
somewhere deep in this horrible
wilderness....

Rachel Zilber paused with her fingers poised over the typewriter keys, staring at the half-filled page. Did that sound right? Despite years of relentless drilling from Dad and nightly exposure to the BBC on the forbidden, battery-powered wireless set, she still worried about her command of English. Those prim-and-proper British newsreaders were no help in learning the slang she needed to write for the American pulps. For that, she had only her precious collection of *Astounding Science-Fiction*, *Amazing Stories* and the rest that her cousin Abe had mailed her from New York the summer before the war began. Three years had passed. Was her slang out of date? And now that the Americans were in the war too, had they lost their appetite for science fiction and started thinking it was a worthless, juvenile waste of time?

If so, they would have a strong ally in Mom. "What are you wasting your time on that rubbish for?" she would cry whenever she saw Rachel huddled over one of the dog-eared magazines with their garish covers. "You've got to stay up to date with your schoolwork! This war's not going to last forever, you know, and when the Germans are beaten you'd better be prepared to finish high school and take your university entrance exams!" Rachel didn't have the heart to share her growing fears that the

Germans wouldn't let them live to see the end of the war. Maybe if she didn't say so aloud, it wouldn't come true. So she studied her calculus and Polish literature textbooks and ventured out into the streets of the ghetto, where the sound of shooting was becoming more common every day, as little as possible. It was safer to stay in the smelly, crumbling little apartment, even though it was barely the size of her old room and she had to share it with her parents, bratty ten-year-old Sonya Goldberg and her even more obnoxious seven-year-old sister Shoshie, and *their* parents. And no one ever let her write in peace! Mrs. Goldberg always complained about "that clack, clack, clacking" while her horrible little girls always pestered her.

Sure enough, Sonya leaned over her shoulder, whining, "Whatcha writing?"

"None of your damn business!" Rachel leaned forward to cover the page.

"Oo, you used a bad word! I'm gonna tell my mommy you used a bad word, and she's gonna tell your daddy, and girl, you are gonna get a spaaan-king...."

"Don't you ever call me 'girl' again, you little brat! You tell on me and see if your precious little dollies stay in one piece!"

Sonya's face worked as if she was about to cry, tainting Rachel's satisfaction with guilt that bubbled from her gut like the sour aftertaste of Mrs. Goldberg's horrible cooking. Not that anybody could do anything much with the moldy potato ration they were getting these days. She huddled deeper into her corner, trying to ignore Sonya's nasty words to Shoshie and the hard little knot of hunger in the pit of her stomach— breakfast had been a half-slice of stale bread. At least she still had her precious though dwindling store of paper, mainly blank pages ripped out of old books that she'd been able to scrounge or barter for here and there. After a moment, she typed:

```
    Princess Anya was beautiful, with
the delicate long-limbed loveliness
of a native Martian raised in the Red
Planet's lesser gravity, and from the
moment he first saw her looking lost
and bewildered as she emerged from the
immigrants' quarantine at Aphrodite
Port, Jack knew that they were meant
for each other and that it was his
duty to protect her. And that was
```

before he even knew that she was a
refugee from the evil Lord Ares II.

Jack swore as he hacked his way
through the thick undergrowth with his
electric machete. It had been almost
twenty-four hours since Anya had run
away into the jungle after catching a
glimpse of a tall, spindly man with
the telltale chin-beard of the police
caste serving the current Martian
tyrant, whom she always referred to
disdainfully as "the usurper." Of
course, she knew nothing of the Great
Jungle that stretched for thousands of
miles in all directions from Aphrodite
Port, so she had stumbled straight
into the Medusa's nest, and there she
would have been trapped and slowly
eaten, one lovely inch of her at a
time, if not for his faithful friend
Karolla, who knew these lands like
the backs of his giant seven-fingered
hands.…

♂

"Time to do your chores!" Ma called from downstairs.

"In a minute!"

"Right now, Katie!"

Kaitlyn Webb sighed and shut the book she had been reading in the
uncertain predawn light that filtered through the battered lace curtains
over her bedroom window. She stroked the cover's fancy embossed
gold lettering for a moment with work-calloused fingers. *Nobody makes
books like that anymore,* she thought. *Leastaways, nobody in Texas. Lost
Classics of Science Fiction* was an anthology of short stories published
in New York City, which told you right there that it had to be at least half
a century old. She felt sort of wistful, and also sort of resentful, reading
about the future those old writers thought was coming. All those flying
cars and cheap space travel to the ends of the universe. What would

the author of "Zap-Gun Jack Flash and the Dame-Eating Monsters of Venus" have thought if he'd known that hundreds of years after his time, folks would be getting around in horse-and-buggies if they were rich like the Montoyas down the road, or on a broken-down old mule if they were poor like her family?

Katie tucked the book into a pocket of her overalls and made her way out to the well with two empty buckets. It was going to kill her to lug them back to the house. "Tough luck," Ma would say if she complained. "You're fifteen years old, almost a grown woman, and you'd better pull your weight around here!" Katie would've bet a whole lonestar that Zap-Gun Jack's "unknown author" hadn't had such problems. The brief blurb said the story was found in an old wooden trunk in an apartment in Warsaw, which had once been the capital of a European country called Poland, "in neatly typewritten manuscript form." It was a romantic enough story, so Katie had invented a romantic figure to go with it. He was tall and dark and debonair (a word she'd learned from another book she'd found along with the anthology in the ruins of the library in the abandoned town of Jodie, on the road to Abilene). She pictured him in his early forties, with a distinguished touch of gray at his temples and a gently amused expression permanently etched into his face. Maybe he was a count! Didn't they used to have counts in Europe? She'd bet anything that counts had exquisite manners, especially with girls like herself, and quite unlike the swaggering way Texas Rangers like that no-good Johnny Marshall had.

When she staggered into the kitchen with the water buckets, Pa was just finishing his breakfast of salted grits. This morning there weren't even any eggs, let alone bacon, so he was in a bad mood and Katie steered clear of him. He grunted as she walked past.

"Now you hush and finish your breakfast so you can get along into town," Ma said to him.

"Not goin' into town today," Pa replied.

"Why not? You know we need more kerosene for the lamps. Also soap, and twine, and——"

"Fred told me he saw more Dixies out in his back forty," Pa interrupted.

"What? When was this?" Ma asked.

"Day before yesterday. Least half a dozen of them, there were, skulking around in those ash-gray uniforms of theirs and stealin' the ripe corn. He didn't dare say nothin' to them, seein' as how they were armed with rifles and all."

Suddenly Mom turned on Katie. "What the heck are you doing, standing around eavesdropping on grown-up talk? Get yourself back out there and feed them pigs!"

"Yes, Ma," she sighed. Wouldn't be worth her while to complain out loud, not unless she wanted a spanking. *No one else my age gets spanked.* She made her way out to their miserable broken-down excuse for a barn. She never could resign herself to the stink of the pigs. But being out of sight of the house gave her the chance to take out the book and read a few more paragraphs:

> Karolla was waiting for Jack in a clearing deep in the jungle. He looked something like a miniature model of Earth's fabled Tyrannosaurus Rex, only with grayish, downy fur, the head of a sheepdog and startling blue eyes that blinked innocently down at Jack as he emerged and sheathed his electric machete. "You're late," the Venusian chided in a clear, high-pitched voice that always reminded Jack of his little brother Jim, lost and presumed drowned in the Half-Shell Ocean these many years.
>
> To clear the lump that rose in his throat Jack snarled, "Wasn't my fault, all right, ya big shaggy lump? I had to dodge Ares' agents back in Aphrodite Port. Always did hate the city. I'd rather fight a Medusa barehanded any day than have to deal with one of those sneaky, hit-below-the-belt tough guys they got on every street corner there. But let's not stand around jabbering. Take me to the Medusa that's got Anya!"
>
> "Right away, Jack," Karolla said sweetly, and bounded off into the undergrowth. Jack charged after him,

```
hollering in vain at the Venusian
to slow down. At least he was easy
enough to follow, because he left
behind a trail of crushed and trampled
joowallah plants oozing their scarlet
juice onto the forest floor. In no time
at all Jack emerged in the clearing
where the Medusa had made its nest,
but he saw right away that there was a
problem.…
```

Rachel punched the typewriter keys as gently as she could while still leaving a mark on the page, so as not to wake up the brats. Mrs. Goldberg would kill her if she did. The late July night was sweltering, their room stifling thanks to the boards nailed over the windows, which did nothing to keep out the drafts on winter nights. There was little light to see by; for the millionth time Rachel thanked her lucky stars she had taken touch-typing lessons the summer before the Germans invaded. Still and all, it was her habit to write for at least an hour every night after the two brats had finally fallen asleep, despite all of Mom's warnings about how she was going to ruin her eyesight, and Mrs. Goldberg's warnings about what she would do if her precious children's sleep was disturbed. Tonight she typed frantically, trying to forget her worry about her parents, who had gone out hours ago along with Mr. Goldberg, chasing a rumor of black-market apples. But her attempt to lose herself on Venus was soon shattered by a furtive knocking. Mrs. Goldberg lit a candle stub and dived to open the door, bumping into Rachel and shoving her out of the way. Mr. Goldberg lurched in, smelling of dirt and sweat, and embraced his wife wordlessly.

"What is it? Where's Mom and Dad?" Rachel whispered. No one answered her at first. Then Mr. Goldberg detached himself from his wife and looked at her. In the flickering candlelight she couldn't read his expression, but she thought she saw his eyes gleam.

"*Maideleh*, I'm so sorry, but the Germans took them. I barely got away myself."

Mrs. Goldberg let out a stifled sob. Rachel just stared at him. "What do you mean the Germans took them?"

"The Germans grabbed them right off the street along with dozens of other people. I saw them being marched away with their hands up. They're all going to work camps, or so the Germans say."

Trust that weaselly little Goldberg to be the one to sneak away. "So how come you weren't rounded up?"

Mrs. Goldberg stopped her soft crying. "Rachel, don't—"

Mr. Goldberg's head and shoulders sagged, as if he were a marionette whose strings had been cut. "I hid," he confessed. "I didn't dare sneak back here till now."

"They should have taken you instead!" Rachel cried, and flung herself onto the filthy, broken-down pallet beside the window that she slept on instead of a bed—only the Goldberg brats were good enough to get actual beds. She buried her face in the pillow, sobbing until her throat was raw and her chest ached, waiting for Mrs. Goldberg to start slapping her and not caring if she did. But nothing happened.

Later, after Mr. and Mrs. Goldberg had settled into their bed, she gazed at the sliver of night sky just visible through the boards over the window. *I'll never sleep again.* Her gaze was drawn to a bright light, too bright to be a star, so bright that it seemed to have definite mass, a shining pewter weight up there in space. Could it be the morning star? Venus was the morning star, wasn't it? She yawned, her eyelids suddenly heavy, and she struggled to keep them open.

♂

A moment later she blinked and opened her eyes to gray daylight. She turned over and something wet seeped through her thin dress. She scrabbled to sit up. An oozing scarlet liquid the consistency of glue covered her hands and dress. *I'm bleeding.* Her guts lurched, but then the smell hit her, an odd, sharply sweet scent. She touched the tip of her tongue to her finger. Raspberries? How could she be lying in raspberry jam? The sugar ration had been eliminated, and when was the last time anyone in the ghetto had had fresh fruit to make into preserves?

Rachel sat up. "Mom?" She stared. Instead of sheets, she had been lying under grayish-tinged green leaves big enough to build a tent with. In fact, Zap-Gun Jack had done exactly that once, when he was fleeing from the Zonds, who hated Karolla's people, the N'Bialys, so much that.... Rachel blinked twice, squeezed her eyes shut and pressed her fingers to her temples. *I made all that stuff up. It isn't real. I'm dreaming about it right now because I'm so upset about.... Anyway I'm going to wake up any second because the brats are bound to be fighting like they do every morning....* But when she opened her eyes she was still not in the apartment. Instead she was surrounded by giant unearthly trees, "with mother-of-pearl trunks that stretched up to touch the featureless ceiling of the world," as she had written just last week. She tried to stand but the decaying leaves on the forest floor were so slippery she landed right back on her rump.

A man charged out of the jungle, grunting with effort and swearing to himself in English. "Darn that Karolla…if that thing has hurt one hair on Anya's head I'll…." He stopped dead when he saw Rachel sitting there and they stared at each other.

"Jack?" Rachel finally whispered. "Zap-Gun Jack?"

"That's my name." Jack hitched his thumbs into the loops of his gun belt and rocked back on his heels. "Who might you be, missy?"

Before Rachel could answer there was a rustling to the left. Jack raised his index finger to his lips and tiptoed in that direction, zap-gun at the ready. Rachel held her breath, waiting for the "frizzing sizzle of the zap-gun, like an enormous steak cooking on the stovetop," as she'd described it, her mouth watering at the simile. Instead there was a thrashing and a yelping and a surprised shout from Jack. A moment later he was back, his face set in a scowl as he pulled a skinny brown-haired boy by the hand. Wait. Not a boy, but a girl about her own age with her hair cut very short, dressed in dirty dungarees and a patched, short-sleeved shirt. She had a dazed look on her face and kept muttering to herself in strangely accented English, "Time to wake up now. Them pigs need feeding…."

"Damn tourists," Jack said. "Pardon my language, ladies, but what in the heck are you doing so far from Aphrodite Port? The deep jungle's no place for offworlders. You can get hurt out here. In fact, I'm kind of in a rush right now because I have to rescue another offworlder who got herself in a pickle. Though she's no tourist."

"Neither am I," the girl who looked like a boy said. "My name's Kaitlyn Webb, but y'all can call me Katie. I was just walking back from feeding the pigs on our farm when I saw the Dixies surrounding our house. Looked like a whole platoon of them! I ran and hid, and then they took my parents away at gunpoint and set fire to our house."

"Far?" said Rachel. "Oh, fire!"

"Yeah, that's what I said." Katie wiped her eyes with the back of her hand. "Damn butternuts! I'd have shot at them myself and maybe bagged me a few, but our guns were in the house, and I saw some filthy Alabama redneck swaggering around with Daddy's best 12-gauge. So I ran to get help from the Montoyas, but there were Dixies there too! It was a regular invasion, and no Rangers around anywhere to drive the damn weevils off. I would've even been glad to see Johnny Marshall's ugly face, but of course he was nowhere to be found. Everyone knows what them Dixies do to girls when they catch 'em, so I just ran and ran and ran till I couldn't run no more, and I dropped and fell asleep right there on the open prairie. Last thing I saw was the morning star."

Rachel started at this detail, and then slowly told her own story. "I also thought I must be dreaming, Katie," she said, "especially because I made this whole thing up."

"Made what whole thing up?" Jack interrupted. "You mean to say you girls have been lying to me this whole time?"

"No, no. I mean all this," Rachel said, waving her hand around at the grayish-green foliage.

Jack looked even more confused, but Katie's brown eyes widened. "You mean to tell me you're the author of 'Zap-Gun Jack and the Dame-Eating Monsters of Venus?'"

Rachel winced and her face heated up. "That's a stupid title, but yes, I'm the one who made up Jack and Princess Anya and the N'Bialys."

"You?" Katie cried.

Jack said, "How did you know my girl—the name of the princess? And how come you're the only offworlder I ever met who can pronounce the Venusians' true name?"

"Because I'm the author. I made all this up. I made *you* up, Zap-Gun Jack. So I know all about you. I know what happened to Jim. It wasn't your fault, and anyway, he's not really dead, he..."

Karolla bounded into the clearing. Katie shrank back, her arm over her eyes, but Rachel only muttered, "No no no, I said seven fingers. Seven! Oh...I see... that one's just so much smaller than the others...." The creature's fur was mottled, providing better camouflage with the jungle foliage. *I don't remember thinking of that.*

"Jack, why are you a-lazing while Anya is a-blazing?" the Venusian piped.

"I thought I told you, no more rhymes! It's gettin' on my nerves!" Jack reholstered his zap-gun.

"But it helps me with my English!" Karolla's big blue eyes narrowed. "Hey, what's the story with these pretty girls, Jack my lad? When Anya sees them, she'll be mad!"

"They're a couple of lost tourists," Jack said. "And Anya isn't going to see them, you furry horror, because they're going to be good girls and wait right here till I'm finished rescuing the princess!" Jack and Karolla rushed into the jungle.

"Oh no we won't." Rachel took off after them. "I have information you need, Jack! I know where your brother is!"

"And I ain't waiting out here on my own!" Katie ran after Rachel. Fortunately Jack needed his electric machete to blaze a trail through the dense growth, so he couldn't get too far ahead. Still, it was hard work just keeping up, and both girls were soon dripping with sweat. Rachel kept staring at the landscape. She knew the names of the major species of trees—the ones with the tent-size leaves were called *wharsawa*, for instance, while the ones that were just a little taller than Karolla and had brilliant yellow flowers were called *czarniy*—but she didn't know the names of all the smaller plants, apart from the *joowallah* and the dark green *klemeth* creeper vines. And she didn't know what the dinner-plate-size fluorescent green ladybug that she almost stepped on was called. In fact she didn't remember inventing so many things, but it was a jungle after all. The profusion of life made logical sense.

Something else was bothering her, though, and it took a while of listening to Jack and Karolla's banter before she figured it out. *The rhymes, that's it. I never said the N'Bialy had a habit of rhyming in English. What else don't I know about?*

Katie interrupted her reverie. "So you're the author, huh?"

"I am," Rachel puffed. *Wish I could keep up with the pace Jack is setting, like Katie can.* For a city girl who didn't get enough to eat, it wasn't so easy.

"I always figured you for a count, since the book said your story was found in Poland."

"Well, I'm not a count," Rachel said. "I'm a Jew."

Katie nodded. "The book said you might have been one, and that maybe you were in the Holocaust."

"What's the Holocaust?"

Katie grimaced and changed the subject. "How come we're here, Miss Rachel? Any ideas?"

Rachel shook her head. "I don't understand it either. I was just writing stories to take my mind off things. I missed our house and the friends I used to have before the Germans made us move to the ghetto."

Katie nodded. "I used to play dolls with Jennie down the road, but then her family up and moved to California. My daddy used to say he never could understand why free-born Texians would want to go live under the Reagan, but Jennie said her daddy had an offer to manage a wind-farm up north of Big Sur, so they got their passports and we never saw them again."

"I don't understand. Aren't you an American? Why would you need a passport to visit another American state?"

"Well yeah, I'm an American, same as you're a European, I guess. But America hasn't been a single country since—"

"Ladies, I hate to interrupt this symposium on Earthside politics, but you're gonna have to keep it down from now on. Medusas have very sensitive hearing," Jack said.

"I didn't write that," Rachel grumbled, but she obediently shut up and concentrated on avoiding the snakelike *klemeth* underfoot. Her mind whirled. Was Katie from the far future? Or from a parallel world of some kind? How exactly had her story come to be published, and how had Katie found it? And most of all, how on earth had both of them been catapulted into a world that she, Rachel, had made up? Mom might think she was a woolly-headed dreamer, but Rachel was no believer in magic. If by some miracle she did survive the war and went to college, she wanted to study physics. She'd read about Einstein's Special and General Theories of Relativity, and the new quantum mechanics that even he didn't seem to understand, and she thought it was the most exciting stuff in the world. That was how she wanted to spend her life, learning about how the universe really worked, cracking God's code. Physics was so much more elegant than the clumsy attempts made at guessing the divine mind back in Biblical times. But this, this was as crazy and illogical as any story about bushes burning and the Red Sea splitting. And yet there seemed to be no alternative but to accept things at face value for now.

♂

Katie's horizons were narrower than Rachel's, but paradoxically this made it easier for her to accept the situation. Hadn't she always dreamed of running away from the farm? It seemed like her prayers had come true, though God was playing a mighty cruel joke if He had taken her parents as the price of her escape. She tried to push the thought away and concentrate on making headway through the jungle. Jack was using his electric machete economically, cutting away only the largest plants and stomping right over the vines and some kind of mushroom-like growth that groaned when you stepped on it. They didn't have anything like that back in the Texas Panhandle, but the farmers who scratched a living out of a prairie that got drier every year often spoke in hushed tones about "you-foes," mysterious colored lights that appeared in the night skies and sometimes took away a calf or a child. Then too, Katie had found a collection of L. Frank Baum's books in the children's section of the ruined library, and while he wasn't as good a writer as Rachel, he had also helped accustom her to the idea that all living things might not look or sound familiar.

"Hey Rachel," she whispered, helping her over a tangle of vines, "what's that important information you said you had for Jack?"

"Remember the part in the story where he first sees the Medusa?"

"Oh, yeah— Hey Jack!"

Jack hissed like the Montoyas' sprinkler system. "Keep it down, I said! I don't want to have to rescue three dames from the Medusa's clutches."

"But that's what we have to tell you about," Katie said. "The Medusa that's got Anya—it's calving."

Jack stopped and turned around. "It's doing *what*, now?"

"What Katie means is, it's having babies," Rachel explained.

Jack let loose with an impressive string of English swear words, some of which Rachel didn't know. When he finished, he whistled and Karolla bounded back.

"Earthlings are so slow, how you don't all get eaten I do not know," he said.

"N'Bialy rush in where angels fear to tread," Jack retorted. "Listen, you big galoot, is this Medusa spawning season?"

"I do not understand, Jack my man."

"Aw, cripes. Are big Medusas making little ones now, you furbrain?"

"N'Bialy brains are not made of fur," Karolla retorted. "The history textbooks Anya brought from Mars, I study with her. She is so patient, she's teaching me to read English real well. Although I still find it hard to spell."

"But not to make annoying rhymes," said Jack. "Anya's studying history?"

Rachel also looked surprised, but then her lips curled in a smile.

"Now's not the time of studies to be dreaming. I can hear Anya screaming!"

"I don't hear anything," Jack said, but just then a distant shriek echoed through the jungle, and he moved faster than Rachel or Katie had ever seen a man run before. They did their best to keep up as he charged after Karolla, dashing down a gentle slope, splashing through a creek, and climbing a tuft of grass along the opposite bank, until they found themselves standing on a blasted patch of ground at least fifty yards across. In the center squatted the Greater Venusian Medusa, every bit as horrible as Rachel had imagined and then some. It was that *thing* in nightmares that grabs you from behind and lifts you slowly, oh so slowly off the ground while your parents and your friends watch with frozen, terror-stricken faces as you struggle to turn in its grasp and get a glimpse of it, and just when you're about to succeed you wake up with your throat too tight even to scream. The Medusa had tentacles in profusion, yes, and claws like giant scimitars that gleamed in the occluded sunlight, and fangs where no fangs ought to be, and malevolent yellow eyes and wicked-looking spines and…and…and it took up half the clearing, and in its center (if the thing could be said to have a center) wriggled a tall, slim woman with flame-red hair dressed in what looked like a filmy white nightgown. Her face was bruised and thin rivulets of blood ran down her arms, chest and legs, staining her toga or whatever it was.

Jack unholstered his zap-gun. "Unhand her, you brute!" he cried.

"That's a little corny, Rachel," Katie said in an undertone.

"It's how heroes are supposed to talk! Duck!" Rachel shouted as something whizzed through the air. Katie dodged and the thing crashed into a tree and fell to the ground with a sickening plop, waving claws and tentacles frantically until Karolla bounded into the clearing and stomped on it with the sound of a sledgehammer smashing a snail shell. That was the signal for half an hour of frenzied yelling, stomping and splattering, all mixed up with the sizzling noise of Jack's zap-gun cauterizing various Medusa limbs. Katie had reason to be grateful for her tough work boots, while Rachel found a *wharsawa* stick and grunted every time she crushed a larva's carapace. At last the mama Medusa let out a squealing bellow, like a woolly mammoth with its foot caught in a bear trap, flung Anya at Jack's feet and scrabbled off into the jungle, followed by all the surviving larvae, which were chittering angrily as they retreated.

"My love." Jack lifted Anya to her feet. "Are you all right?"

"Never better, Jack darling," she gasped. And they kissed for a long time, while Rachel and Katie stood with folded arms and watched.

"You sure do know how to write a love scene," Katie murmured after a while.

"Not really," Rachel said out of the corner of her mouth. "I've, uh, I've never been kissed. I think Jack and the princess figured it out for themselves."

When the lovers surfaced for air the Martian princess looked around, waved shyly at Karolla, and narrowed her eyes when she saw the girls. "Jack, who are these people?"

"They're Earthling tourists who somehow got themselves lost in the jungle. I'm just taking them back to their tour group," Jack said.

But Anya hardly seemed to hear his explanation. Her eyes remained narrowed, focused on Rachel, who promptly broke out in a fresh sweat.

"What? What is it? What's wrong?"

Anya walked up to Rachel, placed her hands on her Rachel's shoulders and said something in a foreign language.

"What? What was that?" Katie asked.

Jack said, "You never talk Martian to me, honey."

"That's because you're lousy at languages, my love." Anya stared into Rachel's eyes. "I called her my sister."

"In Polish," Rachel said.

"Oh, yeah," Katie looked from one to the other. "You do look alike. A lot alike! You could be twins, almost! You both got that long, curly red hair and green eyes, and...." She stopped because Rachel was blushing furiously.

"In N'Bialy we say *peggishah mishpakh'teet*," Karolla said approvingly. "A family reunion, how sweet."

Jack cleared his throat. "Well, when you finish the reunion, ladies, could you please explain to me what you meant about my brother, Rachel?"

"Oh yes," she said, shaking herself. "It's simple enough. It was going to be in my next story. Jim is alive and well, but he's being held captive on Mars by Lord Ares."

"Then," Jack said grimly, "we must rescue Jim, and free Mars from the awful tyranny of Lord Ares! Come with me!" And he strode forth without looking back to see if anyone was following him. But of course, they all were, Jack and the three dames and the furry Venusian monster.

2

The walk back through the jungle was difficult going for Rachel, who envied Katie's seemingly effortless stride, especially when every root hidden under wet, fallen leaves seemed to be lying in wait for her, and she was still sticky with *joowallah* sap, though her sweat had washed some of that away. But the going was even tougher for the princess, who had grown up in Mars's low gravity, so Jack and Karolla adjusted their pace accordingly. Jack offered to carry Anya over the creek that bordered the Medusa's blast zone and several other rivulets they crossed in the next few hours, but she declined with dignity, though sweat poured from her delicate limbs. Katie worried about being caught outside after dark, but Jack laughed and said sunset wouldn't be for another 80 Earth days.

"Besides," he said, "on this planet, the things that hunt in the daytime are much more dangerous than the night-stalkers."

"Gee, thanks, mister, I feel so much better now," Katie said.

"Not at all, missy."

"The name's Katie, mister."

"Katie Mister? That's a funny name." Jack gallantly handed over a canteen. Katie gulped, followed by Rachel, while Jack and the princess took turns sipping from a second canteen and gazing into each other's eyes.

When they were under way again and Jack seemed safely out of ear-shot, Katie whispered to Rachel, "You didn't make him the sharpest tack in the drawer, did you?"

"He has unexplored depths," Rachel said. "I didn't have enough time to get into all of them. Besides, I had an uncle from Chelm who was just as immune to sarcasm as Jack."

An enormous rustling to their right, as of cannonballs crashing into autumn leaves, interrupted. Both girls jumped, then relaxed when they saw it was only Karolla.

"What did you say about Jack?" he asked.

"I'm sorry," Rachel said. "I didn't mean to hurt anybody's feelings."

Blue eyes as large as ponds gazed deep into Rachel's soul for a long moment. Then the sheepdog head bobbed in acknowledgement and the giant gray legs carried the creature back into the jungle.

Rachel shuddered. "This is going to sound strange, Katie, but Karolla reminds me of my grandfather."

"Your grandpa?"

"Yes. My *zayde* was a rabbi in a little *shtetl*—a Jewish village out in the forest called Bilgoray, very backward. He was always going on about *loshon hora,* the need to avoid malicious gossip and hurting people's feelings. My father couldn't get away from him and his scolding fast enough. He ran away to the city and got into the university by sheer stubbornness, even though they didn't want him because he was a Jew."

Katie scratched her head. "So the Venusians are, like, Jews? That doesn't make a lot of sense. No offense."

"You're right, it doesn't. And that's not what I wrote, or meant to write. But somehow my ideas, my background, must have influenced things more than I realized. Also with Anya! I didn't think the Martian language was Polish. That's just crazy!"

"I found a book about Polish Jews in the library once. Didn't y'all speak a language called Yiddish?" Katie asked.

Rachel shook her head. "I understand Yiddish thanks to my grandfather, but we don't speak it at home. My parents are embarrassed by it. They speak Polish and German to me, and now Hebrew since they got all enthusiastic about Zionism. We were all going to move to Palestine before the war started, but we couldn't get visas." She stopped walking and rubbed her eyes.

Katie put a hand on her shoulder. "I understand. My family's like yours in some ways. Leastaways, my grandpa was like your dad. He ran away to the big city to get away from *his* daddy, who was a Baptist preacher. Went to college, too, graduated with honors and was all set to become a computer programmer."

"What's that?"

"Ladies, we need to keep moving!" Jack called. "We got another hour to go till we get to our campsite."

Katie explained what a computer programmer was as they slogged along. The ground turned marshy, and their feet sank with every step. Rachel's shoes had big holes, and wet and muddy feet just added to her misery. But she was transfixed by Katie's story. It sounded a little like the worlds the pulps described. "So how come your grandpa didn't get to become a computer programmer?"

"He did, for a while. But then New York got atom-bombed by the terrorists, and the Internet crashed, and the old United States broke up, and there wasn't much call in Texas for computer programmers, what with everyone scrambling to find enough to eat. So he had to go crawling back to his daddy, who had a little farm up in the Panhandle. Grandpa died when I was a little girl, and all I remember of him is an old guy with a sad face."

Rachel didn't understand half Katie's words, but she knew trouble when she heard about it. Before Katie got upset, she changed the subject. "Did you ever see any of his computers?"

"Sure I did. We actually have his favorite one. But we don't—we didn't have a generator, so the only way to get it to work was to take it over to the Montoyas'. They had beautiful solar panels on their roof, before a big hailstorm wrecked them when I was ten."

"Oh. And what did the computers do? Did they walk and talk? Serve you food, help out with the chores?"

Katie laughed. "No, like I said, they were computers, not robots. But what they could do was a lot more exciting than carrying water and feeding the pigs! They could send messages to other computers, all over the world! They'd patched up a partial Internet by then, and I got to email with a guy in England, and a lady in India!" Her mouth drooped. "But it didn't last long. There was that hailstorm, like I said. And then the Dixies started coming around hassling people, and nobody had time to worry about electricity and all that. Joe Montoya, he tried raise a militia, but my daddy said he could defend our homestead just fine himself."

Katie's lower lip trembled, so Rachel asked her where she'd found her story about Jack Flash. Katie explained about the book, and the ruined library on the road to Abilene.

"But why was there a library in the middle of nowhere?"

"It wasn't in the middle of nowhere, not when they built it. There was a whole town around it, but all the people left during the Troubles. Me and some of the other kids liked to go exploring in the abandoned houses, though of course we weren't supposed to, which just made it more exciting. I was the only one who cared about the library. Well, me and this no-good character called Johnny Marshall. It was in a glass and steel building, the kind of thing they used to build back in the twentieth century."

"Katie, what year was it, where you lived?" Rachel asked.

"Hmm? Oh, 2140. Though the Mormons get pretty mad if you call it that. According to them, it's the year 297, but we don't use the Deseret calendar in Texas."

"What are you talkin' about, little lady?" Jack called back, making both girls jump. "2140 was more than thirty years ago."

"What? No it wasn't!" Katie said.

Rachel elbowed her and whispered, "Don't argue with him. He'll get suspicious. Besides, by me it's 1942! Who says your time is any more accurate in this world? Remember Einstein!"

Katie scowled, thinking it over, then nodded slowly and said loud enough for Jack to hear, "Well, I guess maybe I've been gone a long time."

"I guess maybe you have!" Jack replied.

After a moment Katie continued, a little more quietly:

"All the windows in that library broke long ago, of course. A lot of those books were nothin' more than pulp—real pulp, not what they used to call science fiction magazines. The stink of all that mildew would've driven everyone away if nothin' else did."

"So what drew you?"

Katie shrugged. "I'm not really sure. Mom and Dad taught me to read and write, and to do basic sums so I won't get cheated by some scumball grain buyer, but that was about it. And I didn't know my grandpa long enough for him to get me excited about science. Maybe he had some kind of indirect influence on me, from Dad talking about him. Mainly though, I was just bored and keen for anything that might get me the heck out of the Panhandle, though there ain't, or there weren't, anything like the kind of opportunities a girl like me could have had fifty years ago." She spoke without bitterness: these were the facts of her life, like dust-storms and hostile Dixies.

"So anyways, there were a whole bunch of sci-fi books that hadn't been damaged too bad, because they were buried under a lot of other ruined books. And *Lost Classics of Science Fiction* was my favorite." Katie's dreamy expression faded for a moment, and her lips thinned. "I almost had to fight Johnny Marshall for it. I could hardly believe it—that that snake took enough time off from beating up little kids and stealing people's stuff when they weren't looking to learn to read. But it seemed like he wanted that book as bad as I did. Luckily we found two copies."

"'Lost Classics,' huh?" Rachel mused. "It's nice to be classic, but not to be lost."

"A-men to that, little lady." Jack popped out from behind a tree so abruptly both girls jumped. Jack grinned. "Just came to tell you gals, we're done walking for the day. Past those trees over there is a nice dry clearing where I've got a permanent base camp. We're staying there for the night."

"Sounds good to me," Katie said. "Got any grub, mister? I'm awful hungry."

"Me too," Rachel admitted.

"Course I do! I hope you two are really, *really* hungry, 'cause while you were jabbering away back here, I went and shot a Venusian buffalo!"

Katie looked pleased but Rachel felt a little sick to her stomach. She didn't recall writing about any buffalos. "What's it look like?"

"A Venusian buffalo? It's really a twelve-foot-long reptile covered with grayish-green fur for camouflage, and a head like an Earth alligator. But don't you worry, the meat looks just like regular old beef and tastes great when you mix it in with potatoes and carrots and some of my special New New Orleans hot sauce! But first, we gotta skin it. Either of you two ladies care to help me with that?"

"Sure thing," said Katie. "Daddy showed me how to do the butchering when I could hardly walk. Bet I can do it faster than you!"

"Attagirl! That's my kind of lady!" Jack punched her on the shoulder. Then, glancing back, he hastily amended, "'Cept for Martian princesses, of course. One particular Martian princess, to be exact. Rachel, why don't you two get acquainted while Katie and me fix dinner?" He gave Rachel a second, long look from head to foot that made her feel weird inside, shivery and melty at the same time. "You know, Katie is right, you really *do* look an awful lot like Anya. Well, have fun, girls!"

And Rachel was left alone with her creation. Of course, Jack was hers too, and so was this jungle and the whole planet she was standing on, and maybe Katie as well. But nothing was so completely and obviously hers as Anya, who really did look like an idealized version of herself—a little taller, a little bustier, a lot better proportioned overall, with a much thinner scattering of freckles on her cheeks and jade-colored eyes that positively glowed, even in the muted sunlight. The princess gestured at a fallen log, and Rachel sat down beside her after carefully checking to make sure it wasn't some other creature she might not have made up.

To Rachel's consternation, Anya seemed shy and diffident. She struggled with her words, starting to speak and stopping herself several times before she said in Polish, "I am so happy to have found a fellow Martian here in the Venusian jungle, of all places. Things are worse than ever back home."

Even her voice was a better version of Rachel's, low and soothing and doubtless very sexy to Jack and any other man in range. Rachel tried to remember what she'd written about Anya's home world. The princess's family were the rightful rulers of the Red Planet, but they'd been overthrown more than twenty-five years earlier (fifty Earth years ago). Her father was leading the resistance to "Lord Ares II," and it had been Rachel's vague plan to write a novel in which Jack and Anya helped him overthrow the fun-loving but cruel usurper's son, while also rescuing Jack's brother Jim "in the nick of time." Okay, so far, so good.

Rachel said, "Worse? How could it be worse?" Maybe Ares II was holding wild drunken parties on the holy Mount Olympus, or something.

Anya gave her a funny look. "The original Ares at least cared for the outward beauty of our precious Mars, though he crushed our people's spirit. I admit that some saw it as poetic justice when an unknown soldier of fortune murdered his drunken wastrel of a son and took the throne as Ares III last year...."

What's this all about? Better just keep quiet and find out.

"I'd take a fool whose only interest is pleasure over a real tyrant like the new Ares any day," Anya said. "All he talks about is conquest—'let the Fatherland regain its glory as the Star of War'—but meanwhile he's turned the people into slaves and wounded the beautiful desert with mines and factories to build his warships!"

Tears streamed down the princess's face, and she seized Rachel's hands. "He uses the Grand Canal to dump toxic waste from his weapons plants!" she whispered. "He's turned Valles Marineris into a giant prison for those who dare cross him! My own parents may be there—I was tipped off they had been arrested and so I fled the planet before Ares could catch me too. And there are rumors"—she paused and lowered her voice still further, so Rachel had to lean forward to hear—"there are rumors he's building an altar for human sacrifice on the peak of Olympus Mons, the holy mountain!"

"No!" Rachel gasped. *Is this all my fault? It must be! I'm the one who dreamed up this world.* What did these horrors say about her imagination? She'd thought she was escaping the world of Hitler and Stalin when she wrote about the jungles of Venus and the deserts of Mars, but wasn't the "new" Lord Ares really just another two-bit dictator? She closed her eyes and shuddered, imagining what he must look like when he was ranting away in front of his goose-stepping army. When she opened her eyes she saw Anya through a blurry lens of tears. "I will help you," she whispered, squeezing the princess's hands. "Of course I will help you! Together, we'll overthrow the tyrant and put your father on the throne where he belongs!" At that they embraced.

"Come and get it!" Katie hollered.

Jack was right, Venusian buffalo stew was tasty. Not that it would have mattered to Rachel if it wasn't. Everyone watched in amazement as she put away an entire haunch the size of a Thanksgiving turkey. Well, they couldn't know what it was like to have to survive for years on bread stretched with sawdust and moldy potatoes, how it could turn a noble, cultured man like her father into an animal scrabbling for survival. Anything that filled the hole where her stomach used to be was a good thing, so let the others stare. As soon as she finished eating, Rachel almost collapsed from exhaustion. It was all she could do to crawl into the leaf-tent Jack had set up before her eyes shut. A few seconds later, it seemed, she woke to Katie shaking her shoulder vigorously.

"Lemme sleep," she muttered.

"Huh? Don't talk foreign, Rachel, I can't understand it."

"It's not foreign, it's Polish," Rachel snapped. The light seemed unchanged. Oh, right. Venus's day was actually longer than its year. How odd. When was she going to wake up to the sensible, normal, everyday world of the Warsaw Ghetto? And see her parents again.... She blinked away tears. *Maybe the shock of losing them drove me crazy and I'm hallucinating all this.* But there was so much detail, and the texture of everything seemed so real. Take that caterpillar crawling along her upper arm. It looked like a thick, gaudy orange crayon, complete with paper wrapper, but it was soft and fuzzy and flexible and moving like an inchworm toward her elbow, opening its mouth to reveal gleaming teeth the size of thumbtacks....

Rachel's shrieks brought Jack running, zap-gun at the ready. But when he saw what was the matter he dropped the gun and doubled over laughing, his hands on his knees.

"Aww, you didn't have to stomp all over a little furbug like that!" he said when he had caught his breath. "Them things only want to play! Those teeth may look scary, but they can't use them on anything bigger than a moosquito!"

"You mean a mosquito," said Katie, whose boots had reduced the furbug to orange paste.

"No, a moosquito. Hey, there's one right now!" He pointed at Rachel's neck. Rachel slapped frantically, reducing Jack to more helpless laughter. She glared at him. A loud droning in her ear brought her up short. She winced and dodged violently to the side, knocking her head into the sturdy stick that served as the tent's central support and bringing the whole thing down around her. It was like being smothered by a giant mint leaf.

In rescuing her Jack was treated to an earful of Polish profanity. He raised an eyebrow as he helped her to her feet. "Now I never been to Mars myself, but we have some Martian exiles hangin' around Afro-Port, and I can tell you I ain't never heard language like that except from some of the roughest, toughest, meanest astronaut types as ever sailed a freighter out of Phobos. Certainly not out of a lady like you."

Rachel blushed. "You don't think the princess heard, do you?"

"No, she's attending to her toilet on the other side of the clearing. But I hope you watch your language around her in the future, Miss Rachel."

"I don't normally talk like that. It's just that everything here is so— *Jack, what's that on your neck?*"

"This?" Jack let something that looked like an enormous wasp with water-bug legs crawl onto the back of his hand. "This, here, is a moosquito like the one that made you knock down the tent. Listen." He flicked the part that looked like a stinger with his finger and it lit up red, giving off a droning hum that shaded into a lowing that sounded for all the world like the mournful noise the skinny cows in Rachel's grandfather's *shtetl* made.

"Fascinating," Rachel gulped. "Why couldn't I have made Venus a nice, peaceful park world?"

Jack looked at her quizzically. "See here, missy, it ain't my business, but I wouldn't talk like that when we get to Afro-Port if I was you. Out here in the jungle, you can say whatever you want, but in town they're liable to drag you before Mayor Bellini for a session with the Corrector."

"What's a Corrector?"

"You mean to tell me they don't have any Correctors on Earth? Well, let's just say it's one of the reasons I prefer to spend my time out here in the jungle, zapping Medusas and rescuing stupid tourists, no offense."

"None taken," Rachel muttered. "A Corrector? What is this, a penal colony?"

"As a matter of fact, Venus did start out as a penal colony, like Australia on Old Earth," Jack said. "Thought you knew everything about Venus."

"Apparently not."

"See here, Miss Rachel, I'd love to stand around jabbering all day, but we got to get moving if we're going to make Afro-Port within the next twelve hours. There's a monsoon brewing that's going to hit around then."

"How can you tell?" Katie asked, squinting up into the featureless gray sky that was visible through the gaps in the tree canopy.

"Plain as the nose on your face, Miss Katie. Not that your nose is anything to be ashamed of. I once knew a girl with a nose like yours, and she won the Miss Luna 2160 contest hands down."

"Did he just call me a lunatic?" Katie whispered to Rachel.

"No, Luna's another name for the moon," Rachel whispered back.

"Right. I knew that."

"I'll explain to you how I can tell a monsoon is coming if you help me with this gear, Miss Katie," Jack said.

"Deal," Katie said happily.

As they worked, Anya walked over to Rachel. Glided over, more like, Rachel thought enviously.

"Rachel, I am duty bound to inform you that you if you accompany me and Jack, you will be in grave danger from the moment we arrive on Mars. In fact, Ares' agents will probably spot us as soon as we arrive in Aphrodite Port."

"S'alright," Rachel said, "they can't be any worse than Nazis."

"Nazis?" The princess frowned. "What are Nazis?"

"Something from Earth history. Believe me, you don't want to know."

"But Earth history is my field! I had almost enough credits to graduate when Ares had me expelled from Wandanian University. Then the faculty and students went on strike in protest, and he got rid of them all and turned the place into a military academy." She shut her eyes for a moment. "So much suffering on my account."

Rachel put her hand on the princess's arm. "It isn't on your account, Your Highness," she said. "I mean, I'm sure your people love you, but they are fighting for their own rights. And you, like your father, are their leader and their symbol. You can't give up, for their sake."

"You're right, of course," Anya said. "But tell me about these Nazis of yours. Were they one of the tribes the Aztecs subjugated?"

"Uh, no, not exactly. Look, can we talk about this another time? Right now I need to know about Ares' agents—what they look like, how they are armed, what we should do if we run into them in Aphrodite Port...."

"Breakfast, ladies!" Jack called. "I'm afraid we'll have to eat on the run. Hope you like bananas!"

"Bananas?" Rachel said. "We have bananas on Earth. In Warsaw, even! At least before the war, we did."

"Bet they weren't anything like this!" Jack tossed something to her.

Rachel examined the rose-colored, gracefully curved tube as long as her forearm. It had no obvious stem. "How do you peel this thing?"

"Peel?" Jack laughed. "Earth bananas have peels? That's funny! Just bite into it, Miss Rachel!"

She did, and her eyes widened. "This tastes just like strawberries and cream! My favorite! I haven't eaten that since before the war!"

"No it doesn't," Katie said, matching her pace to Rachel's. "It tastes just like my daddy's barbecued ribs."

"It tastes like whatever you want it to," the princess explained. "The technique was a Martian trade secret, but Ares II sold it to finance one of his palaces." She made a face. "The one with a harem."

"What's a harem?" Katie asked. Jack and Rachel blushed.

The princess said, "It is a place where the tyrant keeps his female, ah, that is, his women—"

"Oh, like par-tay time on Mars!" Katie said. "I gotcha."

The princess frowned. "No, I'm afraid you don't. Not all the women are there of their own free will."

"Oh. *Oh*," Katie blushed in her turn. "Why, that's awful! How come you Martians don't get together and throw the bums out?"

"You mean, have a revolution?" the princess said. "No, I don't think you understand Martian culture. We are a desert people. The climate on our world has been growing steadily drier for thousands upon thousands of years. People from Earth and Venus who visit for the first time often speak of the beauty of our ocher plains, but they do not remember as we do when it was all green and lush, almost as much as this planet where we are now." She smiled at Jack. "In Martian we call this world the Jewel of the Night, it shines so brightly in our sky." Her smile faded slowly as tears welled in her eyes. "Poets and painters travel from the outer system, from Ganymede and Titan as well as Earth and Venus, to capture something of the beauty of our world, but it is the beauty of a young girl dying before her time. And yet, we Martians are a determined people, and we would not let our world die without a fight. So my renowned ancestor Lady Wanda organized the first of the great canal-building projects. Everyone on the planet who was physically able took part. Little children carried little buckets of dirt and pebbles. Together we built the Grand Canal, a thousand miles long, to carry the sweet water from the springs on Olympus Mons into lesser branching canals that irrigate the plains. But we could not have done this without the wise leadership of Wanda, her son Lord Witold I, and his daughter Lady Wanda II."

"And of course, her son Prince Witold was your father," Jack said. "Which makes me wonder how come your name isn't Wanda."

"Because Ares II would have taken that as a direct challenge, and I would not have lived to reach adulthood. As it is, I've still got more than a Martian year—almost two Earth-years—to go before I become an adult. May I continue?"

Jack dropped his wiseguy expression, but Katie frowned. "This is very interesting and all, Miss Anya, but I still don't understand why your people don't give these Ares folks the bum's rush."

The princess sighed. "Any non-Martian would find it difficult to understand, but the fact is that our planet has been in such terrible danger for such a long time that the idea of overthrowing our rulers is unthinkable. If we don't all cooperate, we will all die. Not only will our lands dry out, our very atmosphere will blow away into space. We cannot afford wars or revolutions like the people of the sunward planets."

"But—well—no free-born Texian would stand for that for one minute! We'd chase 'em out with shotguns and pitchforks if we had to!"

"But my dear Katie, I heard you talking with Rachel earlier about how your people live. No, please don't misunderstand me." She smiled as Katie's face darkened. "I am sure you and your parents worked harder than I could ever imagine. But can't you see, without cooperation to build the sort of canals we have on Mars, your country will remain poor and backward—"

"You can't say that about Texas!" Katie roared and jumped Anya, sending her to the marshy ground with a loud mucky splash. Though the princess had a few inches on the farm girl, all those mornings lugging water had given Katie some respectable muscles, and before an appalled Jack and an even more appalled Rachel could pull them apart Anya had suffered a bloody nose and was covered in rich Venusian mud.

While the princess toweled off, Jack advanced on a sullen Katie, fists clenched at his side. "I never hit a girl, but I've got half a mind to leave you to fend for yourself in this jungle, seein' as how you're so tough and all."

"None of that please, Jack." Anya held a handkerchief to her nose. "She was defending the honor of her country, which is only right. I was in the wrong. Kaitlyn Webb, I ask your forgiveness." And she held out her hand.

"Guess maybe I shouldn't have been so quick to use my fists," Katie mumbled, accepting the outstretched hand. "That's just how we do things, down Texas way."

"Seems to me we Martians could use some of that Texas spirit," the princess said. "If you would help us in our struggle once we reach Aphrodite Port, instead of taking the first rocketship back to Texas, my world will be forever in your debt."

"The honor would be mine," Katie said. "I've never had a real princess ask me for anything before." Once they were under way again, she added in a whisper to Rachel, "Besides, I somehow doubt the Texas I would be returning to would be *my* Texas, if you know what I mean."

Rachel nodded. "How can there even be a Poland in this world, where the Martians speak Polish and have Polish names?" she whispered back. "I'm only sorry I marooned you here, Katie."

"Are you kidding? This is the adventure of a lifetime!" Katie grinned ear to ear, but then her face suddenly fell. "Except for my poor folks. I wish I could help them. Or at least find out what happened to them! But that was so long ago. Thirty years...or I guess...."

"It's even worse than that," Rachel said. "It seems like your parents and mine are not just stuck back in the past somewhere, *and* on another planet, but in a whole other *universe!*"

"I guess maybe you're right." Katie's eyes widened. "How on earth... uh, anyway, how are we supposed to help them?"

Rachel shook her head slowly. "I think Einstein himself would have a tough time with this."

"Yeah! But my parents are prisoners of those rotten Dixies and yours," Katie gulped, "of the Nazis! What are we gonna do?" They both fell silent for a long time.

Rachel rubbed her eyes. *I'm not going to cry, I am not.* She had a sneaking suspicion that Katie felt the same.

"Einstein," Katie said suddenly.

"Hmm? What about him?"

"Didn't he say that imagination is more important than knowledge?" Katie said. "I think if he were here, he would be tell us to keep on doing what we're doing—trying to learn as much as possible. That's the *only* way either of us is gonna be able to help our folks!"

"You're right, Katie," Rachel said, looking at her with newfound respect. But then she thought of warmongering Martian emperors and sadistic mayors who liked to "correct" people.

What are we getting into?

3

Aphrodite Port was a bedlam through which Jack led his companions confidently.

Karolla had bid them goodbye at the edge of the city. "Afro-Port is a human town, I fear that Venusians they would hunt down," he explained. Overhead, dark clouds billowed and grumbled.

"Aw, c'mon, ya big furry lump, you know that the Treaty gives Venusians full guest status in town."

"Treaties humans make, treaties humans can break," Karolla replied, blinking innocently.

"Next thing you know, you'll be asking how come you need 'guest status' on your own planet," Jack sighed. "All right, friend, go in peace." He spun around three times, ending with his back turned to Karolla, put his right hand against the small of his back and wiggled his fingers. The Venusian gravely bowed until his head was on a level with Jack's hand, where a small fleshy comb atop his head, like a scaled-up version of a cock's comb, wiggled in sync with Jack's fingers. For a moment the hand and the comb touched, then the Venusian disappeared into the jungle with a single mighty bound.

Katie and Rachel stared at Jack.

"What? Haven't you ever seen a Venusian handshake before?" Without waiting for an answer, Jack took Anya's hand and strolled up to a white, human-size metal gate.

"Who desires entry?" a mechanical voice demanded. Rachel and Katie jumped.

"It is I, Zap-Gun Jack," Jack proclaimed with a grand flourish of his weapon.

"Negative. Not recognized. Admission denied," said a red-eyed metal spider crouching atop the lintel.

"Aw, come off it, you mechanical arthropod. You know very well who I am."

"You must identify yourself properly and surrender your weapon," the robot insisted. Jack opened his mouth to argue.

Searing heat struck Rachel from behind. She opened her mouth to scream, but the planet was apparently splitting open, leaving her deaf and blind. When she came to she was lying on her back in a patch of neatly trimmed grass, lights flickering overhead. Jack, Katie, Anya and a number of other strangers looked down at her with concerned expressions. Seeing that Rachel's eyes were open, Jack grinned and reached down to help her up. "Attagirl, you're a real Venusian now!" he cried, clapping her on the back.

"Ow! That hurt!" Rachel gasped and tears came to her eyes. "What—what—"

"What was that? You, my girl, were grazed by the first lightning strike of this monsoon season and lived to tell the tale! Which is good luck! Take a look up there." Jack took her arm and pointed to the sky.

Rachel looked up and gasped. She had thought the flickering light was from a concussion. But it was real, the result of continual lightning strikes on the surface of an invisible dome that stretched far above the town. The effect was mesmerizing, a writhing of white-hot branches against a velvety background, like a photographic negative of trees lashed by hurricane winds. "Why don't I go blind?" Rachel whispered.

"Ah," Jack smiled, "thank our afro-bucky for that! It's polarized, keeps out the harmful radiation as well as the rain. If you were standing outside right now, well, let's just say you couldn't be standing outside right now. People who've been exposed in the open say it's like having a nice hot shower from a fire hose. Those who survive, that is."

"And you were going to leave me to fend for myself in that?" Katie gave Jack a shove that sent him staggering.

"He was only kidding, he already told you that," Anya caught Jack smoothly. "Come on, let's go inside somewhere. This lightning could set off my epilepsy, and you wouldn't want me frothing at your feet, would you, Jack darling?"

"No, quite right, uh, Annie my love," he said, catching her eye. "Let's go back to my digs, girls! I'm almost caught up on my rent for once!" When they were clear of the crowd, Jack said out of the side of his mouth, "She doesn't really have epilepsy. It's just that you never know when one of Ares' agents might be hiding in the crowd."

Katie gave him a withering look. "We're from Earth, you pistol-waving goon, not the planet Dumbass."

"Yeah, okay, gotcha there," Jack mumbled, leading them into a seedy alley.

Rachel half-listened to the chatter as she glanced around. Things were much messier than she would have imagined. From all those pulps Abe had sent her, she had expected the future to be bright and gleaming, with hard, clean steel and plastic surfaces. Steel and plastic there were in plenty, but everything looked scratched or rusty or both, as if from long use. The poorer parts of Warsaw might look like this in two or three hundred years. *Wait. Has everyone I know been dead for two hundred years?* Abe, a skinny kid with an annoying grin, grown up and married with children and grandchildren and maybe even great-grandchildren, dead longer than Thaddeus Kosciusko? What if she never lived to see the end of the war? So maybe she was dying and only dreaming all this. Or had she been right before, that all that was taking place in another universe? There was one way to find out.

"Ow! What was that for?" Katie yelped.

Rachel shook her aching hand. "Hit me back. Please! Like you did to Anya?"

"Rachel, what the hell is the matter with you?"

"Do you have to talk like that? That stupid Texas accent? I've studied English since I was six and I can't understand half of what you're saying! You sound like Huckleberry Fi—" Lying on her back in the street watching stars sparkle among the dancing lightning flashes in the sky-dome, Rachel croaked, "Thank you, Katie. Now I know I'm alive."

"You won't be if you make fun of me again!" Katie growled as Anya and Jack helped Rachel to her feet.

Jack shot her a warning look. "Miss Katie, don't take this wrong, I've known a lot of hot-tempered space jockeys, and I've been known to throw a punch or two myself, but you'd better get a hold of yourself or you won't last till we get out of Afro-Port, much less on Mars."

"Thanks for the advice, Mr. Zap-Gun," Katie snapped.

"Look, let's all cool out here," Jack said. "We're all tired out from the danger and the long walk. I'll just drop our gear off at my place and we'll go around the corner for some grub and a cold drink at Adrian's."

Anya's lips tightened at the suggestion, but she didn't say anything. Jack ran into a darkened entrance, emerging barehanded less than a minute later. "All done, ladies. Let's go refresh ourselves!"

Adrian's was located in a dark, dank room that stank of beer over a slight savor of vomit and disinfectant. Loud music blared from unseen speakers. The bar supported a solitary semiconscious drinker, a middle-aged man. The bartender was nowhere to be seen.

"Charming," Katie said. "Are all the bars in Afro-Port like this?"

"Afraid not. This is one of the better ones," Jack said cheerfully. "Yo! Adrian! Get your lazy butt out here, you have customers!"

There was an unfriendly rumble from the shadows, and a hulking figure appeared out of the darkness fast enough to make Rachel jump. "Why, if it ain't Deadbeat Jack," it said, with a voice like Karolla would have had in a sensible world.

"Deadbeat? Me? Come off it, Adrian. You know I'm good for it. I know things have been rocky for me lately, but I've got money coming in next week from the city for that surveying work I did out in the canyons."

The man-mountain snorted like a baby tornado. "The city, huh? I got news for you, Jack: They're broker than you are. Any graft that comes in, da Mayor keeps for himself. If you're waitin' on them for your pay, you'll soon find your sorry butt in the Corrector, courtesy of a debt collector." The walls trembled as he laughed.

Jack snickered dutifully. "So what do you say then, old friend? For the sake of old times?"

"You were broke then too."

"For the sake of friendship between worlds?" He gestured at his guests, who cringed. "Here I have two lovely ladies from Earth as well as my best Martian girl!"

"So now I'm financin' you getting' laid?"

Katie raised her fists. "Shut your trap, you big mmmmf!" Rachel clapped her hand over Katie's mouth.

"Not only pretty, but spunky, too! I like spunk. All right, Jack, I'll feed you and your girlfriends this once, even if they do have highly questionable taste in men. But this is the last time, clear?" Adrian shook a finger as thick as a *klemeth* vine under Jack's nose.

"Perfectly, my good man. But I really think this is an awful lot of fuss to make over a 200 zloty debt."

"Two hundred eighty six zlotys and 35 groszys, and that's before I feed you and your hungry pieces, Jack."

Katie asked, "What's he talking about?"

"Polish money," Rachel mumbled.

Anya responded, "Solar System currency."

Katie rolled her eyes. "Oh, brother, Rachel. What's the Solar capital called? New Warsaw?"

"No, that's the Lunar capital. I'm surprised an Earth native wouldn't know that," Anya said.

"Not half as surprised as I am," Katie said. "And here I thought you had so much imagination, Rachel!"

By this time they were all seated around a grimy table on which Adrian sullenly deposited a steaming tray of some type of meat, a plate of buns, and a pitcher of beer.

"I don't really want to know what animal that meat came from, do I?" Rachel said in Polish to Anya.

"Probably not. It's best to close your eyes and hold your nose while eating here. Though it does make you look kind of funny," Anya demonstrated. Rachel put her hand over her mouth and giggled.

"All right, all right, quit jabbering away in Marpolski and leaving us monolingual types out of the conversation," Jack said.

"Jabbering away in what?" Rachel asked.

"Marpolski. It's what we call our language," Anya eyed Rachel.

The food was surprisingly good, however. The meat reminded Rachel of her mother's brisket, and she made sandwiches of it with the buns. The beer was strong, and she sampled it cautiously; her parents didn't let her drink, not that there was any alcohol to be had in the ghetto, unless you were some black-market bigwig.

"We need to start planning how we will get to Mars to end the dreadful tyranny of Ares and rescue my long-lost brother." Jack sounded as if he were going to the store to buy a quart of milk.

"Do y'all actually talk like that?" Katie asked.

"Talk like what?"

"Like that. Like something out of a book."

Rachel sighed. *He is something out of a book, and not a very good one.*

Jack merely blinked at them. "How should I talk then, ladies? Is it not true that Ares is a dreadful tyrant?"

"Well—yes, from everything you and the princess say," Katie said.

"And is it not true that Jim is lost, lo these many years?"

"You're doing it *again!*"

"Doing what again?"

"Talking like a character in an old book! Who says 'lo these many years' in real life?"

"I do," Jack said, puzzled.

Rachel sighed again. *But this isn't real life.* Though it sure felt like it. She wasn't about to repeat her experiment with Katie. People in her grandfather's village might have a lot of silly superstitions about dreams, but in Rachel's experience if somebody hit you in a dream it didn't physically hurt and you didn't wake up with a lump like the one that was forming on her forehead.

"Katie, could I talk to you for a second?" Rachel stood abruptly.

"Huh? Sure, I guess so." She followed Rachel to the far corner.

Jack and Anya stared after them for a moment but then started making out. Rachel frowned. *Is that proper royal protocol?* She turned to Katie.

"Look, I can't explain what's going on any more than you can, but I think we'd better just play along for now," Rachel said. Katie stared at her. "What? Don't tell me the expression 'play along with' is obsolete in the twenty-second century."

"It's not that," Katie said. "But what's the point of getting caught up in this world if it all melts around me in the end? How do I know I'm not just lying out on the prairie dreaming?" The shadows in the room grew darker as she spoke.

Rachel shivered. "That's why I provoked you into hitting me. It hurt enough to break me out of my solipsism. Uh, solipsism means—"

"You don't have to tell me what it means. I ain't stupid just because I grew up on a dusty old farm in the middle of nowhere and sometimes say 'ain't.'"

"Sorry. I didn't mean—"

"Never mind. Y'all are right, I'd better learn to be a little less prickly, before I get into a fight with somebody bigger than me." Katie paused. The silence and the shadows thickened still further. When she spoke again it was in such a low whisper than Rachel had to lean forward until their faces were practically touching. "What do you think, Rachel? If we wanted to go back home, could we?"

"I haven't got any ruby slippers, if that's what you mean." Rachel remembered wistfully seeing "The Wizard of Oz" that final summer before the war broke out. "And I know this seems hard to believe, but I don't understand what's going on any more than you do. *I* didn't make up this bar, and if I had, I wouldn't have made it a filthy, disgusting hole like this."

A faraway look came into Katie's eyes. "Maybe I did."

"Maybe you did what?"

"Maybe I'm responsible for this bar. It looks a lot like the place in Abilene my daddy took me to for my first drink, on my fourteenth birthday. Even smells like it."

Rachel stared. Her breath caught in her throat. "But it's my story!"

Katie shook her head. "Huh-uh. It's just as much my story, ain't it? I mean, once you write it, the reader's got to imagine it in her own mind. It ain't as if I had a TV I could watch it on, like in the old days."

"What's a TV?" Rachel frowned. "So everything in this world is made up by either you or me?"

"Could be," Katie said. "And then that means, if we ever want to go back home, we've *both* got to click our heels three times. So to speak."

Rachel looked across the room. Jack, Anya, the bartender, and the semi-conscious drinker were still visible, but their outlines wavered like trees seen through a heat haze. "Do you want to go home so we can help our parents?" she whispered.

Katie hesitated. "Not yet. Not till we know more. Otherwise we're both liable to get into the same pickle our folks are in. But I miss my parents so much. I don't know what the Dixies did to them. I wish I could bring them here."

"And my parents," Rachel whispered. "The Germans...." Katie's gaze fell to the floor. "What? What is it?"

"I—I don't know if I should tell you," Katie whispered.

"What is it? Why not?"

At that moment, the outside door burst open.

4

Through the door came two big men armed with zap-guns.

"Anya Olympulska, we arrest you in the name of the crown," said the shorter of the two, who had a nasty scar down the right side of his face. He and his taller companion both had little bristly chin-beards. Jack's right hand twitched. "I wouldn't try that if I were you, Flash," said the tall intruder, pointing his gun steadily at him.

"Venus has no extradition treaty with Mars. This is kidnapping," Jack said.

Scarface grinned nastily. "Take it up with the Mayor Bellini after we're gone, Flash. But I think you'll find yourself on the business end of the Corrector if you make too much of a fuss."

"What is this Corrector thingie?" Katie asked Rachel, who shrugged.

"Let's go now, princess," said Scarface, grabbing her by the right forearm and hauling her to her feet. "I think you'll find the Corrector we have back home is the latest model, not like the one Hizzoner the Mayor has on *this* backward planet. You'll be serving the Emperor in no time."

"Ah, now there I musht dishagree with you, shirr," a voice slurred. Everyone turned to see the drunk staggering to his feet. "Our shcum-shucking rulersh are jusht ash shcummy ash your sho-called lord any day!"

"Stay where you are and hold your tongue, sir," Scarface said, waving his gun for emphasis.

The drunk kept staggering toward him. "But you have not yet tashted Venushian hoshpitality, my good man!" he cried, and threw his beer in the Martian agent's face. The man cried out and let go of Anya's arm to aim his weapon, but the drunk was already tackling him and the bolt went wild, sizzling a hole in the bar. At that Adrian, who had ducked down behind the bar when the invasion began, growled and launched himself over it. The other Martian agent pointed his weapon at him only to have Jack kick it out of his hand. He yelped, and as the girls advanced on him he turned and ran out the door.

"You know, that's something I've always admired about the agents of Ares." Jack walked to the man on the floor. "Your rugged individualism. You don't waste energy covering each other's backs, do you? If your colleague had been the one to go down, you would have been just as quick to desert him, isn't that so?" The trapped agent glared at him but said nothing, so Jack shrugged and clapped the man straddling him on the back. "Eagle-Eye Eddie, you son of a gun. I didn't know you were in town."

"Just hoping my ex-wife's lawyers can't trace me here, Flash," he said. "It's a long way from Ganymede, even for someone as greedy for alimony as she is."

"And you're busy falling off the wagon again, I see."

"Hey, I can handle the sauce perfectly well." The Martian agent tried to wriggle free, and Eddie punched him in the throat without even looking.

"Business first, Eddie, then we can catch up later." Jack walked around the prostrate spy until his boot tips brushed against the man's cheekbones. "Now I'm going to ask you this just once, desert rat. How many of you little sneaks did Ares send to this planet?"

The man on the ground grinned a slow, wicked grin, revealing a mouth that would have put a dentist's offspring through college unto the third generation, if its possessor had had any money.

"I see," said Jack. "Well, you can tell your master when you see him again—*if* you see him again—that Princess Anya will always be safe from him, and he should check the temperature of the throne before it burns his bottom."

"Sure we shouldn't just clean his clock for him, Flash?" Eddie growled.

"Nah, let the law deal with him. I understand the jail is suffering from an infestation of lightning lizards."

"What are lightning lizards?" the Martian agent asked.

"Let's just say if one of 'em jumps on you while you're sleeping, you'll never know what hit you," Jack replied.

"All right, what's the harm, you'll never get off this planet alive anyway," the agent decided. "There are dozens of us in Afro-Port. Dozens. The Emperor isn't taking any chances. And he's paid off the Mayor, so security at the space port, such as it is, will be looking the other way when we load our cargo. We have orders to kill anyone trying to protect the traitorous Pretender, and some super-groovy drugs on board that mimic the effect of the Corrector so she'll be nice and docile when we get her home. It'll be good practice for her," he chuckled. "As soon as she finishes getting the full Corrective treatment to cure her of her ridiculous and illegal ideas, she's going to marry the Emperor in a big, beautiful ceremony so the mob finally accepts once and for all that he is the planet's true and rightful ruler. Then he's going to take her back to his chamber and—" Jack punched him hard in the mouth.

"Now you do realize," Eddie said mildly, looking at the blood trickling from the unconscious agent's mouth, "that that's exactly what he wanted you to do."

"Jack, here you are lecturing Katie about temper, and look how you go and act," Anya added.

"Pile on me, why don't you," Jack grumbled.

"No, that's my job," said a man in uniform who walked in at that moment. "John Wilbur Flash, it is my duty to place you under arrest on suspicion of assault."

"Officer Dogberry, you came just in time," Adrian rumbled. "I want to lodge a complaint for property damage against Flash here."

"Just a minute, let me finish handcuffing him," the policeman said, feeling around his rumpled gray camouflage uniform until he located his handcuffs hanging from his belt. "Never could get the hang of these things.... Now, does the little piggy go into the lobster claw here, or is it the other way around?"

Jack rolled his eyes. "You want me to do it?"

"No, no, no, thank you all the same, Mr. Flash. Ah, I see.... This thingie here goes in the piggie's ear over there, and—"

"*Ow!*" Jack yelped, hitting the policeman on the side of the face as he jerked his hands away.

"Oo, now this is getting serious, Mr. Flash. I'm afraid I'm going to have to charge you with resisting arrest and assaulting a police officer, too."

"And don't forget attacking a diplomat." The Martian agent groaned and sat up, holding his right hand over his bleeding face while he flashed an ID card with his other hand. "Which is punishable by up to five years in prison and/or a 50,000 zloty fine. Venusian Code of Law, Section 1302(b)."

Dogberry took the ID card and stared at it with the intense concentration of the questionably literate. Katie peered over his shoulder curiously and did a double take as the cop politely helped the Martian agent to his feet, and, handing him back his ID, proclaimed him a legitimate "diplocrat."

"I don't believe this!" Rachel said. "He came in here and tried to kidnap the pr—uh, this woman over here! Mr. Flash was just trying to defend her! We've got at least three other witnesses who can vouch for him!"

"Yes, well, that's for a court to decide," Dogberry said, scratching his head. "Or Mayor Bellini, if the bribes aren't big enough—I mean, if the judge can't. Come along now, Mr. Flash."

"What about my property damage complaint?" Adrian said, pointing at the bar. "Flash blasted a hole right in my new oak bar! Cost me 129 zlotys to install, that did!"

Dogberry ran a hand through his hair, knocking off his hat without realizing it. "As I say, a court—"

"This is beyond outrageous!" Rachel yelled. "That blast hole isn't even from Jack's gun, it—"

Adrian clapped his hand over her mouth. It was like trying to shout through a two-by-four.

"He is responsible," Adrian said firmly. "I claim my rights as a citizen property-holder to seize Mr. Flash and hold his person here until such time as he makes good on the debt. Venusian Code of Law, Section 1065(a)(9)."

"Well, I…hmf…it seems…ah, it seems you are in the right, Mr. Josephus. I'll be on my way, then," Dogberry said, reclaiming the handcuffs and absent-mindedly snapping them around his own right wrist. "Say, anybody see what happened to my hat? No? Drat, that's the fifth one I've lost this week."

"You're just going to let this ruffian go after he attacked me?" the Martian agent cried. "I shall lodge a diplomatic protest!" And he stomped out of the bar, all wounded dignity, followed by the bemused policeman.

"Thanks, Adrian," Jack said.

"I really *do* want the money you owe me, Jack. With the food you and your friends just ate, your tab is now 432 zlotys and 65 groszys. Venusian scorpion-bunny don't come cheap, you know."

"Venusian *what*?" Rachel said, clutching her stomach, while Katie looked at the men curiously.

"Tell me, are all y'all lawyers?" she asked.

Adrian and Jack looked at each other and laughed. "Nah," Jack said. "It's just that the Mayor passes a new law every time somebody slips him a few zlotys, so it's just good common sense to keep up to date."

"Seriously though, Jack, I need my money," Adrian said. "You keep shootin' up my bar the way you do, I'm going to end up serving drinks out in the open jungle."

"Yeah, yeah," Jack said, waving his hand dismissively. "I'll get you your money. What I'm worried about right now is, we got to get off this planet. Even allowing for some exaggeration on that thug's part, it's gettin' too hot for us here."

He disregarded the barkeep's furious expression, but Anya walked over to the man, turned his head with her hands until he was facing her, and said softly, "The debt shall be paid. I swear it by the name of the House of Olympulski."

"Wow. Um, okay, princess, that's good enough for me," said Adrian, retreating behind the bar to clean up the shattered glass and spilled liquor.

Looking as if she were about to burst with curiosity, Katie pulled the princess aside and said, "Anya, I've got something to ask you."

"Ask away."

"That funny ID card Ares' agent pulled out. Was that the Martian flag in the upper left corner?"

"I didn't see it. What did it look like?"

"It was a rectangle with a fat blue vertical stripe on the left, next to two fat horizontal stripes—white on top and red below. Plus there's a red star smack in the middle of the blue stripe."

Anya made a face. "That's the new flag the latest usurper who calls himself Ares made up. Ugly, isn't it? The old Martian flag was a thing of beauty—a simple red circle for our planet, plus one golden dot each for the moons Phobos and Deimos to the left and right, all on a plain white background."

Katie bunched up her fists, then forced herself to relax. "You shouldn't call the new flag ugly. It's just like the flag of Texas, except for the star bein' red instead of white. But I guess you don't have no way of knowing what the Texas flag looks like. It sure is a weird coincidence, though. The new Ares isn't from Texas, is he?"

"Come to think of it, there *is* a rumor—"

"Come on, friends. This is no time to stand around shooting the breeze. Let's get off this world," said Eddie, dusting himself off. "You can stay at my place on Ganymede till things blow over."

Rachel frowned. "But I thought you said—"

"Yeah, yeah. It's all right, I got me some hidey-holes my ex-wife's lawyers don't know about. Jack, I presume it's not safe to go to back to your place. There ain't nothin' you need back there, is there?"

Jack scowled. "What, and leave my duds behind?" He thought about it for a minute, then shrugged. "I guess I can always buy some more clothes on credit. I'm all packed and ready to go, long as I got Annabelle here." He stroked his zap-gun affectionately.

Katie rolled her eyes at Rachel.

"I know, I know," Rachel whispered. "Unexplored depths, okay? You'll see them, I promise."

5

Climbing on board a rocket ship and blasting off for another planet was even better than having Katie sock her in the nose for convincing Rachel that there was something really real about the bizarre world she found herself in.

The space port was surprisingly sleazy and dilapidated, although given what Rachel had seen so far, maybe that shouldn't have been such a surprise. It reminded her of the rundown train station in Lvov, the nearest sizable town to her grandfather's village, complete with guys slouching against the walls with hands in their pockets, flat caps shading shifty eyes. Among them were three or four men in the same kind of camouflage uniforms Officer Dogberry had been wearing, cops or customs officials apparently, though it was hard to tell since their clothes were slovenly and their faces unshaven. One of them was eating a sausage on a bun, which was smothered in sauerkraut so pungent it smelled like rotting garbage. He swaggered up to Jack, sauerkraut dripping from his chin, and to Rachel's amazement thrust out an open palm. Jack merely nodded and placed several bills in the man's hand, whereupon all five travelers were waved through the departure gate without a second glance.

Rachel kept her mouth shut, but Jack saw the expression on her face, and once they were safely out on the tarmac he started to laugh. "What we like about our 'port is its informal efficiency," he said breezily. "As long as you have dough, all things are possible."

Eddie cocked a silver eyebrow at Jack. "I thought you were without funds, friend Flash."

Jack grinned. "I couldn't let Adrian take my emergency walking-around money, now could I, Eddie? Besides which, I have a certain image to keep up. I'd hate for people to start thinking I was flush instead of Flash, right?"

Thanks to the monsoon, the air smelled fresh and clean as they made their way to the rockets, which were the only things so far that looked exactly as Rachel had thought they would—sleek, streamlined white torpedoes with needle noses pointed straight up at the featureless gray sky. To reach them they had to detour around several puddles that were like miniature ponds, complete with live fish if the ripples were anything to go by. At least, Rachel hoped they were fish—Jack silently took her elbow with one hand and Katie's with his other and steered them away from the instant bodies of water.

"Where's the ticket counter?" Katie asked.

"Who needs a ticket counter? Most of these ships are charters, owned by their pilots. You pay in cash when you board," Jack said.

"Which is convenient," Eddie said, motioning with his head toward the terminal, "for a quick getaway."

Jack glanced back, then tightened his grip on the Earth girls' elbows and started walking faster and faster until Rachel's feet barely touched the ground. Not looking back to see who or what was after them was almost as hard as the physical effort of running. She panted, but Katie seemed untroubled and Anya and Eddie kept pace easily. *That's what I get, coming from a family of professors and rabbis*, she thought ruefully. At least the nearest rocket was no more than a few yards away—but suddenly Jack swerved off to the left, heading for another spacecraft much further away. Eddie asked the question Rachel didn't have breath for.

"I owe that guy money," Jack snapped.

"You ever think," Eddie gasped, "that it might make sense to pay at least some of your debts, some of the time?"

A searing beam of heat struck Rachel's arm. It was like a miniature of the lightning bolt that had welcomed her to Aphrodite Port, and she yelped in pain but found reserves of strength she didn't know she had, speeding ahead of everybody to the metal staircase of the rocket Jack seemed to be steering them toward. The air was suddenly full of sizzling and a sharp ozone tang.

♂

Rachel came to with a gasp and tried to push that fat pig Sonya off her chest. But her little sister Shoshie was holding her hands down. Or anyway, something was crushing her chest and something was pinning her arms to the bed. Even her eyeballs felt like they were being squeezed. She tried to scream but it came out sounding sort of flattened. *G-forces,* her mind belatedly informed her. *The rocket is taking off, so I weigh several times what I should thanks to all that force pressing down on me.* It was elementary, anyone who read sci-fi knew about g-forces, but it didn't stop her from panicking. "Katie?" she called hoarsely. "Jack? Anya?"

"Ain't this *beast*!" Katie called back happily. "We're going up into space, just like you wrote about in your stories, Rachel!"

"Yeah. Beast," Rachel muttered. The pressure on her chest gradually decreased, and soon she was able to sit up. She was in a berth in a cramped room with white metal walls and foam padding distributed at corners and edges. Katie was in the berth above her, Anya in the berth opposite, with Jack underneath her. Rachel looked for a porthole, then felt foolish. This wasn't some little ferryboat like the one she and her parents had taken in Danzig. No, this was a real honest-to-God *spaceship*. Outside the hull was hard radiation and hard vacuum. Nothing to mess with.

Not surprisingly, Jack was in his element. He stood up, stretched and grinned at the girls. "Welcome aboard! You might as well make yourselves comfortable, it's a three-week run out to Ganymede. Anya's an old hand at this, but you two landlubbers should know that you're going to be weightless shortly. That won't last long, though—the grav will come back as the spaceship starts to accelerate outwards."

"You should probably stay put until we're on our way," Anya said with a sympathetic glance at Katie and Rachel. "A lot of people get spacesick. Plus, moving around in zero-gee takes practice, and you don't want to get bruised."

"Wonderful," muttered Rachel. She already felt queasy, but the burning itch on her left arm distracted her. A crude bandage covered her arm.

Anya came over to sit beside her. "I have a paste in my emergency bag that will ease the pain and prevent infection," she said in Marpolski, producing a tiny bottle from a pouch concealed in her waistband. "Let me have a look." She gently peeled back the strip of gauze covering Rachel's forearm.

Rachel muffled a cry. She wouldn't show pain or fear in front of the princess. An angry red patch of skin the size of her palm was surrounded by a long narrow oval of charred flesh, oozing blood. Rachel's head spun.

"That's a nasty flash burn you've got there, Rachel," Jack said quietly.

Startled, she nearly hit her head on the bottom of Katie's berth. His tone reminded her of the pediatrician her parents used to take her to before the war, a kindly balding man with bifocals named Max Kantorowicz. It was so unlike Jack's usual jauntiness that Rachel peered up at him in confusion.

"Mind if I help Anya fix you up?" he asked, and she could only nod, turning away while they clucked and murmured over her wound, swabbed it with something sharp-smelling that instantly dulled the pain, and then applied a professional-looking bandage. "There you go," said Jack, ruffling her hair as unselfconsciously as if she was a girl of five and not fifteen. "You're a real veteran now, with the scars to prove it."

"Thank you," Rachel said in a small voice.

"Don't mention it," Jack said. "Now, the next thing we need to do is figure out where to find some decent clothes for you and Katie. You can't go running around dressed in costumes like that."

"Costumes?" *Look who's talking, when Anya was wearing that ridiculous toga!* The Martian princess had changed into more sensible traveling wear, slacks and a nondescript blouse, though of course she looked like a million zlotys in it.

Jack ran, or rather swam, out the door of the compartment, motioning them to stay put as he sailed off. Rachel tried to follow him and floated away from her berth, moving as if surfacing through shallow water. She swallowed a brief surge of panic, reminded herself that she was not a bad swimmer, at least in water, and stretched her arms out to push off the ceiling. Bouncing off at an angle she found she had gained momentum, and ducked to avoid hitting her head on Katie's berth. This motion in turn sent her caroming off the wall, and she flailed around helplessly until Anya caught her from behind in a bear hug and eased her gently back onto her bunk.

"Jack can be difficult, but he does know what he's doing in space," she said. Rachel said nothing, sitting with her hands on her thighs and staring at her knees. Bony knees, clearly visible through the threadbare skirt she had worn to bed two hundred years ago.

Anya looked at Rachel intently, then took hold of her chin so that she was forced to look into the princess's eyes. "It's nothing, Rachel," the princess said. "Everybody makes mistakes like that when they're new out in space. You've hardly ever been in space before, am I right?"

"I don't know anything about space, but it reminds me of my first time on horseback," Katie chimed in from her berth, from which she'd had the good sense not to move. "Daddy put me on the gentlest pony we had, and I darn near broke my neck."

"And what about you, Anya?" Rachel whispered in Polish. Or was it Marpolski? "When was the last time you made a mistake, ever?" The jade eyes stared into hers, then the long pale lashes came down and she turned her head away. Oh, great. So now Rachel had guilt to add to her humiliation. It wasn't Anya's fault she was a perfected version of Rachel; that's how Rachel had written her. Only she'd never expected to meet her face to face. She only wanted to *be* her in the daydreams she dignified by writing them down on her battered typewriter, and to be Jack, and Karolla too. If this was her world, a world she had created, why did it hurt so much to live in it?

Just then Jack surged back into the room, a shiny bundle under his right arm. "Got what you need, girls!" he called triumphantly. "Feast your eyes on this! The height of fashion in Old and New Paree both! You got your scarlet, you got your turquoise, you got your lemon-yellow! You got your blouses, you got your tights, you got your sexy little skirts and Venusian buffalo-hide boots, you got your.... Hey, what's with all the long faces? Somebody die in here?"

"Jack!" Katie said, beckoning.

He looked at her, looked from Anya to Rachel and back again, then pushed himself gently up until he was within whispering distance of the Texian. He listened, nodded gravely, looked sideways at Rachel, glanced at Anya, winked at her, then descended until he was midway between Katie's bunk and Rachel's. "Hey Earthies. Wanna see the inside of a real rocket ship?" he said.

Rachel glanced at Katie, who lay casually back on her bunk and waved them off. "I'm feeling pretty tuckered out from that rumble through the jungle. Think I'll try on some of them clothes you were kind enough to bring and have myself a nap."

That the others were trying to cheer her up was so obvious they might as well have painted it in four-foot-tall letters all over the cabin walls, but the prospect of a guided tour was too tempting for Rachel to turn down. Jack discreetly ducked out of the room while Rachel changed her clothes. The least gaudy choice was a blouse that didn't have too many sequins on it, and a skirt that barely managed to cover her knees. As she pulled on the "Venusian buffalo-hide" boots, which were a little tight, she realized she hadn't ever described the inside of an interplanetary spacecraft in anything she'd written so far. Did that mean as soon as they stepped out the cabin door, or anyway moved through it, that they would be surrounded by a gray void?

Not far from it, as it turned out. Jack took her hand and tugged her through a sliding metal door into a featureless tube, which was so narrow she could stand at any point and stretch her arms out to reach the far side. From end to end, the tube looked not much longer than the distance from Rachel's old house to the corner where old Witkowski used to have his grocery store. To get her oriented so that the tube would seem like a horizontal hallway rather than a vertical shaft, Jack tugged her through a quarter-turn around its circumference. This was made easier by the hand-holds installed at ninety-degree angles to each other and spaced at regular intervals along the corridor, allowing passengers and crew to move as they pleased regardless of how the ship was oriented at any given moment. Jack showed her how to use them like the rungs on climbing bars, and after a minute or two of queasiness Rachel began to enjoy herself.

Once she had the hang of it Jack took her to a miniature cafeteria, which they had to themselves at the moment. This was arranged like the famous New York Automat Abe had written her about, with sliding glass doors over compartments holding a seemingly endless variety of foods. Jack gave her some change and Rachel managed to find some dumplings that looked vaguely like pierogies, a mug of hot cocoa (which she hadn't had in three years) and a fresh orange (ditto). Jack watched her with amused tolerance.

"We're going to have to call you Rachel Wolf, the way you attack your food."

"That's funny," she said, her mouth full of steaming hot potato dumplings. Now, if only she had some sour cream, she could pretend she was out for Sunday brunch with her parents. Jack looked at her quizzically. "Wolf is my mother's maiden name," she explained after swallowing. "My last name is Zilber."

"Ah? I once knew a propulsion engineer from Earth called Zilber. Mark, I think his first name was, though we all called him B.O. 'cause he never took a shower. Little short guy, probably about forty Earth years old now. Any relation?"

"Earth's a big planet," Rachel said. *Besides which, if he's any relation he's probably my great-great-grandnephew or something.* She shivered. Jack frowned at her in concern and felt her forehead with the back of his hand, a gesture that made her tear up, it reminded her so much of her parents.

"You don't seem to have a fever. Say, are you all right? What's the matter?"

"Homesick," she sighed.

Jack nodded. "I used to get that way. Then I had a jeweler on Luna make me this locket," he said, pulling a necklace from under his shirt. She leaned forward and opened the locket, which looked like it was made of silver. Inside was a tiny color snapshot of a family at the beach: a smiling black-haired woman, a gray-haired man with a slight paunch who was trying to hold onto his dignity despite wearing nothing but a pair of bright orange swim trunks, and twin boys about seven (in Earth years), one of whom was holding up his fingers in rabbit ears behind the other's head. "That's me," Jack said, pointing at the mischievous boy. "I must've wrecked a million family pictures that way. Jim would always try to slug me afterward, but I was too fast for him."

"It's not your fault," Rachel said, putting her hand atop Jack's before blushing and pulling away.

"Isn't it? It was always my responsibility to look after him. I'm older—"

"—by three minutes, yes, I know," Rachel said.

"You do? How do you know that? And how do you know he's alive on Mars?"

How could she explain? If she kept insisting that this whole world was the product of her imagination, they'd lock her away somewhere. But what was the alternative? Letting Jack think she was some kind of spy? "Um. You know I speak Marpolski. My parents were Earth diplomats stationed on Mars, which is how I learned the language. Well, my dad's position as cultural attaché was really a cover for intelligence work. That's how he found out about the Ares dynasty's kidnapping operation. They've been snatching children from other planets for twenty years now. They brainwash them on Mars until they're in their teens, then send them back to their home worlds to serve as secret agents."

Jack frowned. "But I'm twenty-three."

Rachel nodded. "Jim was supposed to return to Venus almost three years ago. But he's never forgotten you or your parents, Jack. His superiors didn't trust him and they kept him behind, pretending he needed more advanced training. But now they've gotten frustrated and put him in a punishment battalion instead. And even that won't save him for long—we have to get to Mars and rescue him, Jack, or they'll kill him!"

"Your father found all that out? Wow, he must be some spy," Jack said. "I'd love to meet him. Plus he could help us out on Mars."

Oops. "No, that won't work, I'm afraid, Jack. You see, well, uh, his bosses in the Earth Intelligence Services didn't like that he was upset over the kidnapping program and Ares' other human rights abuses. They thought it was interfering with his work, so they recalled him and my mother. But I got bitten by the space bug, and I've been traveling ever since we got back to Earth." *Smooth, very smooth. Now I just hope he and Anya don't start comparing notes.*

But Jack seemed to swallow her story without trouble. "Yeah, governments are all like that. And all the Earthside politicians are interested in is trading with Mars and making sure Ares doesn't get all aggro toward the big blue marble." He sighed, then smiled and slapped Rachel on the knee, making her blush again. "Sometimes it takes freelancers like us to keep 'em honest, huh?"

A soft tone reverberated through the ship, and Jack got to his feet, deftly tossing their trash into a receptacle across the room. "That's the escape-burn warning, Ray. We'd better get back to our cabin now, unless you want to make a vertical climb back under rapid acceleration. Which believe me, you don't. You'll have plenty of time to meet the other passengers and crew later."

Rachel nodded and followed Jack out of the room, rolling the sound of her new nickname around in her mind. *Ray.* She liked it.

6

The trip through space was more fun than Katie had thought existed. Jack seemed to think most of the two dozen or so other passengers were boring, "suits in space, not guys in spacesuits," as he put it, but Katie had rarely met anyone from outside the Texas Panhandle, let alone from another planet. Meeting them was a blast. To begin with, there were shady characters like Eagle-Eye Eddie, who tended to talk fast and loud about other subjects when you asked them why they were making the trip.

"The name's Lightning Larry, little lady," one typical specimen said to Katie on the third day out. He was on the heavy side to be lightning anything, Katie thought as she slurped up some noodles in the cafeteria. And did all these guys have corny nicknames? She was going to have to talk to Rachel about that.

"So, do you travel around the solar system selling lightning rods, or is it kites?" Katie asked him.

"Kites? Oh, I gotcha. Ha ha! No, nothing like that," Larry said, absently patting his head and dislodging his toupee. "Say, who do ya think is gonna win the New Wimbledon Open? My money's on Phobos Williams. They got nothing to do on that Martian moon but play tennis."

"So are you from Phobos, Mr. Lightning?"

"Me? Ha ha! Just call me Larry, sweetie. Say, would you like to come to my cabin after lunch and inspect my meteor patches?"

The ship executed a midcourse correction, and Larry's toupee floated away, much to the delight of the other diners, who began to play keep-away with it. Katie slipped out of the cafeteria, leaving a whining Larry lunging after his hairpiece.

Not all of the rogues onboard were so obvious. Katie was fascinated by a fit-looking man in his twenties who wore a sandy mustache and spent much of his time reading in the recreation room. He looked like a man of action, someone who could have repaired a split-rail fence in an afternoon back home in Texas, but when he was reading he could sit perfectly still for hours at a time. Ordinarily Katie was shy around strangers, not that she ever met many of them in her world, but it didn't seem to make so much difference now, when everything was imaginary anyway. So she stood in the doorway and stared boldly at him, until he looked up with a half-smile and said, "Can I help you, miss?"

"What's that you're reading?"

He showed her the spine of the book.

"Nuh-uh, I don't believe you."

"Don't believe me? What's not to believe?"

"There ain't no such book as *Jovian Property Law for Beginners*."

The man shrugged, a rippling motion like a tiger pacing in a cage that made Katie feel kind of hot and mushy inside, like warmed-up grits. "Believe what you want. Now if you don't mind, I'm going to go back to reading my nonexistent book."

He had a few seconds of quiet to do so before Katie asked, "You studying to be a lawyer or something?"

"Nope," the man said without looking up.

"Then you're a, whaddaya call 'em, a real estate agent?" Katie was proud of herself for remembering this word from a library book.

"Not that either."

"Well, what are you then?"

"A very annoyed man," he said, slamming his book shut and standing up.

Katie stood her ground without flinching. "A man of unnecessary mystery, I'd say."

"Cheeky," the man said reflectively, walking right up to Katie and grasping her shoulders with both hands. Their eyes were exactly on a level with each other, a relief for Katie, who was tired of being short stuff. The man's eyes were the color of tea before milk is added.

"Well, my importunate friend," he said, releasing her.

"I am not."

"You are not what?"

"Importunate. You can't intimidate me with fancy words."

"Wasn't trying to. I was only trying to read my book," the man pointed out with some heat.

"What for? If you're neither a lawyer nor a real estate agent."

"Maybe I'm a *secret* agent."

Katie stuck her chin out. "Now you *are* messing with me."

"How would you know? Considering you ain't never been outside the Panhandle."

Katie felt a large, dense lump form in her stomach. "What did you say?"

"You heard me."

"I mean, how do you know where I'm from?"

"Your ac-*cent*," the man said, neatly catching Katie's upswung fist in his hand as if fielding a fly ball.

"Don't you mess with Texas!" Katie cried, drawing back her fist for another swing.

"Whyfore would I want to do that? My mother's from Abilene."

"What? Is not!"

"Is too!"

"Oh yeah? What's her name then?" The population of Abilene had declined drastically since Independence, and Katie bet she knew most of the family names there.

"Helen McSwain."

Katie's knees buckled and she grabbed at the door frame for support. "Helen McSwain?" she whispered hoarsely.

"That's what I said. So?"

Katie knew Helen McSwain, a quiet little girl who lived in Abilene and was the daughter of her mom's best friend Becky. Helen was nine years old last Thanksgiving. Except that that was thirty years ago, right? That is, her home was thirty years in the past and sort of at right angles to this world, if Rachel was right. So Helen could be all grown up now. Except, how could she have a son this guy's age?

"How old are you?" Katie demanded.

For the first time since she had interrupted his reading, the guy looked defensive. "What's it your business?"

"Twenty-five?" she persisted.

"No. I'm younger. People say I look grown-up for my age.... Why am I telling *you* this?"

"Beats me. I don't even know your name."

"I don't know yours, either."

"Katie Webb."

"Pete Kowalski. What?" he added when she rolled her eyes. "I'm half Martian on my father's side, sure. You got a problem with that?"

"Guess maybe I don't," Katie said, and they shook hands. "So why *are* you reading about property laws on the planet Jupiter?"

"Maybe I'm just interested," he said. "You have any idea how complicated it is trying to draw up a deed for a cloud of methane gas moving at several hundred miles an hour?"

"I can honestly say I've never thought about that."

"Well, it's pretty darn complicated. Especially when the property owners are these sort of giant gas bags the size of hot air balloons that reproduce like amoebas. You can imagine how complicated things get, legally speaking, when they start budding."

"Umm. Sounds fascinating. So what do you have to do with it?"

Pete winked at Katie for an answer, making her insides tingle pleasantly, but then retreated to the couch and resumed his reading, where he ignored further questions.

Well, all right, suit yourself. Katie wandered over to the Ping Pong table and picked up a racket.

In walked a woman who appeared to be about Pete's age (but did that mean she was really older than him?). The stranger picked up the other racket. She was slim, with a plain, pale face and brown hair held back from her forehead with a hairband. "So you think you're good, do you?" she asked Katie.

"What? I didn't say anything to you!"

The woman sneered. "I can tell you think you're pretty sharp, just from the way you hold that racket."

"Well, maybe I am good. My daddy plays with me every Sunday after church—they have an old table in the basement."

"Choir girl, eh? Well, let's see ya handle this," the woman said, smashing a serve over the net. Katie returned it just as fiercely, and they had a volley going before the ship made a minor course correction that sent one of Katie's return serves bouncing off Pete's head.

"Sorry," Katie said as he got up and stalked away in disgust.

"Ha! One-love," the woman taunted.

"That's no fair! It wasn't my fault the darn rocket jiggled just as I was serving!"

"Space rules, girlie. You wanna play with me or your dollies?"

"I'll show you!" Katie snarled. A furious volley followed. To her surprise, she eventually won the point. Each point after that was hard-fought, but with the continual minuscule changes in "gravity" caused by the ship's inconstant acceleration, Katie's more experienced opponent had the advantage of her.

When she reached 21 points to Katie's 14, Katie braced herself for some heavy-duty gloating, but instead the woman put down her paddle and walked around the table grinning, her hand held out. "Never had an opponent as good as you," she said as they shook. "The name's Gun."

"Gun, huh? Well, I'm Katie Webb, from the Lone Star Republic."

"Never heard of it, but apparently they raise some good table tennis players there," Gun said as they shook hands. "I grew up on Ceres myself, so I'm a true Belter through and through. Even the biggest of them asteroids don't have enough mass to hold a wad of spit, but they spin the inhabited ones to make artificial gravity. At slightly different rates, though, which is why I can play the game under variable acceleration. Oh, and by the way, my full name is Sherilynn Gunnarson, but if you ever call me Sherry I'm gonna push you out the nearest airlock. Capeesh?"

"Suits me." Katie grinned. Gun was the first person she'd met on this ship—and really the only one in this whole crazy world she'd stumbled into, with the partial exception of Rachel—with whom she felt instantly at ease. That wasn't true of the princess, who despite all her attempts to put Katie and Rachel at ease was still larger than life and just too, too perfect. But Katie had to scrape together the courage to ask to talk to her alone—that business about the "new Martian flag" being a near-copy of the Texian flag couldn't be just a coincidence.

♂

Her chance came one day when she found herself alone with Anya in their cabin. Katie pulled herself even with the bunk where the princess was resting with her hands clasped neatly on top of her head, as if ready at a moment's notice to swing into action. Seeing Katie, she turned and put on her full, radiant smile. "Kaitlyn, I can't believe how quickly you've adapted to weightlessness! You are a natural at it. I only wish it were as easy for Ray."

"Shucks, princess, if Rachel is Ray you can certainly call me Katie."

"All right then, Katie. You look like you want to talk to me about something."

"Yeah, I do. That new Martian flag that the fake Ares forced everyone to use."

Anya's eyes widened, then an unaccustomed scowl tugged at the corners of her mouth. "What about it? That night at the bar, you said it resembled the flag of your Republic of Texas, didn't you?"

"That's right, I did. And you said there was a rumor about the fake Ares...."

"Must we talk about him?" Anya blew a few stray strands of red hair away from her face. Seeing that Katie wasn't giving up, she sighed. "There are many rumors about him. Nobody seems to know who he is, or where he comes from. He speaks Marpolski worse than Jack. Some people whisper that he is actually an Earthling—no offense."

"Just so's you don't say nothin' bad about Texas." Katie paused and bit her lip. "Does anyone say he's from Texas?"

Anya thought for a moment, then shook her head. Katie let out a breath she didn't know she'd been holding. "No, I never heard anyone say what country on Earth the usurper is from. But my mother once heard that he came from some place with a weird name—the Potholder?"

7

For Rachel, the passengers and crew of the ship were a noisy, frightening mystery, and she kept to her cabin for most of the trip. It was one thing to sit in your comfortable room at home—or even in your cramped, shared room in the ghetto—and daydream about men and women "of action." To actually spend time around them, however, was something else again. It wasn't exactly unpleasant—after all the time she'd spent cooped up with bratty little kids and grownups who were helpless to do anything about the terrible situation, it was quite exhilarating to meet people who could buy a ticket to Pluto as easily as she could have bought one to Krakow in the old days—but she'd never had much to do with the kind of people back home who were like the freewheeling space traders and adventurers traveling on the rocketship, such as Jack's friend, Eagle-Eye Eddie. As for the crew, they talked and acted like sailors, or anyway like Rachel's idea of sailors, an occupation she'd only been exposed to once, on that ferryboat ride in Danzig. This meant a lot of jovial swearing and a bluff, hearty manner for the good natured ones ("Hallo, kid, first time in space?") and a get-the-hell-out-of-my-way-can't-you-see-I'm-busy manner for the bad-natured ones. Either way they frightened Rachel a little, which embarrassed her because she was, theoretically anyway, a socialist, and they were her equals. And feeling embarrassed, she resented the cause of the embarrassment. So she avoided them all the more.

Something else kept Rachel from befriending Anya. The Martian princess was an ideal version of herself—stronger and more agile, smarter and more adaptable, braver and more resourceful, humbler and more self-effacing, kinder and more patient.... The list of ways in which Anya was superior to Rachel went on and on, and were topped of course by her beauty and the passionate love she and Jack had for each other. Jack was unapproachable too, because of Anya.

So that left only Katie, Rachel's reader—and hadn't she always wanted readers? But what, after all, could they talk about? Katie had grown up on a farm, which made Rachel think of her grandfather's smelly, scrawny, cackling chickens, and the blood that got on his overalls when he slaughtered one for dinner. The fact that Katie was from the future should have been terribly exciting, and yet despite having read and loved H.G. Wells's *The Time Machine*, it had somehow never occurred to Rachel that the future could be worse than the present. That was depressing, and moreover it was frightening—obviously there was something about Rachel's immediate future that Katie wasn't telling her.

Was Hitler actually going to win the war? It seemed inconceivable, but how else was it possible that America was no longer a single country two hundred years later?

These questions, and her parents' fate, were too threatening to face, and she couldn't do anything about them, so Rachel kept to herself as much as possible. At first this meant she went nowhere but her cabin and the cafeteria, but eventually she discovered a storeroom that was little visited except by a taciturn member of the crew, a squat oriental-looking man whose fine black hair was going gray and who didn't seem to mind her being there. The place was little more than a dusty broom closet filled with mysterious electronic equipment and parts, partly disassembled spacesuits, oxygen tanks missing their valves and the like. Her great discovery there was an unlabeled box full of books; when she found them she let out a little cry. Retreating to her cabin, with trembling hands she took the books out one by one. Most were cheaply printed paperbacks in American English, or "Solar" as people called it here, and the rest seemed to be in Marpolski, so there was no language barrier for her. What she really wanted was a history of the past two centuries. Anything would do, academic or popular, or even a historical novel set in those quaint, long-ago days of 2042, one hundred years after her own time. Instead she found a lot of trashy novels, mostly from the twenty-second century. She knew that a close reading could give her some of the information she was looking for. But she didn't have the patience for it. A typical passage from a bodice-ripper by one Ellie La Tesdene ran like this: "…he took her in his warm, muscular arms. 'Oh, Lauralise,' he breathed, 'I have waited so long to be with you! All those years we were apart while I worked for my uncle building the new settlement on Titan. It gets so cold there, even inside the domes, and all I could think of was taking you in my arms.' Lizzy nibbled Doug's ear and snuggled against his chest. 'I'm here now, my love,' she sighed, 'and I'll never let you get cold again.'"

Sure, this told Rachel that the human race had made it out as far as the moons of Saturn, but so what? The Marpolski books were even less informative than the English ones. There was a small treasury of Martian poetry, which she set aside guiltily, and a number of propaganda works issued on behalf of the Ares dynasty, which she threw aside in disgust. The only one that caught her eye was a lavish hardbound coffee table-style photo album of the "Martian royal family." Just about every picture on every page prominently featured a goatish-looking man with a salt-and-pepper beard. He was dressed in purple robes set with sparkling gemstones and had his arm around, variously, an ethereally beautiful blond lady with sad blue eyes, a curvy brunette who looked as if she wished she could wriggle out of his grasp, a Japanese-looking lady in a kimono who stared wide-eyed at the camera as the man eyed her chest with an evil grin, and a redhead who looked startlingly like Rachel's Aunt Deborah, her mother's younger sister who had run off to America with that no-good pharmacist Marek. Although if they hadn't, her cousin Abe wouldn't have been able to send her all those science fiction books and magazines.

"That's my Aunt Diana, the black sheep of the family," a familiar voice said. Startled, Rachel jumped up, and, since the ship's "gravity" was now only about half of Earth-normal as the spacecraft decelerated toward the midpoint of its journey, she zoomed toward the ceiling. Anya grabbed her by the ankle and hauled her back down.

"Damn it, don't *do* that!"

Anya looked more concerned than abashed. "Poor Diana. I grew up thinking of her as a traitor. My mother wouldn't even speak her name— her only sister!—and my father referred to her as 'Ares' girlfriend.' Though I knew her name and what she looked like anyway because Ares—this was Ares II, of course, not the current tyrant—made sure to splash her picture everywhere. She didn't have royal blood because she wasn't from my father's side of the family, but old Ares must have hoped she'd give him extra legitimacy anyway. And of course, it didn't hurt that she was beautiful." Anya looked wistful. "When the new Ares murdered the old goat, of course, he kicked out all of his predecessor's concubines and mistresses without giving them so much as their wardrobes. Must have worried some of them might have been loyal to the man he'd overthrown. My parents refused to take Diana in, and I'm ashamed to remember how proud I was of them for that!

"I ran into her last year in the tent cities set up after the equatorial dust storm destroyed the central Tharsis Valley villages. I was traveling in disguise, doing what little I could for the refugees, and when I saw Diana, I thought at first that she must be in disguise too. But no, this worn-out looking woman with the lined face and gray hair was really my aunt! She cried when she recognized me. I braced myself for her to start begging me to take her in, but she seemed to know that my parents had turned their backs on her and accepted it as a just punishment. Though what she told me, in the hour before she disappeared back into that wretched crowd, shook my faith in them. 'I had to go to the palace,' she said. 'The old Emperor saw me when he was on a tour of the town where your mother and I lived. I wouldn't get in the air carriage with him, and he smiled and seemed to take it graciously, but when I got home I found your mother crying at the kitchen table, saying that Ares' men had come to her school looking for her and she had to hide in a closet to escape them. I had to protect my little sister, not to mention your grandparents, so I left home without a word that same night.'"

Anya paused for a moment, and Rachel shivered in horror. This was not part of any backstory she'd written or even thought about for Anya, that much was certain.

"I've never told anyone this," Anya said in an anguished whisper, "not even Jack, and don't you dare say a word to him about it. But I confronted Father and Mother when I got back from Tharsis, and they swore up and down that they hadn't known a thing about it. Mother cried like I'd never seen her cry before. She promised she would turn the world upside down to find Diana, but it wasn't long after that that my parents were arrested and I had to leave the planet. So there we are." She smiled sadly. "There comes a time when we all find out our parents are only human beings, isn't it so, Rachel?"

The pulse pounded in Rachel's ears as she thought about the arguments she'd overheard between her parents, these last few months in the ghetto, Dad blaming Mom for not letting him go to America when he got a visa for himself—but only himself—the summer before the German invasion. "I could have got you out from there!" he snarled in what he must have thought was a whisper.

"You're the one who was too tied to your sainted father and all his Hasid friends in Bilgoray to ever leave Poland!" Mom snapped in return.

Rachel shut her eyes. "Yes," she whispered to Anya, "yes, I've had that moment." To her relief a klaxon sounded then, warning passengers about the upcoming ship maneuvers. When they were strapped safely in their berths, Rachel had an idea. "Hey Anya," she said, "Katie and I have a history test after we get back from this, uh, vacation. We lost our textbooks in all that craziness back on Venus, so could you help us study?"

"Yeah, we heard you say how interested you are in history and all," Katie chimed in.

"Do you two go to school together?" Anya asked in surprise.

"Something wrong with that?" Katie said before Rachel could think of anything. "My daddy owns twenty thousand head of cattle, and he can send his daughter to school anywhere he darn well wants to!"

"All right, all right," Anya said. "Well. What period were you two studying?"

"The twentieth century," Rachel said.

Katie said, "The twenty-second century."

Anya raised an eyebrow. "Well, which is it?"

"I'm in the more advanced class," Katie said, "but you can fill Ray in too, I guess."

"Well, of course, the twentieth century, Earth-style, was when we had our first visitors from Earth."

"Girls, can you keep it down? Some of us are trying to sleep," Jack grumbled.

"Jack dear, you're the only person I know who claims to be able to sleep through space maneuvers," Anya said. "Now, where was I? Oh, yes, the first rocket from Earth touched down by the Grand Canal in 5708 on the Martian calendar, which was, hmm, 1948 on Earth."

Rachel stifled an exclamation. So the Martians weren't human beings themselves? Another thing she didn't remember imagining. In a hoarse voice she asked, "But what happened on Earth before that?"

"Before what?" Anya said.

"Before, uh, before 1948."

Anya frowned thoughtfully. "Well, let's see. The explorers were American, of course. Their ship was called the *Edgar Rice Burroughs*, or no, let me think, its captain was an old man by that name."

Rachel swallowed another cry of surprise. Burroughs's Martian novels were a major source of inspiration for her, and her Venusian jungles owed more than a little to his Tarzan stories. Would he—*did* he—actually get a chance to visit the Red Planet? Other questions were more urgent, however. "Yes, but what was happening on Earth? How did the war end, and when?"

"The war? What war? Oh, you must mean the Great War. Really, Rachel, you'd better study up for your tests. The Great War ended more than thirty Earth years before the Martian expedition."

"But what about Hitler?"

"Who?"

Rachel settled back on her bed, staring up at the ceiling as Katie quizzed Anya about more recent history. It didn't jibe with Katie's reality either. Not only did the United States of America still exist, according to Anya; it seemed it was now the United States of Earth, two hundred and thirty white stars in the blue field of Old Glory, which flew proudly over outposts all over the solar system. So her search for a history book had been futile; history here was as much a product of her fantasy as everything else. She was going to have to corner Katie and interrogate her if she wanted to know what the future was really going to be like, although come to think of it, there was no guarantee she would learn anything real that way either; wasn't it possible that Katie was just another product of her fantasies, albeit darker ones? Somehow, though, Rachel didn't think so. Katie seemed too much like a real farm girl, though she didn't talk like the Americans in any book Rachel had ever read, except maybe a little like the people in Mark Twain's novels.

So Rachel steeled herself, and as soon as the maneuvering was over and the passengers were free to move around the ship, she beckoned Katie to follow her to the storeroom.

"So this is where you've been spending all your time hiding, Ray?" Katie said, looking with dismay around the darkened little cubby. "What for? It's downright depressing in here!"

"Never mind that. What did you make of what Anya told us?"

Katie shrugged. "You tell me. It sounded kind of silly. No offense."

"None taken. I never wrote all those things. But what she told you about your own time didn't make any more sense than what she told me about mine, right?"

"Huh-uh. Like I said, silly stories. In real life there's still a country that calls itself the United States of America, true enough, but outside New England it don't amount to much. It don't control Texas, let alone the whole Earth. And it ain't a patch on the old America."

Rachel leaned forward on the box she was sitting on. "And the twentieth century. What Anya said didn't match up with the history you know, right?"

Katie was avoiding her eyes again. "Yeah. But I'm just a country girl. Mom and Daddy couldn't afford to send me to school, they just taught me to read and write and figure enough to get by." Katie's eyes looked suspiciously wet. "You, uh, you do know I was fibbing to Anya about Daddy having twenty thousand head of cattle."

"I don't care about that, Katie. And don't give me that 'I'm just an ignorant farm girl' stuff. You told me yourself about all that time you spent in the ruined library, and I'm sure you read more than just my stuff. So?"

"I don't want to talk about it."

"Why not?" Rachel leaned forward and grabbed Katie's shoulders. "It was July 1942 where I came from, Katie. I was trapped in the Warsaw Ghetto with all the other Jews. You have to tell me—Hitler's going to win the war, isn't he?"

Katie pulled away. "What? Of course not! Nazi Germany was crushed and destroyed less than three years later. The old America kicked his butt, with a lot of help from Texian boys. And the British and the Russians, of course."

Rachel let out a breath she didn't realize she'd been holding. "So we're all going to be okay, all of us in the ghetto. We just have to hold on till the war's over."

8

At midpoint of the trip the passengers and crew had a day of weightlessness to enjoy or to endure, as the case might be. Rachel was more cautious this time, and she managed to enjoy the dreamlike undersea feeling without bruising herself. Though it was embarrassing that Anya had to show her and Katie how the zero-gee toilets worked.

But these matters occupied only a small piece of her mind. She was too busy worrying about what Katie had told her about the "Holocaust." It was worse than anything she or her parents could possibly have imagined. Her parents especially—they were old enough to remember the German occupation of Poland in World War I, which had been a relief compared with the cruelty of the Russians who had dominated Poland for well over a century. What Katie had described didn't even make any sense. Why would the Germans want to put all their energy into killing people who posed no threat to them when they were fighting Russia, America, and Britain? No. It wasn't possible. But if Katie was even partly right, Rachel's parents and the Goldbergs were in terrible danger. She had to get back to the real world somehow and rescue them from the Germans.

But what could she actually do? And how could she get home? She had to figure out whether this spaceship, the jungle world Venus, and everything else in this universe had any reality, or was just a figment of her imagination that she could banish with a thought.

Clearly whatever was going on was more than just an ordinary dream. To begin with there wasn't any point trying to pinch herself, when she'd already been struck by Venusian lightning, burned by a zap-gun, and bumped her head, elbows, and shins innumerable times on this spaceship without waking up. Even more significant, the past few weeks of her life since she'd woken up in the Venusian jungle had a remarkable consistency. Jack hadn't turned into a two-headed purple snake, Anya was still a superior version of Rachel and not a large orange tabby cat, and the rocketship had not become a seventeenth-century sailing ship or a steamer taking her and her parents to America.

Could it be that she had lost her mind when her parents were taken away and was now living in some elaborate delusion? She had no way of proving that wasn't the case, but she didn't think so. In their old house her father had a locked cabinet full of the works of the pioneering psychologists Freud, Jung, Adler, and Krafft-Ebbing (poor Dad, thinking that a simple lock would be able to keep her out!). Rachel had read through many of these, and she was reasonably convinced that she wasn't any more neurotic than anybody else—and certainly not prone to psychotic-type delusions. Nor was there a history of mental illness on either side of her family, Mom's gibes about her crazy Hasidic father-in-law notwithstanding. (It was a terrible thing to think, but what Katie had told Rachel made her feel relieved that her *zayde* had died a few weeks before the German invasion.)

So, she wasn't crazy or dreaming. Her working hypothesis had to be that what she was experiencing was in some way real. The most important questions were how solid this reality was, and whether she could move between it and her own world at will.

She decided to start small. Watching enviously as Anya brushed out her long red hair one morning (frizzy hair being a major hazard of zero-gee), Rachel asked, "Do you ever wish your hair was a different color?"

"Like what? You know red is the most common hair color on Mars."

"Of course," Rachel said. She looked around quickly, but they were alone in the cabin for the moment, so she kicked off her bunk like a swimmer starting a lazy lap and floated up to Anya's berth, a feat that would have been quite impossible for her three weeks before. "What do you think I should do with my hair?" she asked, touching the split ends ruefully.

Anya reached over to finger Rachel's hair. "Let me see, I think I may have some Viking-red lichen," she said, turning her head away to rummage in her toilet kit. Rachel grabbed a perfectly smooth tuft on the back of Anya's head and whispered, in Yiddish in case the princess overheard, "Blond. I meant her to have beautiful, straight, long blond hair."

"What was that?" Anya asked, turning around with a tiny bottle in her hand, the motion pulling her hair out of Rachel's grasp. Rachel looked intently, but Anya's hair remained the same lovely orange-tinged auburn it had always been, instead of the garish carrot color that Rachel always wished she could change (but Mom would kill her if she dyed her hair).

"Hmm? Oh, nothing. I was just wondering if that stuff really works," Rachel said.

"It always did for Mother. Hold still while I rub it in." It smelled like autumn in Mom's garden at the old house. Strike one, as Cousin Abe would say.

Well, maybe thinking she could change things with a whisper was silly. That night, Rachel lay on what had now become the upper berth, above Katie. The ship had started its long deceleration, so the "gravity" had come back on, but in the opposite direction. The bunks could be rotated in place, so there wasn't even any need to change the sheets around, as long as you didn't mind switching from the lower to the upper berth or vice versa. The reorientation of the entire ship was going to take some getting used to, however, with the cafeteria now being a downward climb and the rec room and her closet hideaway now being located above their cabin. But she supposed she could get used to it.

Getting used to writing with a pen that didn't need dipping in an inkwell was something else again. Rachel had borrowed this magic pen from the crewman who frequented "her" closet. He waved her off when she offered to return it the next day. "I got plenty more," he said in what sounded like a flat Midwestern American accent. For paper, Rachel had the endpapers she had torn out of a couple dozen of the paperbacks—making do had become a habit for her.

But how strange not to have to use an inkwell. That habit was so ingrained in her that she couldn't stop stabbing the pillow where the inkwell should have been until the lower right corner of the pillowcase had a blue-black blot on it. She wouldn't make a fool of herself by asking how the thing worked, but clearly the ink was somehow contained within the body of the pen. It was certainly a lot more convenient than a regular fountain pen.

She paused before writing the first words, uneasiness creeping through her. She *liked* Anya, along with Jack and most of the rest of the people she had met—how could she help it, considering that she had dreamed them up? Changing the princess without her knowledge or consent seemed wrong, and what if in altering the color of her hair she somehow altered her personality in some subtle way? But the experiment had to be done. Rachel had created this world through writing, so it seemed only logical that she could modify it through writing.

She looked around one more time. Everyone else in the cabin was asleep. Jack lay face up, his mouth slightly open, looking oddly vulnerable, like a little boy. Katie was snoring gently down below, while Anya lay in her berth directly opposite, the blankets and sheets tucked up neatly around her perfect chin, her red hair fanning out on the pillow around her head. Rachel sighed, drew a breath and wrote:

The princess lay in her berth, the blankets and sheets tucked up neatly around her perfect chin, her long blond hair fanning out on the pillow around her head.

Rachel whipped her head around so fast something popped in her neck. Rubbing it and cursing silently, she looked at Anya, who slept on peacefully, every strand of her beautiful red hair lying undisturbed. Strike two.

For her third attempt, Rachel struck up a conversation with the crewman who shared her closet, whose name turned out to be David Chu. He wasn't a big talker, and he seldom smiled, but when he did you could tell that he really meant it. He told Rachel he was from Independence, Missouri.

"Mark Twain's hometown!" Rachel said excitedly, and was rewarded with one of those rare smiles.

"Yes. I've been a rocketman for twenty-five years, ever since I dropped out of college."

"Dropped out? But—"

"You don't need a higher education for the kind of scut work I do, miss. I wanted to see the universe, but it turns out I don't get to see much more than this closet and the engine rooms."

"But that's terrible! What about the, the surface of the moon? The rings of Saturn? The Great Red Spot?"

"They're not all they're cracked up to be, miss. Though I suppose I shouldn't try and disillusion a young girl like you. It won't do any good anyway."

"You talk like an old man, but you're younger than my dad!"

"Oh, don't get me wrong, this job has its moments. I prefer looking at the stars when we're on the long haul out to Triton, and imagining what we might find out there. That's where the real wonders are, you want my opinion. The solar system must have been an adventure in the early days of space travel, two hundred years ago, but now it's full of people messing it up with their usual greed and stupidity."

Rachel seized his hands, which were dry and calloused, and looked him straight in the eye. "You can't mean that, Mr. Chu! I know this is only my first time in space and I must sound like a silly kid to you, but not everybody is selfish and awful. You should talk to my friend Katie and my sis—I mean, my friend Anya. They'll change your mind."

Chu smiled with his eyes as he pulled his hands away. "Maybe I'll do that, miss. Now, what's all this about a typewriter?"

"I just want to borrow one, that's all. I promise I won't use it long. I can type really fast! And of course I won't damage it. I won't even take it out of the room it's in."

Chu frowned. "There's only one typewriter on board that I know of, and that's in the captain's office. You'll have to ask him."

"Could you please come with me? I, I'm a little shy on my own."

"Of course, miss. We'd better go now, because we'll be coming in radio range of Ganymede soon, and he's going to be tied up with business from tomorrow morning on."

Captain Nelson Turnstone turned out to be a tall, unsmiling black man with a fringe of silver hair and a full gray beard. Chu delivered Rachel's request matter-of-factly, but the captain turned and glared at her. "Seems to me the young lady could speak for herself," he rumbled. Despite his imposing bearing and manner, he was dressed in a rather shabby uniform that reminded her of nothing so much as a prewar Warsaw traffic cop.

"I want to borrow your typewriter, sir."

"Yes, Crewman Chu just told me that. Well? What do you want it for, and what's in it for me?"

Rachel was stymied. What on earth—or what in the universe—was she supposed to offer in return? She looked the captain up and down again. Not only was his uniform shabby, it was missing two buttons. *What kind of captain walks around in a threadbare uniform that's missing buttons? One who can't afford a better one.* Remembering the lessons she'd learned from her mother, who used to work as a bookkeeper, she asked, "Who does your books?"

"What? Er, I do, myself."

"Nobody goes over them for you?"

The captain looked at the floor. "Can't afford an accountant," he mumbled. And so a deal was struck: Rachel would get the ship's books into something resembling proper order, and in return she could actually have the typewriter, "which I hardly ever use anyway."

The ship's books turned out to be so interesting Rachel nearly forgot about the typewriter. They consisted of a single battered ledger crammed with invoices and receipts, some of which were scribbled on the backs of envelopes, napkins, and, in one case, a matchbook advertising "Lil McGill's Fine Eats, New Dakota Black Hills, Io." They went back at least five years. Using a mechanical adding machine that whirred and clucked as if delighted to finally be getting some use, Rachel quickly found that while an unsurprising amount of the ship's budget went to necessities such as fuel, oxygen, maintenance, food, crew salaries, etc., almost a quarter went to "miscellaneous expenses." When she asked Captain Turnstone about this he looked at her with pity.

"You really are young, miss," he said. "You can't fly a rocket in this system without paying bribes."

"Bribes?"

"Bribes to the customs agents on two dozen worlds and worldlets. Kickbacks to fuel and equipment sellers at every greasy little depot between here and Charon. Protection money to the Asteroidal Mafia so that you don't wake up one fine morning to find yourself in a meteor storm with defective hull patches."

"I see, but…did you know they cost you 1,612,389 zlotys last year alone?"

"What? Let me see that." He grabbed the adding machine tape from Rachel. His lips moved as he checked her figures. "You're right," he said soberly. "Must be one of the crew skimming off the top, and now that I think about it, I know just who it is. Plus, it looks like I've been overpaying for fuel in the Saturn system…darned Ring bandits…. Tell you what, Ray, not only can you keep the typewriter, I'll cut your friend Jack a deal on this trip so he only owes me 2,500 zlotys."

Jack would be overjoyed when he heard that! Rachel grabbed the typewriter, a manual Olivetti not too different from the one she used back home, and, holding it and a sheaf of typing paper under one arm, quickly scaled the ship's ladder to her closet.

On the way she passed Anya, who looked at her curiously. "Need some help, Ray?"

Rachel jumped guiltily. "Uh, no thanks, Anya. See you at dinner?"

"Sure. But I'm just heading off to the rec room for the table tennis tournament. There's a woman called Gun who might actually give me a good game.…"

But Rachel barely listened. She hurtled into the closet, paused to catch her breath, then put a fresh sheet of paper into the platen, turned it, and sat for a moment thinking.

All eyes were on the Martian princess as she entered the spaceship's little rec room, Rachel typed. Or meant to type. But the ribbon was as dry as a Martian desert. Spluttering some Yiddish words Dad and Mom would have been very surprised to know that she knew, Rachel climbed back down to the captain's offices, returning a few minutes later with a spare ribbon. After inserting it into the typewriter, she tried again:

```
All eyes were on the Martian
princess as she entered the
spaceship's little rec room. Anyone
else's hair would have looked lifeless
and horrible under the ship's
relentless fluorescent lighting, but
Anya's long golden hair shone all the
brighter. "Sorry," she smiled as she
faced her opponent, "just give me a
second to tie this back out of my
way.…"
```

Rachel ripped the page from the typewriter and hurtled out the door, barely avoiding Chu in her haste. "Sorry!" she called over her shoulder as she climbed to the rec room. Quite a crowd had gathered there, and a fierce game was already in progress. She spotted Jack, his friend Eddie, and most of the other passengers, all hunched around the table. On the far end a leaping, spinning blur with short brown hair must be Gun. On the near side, puffing intently as she returned volley after volley, the princess....

"Ray!" whispered a voice, causing her to conk her head on the door frame.

"Damn it, Katie!"

"What's the matter? How come you look so disappointed?"

Rachel shook her head and handed the typewritten sheet to Katie. Anya had tied her hair into a perfect red bun that bobbed up and down.

Katie's lips were puckered into a puzzled frown as she handed the paper back. "I don't get it, Ray. What's the point of writing that Anya's hair is blond when anyone can see it's a beautiful shade of...."

The crowd gasped and Gun cried out in dismay as a volley passed her. Anya put down her racket and walked around the table to gravely shake her opponent's hand. Then she undid the bun and shook out her hair so it flowed gracefully down her back. Her beautiful, long blond hair.

9

Another world! Rachel's every waking moment was filled with wonder. In Aphrodite Port, you could forget that you were on another planet, because the gravity was so close to Earth-normal and the buildings, though strange, could have been in some foreign city. But here on Ganymede, everything was indisputably, unavoidably alien. Nobody could live on the surface, with an almost nonexistent atmosphere and a temperature of 173 degrees below zero, so everyone on the planet (actually a moon, Jupiter's largest) lived in an enormous warren of tunnels that extended 100,000 miles or more. Ganymede's major industry was digging these tunnels, which also created the major export product—water ice, which made up the bulk of the moon's mass. Any time anybody needed more space, the giant mechanical diggers came in and mined huge chunks of ice that could be exported at a ridiculous profit to the thirsty inner planets, in the same way that people used to cut the ice in blocks from frozen New England ponds in the winter and ship it south in the era before refrigeration. The silicate rock that was mixed in with the Ganymedean ice could be extracted and used to build underground stone palaces for the locals. Even the greediest, most graft-blinded politician (another commodity the Jovian moon abounded in) could see that this happily lucrative situation couldn't last forever. Long before the ice ran out, the hyperactive tunneling would undermine the moon's surface enough to cause major gany-quakes. Already, tunnel collapses were the third leading cause of death on Ganymede, right behind skating accidents and duels. Elaborate digging regulations had of course been drawn up with the help of some of the Solar System's leading exogeologists (those who didn't mind paying a healthy twenty percent of their commissions in kickbacks), but the laws were easily ignored by any contractor who bribed the clerks at the Ministry of Ice Burrows, popularly known as the Slush Fund. The clerks tooled around the Solar System in their Space Corvettes and Stellar Lamborghinis, and the future of Ganymede could take care of itself.

Eagle-Eye Eddie had filled Rachel in on the squalid facts of life in his *pied-à-lune*, but she couldn't get too worked up about it. Everything was so fantastic, with the humblest tunnel-diggers living in stone fantasies out of the Thousand and One Nights, all connected to one another by endless blue-lit tubes of ice where the only sounds were the slow drip of meltwater and distant shouts from "shockey" games, played with granite pucks (concussions from which were yet another leading cause of death locally). The gravity was like that of Luna, just one-sixth that of Earth, so

Rachel weighed less than twenty pounds and could go leaping through the high-ceilinged ice tubes like the Texian antelope Katie had told her about.

Not that I've seen much of Katie lately. She's been avoiding me ever since we landed. But maybe I've been keeping away from her, too. Do we really want this power we seem to have, the power to change everything about the world and the people around us? I know I don't. I'm just glad we turned Anya's hair back, and that no one seemed to notice her instant dye jobs!

Rachel sat on her bunk in the guestroom Eddie had rented for her, hotels apparently being nonexistent on Ganymede. The typewriter glimmered menacingly in the dim light. *But doing nothing seems much worse than messing with Anya's hair. After all, Katie and I have all the power in the world if we choose to use it, don't we? We could rescue Jim in just a few minutes of typing and reading. We could even make it so that Jim would never have been kidnapped in the first place. We could overthrow the wicked Lord Ares and enthrone Anya's father in his place. But if I rewrite the past and change people to suit my will, aren't I as bad as Ares and Mayor Bellini using their little "Corrector" torture devices on people? It's one thing to play with the world's destiny on the printed page, but....*

And Rachel really did seem to be living in this strange future world. The more time went by, the more certain she became that she wasn't having some elaborate dream or hallucination—everything was too detailed and consistent, the new world seeming to follow its own rules, many of which she had never dreamed of when she was writing her silly stories. Take the rampant sleaze. From what she'd seen of Venusian and Ganymedean society, they seemed to function on their own terms, and people accepted the need to hand out bribes left and right to get anything done as a matter of course. But Rachel had never imagined that the shiny future world would be so, well, *grubby*. Or maybe she had imagined it subconsciously—and if so, what did that say about her?

And one more thing. One more BIG thing. What about Mom and Dad, and Katie's parents? If it's so easy to change things around in this world, maybe I could change the real world, too—or at least get back to it and do what I can to help. Admit it, though, Rachel: You're scared. The possibilities are as endless as these damn ice tunnels! Maybe this "imaginary" world sprang full-grown from my brain, like Athena emerging from Zeus's forehead in Greek legend, and then took its own course. Or did it exist independently, in reality or in potential, before I ever wrote about it? In that case, am I really a creator, or just a discoverer and arranger?

The philosophical implications were beyond Rachel. Thinking about it literally made her head hurt, a pain that started as a focused little knot of discomfort in the bridge of her nose and spread until her whole head felt like an overinflated party balloon. Touch her and she might explode, sending colorful shreds of rubber flying. At times like this she left her room and leapt down the corridors, soaring along in giant steps in the endless blue light. The exhilarating motion helped clear her head, as long as she avoided bumping it on the low ceilings. There was a constant steady breeze in the tunnels from powerful fans set in the walls at certain junctions. But she didn't feel cold, or claustrophobic; the tunnels were easily four yards in diameter, so there was little risk of hurting yourself if you were minimally careful and not into "extreme skating." And it helped her forget for the moment that she wasn't doing a thing to help her parents.

On one such expedition Rachel gradually realized that she was on an upward slope in an area where she'd never been before. She wasn't worried, because her locator-bracelet would lead her back to her guestroom through a simple system of beeps and flashes that let you knew whether you were getting warmer or colder, like a game of hide-and-seek. Still, she didn't want to go too far, so she slowed down. And suddenly she stood in the middle of the grandest junction she'd yet seen, a public lounge strewn with soft cushions in the shape of fuzzy pillars, prisms and trapezoids. The ceiling sloped upward to a monitor wider than Rachel was tall, offering a view of Jupiter. Mesmerized, Rachel lay flat on a couch and stared at the screen. She'd seen drawings and photographs of the giant planet back in Poland, but those were taken through early twentieth-century telescopes and showed nothing more exciting than a beach ball, or maybe a nice but unspectacular striped agate. *Those pictures didn't do justice to the king of the gods!* Rachel's breath came in quick, shallow gasps as she studied the seething, boiling cauldron above (below?) her. The screen didn't show the entire gas giant, but the equatorial band visible was spectacular. The summer cumulus clouds she'd watched above Bilgoray were colorless, flabby imitations of what she saw now. Bands of orange, pearly white, and light brown climbed over each other and dissolved like an endless bucket of snakes writhing around stately whirlpools big enough to swallow the Earth without a ripple. If you played the game of looking for animals or castles with *these* clouds, you'd quickly lose your mind.

"Amazing, isn't it?" said a familiar voice.

Rachel let her breath out slowly. "Hello, Anya," she said, sitting up reluctantly. "Any progress on figuring out a way back to Mars?"

The princess's red hair swirled slowly around her face as she shook her head. "Not yet. Lord Ares has done the impossible, watching and controlling every ship that lands on or takes off from my world. He's purged Customs and the spaceport staff of everyone loyal to my family. You can't even bribe your way in—civil servants accused of corruption are fed to Olympus Mons."

"What?" Rachel's skin crawled.

"He feeds them to Olympus Mons. Not only is it Mars' tallest mountain, but it is the biggest active volcano in the Solar System. In the old days my people used to perform human sacrifices there so the gods would send rain to fill the canals. Wanda the Great abolished that barbarism, and my family is even prouder of her for that than for starting the Grand Canal. She had a vision while climbing the mountain, you see—a vision of a thistlecat with its paws stuck in the cleft of a rock, just above a river of magma. It pleaded with her for help and she ran to set it free, when she heard the voice of God telling her to stop murdering the children of Mars, for they were as helpless as the poor beast she wanted to save. And so she ordered, and so it was, but now Ares is returning us to the dark ages."

"A thistlecat?"

Anya gave her a long, hard look. "They're only one of the most famous symbols of Mars, Rachel! Even if you were only on the planet for a short vacation you'd have heard all about them! Jack told me you claimed to be the daughter of an Earth diplomat...but you let me think you were one of us. Either way, your story doesn't add up." The princess leaned toward her, a menacing gleam in her eye. "Just who are you, Rachel Zilber?"

How could I not have prepared something? Stupid, stupid girl! Feeling like she was flying headlong down a dead-end ice tunnel, she leaned toward Anya until their faces were almost touching. It was like looking into a reverse funhouse mirror, one that made you look better than you were. Rachel lowered her voice to a whisper. "You have to keep this secret, Anya, even from Jack," she improvised. "Can you do that?"

Anya jerked backward as if Rachel had spit in her eye. "You would dare insult the House of Olympulska by implying I cannot keep a secret?"

Good grief, she's so prissy. "All right, then. I'm not from Mars. I'm from a country called Poland, on Earth."

"Oh. Well, that explains how you speak Marpolski, then. There are some remarkable linguistic parallels between Polish and what we speak on Mars. There's used to be a whole department at Wandanian University devoted to studying them, before Ares shut it down and had all the professors arrested for treason." Anya paused and gave her the evil eye again. Rachel had to struggle not to gulp. "That still doesn't explain why you let me think you were Martian, and told Jack you were the daughter of an Earth diplomat."

Rachel took a deep breath. "I'm on a secret mission to help you, Anya. You just have to trust me for now. I can't tell you the whole story yet, but I'm an Olympulskan, heart and soul."

Anya grimaced. "We do wish people wouldn't use that term. We're patriotic Martians, that's all."

Rachel's knees buckled in relief. *Time to change the subject.* "What do you want Mars to be like, when your family is restored to the throne?"

Anya smiled ruefully. "There's not much chance of that happening any time soon. I've always thought I'd leave all that to my father—he would be the best ruler since Wanda—but I guess you're right, now that he's abdicated, I really should start thinking about it, in case a miracle happens."

"He abdicated? Why did he do that?"

"I'm sorry, Rachel, but I've been keeping secrets, too. Father got word to me a few weeks ago, just before I spotted Ares' agents on Venus, that he and Mother are in 'protective custody' and that he was going to abdicate in hopes that they'd be released, or at least that the tyrant would leave me alone. He said I should stay away from Mars until everything is sorted out. But I never should have abandoned them in the first place!" Anya stopped and wiped her eyes with a silk handkerchief.

"But really, what would you do if you ruled Mars?"

"Me?" Anya put her hand to her chest and blushed.

Damn it, she even blushes prettily.

"I'm just a child," the princess continued. "Under Wanda's Great Code of Law, a council of regents would have to be appointed until I am of age. But what I would do…well, things can't go back to the way they were in Wanda's time. After all, she ruled so long ago. Almost three hundred Earth-years—before Earth had its Great War. Things were simpler then."

"Maybe it only seems like that from our perspective," Rachel said, hearing her father's voice. "After all, stopping human sacrifice, building the Grand Canal…it all seems so obvious to us now, because we know the end of the story. We know it was the right thing to do. But back then, it must have been so complicated and hard."

"You're right, of course," Anya said, a faraway look in her eyes.

Rachel felt a small spark of pleasure at the princess's approval. She hoped Jack realized what a lucky man he was!

"Anyway, things were different," Anya continued. "Maybe better. After three generations of Ares, each worse than the last, could our people even build another Grand Canal, or write another Tharsis Symphony? Or are they good only for wargames and informing on each other?"

Rachel shivered and hugged her own knees. Just like Poland, even before the Germans invaded. She used to lie awake at night listening to her parents quietly arguing about her father's harassment at the university. Bad enough he was a Jew, but that he taught the truth as he saw it in his medieval history class was intolerable. A death threat had been slipped under his office door the summer before the war broke out, and he had suspected that one of his own students was to blame.

"I told you, we should have gone to New York when Marek offered us the chance," Mom used to say back then.

Dad sniffed. "A pharmacist, what does he know? How would he get us a visa? And I can't just run away from my post and teach at some jerkwater college among the cowboys and the Red Indians! I'd be letting the haters win, proving their point for them that Jews aren't really Poles. No thank you!" How ironic that he'd adjusted his memory after they were imprisoned in the Ghetto, to insist that he was the one who'd wanted to leave the country all along.

"Rachel? Are you all right?"

"Sorry. Just woolgathering. What did you say?"

"I said, it's not like in a fairy tale. We can't just get rid of the evil king so the sun will smile on the blessed Red Land again. It suited a lot of people all these years to go to Ares II's parties with all the sexy, beautiful people and the liquor and the Venusian jungleweed to smoke. He was very generous with all that, and plenty of good Red Martians loved him for it. And even more of them love prancing around in those ridiculous uniforms the new tyrant has dreamed up, and practicing with zap-guns and chanting about how they're going to make the streets of Earth run red with blood. If I became queen tomorrow, what would I do with all those people? I'm not an Ares, I can't just throw them all in jail. What could I do?"

Rachel shook her head. "I wish I knew. Did you ever talk to Katie about it? You and I may know our history, but I think she's got good common sense, on top of having read as many books as we have."

"I hadn't thought about it," Anya admitted. "Where is she, anyway? I haven't seen her around all week."

10

Katie let out a whoop of pure joy as multicolored streamers of Jovian cloud whipped past her spacesuit visor at hundreds of miles an hour.

"Ride 'em cowboy!" she shouted. Pete Kowalski roared in approval. They were both tethered to a spinning-top-shaped platform borne along like a floating buoy by winds that blew five times as fast as the strongest Earthly hurricane ever recorded—faster than the speed of sound. But there was hardly any sensation of motion. It was like floating along on a tranquil river, something Katie had frequently done on visits to family in East Texas. The spacesuit and helmet were comfortably cushioned, and all she had to do was relax and enjoy the ride. Pete was the one who had work to do. His voice came in staticky bursts over her suit radio.

"Now see here, Orangepuff 567, you know perfectly well that we can't get your cloud-clan more than 750,000 Solar zlotys for the larger methane patch."

There was a gloopy sound like mud flowing over a rock ledge.

"Don't give me that, O.P.! We've discussed this before! My client can't get financing for more than 750,000. Those Polar Zone banks, they're really tough. They'll take your arm, leg, and testicles, plus your wife's breasts just to set up a meeting. What?"

Katie stifled a giggle. *Mom would have a cow if she knew I was with a man who talks like that.*

Another liquid noise.

"Oh, right. Sorry. They'll take your tendrils and the honor of your clan, you get my drift? Oh, ha ha, no, I'm following *your* drift. That's what I like about you, O.P.: your sense of humor."

Before they'd set out for Pearlband Station 17, which Pete rented on his frequent business trips, he had explained that seventy-five years of contact had given humans and Jovian puffballs (who called themselves Glorious Balls of Fire) plenty of time to learn each other's languages. Puffballs couldn't speak Solar, however, and it was physically impossible for humans to speak Puffball. Computer technology in what Katie called Ray's World was primitive compared to what it had been in Katie's world before the Collapse, so simultaneous electronic translation was impossible. People and Puffballs simply learned to understand each other's languages, which Pete swore wasn't all that difficult, at least from the human end. Katie figured she'd take his word for it. For her, trying to understand the noises the Puffballs made was like the time she tried to read a couple of books in Arabic she found in the ruined library back home; all those graceful swirls were supposed to comprise separate letters making up words, but to her they made up a lovely but incomprehensible pattern.

So she listened with half an ear to Pete's mysterious "real estate" negotiations and gave her main attention to the sights exploding all around her. Once, her grandfather with the sad eyes and aborted past had given her a kaleidoscope. It was one of her favorite childhood toys, and she had always been fascinated by the infinite variety of patterns made by the little colored flecks. Jupiter was like a kaleidoscope of swirls that surrounded her in every direction, lit by continuous flickers of lightning, each bolt carrying enough of an electrical charge to power a small city. As native-born Texians, Katie and Pete were supposed to be from the Land of the Large, but even he seemed overwhelmed by the planet's immensity. For example, the Mid-Southern Pearlband in which she was bobbing along like a leaf caught in a brook was a streamer of gas visible from space. It was 800 kilometers across and was hurtling eastward toward the Great Red Spot at 900 kilometers an hour, but although it looked from Ganymede as though Station 17 was only a few inches from that enormous storm, in reality it was tens of thousands of miles away (longer than three stretched-out Earths laid side by side, Pete had had to explain to her; she still thought in terms of miles). When it eventually reached the Great Red Spot it would join the endless clockwise swirl around it. The Puffballs called this "returning to the sea," like an Earthly salmon, and it was an important milestone in the life of their community. After seven cycles in the Great Red Spot, they would exit through an eastbound Pearlband that emerged from the far side of the storm.

The negotiations between Pete and O.P. were drawn-out and tedious, but at last they seemed to have been concluded satisfactorily.

"We're done here," said Pete on the private intercom channel.

A powerful motor in the platform began reeling Katie in, and a minute later she was sitting with Pete in a cramped but cozy space exactly like a ship's cabin (ones she'd read about, at least), right down to the gentle rocking and the little round porthole in the wall. Their spacesuited knees almost touched, but they had their helmets off. That meant her breath was mingling with Pete's, swirling together in the tight space like the Jovian clouds outside. Katie's heart pounded faster, and her palms were clammy. *It's just this darned heavy gravity—more than two-and-a-half times Earth's, I think Pete said.*

"So how did your deal go?"

He turned away.

"That? Oh, you know. Just makin' a bargain that's beneficial to all parties, know what I mean? Now, what part of the Panhandle did you say you're from?"

"East of Abilene a piece, and you're changing the subject. *Who* was trading *what* to *whom*? And *qui bono*?"

"*Qui* rhymes with 'me,' not with 'why.'"

"So you're the one who benefits?"

Pete shook his head and looked at the floor. "I'm only a broker, Miss Katie. I just help folks who want to make a deal."

"Now it seems to me," Katie said thoughtfully, "that methane is what we used to call natural gas back in the Panhandle. We still had some of it around, after the oil ran out—that's how come the Montoyas got so rich in the first place. I remember reading that methane makes up less than one percent of Jupiter's atmosphere—but then, everything about Jupiter is so darn big that a little smidgen of methane like that could keep all the houses on Earth warm for, like, the next hundred thousand years. Stop me if I'm riding the wrong horse."

"Miss Katie, you are the finest filly I ever did see." Pete's voice was quiet.

Katie smiled. "But you wouldn't be sneaking around like this, would you, Mister Pete, if taking a share of the methane and shipping it off-planet was all on the up and up?"

"Miss Katie." Pete reached over and tapped her spacesuited knee with his gloved hand. "What you don't know can't hurt me. All right?"

She nodded stiffly, unwillingly. Her head felt like a boulder in the massive gravity. It was one thing to float weightless through the tumbling clouds, but in here she felt like a two-ton Tessie. So with the conversation at a dead end and nothing else to do, she looked around the cabin. It was neat enough—it had to be, like all spacers' cabins in environments where loose clutter could turn into deadly missiles in a flash—and yet, just the same, it somehow had that indefinable masculine edge of disorder that she associated with her father. *Pete must use this place a lot.* Was there something just slightly out of place? A hint of carelessly folded shirts poking out of a tightly closed, miniature dresser drawer, perhaps? Or maybe it was that the eating utensils were lined up nice and regular in their racks, but looked just slightly dirty, as if they'd been indifferently cleaned. Whatever it was, it made the cramped space oddly homey. And Katie was enough of a tomboy that she didn't feel the slightest urge to start tidying up. But in that case, why was there just the faintest whiff of cleaning fluid?

"Hey Pete, do you smell—" Katie began, when suddenly the platform lurched violently. She grabbed her helmet and fastened it, just as Jack and Anya had drilled her and Rachel to do during the slow weeks of their outbound voyage. The lights went out, leaving the lightning flickering through the swirling Jovian clouds as the only source of illumination. Pete had fallen to the floor, bashed his head on something, and been knocked cold before he could get his own helmet fastened. The platform bucked again and again. Katie sprang up and struggled to pry the helmet from Pete's hands and clamp it in place. The air in the cabin was turning a faint brownish color. *Ammonia, it's ammonia. We've sprung a leak.*

At last she fastened Pete's helmet and then lunged for the control panel. She glanced over the unfamiliar knobs, levers, and dials. A big red panic button! She pressed it, screaming, "Mayday, mayday! Emergency on Pearlband Station 17! We've sprung a leak, we're out of control and need help!" Could the suit radio broadcast farther than the immediate vicinity of the platform? Was the panic button hooked up to some sort of emergency power supply? She might as well be a passenger in an old-time jet that had lost its engines and was plummeting thousands of feet to the ground. But she couldn't just wait to die.

Dizzy, she braced herself against the console. Every few seconds the platform lurched. The view from the porthole had shifted, and instead of rainbow-hued streamers of gas there was a sort of brownish billowing. Her stomach twisted, and she shivered; those sewage-colored clouds seemed intelligent and malevolent. But how could that be? They were only gas. *Only gas? Like the Puffballs?* She dragged Pete to his seat and strapped him in before hitting the panic button again. An immense shock shook the platform. The walls cracked, and brown gas poured in through the gap, surrounding her in seconds. She couldn't see a thing. She gasped. Was the stink seeping into her spacesuit through the seals? The feeling of malevolence grew stronger. She groped for the reassuring solidity of her seat and strapped herself in. She coughed and sputtered, describing their desperate situation. Nothing. Only a low oceanic hiss of static broken by crackles from the lightning. *Oh, God, help will never come in time!* Ganymede was half a million miles away, and the other inhabited moons of Jupiter were all on the other side of the giant planet at the moment. Her stomach ached, her head spun. She wanted to throw up. She closed her eyes.

"It just ain't fair. It just ain't! I got clean away from the Dixies, and now I'm gonna die out here."

Her head swam and she fought to stay awake. That was important, wasn't it? Or was it crucial only when you were stuck outside in the freezing cold? Hypothermia, that was they called it. She smiled. *I re-membered that, didn't I? Well, I'm not cold now. I'm nice and toasty warm. A little nap would feel so good...if only the strange voices in my head would be quiet. Shut up, will you? Can't you see I'm trying to sleep?*

What is sleep? a deep, toneless voice responded.

Sleep that knits the raveled sleeve of care. Shakespeare said that. I read it in the library.

What is a shakespeare? What is a library? Why do you steal our food?

Huh? You never heard of Shakespeare? And I never stole your food. Why would I? My favorite food is macaroni and cheese. You blobs eat that?

We ain't blobs, Panhandler. We are the People.

Don't you call me a panhandler! Don't mess with Texas! And I read all about this in Lost Classics of Science Fiction. *Every intelligent species thinks it's the only one in the universe.*

You do not explain why you steal our food! Always till now we fight off the GBFs when they try to steal our food. Now you help them, so we starve! Why?!

GBFs? Oh, you mean the Puffballs. But I don't have anything to do with that. I'm just visiting. You need to speak to Pete...but you knocked him out.

Incomprehension. To speak to one is to speak to all, is it not?

Not with us humans it ain't. And if you kill us, you ain't gonna be speaking to anybody, anyway. Our *People tend to shoot first and ask questions later, if you catch my drift. Like with the Indians in the old days.*

Very well. We'll leave you to explain things to your People, Katie Webb. But if you come back here and steal our food again, we'll be the ones shooting first and asking questions later. Oh, and one more thing.

Yes?

We'd like to try some of your macaroni and cheese, please.

Deal.

Katie dreamily imagined the creamiest mac-and-cheese she'd ever had, with a nice toasty crust on top, and hoped the People could telepathically enjoy it.

Half an hour later, after Jack flew the emergency rescue craft up to the wrecked platform, he found Katie glaring with cool fury at Pete's unconscious form as she muttered over and over, "Everybody benefits, huh, Pete?"

♂

"They call them KLs, or sometimes 'kills' for short," Pete said between hacking coughs.

Jack watched Katie watch Pete. Curious. Jack had never seen anybody hold a hospital patient's hand so unsympathetically. On the other hand, Katie *was* sitting there holding Pete's hand. Jack shook his head. The longer he lived, the less he understood people.

"Charming. And what's KL supposed to stand for?" Katie asked.

"Kitty litter," said Pete. "From the ammonia smell, get it?"

"Hilarious. And neither you nor the Puffballs nor anybody else understood that you were stealing their food?"

"Huh? Of course not! I thought the Puffballs were the only intelligent species in this quadrant."

"Oh, Pete, don't try and BS the girl," Jack snapped. "Even a know-nothin' gunslinger like me knows you can't fart on Jupiter without somebody mistaking it for their long-lost cousin. Beggin' your pardon, miss."

"It's all right, Jack," Katie smiled, "we have heard of farting in Texas."

"No! Honestly! We thought they were just a natural phenomenon," Pete protested.

"Oh, you mean like lightning that just happened to strike every time you signed a contract?" Katie said.

"Yes! I mean no!"

"Now the way I see it," said Jack, rubbing his chin, "your sweet little friends the Puffballs have been getting themselves a two-for-one deal. Not only are they building themselves a nice fat off-planet bank account, they're also eliminating the competition. There are laws against this sort of thing, Pete my man, even if the Solar Federation ain't so good at enforcing 'em."

"Look, I was only trying to earn a living," Pete said between coughs. "I really didn't know the KLs were sentient. O.P. swore to me they were nothing more than dangerous predators."

"Right, like you trust him any further than you can throw him," Katie said. "I heard the way you were talking to him."

"Mr. Kowalski isn't going to be earning his living on Jupiter again any time soon," a new voice put in.

Jack turned. A severe-looking figure in a white coat wearing horn-rimmed glasses and a stethoscope stood in the doorway. He was so stereotypically medical, from his wiry gray hair to his shiny black shoes, Jack almost laughed out loud. His skin was the color of milk chocolate, and his accent was strange. His name, according to a silvery tag on his left breast pocket, was Dr. Thomas Manley.

"Whaddya mean, doc?" Pete asked. Another coughing fit cut off his pitiful whine.

Manley regarded him coolly. "I should think it would be obvious, young man. Your lungs have been damaged by your escapade out on the Gas Balloon. Another exposure to even trace amounts of that atmosphere could kill you. I should even avoid getting into a spacesuit for at least the next six months, if I were you."

Pete's pale face took on a green tinge. "Six months?" he spluttered. "I don't have six months!"

"And at least two weeks on bed rest. What's your hurry? You have loan sharks after you?"

Pete's face turned even greener. "Loan sharks? Me? Ha ha! No, I'm just a man of action. Can't stand being cooped up in bed!"

"Well son, you're not going to stay a man of action very long if you get out of that bed before you're ready."

"Yeah, but I ain't gonna be able to pay for this hospital stay if I don't. And you do like your furniture configured the way it is, don't you?"

"Our furniture? Ah, I see what you mean," Manley said, rubbing his grizzled chin. "Well, I suppose I could patch you up and send you for further treatment to the inner planets in a few days."

"Oh, thank you, doctor!" Pete sat upright and lunged for Manley's hand, only to double over in a coughing fit that ended with blood on his lap. While the doctor scolded and sedated his patient, Katie beckoned Jack out into the icy corridor.

"This could be a good thing for us," she whispered. Her voice echoed down the caverns.

"How so?" Jack muttered in a voice that did not carry.

"We're gonna need lots of help taking on Ares on Mars," she said, imitating his tone. "Ray and me don't know our way around, and with all respect, one gunslinger and three girls don't make an army."

Jack frowned. "You're right, but how can we get him to join up? With all respect, your boyfriend don't seem like the idealistic type."

Katie's eyes were bulging. Interesting.

"He ain't my boyfriend!" she managed to say. "I just think he could help us out, is all. Though why I would want to help *you* out ain't clear to me. Anya is a different matter."

"Of course she is." Katie was unbelievably cute when mad. *Best not say so, if I want to avoid a bloody nose.* Though she certainly was, with her curly brown hair all mussed up and the crinkle lines gathering around her nose and puckered-up mouth.

"All right," he said soothingly. "I'll leave it to you to work it out with him. You know Anya and me have a lot to do to get ready. But I don't need any mercenaries along on this trip! He's got to want to come for reasons other than getting paid, see?"

"I guess maybe I do," Katie mumbled, looking at the floor and un-clenching her fists. Jack breathed a little easier.

11

Rachel was wandering around the ice tunnels, trying to empty her mind of the troubling thoughts her encounter with Anya had raised, when she stumbled right into a shockey game. She ducked behind a solid-looking pillar of ice just as a granite puck came whizzing past and crashed into a nearby wall, gouging out a hole the size of a large man's fist. One of the players sailed past her to retrieve it.

"Gun? I thought you were going straight back to the Belt from here," Rachel said. Katie had introduced them before their ship reached Ganymede.

"Change of plans, but I can't talk right now," the miner panted with a grin. "We don't have any time-outs in this game. I'm about to win!"

Rachel stepped back, her gaze on the players. The game was brutal but not difficult to understand. Each player was their own team. There were six or seven others besides Gun, all large, muscular men. They were all armed with stainless steel "sticks" that did not seem regulation anything, but scraps of metal left over from some gargantuan construction project, with edges so sharp it was hard to see how the players kept from slicing themselves. Moreover, nobody wore any sort of protective gear, not even knee pads or crotch guards. *Where will the next generation of competitors come from?* The goal was a gash the size of a large dog in the ice wall opposite Rachel. All the players were both offense and goalie simultaneously, and there was no concept of a foul. On the other hand, since it was every man for himself, there were few scrums and no pile-ons, at least not that Rachel saw. The object was simply to knock the puck, a dinner-plate-sized slab of dull reddish granite flecked with sparkling mica, into the goal, while avoiding getting a disfiguring facial slash or a broken bone. The scorekeeper was a heavily scarred individual the size and shape of a coffin, who looked as if he had been permanently injured in a friendly shockey game or two himself.

Back and forth the puck sailed, too fast to follow. The players' sticks rang against each other like swords, and the spectators—there were about twenty of them besides Rachel, and unlike her, they seemed to have no fear of getting close to the action—shouted and cheered, creating an unbelievable racket that echoed up and down the tunnels and seemed to explode in her ears. One of the bigger male players fell, howling and clutching his leg. Rachel gasped. Did Gun really kick him in the shins as she scrambled for the puck? She sent it flying triumphantly into the goal, where it hit the chopped-up ice with a solid thunk. The scorekeeper gave out with an eardrum-piercing whistle and pointed at her, whereupon she threw up her arms and the crowd roared.

"Well, what did you think?" Gun grinned, sliding up to Rachel.

"I thought it was the most barbaric thing I've ever seen," Rachel blurted. "That man, is he going to be all right?"

"Rod? Sure he is. Breaks his leg practically every week playing shockey," Gun said.

Rachel stepped back as Rod himself loomed up behind Gun, who was a good foot and a half shorter than him, but all he did was clap her on the shoulder and rumble, "Hey, good game, girl. Next time, though, I'm gonna beat you cold, got me?"

"Better splint that leg up first, Roddy boy," Gun said, twisting her head up to look into his face. "Need my stick to do it?"

"Nah, my bones heal all on their own," he said cheerfully and hobbled away. Rachel watched him open-mouthed.

"Say, Ray, would you mind holding the puck for me a sec?"

"Holding th—" Rachel began. An enormous explosion went off in the middle of her face, and she fell and hit the back of her head. Everything got very dim and far away. Gradually she became aware that she was sitting up, and a hand was offering her a cup of something warm and soothing while another hand pressed some gauze up against her nose. She squinted at the face in front of her. Both hands belonged to Gun.

"You silly girl! How was I supposed to know you have the reflexes of a cow!"

"You beat me up and then you insult me?" Rachel said. Dull, pulsing flashes of pain went off where her nose was supposed to be. She blinked and looked down. Her blood swirled on the ice in complex patterns. That didn't quite make it worth getting a bloody nose, but the flash of inspiration she had next, about Gun's potential usefulness on Mars, surely did. Best to work a little guilt into the equation, though.

"Id really hurds. I think I'm going do need a bedder bandage," Rachel said, eyes watering.

"I think you're going to need an icepack," Gun said practically, eyeing the dribbling blood. "Come on, you'd better come back with me to my quarters." And despite being a couple of inches shorter, she hoisted Rachel up and half-carried her down the corridor, so that her feet barely touched the ground.

So much for guilt.

Once they arrived at Gun's room, she sat Rachel down gently but firmly on her bed and proceeded to fix her up with an icepack and some bandages she took from a compact but professional first-aid kit, doing as good a job at it as Dr. Kantorowicz would have done back in Warsaw.

Then she forced Rachel to swallow a capsule that looked half the size of a shockey puck for the pain.

"You twenty-second century people sure do have quick tempers," Rachel said once the job was done.

Gun gave her an odd look and said, "Everything is quick in space, Martian girl."

"Can you keep a secret? I'm not really Martian." *Some secret, now that four of us know.*

"What? Then how come you have a Martian accent?"

Rachel sighed. "I'm from Poland, on Earth. Apparently Polish and Marpolski are almost exactly the same, for some reason." *As if I didn't know the reason.* "Besides which, I'm kind of love in with Princess Anya." She clapped her hands over her mouth as soon as she said that, but Gun only nodded as if it were the most natural thing in the world.

"You and every other human being on this rotten hunk of ice," she said. "I'm darned if I know how she expects to go around incognito with that face and figure. So, I expect you're going to ask me to join your little restorationist crusade next."

"How did you—well, yes, that's right."

"What's in it for me?"

"A job? You wouldn't be hanging out on this rotten hunk of ice if you had work back in the Belt."

Gun looked at Rachel thoughtfully. "Pretty savvy for a glubber."

"A what?"

"A glubber. It's what we Belters call people who stick to the surface of globes."

"Not worms, or slugs?"

"Not when we're being polite. All right, Ray, it's true I'm out of work at the moment. I got so deep in debt I had to sell my ship, the *Deadman's Bluff,* which was like cutting off my own arm. But we don't do so well on planets, thanks to all that gravity. So it better be worth my while."

Rachel sighed again. *Pity I didn't write any gold mines into my version of Mars.*

12

The seventh and most important member of the Martian Expeditionary Force was Eagle-Eye Eddie, because he was the only one with his own ship. Unfortunately, he was also the hardest to recruit.

"Come on, old buddy," Jack said to him over drinks one afternoon in the Jupiter Lounge.

"Nothing doing," said Eddie. "Lila's lawyers will be on me faster and harder than a Venusian thunderstorm if I haul the *Komodo Dragon* out of her hidey-hole. I'm still hoping they buy my story that it lost an argument with Saturn's G-ring."

"Why'd you name your ship after a reptile, anyway?"

"The *Komodo Dragon*? She used to be named *Lila My Love*."

"Ah. But tell me, how's a process server gonna find you in interplanetary space?"

"They have ways," Eddie said darkly. "I heard Lila told her legal 'team' to search Saturn for the remnants of my ship."

"How they gonna do that? The place is huge!"

"By looking for traces of breathable atmosphere. Once they find there's no air on the G-ring, I'm finished!"

"If your days are numbered anyway, why not let us use your ship? You'll be well paid!"

Eddie laughed so loudly and harshly he nearly fell over backwards. "Jack my friend, I wouldn't trust you to pay me back for a drink. And I should know, I've bought you enough of them."

"I wouldn't worry about any of that if I were you, gentlemen," said a grating new voice. Jack and Eddie looked up. A tall, thin man with a tiny tuft of black chin beard aimed a large, bulbous, late-model zap-gun directly at their heads. The Martian agent smiled thinly as he was joined by two shorter colleagues who were equally well armed. "Your reputation precedes you, as you see, Mr. Flash. Now, as soon as we finish sedating your girlfriend, we—"

Just what happened next would take much longer to describe than it did to occur, but it ended with the shorter thugs lying unconscious on the floor and the tall guy's chest mashed under Eddie's knees, while Jack stroked the Martians' guns respectfully. "Genuine Smith & Wesson, made on Earth. I am impressed."

"Only the best for you, you sneaking, thieving, murdering, fornicating, treacherous son of a snake!"

"Sir, I would advise you not to trifle with Mr. Flash's famous temper," Eddie said mildly, earning him a glare from the immobilized Martian agent.

"We know who you are, too, Eddie the not-so-eagle-eyed! We have all of Flash's known associates pegged, and when we get through helping your ex-wife's lawyers attach your assets, you'll be begging for arbitration—"

Eddie punched him hard in the face.

"Now who's got an anger management problem, Eddie my boy?"

"I hate lawyer talk," Eddie grumbled, rubbing his knuckles ruefully. "Listen, Jack, it looks like now I'm going to have to take the *Komodo Dragon* off planet to keep it out of Lila's clutches. But first, you'd better make sure they haven't got Anya."

"Of course! I must rescue the princess!" Jack cried out in a ringing voice. He gestured grandly with his new weapons, accidentally shot out the light, then dashed off down a corridor, closely followed by Eddie.

"Unhand her, you murdering brutes!" Jack shouted, jumping through the door with his zap-gun leveled. But far from needing rescue, the princess had rescued herself, with a little help from a slightly dazed looking Rachel.

"I can't believe I did that," Rachel muttered. A Martian agent curled on the floor, clutching his groin and moaning softly, while Anya covered his colleague with a pink, very businesslike zap pistolette.

"Umm, right. Looks like you've got things well sorted out here," Jack said, casting wary glances at the Martian on the floor.

"Your women don't fight fair," complained the standing Martian, who was keeping his hands very still, palms raised at shoulder level. Like his luckless taller colleague in the Jupiter Lounge, he had a tiny chin-beard.

"Right. Where did you say you were keeping your knockout drugs again?" Jack snapped. The standing man smiled.

"All right. On your knees, bully boy, hands behind your head," Jack said. "You too, moaning boy."

"I can't believe I did that," Rachel muttered again as her victim scrambled to comply. She looked as if she might throw up.

Poor girl. She seems so innocent, I hope this doesn't scar her, but we've got no choice. "It gets easier with practice, Ray."

"That's what I'm afraid of."

♂

Rachel was upset, but not because of the violence as such—actually, it felt good to be able to fight back, after all those years of being terrorized by the Germans and not being able to do anything about it. *But here, the pain and brutality are* all my fault!

"Hey, what the heck are you doing?" she asked in alarm as Jack placed the muzzle of his pistol against the undamaged thug's head.

"What's it look like, sweetheart? Don't give me that look. I promise you, zap-fried brains don't smell like nothin'."

Rachel gagged and glanced at Anya, but the princess gazed innocently back at her. *What kind of monsters have I created?* "Why don't you call the police? I mean, they barged in here and threatened us and—"

Jack looked at Eddie and they both burst out laughing. Even the princess let out a low musical chuckle.

"OK, OK, that's dumb after what happened on Venus. But can't you just tie them up or something?"

"If there were any rope this side of the inner planets, it'd be a shame to waste it on these goons," Jack said as gently as he could.

"But—"

"I'm gettin' tired of this," said Eddie, and, turning his gun upside down, thumped each of their captives on the head once, hard enough to raise faint echoes off the icy walls.

"Thanks," Rachel said. Had Eddie hit them hard enough to fracture their skulls?

"Anything for a lady," Eddie said with a grandiloquent bow.

"Your friends might not thank you for your qualms if they make it back to Mars, you know," Jack said drily. "Rumor has it there's a whole prison called Valhalla devoted to the torture of failed agents."

"It's true, Rachel," Anya put in softly.

"Now, if everyone is quite finished here, we'd better round up the rest of our crew and get aboard the *Martian Liberator*!" Jack cried.

"Get on board the *what*?" Rachel heard Eddie ask Jack as they dashed off through the tunnels.

"Humor me, my friend. I know what it takes to raise people's morale on a suicide mission like this. Besides, if we do somehow win, you don't really want to go down in history as the pilot of the *Icky Iguana*, do you?"

"*Komodo Dragon.*"

"Whatever. And what was the deal back there in Anya's room? You goin' soft on me?"

"Where's the harm letting the kid preserve her innocence a little longer? You know as well I do the Martian secret police never sends out less than a platoon of goons on these missions. When those guys don't come back, dead or alive, the alarm is going to be raised."

"You really know how to lift a guy's spirits."

"You're the one who called it a suicide mission."

I am not a naïve kid! Rachel wanted to shout, but she couldn't without giving away that she'd been eavesdropping. Also she couldn't help being touched that tough, cynical old Eddie wanted to protect her.

Once Katie and Gun had been located at the ever-active pool tables (the miner was just teaching a fascinated Katie how to do a three-way bank shot) and Pete had been dragged protesting feebly from his hospital bed, leadership of the expedition passed to Eddie. He led the group down a deserted, gently sloping corridor, as the eerie light coming from the icy walls faded from aquamarine to a dusky purple.

Rachel peered through the dimness.

Eddie shouted, "Hey, haven't you girls got enough sense to hold hands in the Midnight Caves?"

As they moved on, advancing more cautiously, the light faded further, and the walls, ceiling and floor began to take on a rough texture, almost like a natural cave. Rachel held Anya's hand tighter as they slowed. Water dripped on stone, one slow drop every five seconds or so. It grew completely dark, worse than a wartime blackout. Rachel shivered. *This is a wartime blackout.* And what if they somehow stumbled on a section that wasn't pressurized? Abe's sci-fi magazines contained lurid descriptions of what happens to a human body exposed to hard vacuum. She squeezed the warm, soft hand she was holding and was surprised to feel clamminess.

"Anya, I'm scared," she whispered in Polish.

The hand squeezed back. "So am I, little sister," Anya whispered back.

Just then a metallic bang and a muffled curse came from up ahead, followed by a rough guffaw from Jack. "Tripped over your own secret entrance, did you, Eddie my friend?"

"Shut up, before I change my mind about letting you borrow the *Dragon* for this quixotic *mishegaas*."

Hearing this space jockey use the Yiddish word for craziness as if it were ordinary English, Rachel did a double take. *That's my fault too! Mom and Dad would kill me if they knew I created a whole world full of people who speak "jargon" like it's nothing.*

A moment later a dim electric bulb came on a few yards ahead, and Anya tugged Rachel forward. They stood in an unadorned metal box that reminded Rachel of the dumbwaiter in the fancy Paris hotel she'd stayed in with her parents the summer she turned eight. It was a tight fit with all seven of them, and as soon as Eddie pulled the folding door shut the elevator floor dropped away. Rachel gasped and grabbed Anya for support.

This is almost as bad as liftoff. It lasted only a few seconds before the car stopped with a sharp bump. Eddie yanked the door open and turned on the lights.

Wow.

An underground chamber dozens of yards across and at least fifty yards high had been hewn out of raw Ganymedean ice and stone. The harsh utilitarian blue of the fluorescent bulbs turned the ice into a glittering array of diamonds and sapphires vaulting to the ceiling high above. The veins of dull gray silicate rock set off the ice, like velvet lining in a jeweler's showcase.

"It's beautiful," she murmured to Anya, who nodded and squeezed her hand.

"It's a dump." Gun strode out of the elevator and making straight for a needlelike rocket ship. "This your deathtrap, Eddie?"

"My ship is up to code," he bristled.

"I'll be the judge of that. I mean, no offense and all, but you icehogs have been known to cut a corner or two."

"Yeah, and you rockrats—"

"Easy, man," Jack soothed Eddie, "what can it hurt to have another professional check things out before we take off? It's gonna be a three-week run back to the Red Planet and we can't exactly call the Space Patrol if we get in trouble."

"There's really a Space Patrol?" Rachel whispered to Anya, who eyed her strangely. Katie ignored them all and walked around the enormous chamber, gawking openly. Rachel watched her enviously. *Why can't I enjoy things like that? I'm the same age as her. Am I that afraid of looking like a silly girl?*

Gun's inspection was quick but thorough, and eventually Eddie stopped grumbling and joined her in running through a preflight checklist. The others dawdled outside as long as they could, for they had nearly a month of breathing in each other's air and drinking each other's recycled piss ahead of them. But soon enough it was time to go.

"All right, everyone. All aboard!" Eddie called from the doorway.

As they started up the ramp Anya frowned, "What's that rumbling?"

"I don't know," Eddie said, and turning inward, shouted, "Hey Gun, ya dumb rockrat, you haven't started the engines yet, have you?"

"Call me a rockrat once more, icehog, and I'll use you for fuel! Of course not! What—"

A huge section of chamber wall burst inward, bringing down an avalanche of ice and rock. As the group scrambled aboard the *Komodo Dragon,* a cluster of heavily armored figures emerged through the gap.

"Stop in the name of the Martian crown!" an amplified voice roared so loudly it made everything on the ship shake.

Jack found the switch for the external PA and cried in somewhat imperfect Marpolski, "Never shall you lay your thistlecat-scat befouled hands on the princess, you spawn of a Grand Canal bottom-feeder!"

"Taunts are kind of a waste of time, Jack!" Eddie shouted. "Help me get this bucket off the ground!"

Just then another enormous chunk of chamber wall caved in several yards from where the Martian secret police had entered, and another group of ominously armored figures loomed in the swirling storm of shattered ice and rock.

Jack stared. "What the—"

Another amplified voice roared, "Process server!"

"YOU'LL NEVER TAKE ME ALIVE, LILA!" Eddie howled. "FULL POWER!"

"Eddie, you're insane! Don't—" Gun dove for the console. She almost made it.

13

"Finally tonight, for our outer-planet roundup, we turn to our ever in-trepid, ever-jovial reporter, Lila Pernod," a sprightly male voice said. "Lila?"

The voice came from a deluxe radio set the size of a child's bed, with a cabinet carved of rare Martian teak and speakers stylized to look like twin mouths singing, or perhaps screaming. The top of the cabinet was covered with what would have looked like fine velvet to the uninitiated Earth-human visitor, but which was in fact the soft orange-and-white-striped fur of a thistlecat. Beside it on an exquisitely carved table made of African mahogany imported from Earth at insane expense, lay a hard-cover book whose title was worked out in fancy embossed gold lettering: *Lost Classics of Science Fiction*.

A desolate woman's voice now came from the radio speakers. "Thanks, Tom. The big news of course is the volcanic eruption on Gany-mede, a moon which was thought to be geologically inactive until now. An enormous burst of heat from under the crust melted the ice in a circle nearly five miles wide. The Ganymedean authorities have rushed to build a top over this lake before it boils away into space, as this new source of fresh water is of course worth billions of zlotys." The radio speakers emitted a sniffle.

"Lila, are you all right?" the male voice asked.

"Perfectly fine, thanks, Tom. I just have a little cold. The other outer system news also comes from the Jovian system. Just after the volcanic eruption that created the new lake on the moon, a ship was detected t-tumbling out of c-control from the direction of Ganymede, p-plunging toward the p-primary p-planet."

"Are you sure you're all right, Lila?"

"N-never better." *Sniffle*. "Authorities are investigating whether there is any connection between the ac-accident and the eruption. The ship was r-registered to one Edward McGregor, who is believed to have been aboard along with several unidentified persons when it c-c-c-cr—" The announcer broke down sobbing, and after a few seconds the radio speak-ers emitted soothing music while a reassuring male voice spoke of tech-nical difficulties. A hand reached over and turned the power knob, which was carved in the fearsome likeness of Moloch, the Martian God of War.

The hand that had turned the knob rose until it met a bushy black mustache, which it stroked thoughtfully. "Well, well, well," a man's voice mused in Texian-accented English. "So it's over. Pity about the lovely Anya. I was looking forward to adding her to my collection for, ah, aesthetic as well as political reasons." A strangely high-pitched chuckle followed, and the hand that had shut off the radio reached down and stroked the book cover. "Guess Zap-Gun Jack ain't coming anytime soon to rescue Mars from my 'dreadful tyranny.' Now I can start making things around here a little more to my liking, like in one of these other fine stories—maybe 'Gunga-Khan and the Solar Conquest.'" The hand left the book and seized a tuft of strawberry-blond hair. "Know what I mean, Nadia baby?"

"Yes, your majesty," a woman's voice whispered breathily. The hand gripped her hair harder.

"Say my name, Nadia baby."

"Ares the Great, Third and Mightiest of that name, Conqueror of Olympus Mons, Ruler of Valles Marineraaaeeeeee—"

"No, my name. My REAL name. Say it. Say it aloud! Shout it! No one can hear you scream in here, you know that!" The hand yanked at the tuft of hair.

"DZHONNY! DZHONNY MARSHALL! TEXASRANGERJOHN-NY MARSHALL!!!!!"

♂

Katie tumbled around the disabled spaceship like the luckless stray cat Johnny Marshall and his dirtball friends had flung into a barrel and set on fire one memorable August afternoon in Abilene. One moment she was fully awake, scrabbling around wildly to grab hold of something so she could begin figuring out some way out of this predicament, before the ship she was in plummeted straight into Jupiter's gumbo of an atmosphere, and the next she was in a disordered dream world, filled with fragments of her childhood, her fantasy worlds and the bizarre new universe she'd found herself in since losing her home and her parents. She glimpsed the cover of *Lost Classics of Science Fiction*, those golden letters turning into real flames that reached for her, warming instead of burning. Her father's tired face, the premature wrinkles gathering around her mother's eyes. The sick calf that died last winter after Katie success-fully pleaded with her parents to let it sleep in her room until it got better, despite all of Thumper's attempts to lick it back to health (such a good cat, that Thumper!) Thunderclouds looming over the prairie, pelting rain that carried the threat of funnel clouds and the hint of something lush and rank, like the jungle on Venus. Karolla's fluffy gray fur and innocent blue eyes. Rachel's shy smile and cultured accent. *What a shame. We were starting to become real friends until that business with Anya's hair. Now we'll never have the chance to patch things up.* Then it was back into the tumbling dream world. Mom's rhubarb pie, fresh out of the oven. The whole fat chicken they'd had last Thanksgiving, Dad making her wait while he solemnly said grace over it. And for some reason, macaroni and cheese. Rich, hot, thick and creamy macaroni and cheese, baked in a sturdy white dish and topped off with crunchy breadcrumbs, just for her. She was just lifting her favorite spoon to break the crust and dig in when there was a whiff of cleaning fluid and everything suddenly cleared, like the prairie sky after a rainstorm.

Oh. You again.

Yes, Kaitlynwebb. Thank you for bringing us the gift we asked for. We had not expected you again so soon.

Yeah, well, about that. I don't actually want to be here right now, no offense.

But why not? You are a hero of the People. You have saved us from the greed of the GBFs and Peterkowalski. Though we sense remorse in his mind. And the Puffballs have had to agree to share the methane with us, like civilized folk. So ask anything of us, and we shall grant it to you, if it be in our power.

14

"This is one terrific course I plotted!" Eddie sounded enormously pleased with himself, but with a hint of uncertainty.

"Is that so?" Gun stood in back of the co-pilot's console, balancing on one leg while the other was draped over the chair, calculating something with dizzying speed on her slide rule while Katie watched her, bemused.

"What's that y'all got there?"

"What? This? Don't tell me you never saw a slide rule before!"

"Nope. Whatcha doing with it?"

"Double checking our course to make sure our clever icehog here doesn't plow us headfirst into Ceres." She jerked her thumb at Eddie, who was reclining in the pilot's chair, pushing with both his feet against the edge of the console. Every spacefarer did his gravity-shift exercises his own way. The *Dragon*'s master looked happy but also quite distracted, and he failed to rise to the bait Gun had set for him. She frowned and went back to her slide rule.

"Why don't you use your computer to help you out with math like that?" Katie persisted.

"Hmm?" Gun scribbled a cluster of figures on a scrap of paper and carefully put down her mechanical pencil before answering. "Computer? You mean the ship's 'brain?' Don't let the word fool you. Even the best of them can barely keep the air circulating and the fuel flowing correctly, and nothing on this bucket is exactly top of the line." Gun threw another glance at Eddie, but he again failed to respond.

"But—" *Shut up, Katie. So what if the old laptop I'd used once probably could have calculated our course to several decimal places in less than a second, no matter how many asteroids were in the way, and without slowing down its Net connection enough for me to notice.* Even knowing what she knew, Katie couldn't really understand the reason for the discrepancy.

Gun turned back to her slide rule, which she flicked back and forth as if she was angry at it, and after another minute or two announced, "Well, that's it. This ship is on a course to slingshot around Jupiter's gravity well and put us neatly into orbit around Big Red a good week ahead of schedule."

"So why don't you say, 'Good job, Eddie. Well done?'" Eddie said.

"Because you know damn well you didn't do it. You weren't even trying to escape alive. You were prepared to destroy this ship and everyone aboard it just to keep it out of your ex-wife's hands. Go ahead and deny it, tough guy."

Eddie developed a sudden intense interest in a crack in his chair's upholstery.

"Thought so. Well, I have no idea how we happen to be not only alive but on a damn-near-perfect course right now, but under the Universal Space Pilot's Code I hereby relieve you of command."

Eddie leapt to his feet, stabbing his forefinger in Gun's face. "You can't do that! This, this is my ship, my livelihood! You can't take a man's ship away from him!"

"Calm down, Eagle Eye," Gun said, gently pushing aside the raised forefinger. "I ain't takin' away your precious smuggler. I'm merely assuming command until we reach Mars. Once everyone else is off this ship, you are free to ram her straight into the nearest asteroid to spite Lila."

Eddie subsided, grumbling.

"Oh, and the next time you stick your finger in my face, I am going to break it off and make you eat it."

"Wow," Katie whispered to Rachel, who had been watching this exchange along with Jack, Anya, and Pete. "That lady is really tough!"

"Yeah," said Rachel. She looked at Katie thoughtfully. "You know how we escaped, don't you?"

Katie nodded slightly. "Can't tell you in front of everyone. Not till we have some privacy." *Which with any luck, will mean waiting until we get to Mars.* There were exactly two rooms on this spaceship, which was designed for a three-man crew; the bridge they were all crowded into at the moment, and a galley-cum-sleeping-room "below" it. Since there wasn't any cargo, the hatch to the cargo bay had been opened, creating a third room larger than the other two put together. This, it quickly became apparent, would have to serve as the women's quarters. At least there were emergency crash "couches" there to sleep on, although they felt almost as hard as wooden boards. Some of the romance was going out of space travel for Katie, though Gun had clearly seen worse and Anya never complained about anything.

But Katie gave in to Rachel's curiosity that "night" and explained in a whisper that the People had saved the ship to repay her for her help with Pete and the GBFs. The two girls lay on their stomachs on their couches and leaned their heads together, while Gun snored and Anya slept peacefully nearby.

Rachel looked puzzled. "But what's the big secret? I don't get it."

Katie screwed up her face. "I don't want anybody calling me a hero or anything. Mom taught me it ain't good manners to brag, especially for a girl. Besides, I was afraid nobody would believe me." She paused, looking with concern at Rachel's face. "What is it? What's the matter?"

"That stuff about nobody believing you," Rachel said, her lips barely moving. "We've both got that problem, seeing that we aren't from anywhere in this universe. I told Anya and Gun that I'm from Poland, but, well, I didn't say that I'm not from *this* world's Poland. And Jack still thinks my father was Earth's ambassador to Mars!"

Katie rolled her eyes. "Gee willikers. Like the man says to Huckleberry Finn, Ray, you sure need experience with lying."

"Thanks a lot. Meanwhile, what are we going to say when everyone starts comparing notes? I got Anya to trust me, I think, but I don't think these hardboiled characters we're traveling with will be so forgiving."

Katie shrugged. "Let's just hope it don't come up. We all have plenty to do anyhow, figuring out how we're supposed to invade a whole planet with an army of seven."

Nobody could think about anything else. As the rocket sped silently through space, Katie watched with growing apprehension as the others made plans that would obviously go to pieces the second they touched red earth, if not before. Because the first problem was making planetfall without attracting attention from Lord Ares' Martian Space Force.

"They can read our call sign," Jack explained to Katie and Rachel. "All ships in the System have one. It's one of the few laws that's really properly enforced. The transponder is hidden deep inside the control panel. You can't rip it out without disabling something vital."

"You talkin' about this thing?" Gun called cheerfully from the cockpit, where she was on duty. Something flew "down" and narrowly missed Jack's head, but he nimbly ducked and caught it. It was about the size and shape of a screwdriver handle, with ends of loose wire sticking out of it. Jack stared at it as if it was a snake that might sink its fangs into him, then let it go. Gun guffawed. "What's the matter, Flash? Afraid of a little transponder?"

"You have just killed us all!" Jack shouted hoarsely. "Even if you haven't wrecked our controls, the Martian Space Force will shoot us down as soon as we come within range!"

"Dry your shorts, Flash. We Belters are old hands at disabling the little robo-spies. Heck, my daddy taught me how to do it on my sixth birthday."

"That's charming, but it doesn't explain how we avoid becoming Mars's third moon."

"Don't worry about it, I have a plan. You boys just concentrate on your little wargames. It'll do you a power of good."

Katie grinned. *If I was a boy, I think I'd want to kiss that Gun.* Rachel asked her in a whisper what "a power of good" meant.

"It's what coming to this world has done for us. For me, leastaways."

"I have to admit I'm enjoying myself too," Rachel said. "I just wish I could figure out how to rescue my parents and bring them here."

"Me too. But how can we even get back?"

Rachel bit her lip. "I've been thinking. You remember how the two of us managed to change Anya's hair color and then change it back, without anyone even noticing?"

"How could I forget? That was really weird!"

"Well, what if we could use my typewriter to go back home…at least for long enough to rescue our parents?"

"Would that work? How could that work?"

"We'll never know unless we try."

Katie thought hard. "Okay. But I think we better wait till we get to Mars. Otherwise we might throw the ship off course or generate a black hole or something!"

"What's a black hole?"

"Ladies, what are you whispering about?" Jack said, throwing them a look. "The princess is trying to figure out our strategy. If you have something useful to say, say it to all of us!"

Katie had to restrain herself from telling Jack to blow it out the airlock. *I seen enough of that swaggering nonsense with Johnny Marshall and all his no-good pals. Even in a whole damn other* universe, *guys gotta be macho jerks to show how tough they are?* But she decided to hold her peace for now.

"The first order of business," Anya was saying, "is to figure out where to land. We don't want to go all this way only to end up being captured immediately. Any suggestions?" Silence was her answer.

Jack said gently, "You're the boss, sweetheart. You have to tell us."

Anya looked a bit disappointed, but nodded. "I guess that's true. I just can't get used to the idea of being in command. I'm too young! My father should be making these decisions."

Jack ran a few strands of her hair gently through his fingers. "But he's not here, honey. He's a hostage of Lord Ares. So is your mother. You have to make the decisions. You're the rightful princess of Mars."

Anya leaned her head against his shoulder while Katie and Rachel looked on with a mixture of envy and affection. Then the princess pulled herself together with an effort and faced the group.

"All right," she said. "Jack, hand me that map you keep in your pocket." Jack handed over something that looked like a folded napkin. Anya ran the tip of her index finger gently along the crease and it sprang open to form a two-foot-by-four-foot glossy chart that had seemingly never been folded, and that smoothly attached itself to the wall without so much as a wrinkle.

"That's amazing," said Rachel.

Katie snorted. *That ain't so great. I've seen better stuff than that at the Montoyas'.*

"Now," said Anya briskly, "we need to find an area that Ares doesn't control, somewhere there are people likely to help us. In the past, I would have suggested Valles Marineris, which makes your Grand Canyon on Earth look like an overgrown ditch. Uh, no offense, Katie."

"None taken," Katie said. "The canyon ain't in Texas. The great California Reagan, Billy-Bob II, conquered the whole Colorado River valley for his thirsty serfs more than 30 years ago."

"Uh, right," said Anya, shooting her an odd look. "Anyway, it's out of the question. Ares has turned the whole Marineris canyon, the biggest in the whole Solar System, into a giant prison camp for people who don't like him, or who told jokes about him, or who looked at him funny, or who maybe just belong to some tribe he doesn't consider trustworthy. He's concentrated them all there, with his secret police to guard them and make them work on his insane projects. It's a kind of *concentration-camp*."

"A what?" said Jack, his puzzled expression mirrored on Eddie and Pete's faces.

Katie felt wild laughter mingling with a shriek struggling to be let out of her throat.

Anya didn't notice. "So it's out of the question," she said. "But there's another big canyon system to the west, also in the southern hemisphere, called Noctis Labyrinthus, the 'night maze.' It's not as massive as Valles Marineris, but it's even deeper and twistier. All sorts of outlaws have been hiding out there since the time of Wanda the Great. Also some tribes who just want to be left alone. Ares sent a division there to clean them out five Earth-years ago, but they got a good mauling and had to withdraw. He claimed it was a great victory, but Father has enough contacts in the military, or he did back then, to find out the truth."

"But how are we supposed to land in a canyon?" Jack asked.

Eddie said, "You ain't takin' the *Dragon* down into any ditch."

"That's rich, coming from a man who blasted his ship right through a two-mile-thick wall of ice and rock!" Gun called back.

"It wasn't really!" Eddie shouted back. "There was a hidden tunnel to the surface for emergencies, what did you think?"

"You still damn near got us killed. And I'm still in charge till the end of this flight. We go where the princess says we go. Don't worry about your precious bird, Eddie. I've landed in the Gash on Ceres itself without a scratch."

"And what is the plan once we land in the Night Maze?" Katie asked.

Jack turned and glared at her, but Anya said, "No, it's a good question, Jack. We have to have a plan."

"A plan? You mean like you had when you ran out into the jungle and damn near got yourself eaten by a Greater Venusian Medusa?" Jack snapped, making Anya blush. Katie opened her mouth, but Jack said, "And anyway, you're forgetting, we have to rescue Jim from Ares' little boot camp."

Anya frowned. "But that's in the foothills of Olympus Mons itself, hundreds of miles away and not far from Krakowicz."

Katie elbowed Rachel. *Huh, like Krakow, Poland. Must be the capital city.*

"We have to save him!" Jack insisted. "And the knowledge he must have of the Martian military will be invaluable!"

"Okay, okay." Anya held up her hand. "Yes, we are honor bound, I agree. But we have to get the lay of the land first. Some of the Night Maze outlaws must know what's going on."

They continued arguing over the details, with occasional contributions from Eddie and Gun. Pete was oddly silent, considering that his father was Martian. Katie looked at him keenly. She'd have to ask him about that.

But she and Rachel were questioned first. They had drifted off to sleep where they were sitting, too tired even to climb onto the couches, Katie with her head thrown back against the wall, Rachel's head on her shoulder. Katie dreamed she was in her own bedroom. Her parents were talking quietly downstairs. Her father's tone of voice was urgent, and she crept to the doorway, trying to make out what he was saying, but the only word she heard clearly was "Dixies." The light came through a crack under her bedroom door, brighter and harsher than it should have been. It fell on Sammy Bear and gave his smile a sinister cast, despite his comforting maroon-colored bow tie. Katie shivered and went down on her hands and knees, putting her ear close to the floor. The door flew open with a bang, narrowly missing her head. She winced at the light in her eyes.

"You'd better tell us why!" a man's voice demanded.

"Why what? Jack?" Rachel asked, sitting bolt upright and staring at him wide-eyed.

"I'll ask the questions, Ray, or whatever your name is!"

"What the heck is this, and why can't your hero talk in anything but clichés?" Katie drawled.

"I resent that! I do not talk in clichés! And I'm not a hero, either!"

"Oh, yes you are!" Katie and Rachel said in unison.

"Stop that! You ain't gonna get around me by flattery!" Jack snapped, his voice cracking. "Now you tell us, and tell us quick! Who are you really?"

"Me? I, I'm Rachel Zilber. I'm just me," Rachel said.

Katie bit her lip. *This may be Ray's world, but I'm going to have to jump in here.*

"And are you the daughter of an Earth diplomat, or a native Martian, or from Poland on Earth?"

"Yeah, get your story straight," Eddie sneered. "Who are you really? And what were you doing in the middle of the Venusian jungle, without so much as a raincoat, just as Jack was hurrying to Anya's rescue? Seems like a pretty neat coincidence to me."

Rachel stammered.

"What's that? Trying to think up another lie? Better think fast," Gun said nastily, "you're standing right on top of the airlock, and the vacuum will kill you pretty quick."

"Gun, please, there's no need for that," Anya said from the darkness. "Rachel, Katie, I know you're not working for Lord Ares. I know you're both really Earth girls. So there must be a good reason why you have kept secrets from us. From me." The statement came out as a plea.

"Let's cut the drama, folks," Katie stepped forward and grabbed the flashlight out of Jack's hand.

"Hey! Give that back!" he squeaked.

"No. Anya, would you please turn on the lights?"

The princess complied, and everyone stood around looking a little afraid and a lot sheepish.

"That's better," Katie said. "Yeah, y'all are a bunch of Sherlock Holmeses. Ray has been telling y'all different things, and I've been keeping my big trap mostly shut, because the truth is pretty incredible. We ain't really from Earth. Nor from anywhere else y'all know about." There was a collective intake of breath, and everyone took a step back away from her and Rachel. Katie guffawed. "Look at all y'all! What do you think, we're gonna rip our faces off and be all lizards underneath? No such luck. I'm stuck with this face, and y'all are stuck looking at it. Thing is, we *are* from Earth. Only not 'the United States of Earth,' all right? We're from a place where Earth is, well, *different*. Mars and Venus, too. They're all dead, like the moon—like Luna outside the colonies. Not Earth, of course! But our history's all different, going back like three hundred years."

"So how did you two end up here?" Gun demanded.

Katie shrugged. "Crack me open and cook armadillo soup out of my guts if I know. We're just *here*, ain't that enough? Can all y'all explain how *you*-all came to be here, on this rocket rushing through interplanetary space?"

"Don't go all existential-philosophical on us, missy!" Eddie said, wagging a finger at Katie, but there was no threat in his voice.

Pete was eyeing Katie. "But I thought you said you were from the Panhandle."

Katie stared right back at him. "Course I'm from the Panhandle! Where else could I be from, with this accent? And something else, Pete. I think I knew your mom, back where I came from."

"What? How's that?"

Katie tried to explain, but Pete just looked more confused. She watched his face with amused sympathy. "Yeah. Helen was a nine-year-old girl when I left home a month ago. Liked to eat long strings of licorice."

"That's Mom's favorite snack! I dunno…I think I'm getting a headache…." Pete clutched his head and slumped muttering against the far wall. That seemed to be the signal for the meeting to break up in confusion.

"Thank you," Rachel whispered to Katie.

"Any time," she whispered back. "Now, if you don't mind, I have to go find a quiet corner I can throw up in."

BOOK TWO

STAR OF WAR

15

Rachel wanted to scream. Only ten more days before the *Dragon* reached Martian orbit, but time dragged. She hadn't reckoned on the endless boredom of space travel in her stories. In the world of the pulps, after all, there was always a sizzling space battle or a sizzling romance. Watching Jack and Anya canoodling as the rocket gradually turned into a giant can of B.O. wasn't exactly what she had had in mind. Except for Saint Anya, people's tempers began to fray. The tension between Gun and Eddie was especially high. It wasn't actually necessary for at least one of them to be in the pilot's chair at all times—even Isaac Newton could have told them that a spaceship, once launched through the void, continues on straight and true until acted on by gravity or another force—but they each considered it a point of pride, not to say a point scored against the other one, to spend as much time at the controls as possible. Often, they'd both be up there at the same time, each monitoring the other. The bickering started off low key but gradually intensified as the days passed.

"Whatcha worried about, big guy," Gun said from the pilot's chair, "afraid I'll mess up the perfect course you didn't plot?"

"No dear, just watching to make sure we don't run into one of your precious asteroids."

"Even a baby knows that the Belt is hardly any denser on average than the rest of the System. You, on the other hand, are plenty dense enough to form your own gravitational field."

"Oo! You slay me, my dear."

"I might just do that, if you keep calling me dear, you washed-up excuse for an icehog!" They sounded like they'd been married for ten years.

Rachel pushed back her greasy hair. *This place is just like the ghetto. All that's missing is the two little brats....* She blinked back tears. Katie had finally told her was happening to the Jews in Poland. The only way she could sleep was to tell herself that Katie was no more real than Jack or Anya or the rest of them, that both futures were equally improbable. But she knew in her heart it wasn't true. Tossing and turning on the thin blanket spread out on the cramped floor of the cargo bay, she gazed at the small bundle of things she had accumulated since leaving Venus, all of which were crammed into a small bin. The typewriter held the rest of the bundle down, and she longed to stroke its keys, to make it sing again. Instead she hardly dared to touch it. What if she typed something by mistake and accidentally killed someone?

Katie seemed untroubled by such thoughts. But she was too busy with Pete to be concerned with much else. Busy doing what, exactly, Rachel couldn't say. She suspected that neither of the two Texians could really say, either. Sometimes they squabbled with as much heat as Eddie and Gun. Sometimes they shared their memories of the Panhandle, laughing at the disparities.

"You mean to tell me there's a rocket depot where Gray Stadium used to be?" Katie cried in disbelief.

"Uh-huh. You people left that old wreck standing? What do y'all put in there? No, don't tell me, let me guess. Y'all use it to store pigs' feet!"

"Jerk!" Katie laughed and punched him on the arm. "No! It's the mustering grounds for the Rangers."

"The Texas Rangers?" Pete said, rubbing his upper arm distractedly. "I only read about 'em in the history books. You people still have them?"

"Have them? Course we do! Don't tell me you don't! How in the heck else do y'all defend yourselves against the Dixies?"

"You people are afraid of Dixie® cups?" He stopped. "Hey, I didn't mean...."

"It's all right," Katie said after a moment. "I'm sure my world seems like a weird joke to you. Just like your world seems like a strange dream to me."

Rachel watched them. *Are they flirting? Is she falling in love with him? I hope not, for her sake. I have a feeling he can't really fall in love with anybody. He's not exactly a bad guy, but he's so self-centered, so interested in making money and having a good time.* Rachel decided not to say anything to Katie, since she would only deny her interest in Pete, and maybe punch her in the nose for her trouble, and there was no privacy anyway.

But she did wish she could talk to Anya about it. Anya seemed so wise. Here she was planning a military campaign while engaging in a passionate love affair with Jack, and yet she had enough of herself left over to soothe everybody's jittery nerves and keep the little crew as cheerful as could be expected under the circumstances. Sometimes the Martian princess even led sing-alongs. Rachel wouldn't have expected hard-bitten characters like Eddie, Pete, and Gun to do anything but sneer at these, but instead they'd join in as Anya patiently taught the non-Marpolski speakers the words, one syllable at a time. "Singing is the best way to learn a language," she told them. And her six comrades dutifully sang:

When Wanda sat upon the throne—Hurrah! Hurrah!
No Martian had to fight alone—Hurrah! Hurrah!
All Red Men joined the common cause

To green the desert with God's laws.
And the waters flowed along, so strong, so deep and strong. ...

Or in a softer mood:

Hush, little baby don't you cry
Mama's gonna sing you a lullaby
And if that lullaby don't calm,
Mama's gonna feed you some Tharsis balm
And if you are still thirsty then,
Mama's gonna buy you a Pavonis hen.
And if that hen won't give green milk,
Mama's gonna wrap you in thistlesilk.
Thistlesilk, it is so soft,
Soon your dreams will float aloft.

Anya even fashioned what she called a "Syrtis flute" out of a spare length of aluminum piping about the length of her forearm, and she would play this while Jack broke out a battered but tuneful mouth-organ and accompanied her. He turned out to have a fine baritone, and he would close his eyes and feelingly sing folksongs of the spaceways, all bloody battles and unappeasable longing. Occasionally Gun would chip in with a traditional Belter chant, all about unfair bosses and mine disasters and "someday Earth, for your bloody iron you'll be a-weepin'."

Rachel smiled to herself. *At least some of my ideals survived in this world.*

"Let's hear it for the Magnificent Seven! Seven against a whole planet!" Pete bawled, shooting Katie a wink. She hid a giggle with her hand. *Trouble ahead,* Rachel thought sadly.

Jack was just winding up a haunting ballad about a boy who ran away from his home on Luna because his girl "so fair, so sweet" had been betrothed to another. He traveled the galaxy on Leviathan's back, "ten clicks long, and gentle as the deeps / Riding Einstein's wave through the slow, slow stars," and returned a year later to find his girl had never married, but lived to be one hundred, waiting for his return, "and now she lay a-buried under Luna's cold black sky."

Suddenly a blast of static as loud as a waterfall came over the ship's speakers. Everybody jumped. A harsh male voice spoke, but even though not everyone could understand the words, the threatening tone was clear enough.

"ATTENTION, UNIDENTIFIED SPACECRAFT. YOU HAVE ENTERED MARTIAN NEAR-SPACE. IF YOU DO NOT REVERSE YOUR TRAJECTORY AT ONCE, YOU WILL BE DESTROYED."

Anya finished translating, her face pale, and added, "This is illegal! Under the Treaty of New Warsaw, all space traffic controllers are supposed to speak Solar—"

Up in the cockpit, a brief struggle ended with Eddie sailing headfirst into the cargo bay, where he came to a thumping halt on the floor, narrowly missing Jack. Rachel and Anya looked up in surprise as Gun, now firmly seated in the pilot's chair, said in passable Marpolski, "Attention Mars control. We are badly damaged from a meteor strike. Our transponder isn't working. Request permission to land in an uninhabited area."

There was a short pause filled with dead quiet, except for the sound of Eddie moaning.

"NEGATIVE, UNIDENTIFIED CRAFT," the speakers bawled. "YOU POSE A THREAT TO THE HOLY STAR OF WAR. TAKE COMFORT IN THE FACT THAT YOUR DESTRUCTION WILL GIVE OUR SPACE FORCE TARGET PRACTICE FOR THE COMING WAR WITH EARTH!"

"The coming—" Rachel gasped.

Gun shouted, "Strap yourselves in, everybody. This is going to get bumpy."

Jack, Anya, and Pete sprang into action, helping Katie, Rachel, and the semiconscious Eddie into the crash couches.

"Everybody ready? 'Cause I got to start dodging NOW!" Gun called back.

Jack and Anya shouted, "Yes," and the world turned upside down.

* * * *

An hour and a half later, after the rocket had settled, with a final almighty bang, onto the ground, Gun called back, "Everyone all right back there?"

"I think so," Anya called back gamely.

She, Rachel, and Katie were the only ones still conscious, and Rachel mightily wished she wasn't. A fresh smell of vomit overlaid the weeks-old smell of unwashed bodies. Was it really possible, she thought as she retched weakly, that Anya hadn't thrown up even once? Her face looked completely clean, so apparently it was true. She was even doing well enough to walk over and gently untangle her and Katie from their harnesses so the three of them could help their unconscious comrades.

Eddie groaned as Gun unbuckled him. "Call the captain. I want a refund!"

"You are the captain, icehog."

"I want a refund anyway," he said, coughing up a teaspoonful of black bile that Gun nimbly dodged. "Wassa big idea anyway, trying to shake my ship to pieces? Lila payin' you or somethin'?"

"You're welcome for saving your life," Gun snapped. "I did such a good imitation of an uncontrolled plunge while dodging missiles, that the reds should think we crashed with no survivors."

"I don't think I did survive," Pete groaned as Katie unbuckled him. "No! I didn't! I must be in heaven! Look, an angel!"

"Spare me your cornball lines," Katie said, suppressing a grin.

"We don't like being called reds, Sherilynn," Anya said mildly.

"What? WHAT did you call me? I oughtta make you—" Gun clenched her fist, but she sighed and stood down. "Sorry, princess."

Anya gave a low chuckle. "That's all right. Welcome, my friends, to my kingdom. Welcome to Mars!" And she undogged the inner door of the airlock, then the outer. A gust of air brought a drift of pinkish sand into the cargo bay. Horrible as she still felt, Rachel came wide awake and stumbled toward the door. Her eyes widened. "It's—it's incredible!" she whispered.

Anya came up beside her and squeezed her right arm. "It's home," she said simply.

"Not for me. But it's everything I—I—oh God, I don't believe it," she groaned, and covered her face with both hands.

16

Anya threw Rachel a puzzled look and, stepping out of the ship and down the gangplank onto Martian soil, bowed low to the little delegation that had come to greet the rocketship.

Rachel peeked between her fingers, hoping against hope that she was mistaken. But no. Facing Anya were three men dressed just like her grandfather's benighted Hasidic followers, in black coats over white shirts and black trousers, with sidecurls hanging down around their ears. Emerging over their belts, just in case there was any doubt of their identity, were the ragged white strands of the *tallis katan,* the fringed undergarment worn by observant Jews in accordance with God's commandment in the Bible's Book of Numbers. True, the splendid round fur hat their leader wore was a strange bright orange color, unlike the brown fox fur that such *streimels* were made of back in Poland. But when the rebbe, for such he must be, opened his mouth to address Anya, there was no mistaking the Yiddish accent that tinged his Polish. Or Marpolski. In which case, was it a Maryiddish accent?

"No, ours is the honor, princess," he said gravely in an unexpectedly high-pitched tenor. His beard and sidecurls were tinged with gray, and Rachel expected his voice to crack, but somehow it didn't. "Please forgive our failure to bow. We mean no disrespect, but our custom...."

"Is not to bow except before the Almighty in prayer. Yes, rabbi, I know. It does you credit," Anya said.

The rabbi gave a humorous shrug. "The pretender in Olympus City doesn't think so, princess. That is why we thought it, ah, prudent, to remove our village to the Night Maze."

"Very wise, I'm sure," Anya murmured.

He scowled. "And we really had no choice, because His Majesty has also commanded all the people to attend some strange new religious observance on Friday nights, which is when we begin observing our Sabbath."

Anya frowned too. "A new religious observance?"

"Yes. All the people are commanded to gather on enormous elevated platforms surrounding a green field called a 'gridiron,' where helmet-wearing soldiers fight to control a strange idol—a brown thing like a giant egg with points on each end. The penalty for failing to attend these barbaric pagan celebrations is death!"

"Barbaric, huh? Sounds like you're talking about Friday night football. This so-called Ares *must* be from Texas!" said Katie, who had also come out of the rocket and was standing beside Rachel listening with a look of intense curiosity on her face. Rachel blinked. Katie's Polish was still a little rough, but most non-native speakers complained how hard the language was to learn, and here Katie was already much more fluent than Jack after just a few weeks of talking to her and Anya.

Rachel was scarcely listening. *Please, please, please, let them all disappear, or let* me *disappear.*

Katie nudged her and said cheerfully, "Hey, ain't those your people?"

"No, they are NOT 'my people!'" Rachel charged down the gangplank, flying higher with each step in the low gravity, and cannonballed straight into the rabbi, who managed to retain his balance with the help of his two companions while Rachel bounced off and landed flat on her butt in the red dirt. She leapt to her feet and shook a trembling finger under the rabbi's nose. "What are you fossils *doing* here?" she shouted in Yiddish.

"I think I just explained that to the princess," he responded calmly in the same language.

"No! On Mars! What in God's name are you doing on Mars in the twenty-second century?"

He scratched his beard thoughtfully. "Please don't take the Lord's name in vain, Miss, ah—"

"Rachel Zilber, if it's any of your business! I asked you a question! What are you *doing* here in my dream?"

"What are you doing in mine?" the rabbi responded.

Why had she called it a dream, and why had the rabbi responded in kind? She wasn't about to wake up again in the Ghetto with her parents still missing, was she? A painful grip encircled her arm. Whirling around, she saw Anya gazing at her with an expression she'd never seen before on that perfect face. Anger.

"Rachel, what has come over you?" she hissed in English.

"What has come over *me*? What are these medieval relics doing on Mars?"

"The Fredonavitchers have been here for more than a hundred years. Their first *rebbe*, Shmuel of Fredonavitch, was an astronaut on Edgar Rice Burroughs' original crew that made the first Earth landing on Mars, back in what you call 1948. He was the second Earth human to set foot on our planet, right after Mr. Burroughs himself. And he said—"

"'Here we can live, and have our very own Jewish state,'" Rachel murmured. Her knees felt weak, and she sat down abruptly on a reddish boulder. All the boulders were reddish, of course. This was *Mars*, after all. But there was something dismayingly familiar about it.

Anya was looking at her quizzically. "I thought you said you had no idea what they were doing here."

But Rachel was realizing that she *did* know. She had written that story as a satire years ago, before the war and the Germans and everything. "Hasidim on Mars," she had titled it. It was all of two typed pages long, and was the longest thing she'd ever written on the typewriter up to that point. She was so proud of it, she showed it to her father. Maybe he was just tired from grading papers, or maybe the Jew haters in the university were already getting to him, but he snapped, "This isn't funny, you know." She was so shocked that her sweet, kind father was angry at her, angry over something she had written to amuse him no less, that she only half heard his rant. She'd heard a lot of it before, anyway. How he got away from all that religious *mishegaas*, all that craziness, as soon as he was old enough to run away to Lublin, where he had a modern-minded cousin willing to take him in. How his father, the *rebbe* of Bilgoray, had sat in mourning for him and even chanted the *Kaddish*, the Jewish prayer for the dead, and only relented when his wife was dying and had begged to see her baby granddaughter Rachel just once before passing on to the next world.

"And it's thanks to backward fanatics like him that our lives are becoming impossible!" Rachel's father said, shaking his finger in her astonished face, his voice nearly a shout. "Other people think we're all religious nuts like the Hasidim, and they won't leave us alone because of it. That's why we have to have a state of our own, so we *normal* Jews can live like *normal* people. I thought you understood that! You think *those people* could make a Jewish state? All they do is sit around praying, get drunk, and wait for the Messiah to come save them! If you write trash like this," he said, shaking the typewritten pages at her, "you make it that much harder for people to take us seriously. Is that what you want? You want to make it even harder for us to get to Palestine?"

"No, Daddy, of course not," Rachel had whispered. She had never really thought of getting that stupid old story published anyway. She had only hoped to make him laugh. So she snatched the pages back from him, tore them into little bitty pieces and burst into tears. Immediately he was all hugs and apologies, and she'd forgotten about the whole thing until now. But it seemed that someone, or some*thing*, hadn't forgotten at all. How did that work? And what other surprises did "her" world have in store for her?

"I thought you said your granddaddy was a Hasid." Katie said.

"Yes he was!" Rachel snapped, pulling herself together. "And it's a good thing my Dad got away from him and all the rest of those Hasidic freaks. Otherwise we'd all be shriveling up back in that cholera-ridden *shtetl* instead of—"

"Imprisoned by the Nazis in the ghetto along with the Hasidim?" Katie whispered.

Rachel slapped her across the face, the sound echoing like a gunshot off the canyon walls.

Katie looked up slowly. "I deserved that," she said quietly. "But Ray, you—you oughtta have more respect, is all." Katie turned her back and walked off into the alien underbrush. Rachel stared after her, started back up the gangplank, then caught a whiff of the smell and ran off into the canyon.

♂

Rachel, watching from a distance, saw Katie emerge from the purplish underbrush fifty yards away and sheepishly rejoin the group.

I should do the same thing. She was too embarrassed to make a move. It was quiet where she was, in a crevice between two boulders that looked like sandstone but seemed to be made of much harder stuff; when she hit them idly with a rock nothing came off. She leaned her head back and stared at the wedge of sky overhead, pale blue shading to indigo. A shrunken sun nearing the horizon cast shadows that spread down the canyon walls. Rachel wasn't sure what a canyon was supposed to look like, apart from the color plate of the Grand Canyon in her father's *Encyclopedia Britannica.* This seemed less spectacular, with alternating horizontal layers of rust orange, pale pink, and washed-out reds. *A study in pastels.* She remembered how Mom used to like to draw on big pieces of white paper with colored chalk. Her eyes closed.

♂

When she woke disoriented, two miniature moons chased each other across the alien sky. She shivered in the chill and drew her knees up to her chin, listening intently. The only sound was the thin noise of the wind blowing hard little grits of sand along the canyon bottom.

It sounds like sleet. She tried to stand but slipped and twisted her ankle, letting out an involuntary cry that echoed strangely off the canyon walls. Something answered with a bubbling chuckle that started far off but seemed to come rapidly closer. Rachel gulped and struggled to her feet, launching herself into an unintentional skimming flight up out of the crevice, crashing back to the ground a few yards away. *Lower gravity. You would think I'd be used to that by now.*

The strange chuckling noise drew nearer still, and something whizzed by her ear, like the wasps out on her grandfather's farm but larger and louder. She screamed and charged blindly off into the night.

♂

Anya turned to her crew and the rabbi, who was called Rebbe Yitzchok. "We should send out a search party right away. I don't like the idea of her spending her first night in my kingdom alone and afraid." To make sure Jack, Eddie, and Gun could understand, she was speaking in Solar.

"Your Majesty, I don't like the idea either," the rabbi said in the same language. "But I know this canyon bottom. There's nothing down there to hurt her, unless she trips over a rock."

"She might just do that," Katie muttered.

Yitzchok's wife, the *Rebbetzin* Sarah, elbowed him and whispered something. The rabbi scowled. "Sweetie, I don't think—"

"Don't you sweetie me, Yitzie," she snapped in fluent Solar. Everyone looked at her, a small round woman with a flowered kerchief on her head. "The poor little *maidele* wandered off in the direction of that nest of Phobos-flies I've been asking you to clean out since Rosh Hashanah."

The corners of the rabbi's mouth turned up in a crooked grin. "But they're so harmless, Sorele! They're really quite pretty. I like watching their orange glow while I study Talmud at night."

"They may be pretty, but they're a darned nuisance. And they're liable to give the poor *maidele*, the poor little girl, a heart attack. Why do you think they're named after the fear-moon?"

"It's not a real moon. Only Luna is the real moon," he grumbled. "How can you use those little matzah balls Phobos and Deimos to calculate when the Jewish holidays are? It gives me a headache. All right, we'll go out and look for the little *apikoros*. But you can deal with her and her foul mouth when we find her."

Katie scratched her head. She'd *thought* everyone was speaking English, and then the rabbi had to go and use a funny foreign word. "What's an *apikoros*?" she asked.

The rabbi looked at her. Again that crooked grin. "An unbeliever—that is to say, a Jewish unbeliever, not a follower of another religion like you, miss."

Katie took her time before replying. "Seems to me that if you want her to respect you, you might try respecting her, rabbi. With all respect."

Anya smiled.

Yitzchok flushed, opened his mouth, closed it, opened it again, closed it again. Anya and the others looked away, but Sarah laughed gently.

"Can we go look for the poor lost *maidele* now, Yitzie, while you try to come up with a clever response?"

"Why do I have to respond to anything a non-Jewish *shikse* girl like that says," the rabbi grumbled under his breath, but he described the canyon bottom they would be searching, handed out glow-sticks and let Anya organize the search party.

♂

Anya found Rachel huddled against the canyon wall, arms over her head, sobbing quietly as a swarm of Phobos-flies circled her head.

They really would be quite terrifying if you had never seen anything like them before. They were bigger than Venusian *moosquitos*, in fact they were about the size of a small Earth bird like a starling. But although they were also flying creatures, that was where any resemblance to anything Earthly or Venusian ended. They had six sets of diaphanous wings which could be neatly cupped within one another like Russian dolls, and when extended in flight, ranged from a few inches across for the smaller stabilizers up to a foot and a half long for the major air beaters. They needed such large wingspans because, despite the lower Martian gravity, the thinner Martian air made true flight difficult, although there were many gliders among the Red Planet's fauna. The glow-lights that extended from their thoraxes were irregular balls a few inches in diameter marked with dark splotches that made some visitors from Earth think of the eyeholes in skulls.

The princess gently batted the swarm aside, squatted down, and placed her hand on Rachel's shoulder. Rachel gasped.

"It's all right, Rachel, it's me, Anya."

Rachel's sobs died, but she refused to uncover her face.

"They're Phobos-flies, Rachel. They're harmless. Travelers often welcome them, because they're attracted to people's body heat and can help light the way at night."

Still Rachel kept her hands over her face.

"What's the matter, Rachel? Why don't you come with us? You obviously don't like the Hasidim, but I'd think you would welcome anything familiar on an alien planet. When I visited Earth, I liked to walk along riverbanks and imagine I was back by the Grand Canal."

Rachel turned her red, swollen face toward Anya. "I should never have left home, even though they were going to kill me."

Anya pulled away. "What are you talking about?"

"Never mind. But I don't belong here. Certainly I can't help you free Mars. I'm completely useless. All I do is trip over things!"

Anya bit back a smile. "Well, you are a little clumsy. But I need you, Rachel. You've read more history than anyone else, including me. So you can help me avoid mistakes."

"Ha," Rachel said miserably. "You should just leave me with those ridiculous Hasidim. When you come back as queen in a few months' time I'll already be married and pregnant."

"Now that's enough of that," Anya said. "They're my subjects too. And Ares wants to get rid of them. So they can't be all bad, right?"

Rachel winced when Anya pulled her to her feet.

"I think I've sprained my ankle."

Without a word Anya put her arm around Rachel's back and supported her all the way back to the village.

17

Waking up the next morning atop a straw-filled mattress that rustled as she turned over, Rachel was sure that she was in her grandfather's village. She braced herself for the old man to start yelling at her to get her lazy *tuchis* out of bed and gather the eggs, a task she dreaded since the chickens in his yard were especially vicious.

"For what do I need you *apikoresche* city slickers lazing around my house?" he'd yell.

"Nice to see you too, Zayde," she always wanted to respond, except that Dad had warned her many times that he and Uncle Jacob always used to call their father "long hands" behind his back for the alacrity with which he delivered a *potch im tuchis*—an educational smack on the behind.

Sure enough, there were voices approaching, speaking in that whining nasal Yiddish. Rachel gritted her teeth and jumped out of bed, landing on her bad ankle and promptly collapsing. That was when it all came back to her. The rocket ship. Mars. She was lying in a heap on the floor on *Mars*.

"Are you all right, *maidele*?" the rabbi's wife asked as she entered the room and extended a hand to help her up.

"I'm fine! Just fine, thanks," Rachel gasped, pulling herself upright on the metal bedpost. Anya stood in the doorway and Rachel's face warmed.

Wonderful. Not only does she see me fall, but she hears me speaking Yiddish. Her parents had drilled it into her that modern people simply did not speak that ridiculous language. Being Zionists, they had made sure she learned Hebrew as well as Polish so that she could do her part helping the Jewish people regain their independence in Palestine. Yiddish? Yiddish was a pidgin German spoken by old fossils like her grandfather and the *rebbetzin* here.

"Well, if you're fine," Sarah said smoothly, "do you think you could give me a hand gathering the eggs?"

Rachel could hardly believe it, but the job was actually worse than it had been back in Poland. It wasn't that the chickens were some bizarre Martian bird—no, they were the same ornery, smelly beasts she knew and hated. But thanks to the lower gravity, the useless fluttering about they did back on Earth was transformed into actual flight—and the nasty little creatures had rediscovered the fact that their beaks were good for something more than pecking at corn. In less than a minute Rachel fled for the safety of the rabbi's house, losing her balance on the lintel and spilling all three of the eggs she had gathered onto the floor.

The rabbi's wife stood with her hands on her hips and shook her head slowly. "One simple thing I asked you to do."

"Why didn't you ask someone else?" Rachel wiped egg white from her face. "Katie's a farm girl."

"But you're one of us," Sarah pulled Rachel to her feet.

"Oh great. I feel so chosen."

Sarah shrugged. "I would have asked my daughter, but Ya'akova Beile is scared of chickens. Can you imagine such a stupid thing?"

"No, I can't imagine why anybody would be frightened of chickens," Rachel said sarcastically, rubbing at the sore spot on the back of her neck where she had been pecked.

"Exactly! It's not like the curly-headed little monster is scared of anything else," Sarah said, reaching for Rachel's face with a rag. "Now hold still, *maidele*, and I'll clean you up."

"Get off me! You are not my mother!" Rachel took a step back.

"May the Holy One be praised for that. Still, you are one of us."

"Stop saying that! I am not!"

"Right. You're a Yiddish-speaking *shikse* with curly red hair and a big nose."

"How did you people get here anyway! This doesn't make any sense!" Rachel cried. But *she* was responsible for their being here. She clutched her head.

"Ray, can I talk to you for a minute?" Katie looked at her narrowly, her arms folded.

"You again! Fine, what do you want?" Rachel said, stalking over to her and lowering her voice.

"You seem awful mad at people who haven't done a thing but take us in and feed us when we're a bunch of desperados."

"I seem 'awful mad,' do I? All right, come with me," Rachel said, grabbing Katie's arm and steering her outdoors. The street was nothing but a dusty path lined with tents and a stone hovel or two, like the rabbi's house. Everything was still in shade and would be until the sun was high enough in the sky to peep over the canyon walls. But the villagers were all up and about. A weary-looking fortyish woman was hauling a bucket of water down the street while a girl of about Rachel and Katie's age struggled with her own load and scolded a squabbling group of younger children. Were there six of them? Seven? Was that the way Katie wanted to spend her life?

"Course it ain't," the Texian snapped, "why do you think I don't ever want to go back to the Panhandle, except to rescue poor Mom and Dad?

I told you, my great-granddaddy was a Baptist preacher. I know what life is like for those people, especially their women, and it ain't too different from this. Except that they have pigs, which stink even worse than chickens. Come to that, life isn't much better for anybody back in the Panhandle, leastaways not in our world. But still, what's it to you? What makes you so darn mad about it? And don't go telling me it's only about your sense of fairness. I ain't as simple as all that. You're just upset that these Hasids sneaked their way into your shiny space fantasy, aren't you?"

Rachel did a double take. Katie leaned in even closer. "What you don't get, Ray, is that this ain't your private daydream. Not anymore. And it hasn't been since you rolled that first sheet of paper into your typewriter."

"Of course it is! I created it! I'm the writer!"

"Yeah, but you ain't God. Not even the god of this world. The minute somebody else started reading your stories—and fine stories they are, Ray, make no mistake—they started having a say in them. And even before that, the stories didn't always quite turn out the way you expected, did they?"

Rachel looked at Katie, startled again. "How did you know that?"

Katie shrugged and studied her shoes. "I just know. I tried writing some stories myself, okay? But I gave it up because I didn't have a prayer of writing as well as you. But I know that the things you make up don't always turn out the way you expect. There's something else at work when you write. I don't pretend to know what it is, but it's there, ain't it? And that's how come you've got Hasids messing up your shiny space world. And also how come there are all kinds of nasty people and things around that you never meant to dream up. So how about you stop blaming yourself for all that?"

Rachel burst into tears and grabbed Katie in a bear hug. After a minute, Katie started wriggling. "Come on. We've got to go help Sarah get breakfast on the table. I think maybe I'd better gather the eggs this time."

♂

Not everyone was interested in breakfast, though. Gun wandered away from the village and watched with her arms folded as Eddie ran around the ship, checking things and muttering to himself.

"Where ya goin', hotshot?"

"As far away as possible from this stupid planet," Eddie snapped. "If you people want to try to fight the most powerful dictator in the Solar System, more power to you, but I'm getting out of here."

"In your ship."

"Yes."

"Which the Martian Space Force thinks crashed and killed everyone on board."

Eddie yanked his hand out of an access panel so fast he cut it. Gun listened appreciatively to the stream of inventive curses Eddie produced in at least three languages, only winding down when he ran out of breath.

"—son of a mutilated six-legged Venusian tree frog and a Titanian methane dung beetle!" he concluded.

"Yes. But you know, Eddie, there *is* a bright side to all this," Gun said, sitting beside Eddie and draping her arm around his shoulders as he buried his head in his hands.

"Oh? And what's that?" Eddie said through his fingers.

"Long as your ship is parked here on Mars, protected by the Martian Space Force, ain't no way your ex can get her hands on it. The Martian courts won't enforce rulings from anywhere else in the System."

Eddie turned and stared at her. "How do you know that?"

Gun pulled away. "Let's just say you ain't the only one that's been married."

Eddie stared even harder, looking as if he wanted to laugh. "You?"

"Yeah, me. What a joke, huh? To a genuine full-blood Martian, blast his cheatin' lyin' heart. Martian men, ucch, don't get me started. That's how come I speak Marpolski. Now, if you're done feeling sorry for yourself, you can come back with me, have some breakfast and help *your* good friend Jack plot to overthrow the government."

"I feel so much better already," Eddie grumbled, getting to his feet. The first beam of morning sunlight to make it over the canyon rim hit him right in the eye.

♂

Rachel stood on a perch high up on the canyon wall, her gaze on Gun and Eddie. She'd fled as soon as breakfast was over, lest Rebbetzin Sarah collar her and demand she do the dishes. *I hate doing dishes. But what am I good for, anyway? These Hasidic women, they need to have a revolution now, but at least they know how to do stuff! So does everyone else—Jack and Eddie are good at gunslinging, Eddie and Gun at piloting, Pete at whatever his shady business is, Katie adapts herself without complaint to whatever crazy situation she finds herself in, and Anya, of course, is good at everything. So, what am I good at? Apparently nothing except flicking pebbles off this ledge.*

"Ow!" a voice shouted from below.

I guess my pebble-throwing license just got revoked, too. "Sorry," she called out in Yiddish. Somehow it had sounded like a Yiddishy ouch.

"You better be!" the voice called back. There was a scrabbling noise, and a head full of brown curls hove into view. Beneath the curls was a very energetic and very dirty little face. "You must be the Yiddish-speaking *shikse*," said the injured party.

She wore a skirt, so she must be a girl. *Who goes rock climbing in skirts? The rebbe's daughter, that's who.*

"I'm as Jewish as you are," Rachel snapped. "You must be Ya'akova Beile, who's scared of chickens."

To reply, the hellion had to remove her thumb from her mouth where she'd planted it as soon as she sat down. It made a popping sound, and a little drop of spit flew up and hit Rachel on the nose. "I heard you ain't too happy around those nasty birds, neither."

"No, I'm *not* too happy around them *either*," Rachel growled.

"But I bet you'd love to meet my friends the *deestelketz!*" the little girl cried, leaping to her feet so quickly Rachel was afraid she'd pitch herself headfirst into the canyon.

"What on Earth—on Mars is a *deestelketz*?" Rachel translated the words to herself. Thistlecats? The ones Anya had told her about? But she'd gotten the impression that those were mythical animals.

Ya'akova Beile rolled her chocolate-brown eyes. "Duh! *Everybody* knows what a deestelketz is! You're so dumb, you must've been born on Old Earth!"

"I *was* born on Old Earth," Rachel said.

The little girl's face rearranged itself into an expression of awe under all the reddish dirt. "Really? Is it true then that Jerusalem is made all of brass and gold?"

"I wouldn't know. I've never been to Palestine." The girl looked puzzled. "I've never been to the Land of Israel," Rachel explained.

"But you're from Earth, so you must have been to the Land of Israel! On Earth you don't even have to get on a rocketship to go there.... Hey, how come you're crying?"

"I am NOT crying!" Rachel swiped at the tears rolling down her cheeks. "And I don't believe there is any such thing as a deestelketz! You're making it up to fool me!"

"Am not!"

"Are too!"

"Am not! There's a *deestelketzel* right behind you, the one I've been looking for all morning!" Ya'akova Beile exclaimed, pointing over Rachel's shoulder.

She wants me to think that not only is there such a thing as a "thistle-cat," there's also such a thing as a "thistlekitten"?

"You can't fool me! That's the oldest trick there is, saying 'look behind you!'" Rachel snapped. Just then she felt a hand on her shoulder. It must be Rebbetzin Sarah, come to collect her bratty daughter. Rachel turned around with relief.

An orange-and-white striped beast as big as a baby elephant, with a basketball-sized white fluff ball like a giant dandelion going to seed where its head should have been stood before her. One of its eight or ten paws—or maybe it had sixteen or twenty, Rachel couldn't count in the terror of the moment—was planted firmly on her shoulder.

♂

Rachel curled up in a fetal ball behind a rock on the canyon floor. Less than a minute later, Ya'akov Beile leaned over her.

"You scared the poor thing!" Ya'akov Beile said.

Rachel made a choking sound.

"Yes you did! You scared him! I've been tracking him ever since he got separated from the herd this morning! It's my job."

"Your job," Rachel repeated faintly.

Ya'akova Beile puffed out her chest. "That's what I said. It's my job! When I grow up, I'm going to be the head shepherd for the whole *shtetl*!"

"Do they let girls do that?"

"They will if I have anything to say about it! It ain't fair for the boys to have all the fun around here!"

"All the fun?"

"Yeah. Shloimie, he's the head shepherd, and all his assistants are men and boys, and Yomtov, he's the head shearer, and almost all of *his* assistants—"

"Head shearer?"

"Are you repeating everything I say? I thought only little kids did that. I don't do that anymore now that I'm big. I'll be four at Rosh Hashanah."

"You'll be four?"

"You're still doing it! Cut it out! Four in *Mars* years, of course. In Jewish years I'm almost eight."

Earth years. She'll be eight in Earth years.

"Now I'll have to go tell Shloimie that the poor little deestelketzel is still hiding somewhere, thanks to you. I mean, I don't blame you for being afraid of chickens, but a poor harmless deestelketzel?"

"Why does the village have a herd of deestelketz, anyway?"

"Duh! For their wool, of course! I just said we have shearers, didn't I? We sell the wool, that's how we make our *parnausau*, our living. It's also how Daddy has his nice *shtreimel*, and Mommy has her beautiful winter coat. For my birthday I'm getting a coat just like hers."

"That was supposed to be a surprise, sweetie," a man's voice said. Rachel looked up and saw Rebbe Yitzchok smiling affectionately at his daughter.

"Well, since Cousin Moishe spilled the beans, can I have it now?" Ya'akova Beile retorted.

For an answer, the rebbe scooped her up and said, "You're late for learning your *aleph-beis*, cookie. Let Shloimie send Kalman or Alex or somebody to look for the lost deestelketzel. In fact, I'll go have a look myself."

"You're going to go look yourself?!" Rachel exclaimed.

The rebbe raised an eyebrow. "Doesn't that meet with your approval, Miss Rachel?"

"But you're the rebbe! Don't you just sit around and study Talmud all day while Sarah waits on you hand and foot?"

The rebbe chuckled. "The day Sorele waits on me is the day I'll know the Messiah has come to lead us back to the Land of Israel and rebuild the Temple. Besides, we all have to earn our keep here, miss, and our ancestors Abraham, Isaac, and Jacob were shepherds, so what more honorable occupation can there be? Now, are you coming with us? Ya'akova Beile needs to learn her letters and you need to prepare for your journey. Sarah's brother Moishe has agreed to take you where you need to go in his mule cart."

Rachel followed Rebbe Yitzchok and his daughter as they walked the winding path up the canyon wall. *Have I been too hasty in judging these people? But Dad couldn't have been wrong about them! The Martian Hasidim must just be different from the ones back in Poland.*

18

"Explain to me again," Pete said in a muffled voice, "why this is the best way to travel on Mars?"

Pete and the rest of the would-be rebel army were huddled under a tarpaulin inside a cart drawn by two mules called Azriel and Shimon, bumping along a desert track under a noonday sun. The cover kept away the breeze and made what air there was stifling hot, but was no barrier to windblown grit. Everyone was squeezed in tightly among the bulging duffel-bag-type packs containing their belongings, battered gray canvas ponchos in case of dust storms, and giant jerrycans of water. The fact that the cart was made of aluminum due to the scarcity of wood on Mars made it even more uncomfortable.

"It's the only way, seeing that our dear leader Ares has nationalized all the mechanical surface transport," Jack pointed out. "Besides which, it'll be a little easier to get into the base where my brother is a prisoner if we're hiding in a mule cart than if we drive right up in a groundcar and ask for him, right?"

"A sort of Trojan mule strategy," Gun said. "Pity we haven't got any guys here with the wit of Odysseus."

"On behalf of myself and the other two male members of the Magnificent Seven, I protest," Eddie said. "Ow," he added, as the cart went over a rock and he bumped his head.

"Keep it down back there," Moishe called back. "We're coming to a checkpoint."

"A checkpoint way out here in the desert?" Pete whispered. "This Ares must be one crazy paranoid dude!"

"We've been trying to tell you," Anya whispered back.

The cart bumped to a halt. "Stop right there," said a grating voice that made the hairs stand up on the back of Rachel's neck. "Let's see your papers."

Now I really do feel at home.

For a few moments everything was quiet. Then they heard footsteps approaching. "Hey, Ryszard, what's with the freak in the black suit? Carnival come early this year?"

"Nah, it's just a Jew. Some medieval fossil," said the first voice.

Rachel's hot face grew even warmer.

"Oh yeah? Well, I think he's cruelly mistreating that thistlecat on his head."

"We do not mistreat our deestelketz, Your Excellency, we herd them and shear them every spring.... Hey, give it back!"

"Keep away," the soldiers chanted. "Keep the fur away from the nasty smelly Yid."

"Good thing you're not one of them, right?" Katie whispered.

Rachel burst into silent, angry tears. Was there nowhere she could escape from the curse of being Jewish? Many science fiction writers were Jews like her, even if they were lucky enough to live in America. Didn't they all hope that the future would be shiny and clean, free of superstition and unreasoning hate?

"C'mon Anya, let go of my arm and let me go sort those jerks out," Jack whispered.

"You do that and we'll never rescue your brother!" Anya whispered back.

Rachel smiled through her tears. Her hero was acting like, well, her hero. Fortunately the soldiers tired of their fun soon enough, and after extracting a hefty bribe from Moishe, let the cart go on its way without a search.

"I'll pay you back, Moishe," Anya called.

"Don't worry about it, princess. It's the cost of doing business out here."

"You mean this happens all the time?"

"Yes, princess."

A little sunlight seeped under the edges of the tarpaulin. Anya frowned.

Poor Anya. If she or her father ever came to the throne, they would have a hard time turning Mars back into a civilized planet, what with all these bullyboys who had got a taste for pushing people around. What were they going to do with them? They couldn't just put them all in jail, unless they'd actually killed someone, and they couldn't all be murderers, could they? Or could they? Rachel shivered despite the heat. It was all pretty academic for the moment, anyway. If they didn't win, they were going to find themselves in Valles Marineris. Or in front of a firing squad.

♂

After bruising hours Moishe decided they were in an area remote enough to chance taking a rest break. Besides, Shimmie and Azri needed to eat and drink. All seven passengers clambered stiffly out of the cart. Rachel stumbled, went down on her hands and knees and retched weakly.

"Now, now, I thought we agreed, no discussions about Ares," Jack joked.

Anya folded her arms and glared at him. "You think it's funny?" She gestured at the surrounding desolation of broken pink rock. "This area was farmland from the time of Wanda the Great right up through the reign of Ares the Usurper. Now it's all going back to desert since Ares III is too busy building up his little boy-toy army."

Jack held up his hands. "Come on, Anya honey, I'm on your side, remember?" He moved to embrace her but she slipped away from him.

"No offense, darling, but you stink," she pointed out.

"Not as bad as when we were on the *Martian Liberator*."

"We're all a bit worse for wear," Gun said. "Moishe, dude, how soon can we get to a bath?"

"Did I just hear a Belter talk about getting clean?" Eddie rasped. "The situation must be worse than I thought. You guys smell like blue cheese dipped in cat poop, and that's after a bath."

"Yeah? Well you icehogs ain't exactly winners of the Ivory Soap Awards."

While the ill-natured banter continued, Rachel got shakily to her feet and beckoned to Katie.

"You all right, Ray?"

She nodded and took a swig from her canteen. "Have to talk to you before we get under way again," she gasped. "Somewhere away from the others."

"This desert isn't a real good place for privacy."

"I'm worried we won't get another chance before the Second Trojan War starts. Behind that boulder?"

They brushed off their space-bought jumpsuits, which had lost their sheen almost instantly once they landed on Mars, and squatted in the scanty shade of a rock that had been sculpted by the wind into a vaguely daggerlike shape. Rachel scratched at it idly with her index finger, expecting pale red grains of sand to flake away, but instead it was her fingernail that broke off. She sighed and pushed her hair back, feeling the gritty tangles twining between her fingers.

"Katie," she said, "you know what we talked about when we were on the ship? I didn't want to say anything when we were in the village, there were too many people around all the time, but now...."

"You mean about using your typewriter to try and rescue our parents? Yeah, I've been thinking a lot about that," Katie said. She had found a round orange pebble and was tossing it from one hand to the other and back again. "It ain't gonna work the way you were talking."

"Why not?"

"What're we gonna do for our folks back there? I can tell you, I'm not in any better shape than when I left. Probably I'm in worse shape, what with the low gravity and all. And what're we supposed to do for weapons? Borrow Jack's zap-guns?"

"What if we could borrow Jack instead?"

"But—but—that doesn't make any sense!"

"Neither does the fact that we're breathing air on Mars, Katie." Rachel took a deep breath. "But suppose we could talk him and Anya into helping us? If I made 'em up on my typewriter and told 'em what to do in the first place, surely I could send them to Earth the same way."

Katie shook her head. "It still doesn't make sense, Ray. And how are we gonna explain it to them? I think they just about buy our story about being from another universe—heck, I sort of think it's true myself—but they're gonna just freak out if you put on your witch hat and sit down in front of your magic Olivetti!"

"Leave that part to me. I'm the storyteller, remember?"

Jack called them back to the cart. Rachel glanced quickly up at the sun, trying to make out how close it was to the horizon. It looked so much smaller than it did from Earth. *I really am standing on a planet where I shouldn't even be able to breathe.* She straightened her spine. *Okay. How should I put my plan into effect?* Presumably they would have to stop at nightfall. That was probably the best time to try it, anyway. In the dark, maybe no one would notice exactly what kind of sophisticated device she was using for travel between universes—another thing she probably couldn't have gotten away with back in the *shtetl*. On the other hand, it would be hard for her to see. *Is there any wood for a fire, or does Moishe have lanterns or flashlights? If I have to, I guess I can use one of Jack's zap-guns for light.*

The afternoon ride was more comfortable. The stretch of desert they were passing through was so empty Moishe figured they were safe enough sitting out in the open. The heat bothered Rachel, though, so she pulled a corner of the tarpaulin over her. Anya drowsed with her head in Jack's lap. With her curly copper hair she looked like an orange cat napping there, while Jack had his head thrown back against the side of the cart and was snoring loudly. Eddie and Gun had exhausted themselves bickering, and he had dozed off on her shoulder. Rachel smiled to herself; anyone could have seen that coming. In the opposite corner of the cart, Katie crouched beside Pete, letting him take her arm and point out features of the landscape. That left Rachel alone with Moishe, who was intent on driving and didn't seem up for conversation. What could she discuss with him, anyhow? He wouldn't believe her predicament even if she described it to him. But who else could she talk to? She reached out and touched his arm. He jerked the reins. The cart swerved sharply and almost overturned. Moishe leapt out and spent several minutes calming Shimmie and Azri. The peaceful moment was shattered. Gun shoved Eddie off her shoulder, muttering something about icehog perverts.

Can't I do anything right? Rachel closed her eyes. *How would I have written the scene?* Moishe would have turned around with a kindly smile and asked what she wanted. She would have explained the terrible danger her parents and Katie's parents were in, and he would have given practical advice, perhaps with a touch of mystical wisdom and a twinkle in his eye.

Instead he growled at her in Yiddish. "*Maidele!* What's the matter, you cause trouble, it tires you out and you fall asleep?"

"Leave me alone, Moishe," she said without opening her eyes.

"From these *goyim* I expect anything, but from a Jewish girl like you, even if you are an *apikoros*, I expect more modesty!"

"Modesty?" Rachel opened her eyes. "You mean I was coming on to you because I'm wearing a jumpsuit and I touched you on the arm?" Suddenly all the terror and misery she'd been feeling for weeks broke, and she began to laugh. "Do you think I want to go out with a pasty-faced, unwashed, scraggly bearded, *yeshiva bocher* like you? Find some other girl to wash your floors and mend your shirts!"

Moishe turned back to the mules, muttering curses to himself in Yiddish. Katie tapped her on the shoulder and Rachel turned.

"I suppose you're going to tell me I should have been more respectful."

"No, he was being a jerk. I just wanted to ask if you know what you're going to say tonight."

Rachel nodded slowly. "I'm beginning to get an idea. Just back me up, okay?"

"Whatever you say, boss!"

A moment later Azri kicked his hind foot and Moishe let out a yelp and began hopping around on one foot, swearing in a higher register. "May the Holy One put a curse on your entire breed! May they all be born with two heads and a stomach outside the body!" he howled, shaking his fist at Azri, who seemed to glare back at him. Hobbling back to the cart, he gloomily told his passengers that they were going to have to stop where they were for the night.

Gun eyed his torn right trouser leg and said, "That looks like it might be broken. Mind if I have a look?"

Rachel kept her face carefully neutral as she translated this offer into Yiddish. Moishe spluttered and touched his wound, but his eyes watered and he fell backward in his seat with a groan.

Taking that as permission, Gun pulled out a pocketknife and cut away the black fabric. She grunted at what she saw and began wrapping an improvised bandage around his leg. "Not broken, but he's gonna have one painful bruise," she explained.

Rachel looked out across the desert. The shrunken sun was nearing the western horizon.

"It gets cold out here at night, doesn't it?" she asked Anya, who nodded. "So what are we going to do to keep warm? I don't see lots of firewood lying around."

Anya frowned. "You're right. I'd better go out with the guys and see if we can find any clingerweed."

"Clingerweed? What's that?"

"You really haven't ever been out in the Martian outback, have you? The stuff grows in almost every deep gulch. Once the seed-pods get on your clothes or skin, they're almost impossible to get off. That's how they spread. A bit like burrs on Earth, but much stickier. If you can avoid getting covered in the pods, though, the stalks and leaves make a really nice fire."

"Sounds neat! Can I help gather it?"

Rachel had the impression that Anya was the one controlling her face now. "Why don't you, um, stay behind with Moishe and help him pitch camp?"

"You're afraid I'll come back a giant burr, aren't you?"

"Well—"

Rachel sighed. "All right. But it's going to be hard helping someone who thinks so little of me."

"What?"

Rachel explained what had happened.

Anya shook her head. "Rachel, my friend, I usually find people are practical when they need to be. Just be polite to him, all right? For my sake, please?"

Rachel managed to take instructions from Moishe and they both managed to stay civil until the firewood-gathering party returned. By then it was sunset, the long orange light casting stretched-out purple shadows across the alien landscape. It would have been beautiful if it wasn't also frightening; it was all too easy to imagine bandits or Martian soldiers hiding behind every one of the desert's myriads of strangely sculpted rocks. Things looked more cheerful, though, once the fire was going and the giant Martian *kruckle* beans were making the rounds. These tasted vaguely like buttered corn, although the texture was closer to peanuts and they made disconcerting popping noises when you bit into them. But with a homey chicken gravy that tasted like her grandmother's, they were irresistible, and she had three helpings before coming up for breath. It was time. So she took a sip of water from a tin mug, stood up and cleared her throat.

Everyone ignored her. Anya was deep in conversation with Jack, Gun was jabbing her finger into Eddie's paunchy gut, and Pete was staring into the fire, his eyes shining like an animal's. Moishe had fallen asleep sitting up, gravy dribbling into his beard.

"Hey folks," Katie said. "Stop jabbering a sec and listen to what Ray's got to tell y'all."

All eyes turned Rachel's way. She had always hated speaking up in class, but now a strange thrill went through her.

"When Katie and I told you where we're from, we never said how we got here. An experiment went wrong." She paused, but everyone just kept looking at her, so she took a deep breath and went on. "My father is a professor at the University of Warsaw. I take after him, I guess." *As a writer with an interest in history.* "I started messing around with his machines when I was three." She didn't actually say "his typewriter." "And, well, one thing led to another and I—I found the gateway to other worlds." She paused again, her throat tightening as she fought back tears. She swiped at her eyes and spat into the fire, an action that would have horrified her parents. "But by the time I was getting halfway decent at exploring these—other worlds, a terrible war had broken out. The invaders came into my country and forced my people—my family, into a ghetto. We lost our house. I can't talk much about it, forgive me. Maybe Katie can explain if you want to know more. But the thing is—" Her knees shook. Katie quietly stood and put her hand on Rachel's shoulder. Rachel nodded twice, vigorously. "My parents are trapped back there in the ghetto. And Katie's parents too—in a different country, someplace else entirely, but they're in trouble too—they've been kidnapped by enemy soldiers. We need your help to rescue them. That's—that's it, I guess."

The silence was unbroken for a long time, except for the faint crackle of clingerweed burrs bursting, like tiny firecrackers. Finally Jack looked up from the fire, looked Rachel straight in the eye. "I only have one question," he said.

She tensed. *Why should I believe you? How much has Ares been paying you? Would you hold still a sec so I can shoot you?* No, that would be three questions.

"How can I get to your world and free your folks? And why didn't you tell me this before?"

"That's two questions, Jack."

She slumped against Katie, who explained that their experimental device for traveling between dimensions was—a typewriter.

"A typewriter?" Anya said with a quizzical expression.

"That's right," Rachel said, recovering herself, "a typewriter. Anyway, it *looks* just like a typewriter. I use the keyboard to set coordinates. The, uh, interdimensional wave differential generator is inside the bell."

"The bell?" Pete said. Moishe leaned against him, snoring loudly, and Pete shoved him away.

"Yeah, you know, the little bell that goes off before you reach the end of a line. The interdimensional dynamicalizer is hidden in there."

"You just called it an interdimensional wave differential generator," Gun pointed out.

"Who cares what it's called! It works, that's all that matters, right?"

"It better," Katie said under her breath.

19

"This is ridiculous," Katie murmured, "what are we, witches? Double, double, toil and trouble."

It was late. In the distance, the campfire burned low, with Gun, Eddie and Moishe huddled around it, while the slim, flame-haired figure of Anya stood gazing off into the desert. Katie bent over Rachel's type-writer, holding Eddie's lucky flashlight.

"Shh," said Rachel. "I'm trying to concentrate."

"You ready for us yet?" a voice with a Texas twang called out of the darkness.

"Not yet! Just keep your britches on, Petey," Katie said loud enough to make Rachel jump.

"Don't call me Petey," he grumbled.

"Petey! Petey!" Jack cackled.

"Will you all BE QUIET!" Rachel shook her head. Maybe it wasn't such a hot idea sending two guys off on this first mission. At least, not these two guys.

She and Katie had agreed that it made sense to send the rescue mission for Katie's parents first, since it would likely be easier and would give them a better idea of the logistics of interdimensional travel.

"Those Dixies are a bunch of yellowbellies," Katie said. "They have to bring their own guns, which ain't even good for shooting possum, some of 'em. They'll be a pushover for our Mr. Flash. The S.S., on the other hand...." Both girls trembled.

It was Pete's idea that he should come along. In fact, at first he said that he should go *instead of* Jack.

"You crazy, you big blowhard?" Katie demanded, her hands on her hips.

"No, all y'all are crazy," he retorted. "Jack doesn't know his way around the Texas back country. I do."

"Peter, my friend, no offense, but you ain't half the shot I am," Jack said, clapping a hand on his shoulder.

Pete narrowed his eyes and opened his mouth, then closed it and shrugged. "Still, you need a man who knows the lay of the land."

"Which you don't, you big tumbleweed," Katie said with a gruffness that sounded suspiciously like affection. "No matter how much time you spent in the Panhandle, *here*, you ain't ever been to the Panhandle, *there*. They might as well be different countries. In fact, they are."

"So what's so different about 'em, other than the names of the corrupt politicos running the place?"

Katie snorted. "How about the minefields fifteen miles out of town?"

"The WHAT?" Pete and Jack said in unison.

"You heard me. Damn Dixies have laid mines all along old I-40 to block the way east to their promised land in Oklahoma, not that any decent person has any desire to so much as visit the place. And that's the way they probably went with my parents. So if you were thinking of just taking a nice leisurely drive down I-40 to rescue 'em...."

"I don't know what you're talkin' about," Pete interrupted. "Eye-forty? Forty eyes? There are only twenty of these 'Dixie' soldiers?"

"No, dumb-bell," Katie said, pushing him in the chest. "I-40! The interstate highway! Don't tell me you rich folks don't have cars...."

"We don't," Pete said, "not internal-combustion ones, anyway. The old 'interstates' are all parkways now, planted with trees and grass. They even grow corn on some of 'em."

"Ain't that a purty picture," Katie said. "I can see you ain't prepared for what you'll find. Jack, here, is a genuine hero. He'll manage. But you—"

"Are just a schmoe," Pete finished.

"I am NOT a hero!" said Jack.

"Didn't say that," Katie said, ignoring Jack. "But don't go thinking you're gonna impress *this* country gal, Mr. Half-Texian Half-Martian half-breed, with any stupid heroics!"

"I don't think any such thing," Pete snapped. "I just want to find your parents so I can tell 'em what a loudmouth, rude little tomboy they raised!"

Jack held up his hands. "Cut it out, you two. We've got to get a move on if we're gonna be out of here by dawn. Now, Katie, I'm sure everything you say is right, but it would be very handy for me to bring a native along with me. Somebody sorta like Karolla, big, furry, and dumb."

"Thanks a lot, gunslinger," Pete said.

"You're welcome," Jack said without looking at him. "Bottom line is, Miss Katie, it improves my chances of saving your parents."

"Okay," Katie whispered, her eyes welling up. "Their names are Mike and Mary. She calls him 'Boo' and he calls her 'honeybunch,' got it?" Both men nodded. "He's a wiry guy with gray hair and mustache, stands about five foot eight in his socks. She's a strawberry blonde who hardly comes up to his shoulder blades. You take good care of my folks."

They swore it. And so there they were, making nervous jokes standing out in the darkness of the Martian night so that the "interdimensional transport" effect wouldn't catch the others, while the yellow light of the flashlight illuminated the scariest sight Rachel knew: a crisp white piece of paper, its top peeking out above the platen, the carriage holding it shoved out as far left as it would go. Anything could happen. Until now, all she'd had to worry about was that a story wouldn't turn out right, and she'd have to ball it up and toss it in the wastebasket. Or that she'd run out of paper or typewriter ribbon. But it was all so different now. Her fingers rested lifelessly on the keys.

Katie put her hand on Rachel's shoulder, bent down and whispered, "It's all right, Ray. Whatever happens now, it's all right."

"Is it?" Rachel murmured. She crooked her fingers, took a deep breath and moved them off the home keys. Their clackety-clack noise sounded flat and echoless in the stillness of the alien night. The bell sounded to mark the end of the line, and the carriage swung smoothly back to the left. As reverently as if reciting a prayer, Katie read aloud:

```
Jack and Pete blinked as the
lightless Martian sky vanished and the
white heat of a Texas noontime beat
down all around them.
```

"That's it? That's all you're gonna write?" Katie said, her voice rising.

"Check if they're still here."

"Hey Pete! Jack!"

Silence.

The quiet didn't last more than a few seconds before the typewriter started clacking away again, the smack of the individual keystrokes merging into a miniature thunderclap so that Katie had to raise her voice. "Are you sure that's wise, Ray? I mean, you know what you mean to write?"

"I'm not writing anything," Rachel's hands lay in her lap.

"Then who—"

A stream of words appeared on the paper.

♂

Jack and Pete blinked as the lightless Martian sky vanished and the white heat of a Texas noontime beat down all around them. They staggered, disoriented by the bright sun and the doubled gravity, but kept their balance and looked around warily. Jack and Pete drew their zapguns, but left the safeties on.

They were standing in a ruined farmyard, beside a pile of charred and splintered wood that looked as if it might once have been a picket fence. The effort that had gone into destroying it seemed excessive, as if the vandals had been motivated by malice. There was worse in the direction of the barn, which had been burned to its foundations like the farmhouse. In fact you could only tell it had once been a barn by the animal skeletons lying in the ashes. Jack and Pete both shook their heads over the sheer waste.

"You'd think an army in a non-mechanized society could have used horses," Jack said.

Pete spat. "I expect they took the good ones. Looks to me like there's only one horse skeleton in there. Probably an old nag Katie's family couldn't bear to put down."

Jack nodded. "Let's not tell her about that when we get back, okay?" They set off toward the house through a field of stubble. Along the way they passed the well, whose sturdy housing had been smashed. A faint breeze carried a rank smell from its depths.

"Why the heck would anyone go and spoil a well in dry country like this?" Pete said.

Jack shook his head. "The 'Dixies' weren't coming to conquer, I think. They were raiding for whatever spoils they could grab, and to wreck whatever they couldn't carry away with them. Makes rebuilding that much harder."

Pete wrinkled his nose. "Pretty disgusting."

"Welcome to war, my friend." A tiny rustling noise came from within the ruins of the house. Jack spun around, zap-gun at the ready. A very dirty and scruffy calico cat crawled out and looked calmly at the intruders with yellow eyes set in a soot-covered face.

"Hey, Thumper," Pete said, tucking his gun under his arm and crouching down to rub the cat under the chin. It sniffed his fingers and mewled pitifully.

"How do you know the cat's name?"

"Katie told me," Pete said without looking up. "Who's a wuzza wuzza wuzza? Hey? Who's a wuzza wuzza woo."

Jack rolled his eyes. "I hope you're not like that with Katie. She seems like a tough girl."

"None of your business," Pete snapped. "Well, what next, o captain my captain? Do your mighty tracking skills tell you where in the heck Katie's folks are?"

"No, but I think he might." Jack's zap-gun was trained on the stone base of the well. "Right, you can come out from inside there. Real slow, like, and keep your hands in the air."

"How in the heck am I gonna do that?" a voice echoed from the well. "I got to pull myself up with my hands 'fore I can come out." The voice was squeaky but sounded masculine.

"Just don't try anything funny!" Jack called.

"Yeah, we got a whole platoon out here!" Pete added, his own gun trained on the well. "Plus a fierce attack kitty," he muttered under his breath.

"Just keep your mouth shut," Jack hissed at him. They both watched as a shadowy figure emerged headfirst from the ruined well, grunting and struggling. They kept their guns leveled and cast nervous glances around for any sign of an ambush.

Finally their new captive flopped on the ground and put his hands behind his head. He was a tall, skinny young man dressed in the remains of an ill-fitting uniform. Pete searched him clumsily, coming up with a primitive-looking pistol in his waistband and a dagger hidden in his worn-looking boots.

"Ain't too friendly, are you?" Jack said, casually kicking the gun away into the ruins of the house.

"What business is it of yours?" the captive complained. "Who are you people, anyway?"

"We're Texas Rangers, idiot," Jack explained.

"No you ain't! You ain't got them stupid hats!"

"We're undercover, dogface," Jack said. "Now shut up and stay put while we figure out what to do with you." He beckoned to Pete and they walked a few steps toward what had once been the Webbs' farmhouse.

Pete spoke first. "He's not Texian, I can tell you that much."

"How can you tell?"

"Well, number one, he ain't too respectful of the Rangers. Number two, he said 'business' instead of 'bidness.' Number three, he had this-here ID card on him." Jack squinted at the piece of cardboard Pete handed him. A poor likeness of a pimple faced, squinting individual stared back at him. Was it a photograph or a drawing? It was so bad Jack couldn't tell if their captive, doubled over coughing in the dirt, was really "Pfc. Kyle Stevens, Army of the Southland." Well, maybe there *was* a way.

"Hey Stevens! On your feet!" Jack called. Their captive scrambled to comply. "Keep your hands behind your head if you wanna stay in one piece!"

"What kinda gun do you guys have anyways?" Stevens asked.

For an answer, Jack fired a beam at a stone that had rolled away from the well, which promptly turned into a miniature stream of magma the Dixie had to leap aside to avoid.

"We're licked if Texas has them babies."

"Do tell. Now, Private, please explain what you are doing on private property in Texian territory."

Jack and Pete watched with some interest as Stevens' calculations about what to say worked their way visibly over his acne-scarred face. At length, he said, "Aw, what the heck. Me and my buds came out this way to see if we could scavenge some clothes. You can see my boots ain't worth nothin', but the officers took all the good stuff when we burned Abilene."

Jack and Pete exchanged glances. Katie hadn't said anything about the Dixie army actually invading with the force that implied. Were they trapped behind enemy lines?

"How long ago was that?" Jack demanded.

"How long ago was what? That we took Abilene? Night 'fore last. But General Greeley says we gotta move out 'cause he's afraid— Hey, I probably shouldn't be telling you this."

"Probably not." Jack melted a pebble near Stevens' right foot.

"Ow! Stop doin' that! What do you want?"

"I don't care where your 'buds' are at the moment," Jack said, "what I want to know is, what you've done with the people?"

"What people?"

Jack sighed. "Are you really as stupid as you look, man? The people who owned this farm your people torched, that's who."

"Those clodhoppers? Heck, we cleared this area out weeks ago."

"Yeah, I can see that, genius. But where did you take them?"

Stevens attempted to look sly. Jack started to feel sorry for him again, but he raised his zap-gun anyway. "All right, all right!" the Southerner said. "We've got 'em in a big camp just east of the Barbour Line."

"What is the Barbour Line, Stevens?"

"You don't know that? Where in heck are y'all from? The minefields we got east of here, that's what!"

"Well, Stevens, if there are minefields, you'd better lead us across them so we can find our 'clodhopper' friends."

Stevens looked genuinely horrified. "But that'll take days!" he protested.

"Then we'd better get going now," Jack said, with one more flourish of his zap-gun. Stevens opened his mouth and closed it a few times without making a sound, then turned around slowly and started walking away across the empty plain.

"I said, keep your hands on the back of your head!" Jack said as he caught up with the Dixie and grabbed his elbow.

"But they're really starting to hurt!" Stevens whined.

"I got an idea," Pete said. "Why don't we have him carry Thumper? That'll keep his hands busy." And before either Jack or Stevens could protest, he shoved the wriggling animal into the captive's arms.

"I hate cats!" Stevens blubbered. "Plus I'm allergic. My eyes and nose are gonna be all runny."

"Good," Jack grunted, "decreases the chances you'll try anything. Forward march."

"Are you sure this is such a good idea?" Pete whispered in Jack's ear.

"You got a better one? We're here to rescue Katie's folks, remember?"

"Well yeah, but—how are she and Ray going to know where we are? Don't we have to hang around where Katie's house used to be or something?"

That was an unwelcome thought, so Jack waved it away. "I'm sure they have some way of watching us, seein' that they've got the power to transport us to a whole other universe and all."

Pete looked dubious, but he nodded, and the three men and a cat trudged off across the dry Panhandle plains.

♂

Katie and Rachel stared at the chattering typewriter. "How long is this gonna take?" Katie whispered.

Rachel shook her head slowly. They both jumped when the noise stopped abruptly.

"Oh. End of the page. I'd better put another one in," Rachel said. She felt weirdly calm.

Katie clamped her hand on the other girl's wrist. "Oh, no you don't. I'm not letting you feed this-here possessed machine till I see what it's done with Pete and Jack so far."

Rachel nodded. Katie had mentioned Pete first. Interesting.

Katie snatched up the finished page and shone the flashlight directly on it. Almost immediately she cried out.

20

"What! What is it?" Rachel said, jumping to her feet. Out of the corner of her eye she saw Anya running toward them.

Katie looked at Rachel with teary eyes. "They killed Daisy! The no-goods just up and killed her! Those Dixies ain't human!"

"Who's Daisy?" Rachel asked.

"What? Only the best darned horse in the whole darned universe! But wait... Thumper... My cat Thumper's okay!"

"What about Pete and Jack?" Rachel prompted after an awkward silence.

"Hmm? Oh, of course! They're fine!" Katie said with a guilty start. "They're gonna get this Dixie they caught looting our farm to take them to where Mom and Dad are being held captive."

"How long is that going to take?" Anya asked. "And how do you know all that, anyway?"

"Why, um, it's all in this here report!" Katie said.

"Yeah, from our computer," Rachel said hastily. "It takes a real powerful computer to travel between universes. And it can keep track of where the, uh, interdimensional travelers are."

"Wow, that's some computer," Anya said, dubiously eyeing the battered typewriter. "Well, let me know as soon as you hear anything. I'm going to go try and get some sleep. I hope they're back by morning so we can move out. I feel exposed out here."

"Me too," Rachel said feelingly. She and Katie waited until Anya had walked back to the campfire, where Moishe, Gun and Eddie lay drowsing. Then Rachel sat down again and, hands trembling a bit, rolled the same sheet of typing paper into the machine, blank side up. She'd barely got the paper into position when the typewriter started clattering away again, the typebars leaping up and striking the page almost too quickly to see. Both girls leaned over and read the rapidly emerging words.

♂

As the swollen red sun sunk toward the horizon behind them, casting grotesquely long shadows in their path, Jack, Pete, and Private Stevens, who was still carrying the drowsing Thumper, reached the abandoned highway. It was completely deserted. The median strip was overgrown with tough-looking weeds that were colonizing cracks in the tarmac, making the road all but impassable to anything on wheels.

Jack studied the ruined highway. "It's just as well we're on foot."

Pete snorted. "Maybe we'd be better off striking off across country," he said as they forced a grumbling Stevens to climb over the battered and rusted guardrail with his feline burden.

Jack shook his head. "I don't think so. We don't know what's out there. Even you, Pete, meaning no offense to your knowledge of the countryside."

"None taken. I've never been out this way, even in the real world. By the way, it's a pity you kicked our friend's gun away. We could've used a spare weapon."

"That piece of junk he was carrying looked as likely to explode in your hand as to get off a shot. The so-called Army of the Southland is nothing but a poorly armed rabble, if you ask me."

"I heard that!" Stevens called.

"And? Ain't it true?"

"No it ain't! They don't give us any weapons at all! We have to bring our own guns!"

"And your own uniforms and boots too, from the looks of it," Pete said.

Stevens bristled. "My momma made me these boots herself. She gave 'em to me for Christmas three years ago. They was perfectly good until we started going on all these stupid forced marches into cow-kicker country here."

"We ain't insulting your momma," Jack said soothingly, "even if she did give birth to a halfwit like you. Now, why don't we pick up the pace a little. I'd like to make another couple miles before it gets dark."

"But I'm tired! And hungry, and thirsty too! I hope you guys brought water with you! And my feet hurt fit to fall off! And my nose is running and my eyes are watering thanks to this furry nuisance you're making me carry! And—" A tumbleweed at Stevens' feet burst into flame, and he took off with a yelp.

"I do love my zap-gun," Jack sighed happily as he and Pete hurried to keep up. The long summer dusk allowed them to get in another two hours of slogging before Jack finally called it quits.

"Do you guys have any grub?" Stevens said. "I'm starving! And I suspect Puss here is, too."

"Don't tell me you Dixies have to go out and shoot your own food," Jack sighed, taking off the backpack he had brought.

"Huh? Don't all armies do that?"

"This isn't good," Pete whispered to him as the soldier and the cat fell on the leftover chicken Jack gave them. "I don't think we have more than a couple days' worth of food between us."

"We'll have to make it last," Jack whispered back, "or else we might end up enjoying the taste of zap-gun-fried jackrabbit."

Water was an even bigger worry, but the following afternoon the highway crossed a small, muddy creek almost hidden beneath dried-out brush. Stevens threw a startled Thumper to the tarmac, jumped off the bridge and was dipping his hands into the stream before Pete or Jack could react.

"Hey Stevens!" Jack shouted. "Stevens, you numbskull!" Since there was no reaction Jack used the zap-gun again.

"Ow! What the hell, Ranger Flash! You tryin' to kill me?"

"No, you moron, you're doing a good enough job of that yourself!"

"Huh?"

"Ain't you ever heard of boiling water?"

"What—oh."

"Yeah, 'oh' is right. Especially with your colleagues trampling all over the countryside using all the water holes as toilets. You want to end up with cholera? Because Pete and I really haven't got the time to clean up your diarrhea."

A sullen expression fixed on his face, Stevens moved away from the water while Jack directed Pete to fill up everybody's canteens. Then he switched the zap-gun to its lowest setting and used it to boil them all, after which all three men shared a Spartan lunch of half-dry *kruckle* beans and hot water while Thumper nosed at each of their bowls in turn before turning his nose up.

"What kind of beans are these? I ain't never had 'em before," Stevens asked through a mouthful.

"*Kruckle* beans. Staple food on Mars," Pete said before Jack could stop him.

Stevens looked from one of his captors to the other and let out a nervous chuckle. "You guys sure are some jokesters!" he said.

"Yeah, we are that," Jack glared at Pete, who merely shrugged. "But we're not great ones for taking a joke, and we're also in a hurry," Jack said, gesturing with his zap-gun, "so why don't you finish your damn beans and hop to it?"

"Yessir," Stevens gulped, scooping up the cat. They made more satisfactory progress that afternoon, except for one patch where Stevens had to consult a pocket map to avoid a minefield. That night they camped under the highway at another spot where it forded a creek, although this one was dry. As soon as Jack said they could stop walking, Stevens dropped as if he'd been shot and started snoring loudly, Thumper curled up at his side.

"I'll take first watch tonight," Pete offered.

"Thanks," Jack said, holstering his zap-gun and stretching out beside Stevens and Thumper, who half-opened one sleepy yellow eye before settling back down on his outstretched paws. Jack had just gotten comfortable when Pete asked softly if he was awake.

"Yeah man, I am, what is it?"

"I was just lookin'," Pete said making a sweeping gesture. It was a cloudless, moonless night, and the sky was a dome of twinkling infinity. "Over there," Pete said, pointing at a pale reddish star, "that's Mars, ain't it?"

Jack squinted up as sleepily as Thumper had done a moment before. "Think so. What about it?"

"Katie told me it's a dead world here, dead as Luna outside the bases. And there ain't no bases on Luna, here, either."

"Yeah, she told me that too. So?"

"It's just weird, that's all. I mean, apart from visiting the moon like two hundred years ago, these people never even left Earth. They didn't have anything to leave *for*. There ain't no life anywhere in this universe but here, far as anybody knows. It's just freaky... scary."

"You know what freaks me out?" Jack said, his eyes closed.

"What's that?"

"Not being able to sleep!"

"Oh. Okay." But he was only quiet for a few seconds before he said, "Remember that ID card of Stevens'?"

Jack sighed. "What now?"

"His ID card. You saw the date on it—August 2140. That's thirty-one Earth years ago, our time."

"So?"

"So what's that about? Something to do with relativity? I mean, this ain't 2140, our time. This here is more like the Middle Ages."

"Lucky for us," Jack said, still without opening his eyes. "Now, please shut up about the wonders of the universe. I'm not a science guy, I'm just a gunslinger. You can talk all that over with Katie when we get back. I need to catch a few winks now so I can concentrate on keeping us in one piece and rescuing your future in-laws. All right?"

"They are NOT my future in-laws!" Pete shouted loud enough to raise echoes in the desert night. But this time Jack would not be goaded into responding, and at length Pete sat down with his own zap-gun in his lap and stared off into the starry sky, his thoughts swirling with no fixed center.

♂

"It's reached the end of the page again. We need more paper," Rachel said into the dark Martian night. "Katie. Katie!"

"Hmm? Oh, of course!" Katie said, pulling the paper out of the typewriter. "Here, Ray, this is a little weird."

"What is, Katie? Please hand me fresh paper!"

"Here."

Rachel rolled the blank page into the typewriter and the clattering started up again immediately.

"Now what is it?" Rachel said, not daring to take her eyes off the moving page.

Katie's gaze was riveted there too, but she said, "The date on the Dixie's ID card. August 2140."

"Yeah?" Rachel said distractedly. "Oh, Jack! Watch out for that coyote! Good. What now?"

"August 2140. The Dixies attacked our farm in April."

"So?"

"So how long would you say has passed for us, here, since we showed up on Venus?"

"Umm. Two months?"

"See? Time is passing faster there, in the real world."

"Well, we don't know what the rules are," Rachel said. "It could be time sometimes passes more slowly back home than here, and—oh. OH!" She leapt to her feet.

"Yeah," Katie said softly.

"If four months have gone by back in Poland, it'll be November! My parents'll never survive winter in a labor camp."

"If that's even where they are."

Rachel stared at her, then smacked her forehead with the palm of her hand. "So what! I can make the story go any way I want! We can rescue my parents *before* the Nazis take them away!"

Katie frowned. "How would that work?"

"Who cares! We have to save my parents!"

Rachel and Katie stared at each other again for a moment. Then Katie said in a small voice, "What about my parents? What's happening to them?" They both realized at the same moment that the typewriter had stopped again. Rachel reached it first and pulled the paper out.

"They're already there."

"Where?"

"At the prison camp. Another day and a half has passed for them. You're right, time is passing *much* faster back there."

"Prison camp?" Katie whispered, snatching the page away as Rachel put another one in the typewriter. Katie read aloud.

♂

Shadows were lengthening as Jack, Pete, Stevens, and Thumper arrived, dusty and tired, at the top of a steep hill above a tent city. The prison camp covered the floor of an elongated valley between other, similar hills. At a quick glance, Jack estimated that there were hundreds of tents scattered down there, and more than a thousand people of all ages, most of whom were digging, moving wheelbarrows here and there, and filling sandbags, all under the supervision of sloppily uniformed guards armed with shotguns, rusty rifles, and antiquated pistols.

Stevens had a quizzical look on his face. "I thought I was joining up to protect my family from the maraudin' Texians," he said. "Looks like them's the ones that need protectin' from us."

"How the heck," Pete said, "are we supposed to find anyone in that chaos?"

"Well," Stevens said, "you want my opinion—"

"Actually, no," Jack said, turning toward him.

"You can't shoot me," Stevens said, "I'm holding Thumper."

"Put the cat down real slow and step away," Jack said, leveling Annabelle.

Stevens did as he was told, putting his hands behind his head as he straightened up. His eyes on the gun, he said, "L-listen. Please just shoot me."

"What?" Jack said. He moved his head slightly, and Pete stepped up quietly behind Stevens, pulled his hands down from his head and began tying them behind his back with Stevens' own greasy-with-sweat bandanna.

"Just shoot me, and please don't eat me," he begged, his eyes welling up. "My poor mama would be so upset."

"Excuse me?"

"That gun. Your ray-gun."

"It's called a zap-gun."

"It's got that low setting for boiling water. Perfect for cooking humans too, huh?"

"We ain't gonna eat you, Stevens," Jack said as Pete moved on to tying his ankles together.

"Huh? But why not? You guys are Martians, ain't you?"

Jack shook his head. "Naw. Too stringy. No, seriously, I grew up on Venus. And Pete, here, he's only half-Martian."

"But you came here in a you-foe, didn't you? Well, didn't you? And Pete's other half? Alien, right?"

"Naw. My mom's Texian. I was born and raised in Abilene, in the Lone Star State!" Pete said, and conked Stevens on the head with the butt of his zap-gun.

"You didn't kill him, Pete, did you?" Jack asked, looking at the fallen Dixie soldier.

"Course not! I'm no killer. I just don't like folks messin' with Texas."

"Good. I was getting kind of fond of the yellowbelly. But, luckily for Mike and Mary Webb," Jim added grimly, "I *am* a killer, when I need to be." And sighting along Annabelle's barrel, he felled the man he'd singled out as the chief overseer, at a distance of half a mile.

It was like kicking over the proverbial anthill. Pandemonium broke out, people running this way and that. When the guards found that shouting didn't restore order, they fired shots in the air. A few, not in the air.

Jack shot down two of the trigger-happy men and bellowed, "Texas Rangers! Put your weapons down now!"

"The cavalry is here!" Pete cried.

"What the hell did you say that for?" Jack demanded.

Pete looked sheepish. "I always wanted to!" It didn't matter, anyway, because the guards had panicked and were running pell mell for the hills opposite where Jack and Pete were standing.

Jack grinned at Pete. "Guess you Texas boys are good for somethin' after all!" he drawled. "Come on, partner, let's go down and find your future in-laws."

"They are NOT my future in-laws!" Pete snapped. "And aren't you forgetting something? Two things, in fact?"

"What's that?"

"This is first," Pete said, bending down and gathering up the yowling Thumper, "and *that* is second," he said, pointing with his chin at Stevens, who had begun to snore.

"What about him?"

"Them Texians down there will kill him for sure if they get hold of him."

"Ah. Good point." Jack squatted down and untied Stevens' hands and ankles, then slapped him gently to some semblance of consciousness. "Come on, friend. Time to be movin' along."

"Wha? Lemme sleep, Ma, them pigs can wait a few more min—Oh, it's you. What the—?"

Jack hauled him to his feet and turned him around so he was facing toward the rapidly disintegrating prison camp. "That's those Texians you thought needed protecting a few minutes ago, friend. Shoe's on the other foot now, I'm afraid."

"Hmm? Oh! Be seein' ya!" Jack and Pete watched in amazement as he skedaddled. Neither of them had ever seen anyone run while clutching his head in both hands before.

"All right, then, time to find the father and mother of the bride!" Jack said as they started down the slope toward the milling crowd.

"I'm telling you one last time, I am NOT planning on marrying Katie!"

♂

"Well, who says I'd have you, anyways?" Katie said, her eyes flashing as she stood with her hands on her knees, watching the words emerge out of the typewriter. "Hey, it's stopped halfway down the page! Ray, what happened?"

"Don't know," Rachel said. She leaned forward on her haunches and read out loud:

```
    While Pete attempted to explain
to Mike and Mary where they had come
from, Jack stood still, the man of
action suddenly at a loss for what to
do, and called out to the pale blue
sky, "Ray? Katie? We're done now. Can
you bring us back to Mars?"
```

"Oh! Of course!" Rachel said, and swiftly typed:

```
    The bright, hot day went out like
the lights failing in a thunderstorm,
and the four travelers
```

"Hey! Ray!" Katie said.
"Oops! Sorry!"

```
    The bright, hot day went out like
the lights failing in a thunderstorm,
and the FIVE travelers found
themselves standing, disoriented, in
the Martian night.
```

Katie was on her feet. "Mom? Dad?"
"Katie? Katie, where are you?" Mary called.

"Baby girl? Where are you?" Mike added. "How come I feel so light? We ain't Down Below, are we? Granddad warned me—"

"No, Dad, you ain't Down Below!" Katie said, half-sobbing. There was a startled yowl. "Oh, Thumper, you're okay too!" Then it became impossible to make out what anyone was saying in the happy babble.

After a moment Jack stepped into the small cone of light shed by the flashlight, which illuminated only Rachel's knees and a corner of the typewriter. "Ray," he said softly, reaching down and grasping her shoulder, "it's all right. We're going to save your parents next." She leaned against his legs, too tired to respond.

21

By the time Rachel, Katie, and Anya had gathered for the second interdimensional mission, the Martian night sky had cleared and the stars shone as brilliantly as they had for Pete and Jack back in the Panhandle.

"Why was it so dark earlier?" Katie asked.

Rachel looked up. Why hadn't she noticed that the sky had been as featurelessly black as if she was huddled under her blanket at home?

"Probably a volcanic plume from Olympus Mons," Anya said. "It's been acting up a bit lately."

"But isn't Krakowicz right under it?"

"Well, yes. Actually Krakowicz is on top of a biggish hill all its own. It's built on top of older versions of itself, going back 2,500 years—Martian years, that is, so about 4,700 Earth years."

"Wow, you mean that every few hundred years your capital gets buried by an eruption like Pompeii, and you just keep rebuilding in the same place?"

Anya nodded. "The thing that surprised us, when we heard about Pompeii, was that you people would abandon the place for so long."

"What, you don't think it's a little weird to keep rebuilding on a spot you know is going to be buried in lava sooner or later?

"Well, it *is* a holy spot," Anya said. "Besides, ah—well, this is a little embarrassing...."

"Yes?" Katie prompted. Rachel stopped stargazing and turned her full attention to the princess.

"Well," Anya said hesitantly, "after each eruption—sometimes *during* them, if they started slowly enough—the king, who was also ex officio high priest, would sort of, um, you know, well—"

"Yes?"

"Well, sacrifice a virgin to appease the volcano god Moloch. Just a little, you know."

"A little what? A little virgin? Like five years old, maybe?" Katie snapped.

"Wanda the Great put a stop to it!" Anya said defensively. "You see, there was this thistlecat...."

"Not now, Anya, please," Rachel said. The sound of her heart in her ears could have drowned out a rocket takeoff. "Please, we have to save my parents. We have to try!"

"Of course," Anya said. "Where do you want me to stand?"

"Oh, anywhere," Rachel said, waving vaguely, "it doesn't matter. Our, ah, our computer is powerful enough so it doesn't matter."

"I still say you should let me go with you, Anya!" Jack called out.

"Jack darling, you can't ask for a glass of water in Marpolski, or Polish, without making five grammatical mistakes. I'll be right back, my love!" Then she turned her gaze back to Rachel and Katie. "I'll stand right here then, with my friends. Now Rachel, are you sure I'm dressed all right for Warsaw in 1942?" She gestured at her traveling clothes, which would have made anyone else look like a sack of potatoes, but might as well have been a coronation gown on her.

"Well, it's the ghetto. People wear whatever they have. Most people have already sold their best and even their not-so-good clothes so they can buy food. Nobody's going to be looking at your clothes, Anya." *I hope not, anyway.*

"So I guess I'm ready, friends," Anya said. "I can't wait to meet your parents, Rachel!"

"Yeah. Me either," Rachel whispered, rolling a fresh sheet of paper into the typewriter. Hesitantly, she typed:

```
The starry bowl of the Martian night
sky vanished from over Anya's head and
was replaced by a narrow gray strip
of sky between tenement buildings. In
the ghetto, even the sky looked worn
out and dirty. She looked down and saw
a narrow door, number 21 like Rachel
had told her. She approached and
knocked hesitantly. A babble of voices
erupted, and before she could lower
her hand a short but distinguished-
looking man with a neatly trimmed gray
beard opened the door, took off the
black homburg hat he was wearing, and
said, "Can I help you, miss?"
```

Rachel stopped typing. *Dad always takes his hat off for a lady.* She and Katie, who had been bending over with her hands on her knees to see what Rachel was writing, both looked up expectantly. But Anya was still standing there, looking at them uncertainly. "When does it—" she began, and the typewriter started clattering away on its own, startling the two Earth girls. When they looked up again Anya was gone. Even the faint scent of flowers that always clung to her seemed to have dissipated.

♂

The starry bowl of the Martian night sky vanished from over Anya's head and was replaced by a narrow gray strip of sky between tenement buildings. In the ghetto, even the sky looked worn out and dirty. She looked down and saw a narrow door, number 21 like Rachel had told her. She approached and knocked hesitantly, getting no response. Feeling as if she was moving through glue in the heavy gravity, Anya raised her hand to knock again.

"There's nobody in there," said a voice that sounded as if it was coming through broken glass.

Anya turned to see a short, gaunt, stooped woman with a canyonlike vertical line over the bridge of her nose glaring at her. Unkempt salt and pepper strands of hair were plastered to her temples like exhausted worms.

"I'm sorry?" Anya said.

"Nobody home. Kaput. The Goldbergs were all taken in the last big roundup a few days ago. That froggy little man, his crabby wife, and the younger of their two bratty kids. I don't know what happened to the older one."

"What about the Zilbers?"

"You're wasting your time. The professor and his wife were taken in the roundup before last, and nobody's seen their girl since. Too bad, but I wish the Council would reassign their place already. I've got eight to look after myself, now that my sister Zelda's gone to the work camps. A good thing, too! That woman never did a stitch of work in her life, even when we were kids. Our dad—"

"Thanks. I need to go check inside anyway. I'm a cousin of the Zilbers'."

The woman took a half step toward Anya. "Yes," she said, "I do see a resemblance to the girl, Rivka."

"Her name is Rachel."

"Rachel, right. You really do look a lot like her."

"Uh, thanks. Anyway, I have to at least have a look around inside, so I can tell my mother I tried. She's Mrs. Zilber's younger sister."

"Go ahead, but I think it's locked."

The doorknob was only stuck, though, and Anya wrenched it open with a sharp tug. She stepped into a mildewed, windowless room that felt as if it hadn't been lived in in months, if not years. "Hello?" Anya called softly. It was hard to see because of the boarded-up window, but the room seemed to be strewn with junk. There were three or four mildewed mattresses that had been slashed open with knives and their straw stuffing pulled out, as if someone had been checking for hidden valuables. In one corner was a broken-down bed frame, and in the other a smashed typewriter like the one Rachel used. The princess turned to go but a tiny rustle stopped her. It seemed to be coming from under the bed. Anya got down on her hands and knees.

"Hello?" she called again. It was dark and still under there. "Hello? I know you're under there. I won't hurt you, I promise." A pause. "I'm looking for the Zilbers. I just want to know where—"

"Rachel?" a voice like autumn leaves whispered. Anya felt a chill go down her spine. She didn't believe in ghosts, but....

"No, I'm her cousin, Anya." She took a deep breath and said what Rachel had taught her to say. "I'm with the underground. I'm here to help the professor and his wife escape to England."

Something started to drag itself along the floor under the bed. Anya backed against the wall. There was a hollow knocking noise, and a scrambling. As Anya watched, petrified, a head emerged from under the bed, a small head covered with yellow hair streaked and discolored by dust. This was followed by a neck so thin it looked like a strong man could snap it between his fingers and a torso through which the bones showed. Anya gasped and leapt forward to help the child to her feet. She looked like a girl of seven or eight, with enormous blue eyes that regarded Anya with an out-of-focus stare. "Rachel?" she rasped again.

"No honey. My name is Anya." She knelt and grasped the girl's frail shoulders. Tears spilled silently down her cheeks.

"Oh, yes. I d-don't know where Professor Zilber and his wife are. I h-haven't seen Rachel since the night they disappeared."

"She's safe now on—in England."

The girl didn't seem to hear. "They took away my parents and my little sister. I've been hiding here since then. My name is Sonya. I'm ten years old."

"What have you had to eat, Sonya?" Before the girl could answer, there was the sound of booted footsteps and rough voices in the street. Sonya slid back under the bed, followed closely by Anya.

"I can't understand what they're saying," Anya breathed.

"You don't speak Yiddish? They're the ghetto police. They're Jews, but the Germans make them do their dirty work. If they refuse, they kill them *and* their families." She scrunched up her face and started to cry in dry sobs. "But they took away Mom and Dad and Shoshie! How could they do that!"

A man's voice rumbled, close enough to be in the room with them.

"What are they saying, Sonya?"

"'There should have been two more girls on that transport. The professor's ID card said he had a daughter. Also that Goldberg character. He had another daughter in addition to the one they found.'"

The neighbor's grating voice cut in. Sonya kept translating, in whispers like the noise of dead leaves blown across concrete.

"'The Zilber girl came back. She was nosing around here not ten minutes ago. I saw her go inside.'" There was a pause as heavy as a planet. "'Well? I helped you, so I better get their place when you arrest those two. I've got eight of my own to look after.'" Another rumble. "'We don't have the final say, but we'll put in a good word for you with the Council.'"

Footsteps entered the room. Sonya shrank further back against the wall and Anya followed, covering her with her own body as if that could protect her. The hard weight of Jack's zap-gun, which he'd made her take with her, dug into her hip. She gripped it as a pair of ragged black boots walked into sight and stopped. A pale face lowered itself into view, the lips distorting themselves into a grimace that might have been intended as a smile. *I could vaporize him*, Anya thought. *But what then? It sounded like there were at least three men in the street. Am I going to kill them all? And then the German soldiers who come to investigate?* The lips began to move. Anya didn't need a translation this time to know that the policeman was saying to come out, little girls, come out, it's all right, we've got a nice bar of chocolate and a glass of milk out here for you if you'll be good little girls and stop playing hide-and-seek like this. Your parents are waiting for you, they're so worried, your mothers are crying for you....

A hand reached for her and began scrabbling around on the floor. Anya shrank back, pressing up against Sonya. In a moment the policeman was going to lose his patience and call for his colleagues to come help him drag the girls out.

♂

Oh Rachel, I'm sorry I failed you.

Then something coursed under the sorrow and washed it away.

I'm a descendant of Wanda the Great. If I'm going to die I won't go to my death hiding like a rat.

She tensed her finger on the trigger of the zap-gun.

♂

Rachel had been staring paralyzed at the typewriter ever since it raced backward and crossed out the last sentence she had written with a row of XXXs. *How can it do that?* She was mesmerized by what was happening to Anya and Sonya. Then she let out a howl that brought Jack running and woke everyone else up.

"What is it?" Jack demanded. He pointed at the typewriter, which had stopped dead in the middle of a page. "Is Anya all right?"

"She will be, Jack," Katie said. "I'll get the computer to take care of her. Just take care of Ray, please."

"What's the matter?" he asked Rachel, who had curled up in a ball with her hands clasped over her face and was rocking back and forth on the stony ground. Jack knelt down and put his arms around her, murmuring softly. While he was distracted, Katie took a deep breath and, holding the flashlight under her chin, pecked slowly out on the typewriter:

```
The dusty darkness under the broken
bed frame vanished abruptly as the
cool breeze of the Martian desert
night washed over Anya and Sonya.
```

Katie read the words aloud softly.

Jack looked up. "They're here?" he asked.

And there they were, on the ground not six feet away—Anya, who blinked once, got to her feet and brushed herself off, and a crumpled form that had to be Sonya.

Another shriek split the night. Katie turned, startled. Rachel shook Jack off with such force he went over backward, hit his head on a stone and lay there groaning. Before Katie or Anya could react Rachel reached down, picked up the typewriter, and lifted the bulky machine over her head. For a frozen moment of time she stood silhouetted against the stars. All those Sunday mornings being bored in church welled up in Katie's mind and she recognized the pose: Moses holding the tablets of the Law over his head, enraged that the Israelites had sinned with the Golden Calf. And then of course, he had smashed them. Katie darted forward. But it was too late; with a scream Rachel dashed the typewriter to the rocky ground. It broke into dozens of pieces. Katie looked up at the sky and waited for the stars to start going out. Instead they just sat there, hardly even twinkling in the thin Martian atmosphere, shining coldly down on the human anguish below.

22

Morning dawned bright, clear, and a little chilly, but Rachel ignored the outside world. She sat with her hands clasped around her knees staring off into infinity, while Katie tried to explain things to her disoriented parents, leaving the remaining four members of the Magnificent Seven to hold a council of war with Moishe. Snatches of the conversation drifted to Rachel on the thin breeze, as if from a half-remembered dream.

"I'm very sorry, but my poor Shimmie and Azri can't possibly haul all these people," the cart driver said, gesturing at the mules as he wiped his neck with an already soaked handkerchief.

"I figured as much," Jack said. "Don't worry about it. Pete and I will walk."

"Me too," Gun said.

"That's fine, but there's still too many of you to hide when we're on the open road, let alone when we get to that army base."

"I've been thinking about that too," Jack said. "There's no reason for anybody but me to go there. Everybody else should wait in the nearest town for me to escape with Jim. Where would you recommend, Anya?"

Anya looked up with eyes swollen from lack of sleep and silent tears shed. "What? Oh…Lvovinsk, I think. If we detour there it shouldn't add on more than half a day. And I can't imagine they'd bother setting up checkpoints around such an out-of-the-way place. On the other hand…it *is* an out-of-the-way place. How are we going to explain so many aliens showing up there?"

"Leave it to me," said Pete, "I spent a year there when I was a kid visiting my father's family. Somebody's bound to remember me."

But they couldn't actually go anywhere until Sonya seemed strong enough to travel. She wouldn't speak to anybody in any language, though she clung to Anya's neck like a hurt toddler and her eyes seemed to flicker with recognition whenever she saw Rachel.

"Be careful what you feed her," warned Gun. "If she's been starving for weeks, and not getting enough food for God knows how long before that, eating too much too quickly could kill her."

But for the next few days, as their supplies dwindled, everybody's instinct was to give up their own rations for Sonya's sake. They started out giving her plain water, but quickly moved on to a broth made from the leftover chicken. They left pieces of meat in that to see if she could keep solid food down. When she proved unwilling to touch them, Moishe unexpectedly stepped in, cajoling her in Yiddish as if she was a baby.

"Come on, sweetheart. Just a little bit, there, like a big girl. Hopa! Mazel tov! A big bite! Here, I'll cut up the next piece for you...."

This domestic scene was the first thing in days to arouse Rachel's interest. She asked Moishe, in a voice made hoarse by disuse, "Why?"

"Why what?" he said gently. "Why am I caring for and even touching a strange girl? *Maidele*, she's a child, a child who's lost her parents, and she needs to hear *mamaloschen*, her own mother tongue, just like she needs food. And saving a life is more important than anything. I know you know that, because I know what you and that *shikse* girl Katie did, Rachel."

"I didn't do anything," Rachel whispered, "I forgot all about my parents and left them to die."

"Who do you think you are, Rachel, God?" the Hasid snapped, his voice incongruously cracking on the last word. "Only He decides who lives and who dies." But a strange expression came over Rachel's face and she turned away from him.

Katie, meanwhile, had given up trying to explain to her parents how they had got to where they were. "Just enjoy it!" she said in exasperation. "Pretend like it's a dream, a dream that never ends. I don't understand it either, but that's how I cope. Aren't you glad not to have to try to rebuild that farm after the Dixies trashed it?"

"But it's my farm. It's been in our family near four hundred years," Mike said softly.

Mary said to him, "But Boo, it never was worth much. We were on the verge of starving even in good years, for all the hard work any of us did."

"Anyway, it ain't like we have a choice," Katie said. "Ray sure burned our boats for us. Like Cortés."

"Like who?"

"Hernando Cortés? The Spanish conquistador?"

Her parents looked at her blankly, and Mike shook his head. "Never did see the point of your reading all those books, Kaitlyn, until now. Explain to me again why I feel like I lost a hundred pounds?"

On the afternoon of the third day there was general agreement that they had to move on before they ran out of food and water. Sonya seemed better, and in fact was demanding more food, but Gun insisted she stay on a limited diet.

"But I'm hungry!" the girl wailed. "And I don't understand where I am! The air smells funny. And I'm so light I feel like I might blow away!"

Rachel opened her mouth to yell at the brat, but "primitive" Moishe gave Sonya a little piece of bread and Rachel turned to look at the desert, tears of shame filling her eyes. *I'm on another planet. I'm in a whole other universe, but I'm still a miserable, selfish person who didn't even care enough to save her own parents!*

Watching the landscape roll slowly by was scant relief. Mars might be another planet, but this featureless desert reminded Rachel strangely of the flat countryside she used to see through the windows when they took the train to visit her grandfather.

♂

"Hey, look over there, honeybunch!" Mike said, pointing at a shallow wash between two low hills. "Don't that look like it would be a good place to start a farm?"

His wife glanced over, pushing back a stray strand of graying blond hair. Her best feature was her clear blue eyes. She was solidly built, like her daughter, while her husband was on the lanky side, with a slow smile when he was pleased, as he was now. Mary thought for a moment before rendering her verdict on starting a farm in the Martian outback. "Looks a bit dry," she drawled.

Anya sighed. "Truer words never were spoken," she said, and pointed toward the horizon. "You see that faint line there?" The elder Webbs squinted, Mike shading his eyes with his hand. "That's supposed to be a major trunk of the Grand Canal. But if we went over there now, I'd be surprised if we found more than a trickle of water in the bed. All the usurpers starting with Ares I have neglected the canal system, but the current one is the worst. This *should* be the breadbasket of Mars, but unless he is overthrown soon, it will be past reviving. The whole planet could dry out. And then of course, the tyrant will say we need to invade other planets just to survive. It's diabolical!" She took a breath and forced a smile. "But when things are put right on this planet, we will have need of honest yeomen like you."

Mike stopped walking for a moment and took a bow. "Miss, I don't know what a yeoman is, and we Texians don't cotton to tyranny of any sort, nor royalty for that matter, but if we have to have lords and ladies we could do worse than your sort. We would be honored to bring a little piece of Texas to your kingdom."

Katie looked faintly embarrassed, but Anya smiled again. "Do forgive me for not curtseying, Mr. Webb. I'm not wearing a proper dress, and under the circumstances it would be impossible anyway, but it is the king who should bow to his people, not the other way around."

After that, the slow hours passed with little change in the scenery. Eddie and then Pete took their turns walking to give Mike a break, while

Jack led the mules the entire time, scanning the horizon for trouble with his zap-gun within easy reach at his waist.

♂

Rachel sat passively while Gun fussed over Sonya, but when the miner turned her attention on Rachel, she protested. "I don't need looking after!"

"Shut up," Gun explained kindly. "How much have you eaten since the night Katie's parents arrived? Well?"

"Hardly anything," Rachel admitted in a whisper.

"Trying to starve yourself? It's a nasty way to go. Slow, too. If you want to kill yourself, I can find you a nice pocket canyon and you can throw yourself into it."

What a good idea! Rachel thought.

Gun, who was watching her closely, lowered her voice. "Listen, you silly girl, if you leave us, who's going to take care of Sonya?"

Rachel felt annoyance stir in her gut. It was the first thing she'd felt in days. "That brat? What does she need me for?"

"You're the only person she knows in this world," Gun said. "You can't just leave her to fend for herself."

"Why not? I was left to fend for myself."

Gun looked at her and snorted. "With Katie and Anya both looking after you? I don't think so."

"Why is everyone so concerned with my—with improving me?" Rachel blurted.

"Because we all expect more from you," Gun said quietly.

"More than from Anya the perfect princess? How can that be? If she's the standard I'm supposed to live up to, maybe I *should* go throw myself off a cliff!"

Gun leaned back against a barrel, started to say something, stopped, started again, and finally said, "Everyone knows you're in mourning, Ray. But—"

"You don't know the first thing about it."

"You're right," Gun agreed, "I don't. Because I don't know who my father is. Not only haven't I ever met the little creep, the only evidence I have of his existence is the fact that I'm here. And my mother was too busy partying to take care of me. She gave me to her friend Barb to raise when I was four. I have a lot of respect for Barb, hardest working person I've ever met, but she ain't my mom and never pretended to be. No, don't look at me like that. The whole point is I don't want or need pity, and neither should you."

Rachel wanted to cry, but once again shame overwhelmed her, and she crawled across the cart to Sonya, who was huddled in the far corner looking miserable.

"How's it going, Butterfly?" she said, using Mrs. Goldberg's nickname for her daughter.

Sonya stared back at her before replying, "Don't call me that."

"Okay."

She started to suggest a game, but Sonya said, "Just be quiet."

"Okay," Rachel said again.

♂

The cart rattled along through the afternoon heat. After a time Sonya dozed off with her head in Rachel's lap, and Katie came over to sit beside them.

Rachel stared out over the desert for a long time, trying to ignore Katie. *You've got your parents, haven't you? Why don't you go bug them? All I've got are a bunch of X's on a piece of paper. X, X, X, and Dad is gone!*

"It doesn't make any sense!" she finally said.

"No, it don't," Katie agreed.

"I mean, we saved your parents! Why couldn't we save mine?"

Katie looked uncomfortable. "I wish I knew, Ray. Chances are, the Germans killed them right away…before you left Earth, even."

"That's why I tried to send Anya to save them *before* I left Earth!"

"But, well, that don't make any sense. It's a paradox. If Anya saved them *and* you, and brought all *three* of you back to Mars, then you wouldn't be here to greet them, I mean the other you, *you* you…see what I mean? And you wouldn't have been there in the first place to send Anya on the rescue mission."

"But…. But I…." Rachel ran out of things to say. *It isn't a lesson in logic I need, anyhow.* "It just isn't fair," she said, starting to cry.

"No," Katie said softly. "No, it ain't."

♂

Rachel was dozing when they arrived in Lvovinsk, waking up because the ride had turned bumpy. She sat up and saw that the dirt road they had been following through the desert had turned to cobblestones. Dusk was falling, the dry heat of the day giving way abruptly to a night chill. Low adobe buildings were scattered around a square, which contained a covered well with a metal bucket on a rope. The thought of water made Rachel realize how thirsty she was. A few people were out on the streets, but their arrival attracted no attention at first.

"Hey, Pete! Is it really you?"

A tall man with the spindly look Rachel was beginning to recognize as typically Martian darted up, his arms stretched wide.

Pete had been plodding along beside the cart, but he looked up and exclaimed, "Andrzej Walenski! You haven't changed at all!"

Rachel peeked cautiously and decided that Pete had to be lying, unless Walenski had been a balding kid with a sizable paunch. He and Pete embraced and kissed each other on both cheeks, rather like Rachel's maternal uncles, who were from Minsk, used to do.

"Man, it must be what? More than six years since we used to chase each other down in the gully!" Walenski said.

"Almost twelve Earth years," Anya whispered. She had slid up next to Rachel, her face concealed under a dust-storm poncho. Rachel nodded slightly.

"Remember when some old lady came out and yelled at us for drinking *yaszt* in her backyard?" Pete said. "She was waving a broomstick, too! I never knew you could run so fast, especially drunk!"

"Drunk? Who was drunk? Us Walenskis can hold our *yaszt* better than anyone! Certainly better than a half-breed like you!"

Pete's fleeting expression was the same one on her father's face every time a student casually called him a dirty Jew.

"Martians never used to talk like that," Anya whispered. "At least, not decent people. My father should have made his move long ago."

It was the first time Rachel had ever heard the princess criticize her father, even by implication.

"But what are you doing back here, Pete? And who are all those people you've brought with you?"

"Aww, you know. Just some relatives of my mom's. You know the story—barely ever left the Texas Panhandle, let alone Earth, and eager to see the wonders of the Solar System!"

"And how is good ol' Helen McSwain, anyway?"

"Mom? She's, uh, well, she's good. At least as far as I know. We haven't actually spoken in a while."

"Hey! How come that Martian said Becky's kid's name in the midst of all that jibber-jabber?" Mary whispered to Kate.

"I'll explain later. Hush now!" Katie whispered back.

The Martian was shaking his head. "You picked a heck of a time to come back and visit, ol' buddy. The tourist trade has dried up so much the past few years, old man Polansky shut down the Hotel Athena on Canal Street last winter."

"Really?" Pete said. "That's unbelievable! Doesn't anyone come here for day trips to the Mountain anymore?"

Walenski chuckled nervously and said in a lowered voice, "You really have been gone a long time, my friend. They don't allow tourists within fifty stadia of Olympus Mons anymore. Not with this new warrior cult Ares has started. Can't have no foreigners polluting the holy mountain, don't you know. That crazy stuff was kind of fun at first, all those parades and fireworks, but you know, it's a bit much these days, what with the public executions and all."

"What public executions?" Pete asked.

"How long you been on the planet, man? They just had that big one last week. You know, the Pretender and his wife."

"No kidding! He had Witold and Martina killed?" Pete said loudly, with a surreptitious glance at where Anya was hiding.

Rachel stiffened. *He's trying to warn her....*

"Yeah! Kids begged me to let 'em watch it on tri-vid and you know me, soft touch, I was gonna let 'em do it...."

Anya doubled over, gasping. Rachel threw her arm around the princess's shoulders and put her face right up against Anya's. Anya couldn't give herself away. The effect was eerie, like looking at herself in a mirror that removed every imperfection.

"Hey, what's the matter with your cousin there?" Andrzej asked, pointing.

Pete glanced at the cart casually. "Oh, that's just Annie from Lubbock. She had colon cancer when she was a kid, so she still has trouble with the food anytime she goes anywhere. Can't even show her Mexican food, poor thing."

"Yikes. Well, look, you guys all better come 'round my place at least for the night. Can't have you camping out in the town square after dark, and those mules look like they could use some grub too."

"Much obliged, sir," Moishe said in his heavily accented Marpolski.

"So you have kids now?" Pete said. "You're married? Andy Walenski, a married man? Get out! Who's the lucky girl?"

"Remember Elzbieta Charlinska?"

"You got Blonde Betty? You old devil, you!"

"Yeah, who would've thought it? Now, Pete, just what have you been up to all this time?"

"Oh, a bit of this and a bit of that. I dabbled in Jovian real estate...."

"Anya! Anya, you have to get a hold of yourself till we're safe inside!" Rachel whispered urgently. The princess was moaning as if practicing musical scales, up and down, down and up.

Jack had climbed back into the cart and was supporting Anya from the other side. "It's the Olympian Dirge. Martians must chant it when a family member or close friend dies," he said quietly. "She should be screaming it at the top of her lungs, so she's actually exercising all the self-control she possibly can. Anya. Anya, honey. It's not your fault. We were on the way to rescue them."

Still, the minutes it took to reach Andrzej's home seemed to last years. Even Jack looked worried. "Honey, they're going to hear you and realize you're chanting the Song for the Dead," he whispered urgently.

But Anya didn't stop, didn't even seem to hear him. The dirge went on and on, wordless and eerie. It sounded like the moaning of wind through leafless trees in winter. It was a keening and a wailing that made Rachel's hair stand on end, that made her have to pinch her own nose so she didn't burst into tears herself. And then, just as they were clattering up the cobblestones to a trim single-story adobe house on a back street, Anya added words in a low growl:

> *Olympus Mons stands tall, his head in clouds*
> *And I shall be revenged.*
> *So deep the depths of Valles Marineris*
> *And I shall be revenged.*
> *I swear by Phobos's fear, by Deimos's terror*
> *That I shall be revenged.*
> *As Mars himself is reddened god of war*
> *Know I shall be revenged!*
> *Although I fall and perish in the deed,*
> *Know I shall be revenged!*
> *Revenge! Revenge! Sweet vengeance shall be mine!*

23

"Hey Betty! Better get out the extra dishes! We have guests for dinner!" Andrzej was calling as he walked into his house.

"Not more of your drinking buddies, are they?" a woman's voice called out, half-joking, half-hectoring.

Rachel climbed out of the cart as Andrzej embraced a willowy blonde who had limped from the house to greet him, favoring her left leg. Pete was right, it was a mystery how a dumpy little guy like Andrzej had snagged such a beauty, especially since blond Martians were so rare. And here came their kids, two little moppets who looked more like her than like him, luckily for them. They interrupted their frolicking over their father to stare with unabashed curiosity at the "guests" who came clomping in.

"Andy, who *are* these people?"

"They're Earthside relatives of Pete Kowalski. Don't tell me you don't remember Pete!"

"Oh yeah. Hi, Pete," Betty said, a little too casually.

"Hello yourself, Betty. You, ah, you haven't changed at all. In fact you're lovelier than you were when we were all seven."

Rachel did the math in her head. When they were all fourteen? That must have been an interesting year. Betty ducked her head, but she was smiling. "Don't be saying stuff like that to my wife, you old half-breed you. It'll go straight to her head and she'll be insufferable for weeks!"

Pete stiffened momentarily, then relaxed. "Listen, we're all tired out from the trip. Andy saw we came in a mule-cart because we couldn't find any other transportation. Is there a place for everyone to wash up while the driver and I go take care of the mules?"

"Of course," Betty said with a smile. "I'll have the girls go fetch some water so you can take turns bathing in our tub in the courtyard out back. Maria can carry the most, can't you sweetheart?"

"Mom, it's Kristina's turn to haul water!"

"And she's so nice about it too," Betty said, ruffling the hair of the taller of the girls, who looked to be about seven, in Earth years. "We don't have a lot of food on hand, seeing that Andy didn't give me any forewarning—"

"How could I have?"

"—but I'll see what I can rustle up. Pete, why is your cousin there pulling a hood up over her head? Isn't she hot?"

"Smoking," Pete mumbled. "Oof," he added when Jack elbowed him in the ribs. "It's a sad story, Betty," Pete said, drawing her aside, "Annie here's from Lubbock, which is no bigger than this town, and this is her first time outside of it, let alone off planet. She hardly ever goes out when she's at home because when she was three, a pot of boiling water tipped over on her and burned her face horribly."

"Poor thing!" Betty gasped, her blue eyes round as little Earths.

"Yes, so, uh, um, you see, well, she's not going to be able to join the rest of us for meals or anything, because it's too painful for her to be around people."

"Plus she had colon cancer," Andy put in helpfully.

"Yeah, that too," said Pete.

"And the guy driving the cart?" Betty asked, glancing out the door. "Why doesn't he come in and eat?"

Because your food isn't kosher. Pete mumbled some explanation about how Moishe too suffered from terrible digestive diseases.

Betty narrowed her eyes. "Ain't he one of those Hasids?" she said. "He's too good to eat our food, ain't he? Well then, he can go hungry."

Rachel ground her teeth. *I have the right to say the kosher rules are stupid, lady, but you don't!*

"Anyhow, I still don't really get why all your relatives seem so sad, when they're supposed to be on vacation," Betty said.

"Sad? Well, that's just Texians for you."

"I thought they were called Texans."

"Texans, Texians, what's the difference? They're as dour as the Scots."

"I thought you were an exuberant bunch. At least, you were when you were seven," Betty said with a wink.

Pete let out a tiny moan. "Y-yes. Exuberant, yes. Except when we're on vacation. Then we're very grouchy, even sad. Don't ask me why," Pete said, and hiccupped.

"Well, that's just awful! I always have fun when we go on vacation!" a little voice exclaimed. Rachel turned and saw Maria's little sister, who looked eerily identical to how Betty would have looked at that age. "You must be Kristina," she said.

"That's right! Hey, what's your name?" she said, walking over to Sonya, who hid behind Rachel. "Jeez, you people sure aren't a lot of fun," Kristina pouted.

"That's not polite, dear," Betty said.

"Never mind," Pete said jovially, "most of 'em don't speak any Marpolski."

Which was true enough, and made dinner a bit of a strain. Since Anya couldn't be there, Rachel played translator, though Gun insisted on trying out her slightly rusty Marpolski.

"The butter, please to walk."

"Here you go," said Andrzej, suppressing a grin as he handed it to her.

"So, Andy," Pete said, "what have you been doing with yourself?"

"Me? Oh, you know, a bit of this and a bit of that. Kind of like you. Mainly I work down at the factory."

"The textile plant? I thought they were going to close it down."

"They were, yeah, but since the new Ares came to the throne orders for uniforms have kept the place humming. Old man Jaworski put more money in our pay envelopes twice this year, can you believe it? At least as far as business goes, the new Ares has been great."

"Really dear," Betty said with a dazzling smile, "in what way has he not been great?"

"What? Oh, I didn't mean nothin'," Andrzej muttered, looking as his feet.

"*I* think he's *hand*some," Kristina opined. "We had a contest in my class to see who could make the best copy of his portrait, and I won!"

Betty beamed. "She got three gold stars and a commendation from the principal!"

"Really? That's fantastic," Pete said, pushing his *kruckle* beans around his plate.

"Yeah. Not like that stinker Teddy Gdanski. He drew horns on his portrait and got in biiiiig trouble," Kristina said. "He may be expelled!"

"That family's a bad bunch, all of them," Betty said. "I'm not surprised. Agnieszka Gdanska lets her boys run wild, and she's rude when I run into her at the store."

Rachel was desperate to turn the conversation away from the dangerous subject of Ares. "What are these crunchy, buttery nuts you've mixed in with the *kruckle* beans?" she asked Betty.

Betty preened. "Do you like them? They're thescnuts. We used to have them all the time, but they grow on trees along the sides of the canals, and now that you Earth people are stealing our precious Martian water they're more expensive than they used to be."

"Well, our Emperor is going stop Earth from doing that," Kristina said brightly. "Wanna see my picture of him?"

"Uh," Rachel began, but the girl had already darted into the other room, returning with a not-half-bad watercolor of an arrogant, extravagantly mustachioed face under a bright golden crown.

Katie, who had been toying with her food like Pete, glanced up without interest, then did a double take. "Who is *that*?" she asked, pointing.

"I can't understand what she's saying, but I don't like her tone," Betty said. "Tell her she can't point like that at the Emperor."

Rachel gulped and told Katie what Betty had said.

"*That's* Ares?" Katie said. "That's pretty strange, because he's the spit and image of that no-good Johnny Marshall back in Texas."

"It's a coincidence," Gun said. "It has to be. Think how many billions of people there are between our world and yours. A lot of people are bound to look like each other."

"I guess you're right," Katie said, frowning, but she elbowed Rachel and whispered, "It's him all right! I'd recognize that horrible twisted scowl anywhere! I told you he was reading your book too. He must've found his way *into the story*, somehow, just like we did."

Rachel shivered. "Maybe so," she whispered back, "but even if you're right, what can we do about it?"

"We've got to get him off the throne of Mars, that's for sure. No offense to your imagination, Rachel honey, but Johnny Marshall is a worse bad guy than even you could come up with!"

Betty glared at them and turned to her husband.

"Please the *kruckle* beans to send walking," Gun said to Kristina in Marpolski.

"Okay," Kristina said with an impish grin, and slid her right hand under the bowl, making walking motions with her fingers. The bowl started to tip over and a handful of beans fell into her mother's lap.

Betty smacked her arm lightly and handed the bowl on to Gun. "It's not nice to be rude to foreigners just because they're not lucky enough to have grown up speaking Marpolski," Betty told Kristina.

"I can speak some Solar," Maria offered. "I used to get A's before they cancelled all the foreign language programs last year. I speak Solar much good, yes?" she added in English, looking at Katie, who smiled back.

"Pretty good, Maria. Maybe I can help you with your Solar and you can teach me a little Marpolski," Katie said.

"Deal," Maria said with a grin.

Rachel folded her arms. "You never wanted to learn Polish from me," she said to Katie.

Katie looked a little embarrassed. "Well, Rachel, you're a little intimidating. I mean, you're so smart and all, I just don't feel comfortable trying to learn from you."

Rachel opened her mouth, closed it, then got up from the table without a word and went to look for Anya. If she was intimidating Katie, then maybe she deserved to go and be intimidated by the princess. Anya was sitting in the back room that Betty had designated for the female members of their party, her head bowed, holding a purring Thumper in her lap. She didn't even look up from stroking the cat when Rachel walked in.

"Anya," Rachel began, and stopped. *Maybe it's better just to keep quiet*. After a while, Thumper wriggled out of Anya's grasp and climbed onto Rachel's lap. Rachel bowed her head and began to stroke the cat. A few seconds later large, silent tears began to fall onto his orange and black fur, but he never stopped purring. Then the door opened. Footsteps ran in Rachel's direction until Sonya cannoned into her, curled up beside her, and started stroking Thumper's head in her turn. From the other room came the murmur of voices and dishes being cleared away. Mother and daughter Webb peered into the room as Sonya had done, but when Katie saw the silent conclave she whispered to her mother, who nodded and quickly withdrew. The night deepened outside the room's lone window, and a rising Phobos cast strange shadows across the oddly shaped furniture, the chairs that looked half-melted and the love seat that looked like something out of a painting by Salvador Dali.

Without raising her head Anya said in a low voice, "It is a custom on Mars, after a family member dies, to share memories. I know you two are from Earth, and your customs may be different. But I hope it will not offend you if I speak of my parents. And if you wish, you may speak of yours." Neither Rachel nor Sonya said anything, so Anya began, "When I was a little girl, a bigger boy who lived down the street yanked on my pigtails so hard one day that he tore some of my hair out. I ran home crying to my father. After he kissed me and helped me clean up, he took me out in the courtyard and taught me *krav Marpolski*, the Martian way of fighting without weapons. The next time that Jurek tried to pull my pigtails, he ended up with a black eye."

She added a short chant:

> *Bless our memories, You who created Time and World.*
> *Bless those we loved, keep them in Your bosom curled.*

A few minutes later, Rachel said, "The first thing I remember is crawling into my father's study and pulling down a big fat encyclopedia of some kind. I was fascinated by the pictures, but I thought I could improve them. When he caught me scribbling over Tadeusz Kościuszko's face in purple crayon, do you know what he said?" She started to giggle, but it turned into tears. "He said, 'It's about time you started taking an interest in Polish history, young lady.' Then he lectured to me for an hour about the eighteenth century."

When Anya was sure Rachel had finished speaking, she chanted again:

Bless our memories, You who created Time and World.
Bless those we loved, keep them in Your bosom curled.

A long silence followed. If anyone had walked in at that moment, they might have thought all three girls had fallen asleep. But finally Sonya piped up timidly, "When I was four, Mama took me out for ice cream. I got it all over my face and down my shirt, and I was so worried she would yell at me, but instead she just laughed and cleaned me up with her good lace handkerchief." This time, Rachel joined Anya in the chant.

24

In the chill of the night air, Jack, Pete, and Eddie sat in chairs around the courtyard. Moishe had elected to sleep in his cart, and the Webbs were nowhere to be seen. Gun was making the most of her Belter's gift for falling asleep in cramped and uncomfortable circumstances and was snoring away on a balled-up sweater. Eddie too had drifted off, his head lolling over the back of his chair. Jack was examining his folded arms with apparently great interest. *In a moment he'll be asleep too*, Pete thought. *It's now or never.*

"Hey, Jack."

"Mmf."

"Whatcha thinking about?"

"Catching some winks. Moishe and I are going to start out early."

"Yeah." A pause. "Do you get nervous before, um, missions?"

Jack shifted in his chair. "I won't say no, but I just try and concentrate on the details of what I have to do. You can't predict or control what's actually going to happen, of course, but pretending like you can keeps the willies away." He paused, then added in a softer voice, "It's not for everyone. It's not for most people. Having second thoughts?"

A nervous chuckle. "It's a bit late for that. Anyway you're the one who's got the dangerous job. I just have to stay here and look after the womenfolk and kids. And Eddie."

"Uh-huh. Watch out for hidden traps."

"What do you mean?"

"Just look over your shoulder. I seen the looks you gave that Betty and she gave you. Those dangerous blue eyes of hers. Don't bite the hand that feeds ya, man."

"What the heck is that supposed to mean?" But Jack turned away, and, taking his zap-gun out of its holster, started stroking it like Anya, Rachel, and Katie stroked Thumper. He sighed happily.

Pete slumped in his chair. *Great, here I am with a gun-toting psycho, a washed-up pilot and, for female company, a tough-as-nails Belter. I hope Jack has the safety on that thing.* With that happy thought, he tried to imitate Jack's posture so he could fall asleep too. Not surprisingly, he didn't succeed. A Martian thistle-wicker recliner is not the most comfortable furniture for tossing and turning. Those fine, tough fibers that are treasured by antique collectors on Earth turn into thousands of miniature thorns exquisitely designed for pricking exposed skin. Martians are reputed to have thick hides, but in this regard Pete evidently took after his mother's side of the family. With an irritated sigh he finally flung himself out of the chair and wandered into the house for a glass of water. In the darkened kitchen he bumped into Betty and her glass of *yaszt* spilled over them both.

"Oh! I'm, uh, I'm sorry, Betty."

"No, no! I shouldn't have been standing here drinking with the light off."

"I should've watched where I was going."

"I should've been sitting down."

The silence that fell seemed to crackle, as if there was a slowly building electrical charge behind Pete and Betty. *It's a good thing I'm not touching anything metal.* Her golden skin looked as if sparks might actually start flying off it. She put her mostly empty glass on a table and pulled up a rickety-looking stool, gesturing at Pete to take the only chair in the room.

"So," he said, "you and Andy. I never would have seen it coming." That was a baldfaced lie.

Betty shrugged with her right shoulder only, a motion that speeded up Pete's heart.

This is ridiculous. We're not kids any more.

"I was almost ten years old when we got married." *Nineteen, Earthstyle.* "If I'd hit my tenth birthday still single, I would have been considered an old maid by the standards of Lvovinsk. You know that."

"Well, sure, but it hardly seems—I mean, you could have moved to a bigger city. In Krakowicz people sometimes wait to get married until they're fifteen! Or even older."

"So I've heard. But things have changed since you were here, Pete. People's expectations are different. Ares wants lots of little soldiers for his army. He's introduced paramilitary training for boys starting in kindergarten. And a good thing, too! Keeps the little animals out of trouble. A nasty little boy called Frantizek—he's Jola and Leo's boy, you remember them—used to like to yank on Kristina's pigtails, but that stopped real fast when he got a week in the stockade."

"Stockade? Yikes. You people are getting really tough."

"It's mostly for the better, I'm telling you. Though I'd like the girls to be able to wait a little longer to get married than I did. Don't get me wrong, though—Andy's a great guy! He's so good with the girls. He hardly ever lets it show how much he wanted a son."

"Wanted?" Pete heard himself echo. His right hand reached out of its own accord and grabbed Betty's. "What's stopping you from trying again?"

Betty didn't pull her hand away. She gestured with her left hand instead. "Oh, you know. It's money, mostly. I feel so bad for Andy. He works so hard, comes home so exhausted he can barely play with the girls."

Pete rubbed the ball of his thumb absently around Betty's cool, soft palm. He didn't know very many married people, it was true, but somehow pity didn't seem like a good basis for a marriage. "What about his parents? Can't they help out?"

That bewitching shrug again. "Karl died in the Great Dust-storm of 5823, two years ago. His mother won't leave the house since then. I have to bring her meals or she'd starve."

Fifty-eight twenty-three? So they're back to using the classical Martian calendar, are they? "What about your folks?" he asked, stroking the inside of Betty's wrist. She shivered.

"Oh, they're the same. Dad's down at the bar every day except Deimos-Day. He's always drinking Andy under the table, though usually he's good enough to carry him home himself afterward. They're great company for each other, but I'm afraid I'm turning into my mother. Next thing you know I'll be knitting dust-breakers and baking *kruckle* pies."

She sighed and closed her eyes, while Pete moved on to kneading her forearm, and then her shoulder. Slowly she tilted her head back, and Pete's lips brushed first her neck, then her chin, then that lightest of smile lines just to the left of her mouth.

His eyes closed, Pete no longer saw the dark, cramped kitchen, but a place called Bradbury's Gulch south of town, a baby box canyon named after one of the members of the first expedition from Earth. In the brief Flood Time of the Martian winter, the place was a raging small river, but on a cool autumn day it was a place of subdued natural beauty, all pastel stones, tough, waxy evergreens, and mysterious shadows, a few of which actually concealed cave entrances. Pete, Andy, and Betty were old enough to know better, but what else was there to do in Lvovinsk on a slow afternoon but go exploring? The sun burned warm through the chill in the air and a daytime Phobos shone with a diamond-hard light amid a swaddling of mare's tails high in the eastern sky. Homework could wait till dinnertime. They weren't calling it hide-and-seek, which was for babies.

It was Andy who first noticed that neither he nor Pete had seen Betty in close to half an hour. "She must be hiding really well, I guess," he said, the corners of his mouth turning down as he said it.

"Yeah," said Pete, "but we better get started back soon. Her mom serves dinner early."

That gave Andy all the excuse he needed. "Her mom's a real kill-joy," he grumbled, the corners of his mouth turning down even further. "Wouldn't like to see Betty get a hiding for that. Hey Betty! Come out, come out, wherever you are!"

"Game's over, Betty!" Pete added. The wind playing a low note on the canyon rim was their only answer. Somewhere a thistlecat let out the kind of warbling cry that brought non-Martians running, convinced that a baby was dying horribly. Without another word, Pete and Andy took off searching in opposite directions. By the luck of the draw, this meant that Pete discovered her lying on the ground with her eyes half shut and her right ankle caught and twisted between two massive boulders. On Earth, they might have weighed over a quarter of a ton each. Here of course, the weight was less than half that, so by straining what felt like every muscle in his body he was able to shift one of them just enough to free Betty's foot, which had turned purple and swollen so badly Pete had to look away.

He bent down close enough to hear her raspy, irregular breathing. It scared the hell out of him. "Betty, can you walk on your good leg if I help you?"

She mumbled something. He'd take that as a yes. The blue of her eyes that showed through the crack between her eyelids was hazed over, like the sky before a doozy of a Texan or Martian dust storm. He reached around and grabbed her under her right armpit, straining to lift her dead weight. He grunted. *It shouldn't be so hard, not in this low gravity!* And then, despite his best efforts, her right foot scraped against a rock, and her screams echoed down the canyon, startling a flock of bright yellow starbirds into flight. He nearly dropped her. *At least she's alive.* In dreams for years afterwards, he could feel her weight against his and the tiny, re-peated strain-and-release of her leg muscles as she attempted to hobble. He'd wake from these dreams with twinges of pain in his lower back.

"Maybe I should carry you." His dreams would make the obvious rhyming pun. *Maybe I should marry you.*

"No—belava'ed fool that I am—I can walk. Well, hop," she whis-pered with the ghost of a smile.

"I didn't know you knew such language," he teased.

That smile again. Oh those eyes, that starbird-golden hair. "Lot of things you don't know about me, Texas boy."

In the distance, he could hear Andy calling hoarsely. He caught a glimpse of his friend's black silhouette leaping from rock to rock with never a misstep, for all the world like a thistlecat himself. Pete felt his eyes tearing up and reached up with his free hand to wipe them clear, mumbling something about sweat for Betty's benefit. He'd been on this stupid red rock for six solid Earth months now, he was going back to Earth in another two weeks, and Andy and Betty were the only kids his own age who would even speak to him. The others called him mudboy and earthball, while Andy offered his shy friendship and Betty—well. This might be the only chance he would ever get with her. He stopped his shuffling walk. Betty turned to him, tears of pain welling in those eyes.

"What is it, Pete? What's the matter?"

"I—" Words dried up in his throat like the canyon in summer, and he leaned in desperately toward her face. But she turned away. She turned away! She turned her head away, and his lips just grazed her burning hot cheek. In all the years to come under all those different skies, he'd curse himself for a fool and worse, thinking of the agony she must have been in. Or to the contrary, he'd remind himself that in the next instant, Andy's head popped up above the miniature ridge in front of them, so maybe she'd just turned her head because she heard him coming. And not to avoid his kiss. Not to avoid his kiss because it was loathsome to her.

And here was the proof! Here was the proof before him. Right here in his arms in the darkened kitchen. But she was pushing against his chest, pushing him away, and in the hard Phobos-light that shone through the window into her eyes, he saw tears like those she had shed so many years before.

"Pete. Pete, I'm sorry. I can't, I'm sorry." She looked him in the eyes for another endless moment, her fingers splayed against his chest. Then she turned and silently fled the room.

25

The shrunken sun of Mars was already well past the zenith when Drakon Base came in view from Moishe's cart.

"I suggest you hide yourself now, Mr. Flash," Moishe said in his formal Solar, absently rubbing the bandage over his bruised and sprained right leg.

"Good idea, Moishe." Jack climbed into the false-bottomed barrel he had built during the days out in the desert waiting for Rachel and Sonya to get better. He was rather proud of the simplicity of the contraption. All he'd done was to empty out a barrel full of *kruckle* beans, solder it to the floor of the cart and drill a hole into it from below, using a set of power tools Moishe was hoping to sell. The barrel's false bottom had been easy enough to make out of the scrap metal, and underneath he'd attached a large tarpaulin, so that one could enter through the top of the barrel and, after shutting the false bottom, lie snugly in a sort of canvas hammock suspended about a foot and a half above the ground, with enough air entering through the seams to breathe comfortably. Moishe had to shovel enough beans back into the compromised barrel to make a convincing camouflage, but the two men had practiced enough that it took them less than three minutes for Jack to ensconce himself and Moishe to replace most of the barrel's original contents.

"Good luck, my friend," Moishe whispered before spurring Azri and Shimmie back into motion. There was already too much noise for any reply to be heard, so Jack concentrated on what he would do once he got inside the base. Moishe had explained that he was allowed to set up shop beside the canteen, which in turn backed into a largish warehouse.

"I'll just set up right against the warehouse walls this time," Moishe had said. "Those walls are made of rusty metal sheeting. I'll look for a particularly rusty patch so you can just break through it. After I leave, I'll hide the cart in a gulch on the north side of the camp and wait for you and Jim."

Jack rubbed his chin and nodded, reflecting that Moishe reminded him a bit of Karolla, in that his apparent simplicity masked a shrewd mind. He missed the big gray pest. "All right. So should I wait until things quiet down a bit before I try to sneak out?"

"*Davka* no," Moishe said. "It's better to make your escape when there's a lot of noise."

Jack nodded and grinned. "Hey, that's not bad thinking, little rabbi," he said, clapping the Hasid on the shoulder so hard he winced.

"My uncle is the rabbi, not me," he muttered, "but a little bit of *seichel*, street smarts, I've got to have to survive on this planet."

As he huddled in his canvas cocoon Jack still found it hard to believe that Martian soldiers would be interested in buying the odds and ends Moishe carried. He'd had a look at the goods: there were dried fruits and vegetables, salt and other basic condiments, soap, shoe polish, blankets, bolts of cloth, khaki patches, writing paper, envelopes, pens and pencils, even needles and thread of various colors, as well as the power tools. Didn't Ares supply his would-be-conquering troops with such basics? It seemed not, because they were still outside the gate when Jack heard an excited hubbub. He barely had time to brace himself for an inspection when the cart was waved through and immediately mobbed by clamoring soldiers.

They're going to tear the cart to pieces!

"Boys, boys, clear a path! Clear the way for myself and my poor animals!" Moishe shouted in Marpolski. "We need air and water after such a journey! Make way, I say, I am as eager to sell as you are to buy!"

Like Moses parting a khaki sea. Jack grinned.

"Hey little man! Did you bring some toilet paper?" The voice cracked like that of a boy just hitting puberty. "The barracks is really starting to stink!"

"That's just you, Nemerovski!" someone else shouted to general merriment.

"Nothing but the softest for Lord Ares' loyal soldiers I bring!" Moishe half sang, half-chanted as the mule cart bounced along. Jack wished he'd take it a little easier on the curves. It would be very inconvenient if his usually iron stomach was to go weak on him right now.

"What about that book of famous love poems I asked you for last time?" Nemerovski asked. "I got to show my girl Irina I still care so she don't run off with that lousy good-for-nothing Ivan!"

"Right here, my young friend!" Moishe sang.

"Better perfume your letters before you send 'em, Nemerovski!" the wise guy yelled, to an even bigger laugh.

"You wanna shut up, Kristof?"

"You wanna make me?"

The cart fetched up with a bump against something that clanged dully. The sound of fisticuffs and a bunch of bored soldiers chanting "Fight! Fight! Fight!" filled the air, and Jack figured this was his chance. He pulled out his trusty knife and sliced open the tarp with one swift motion. He hit the ground on all fours, prepared for anything, but the fight was still going on. In the distance he could hear whistles and what sounded like MPs bellowing. Better move fast, then.

Jack scooted over and examined the metal wall beside the cart. Sure enough, Moishe had chosen a spot with a huge orange rust stain. Silently thanking the Hasid, Jack took a deep breath and kicked as hard as he could. He braced himself for the shriek of metal failing, but instead a section of wall almost tall enough to let the mules through dissolved in a shower of ugly brown flakes. Jack leapt through the gap and found himself behind a tower of crates stacked so close to the wall that he could barely squeeze past. He cautiously peered around a corner, but the place seemed to be deserted. At a glance, he estimated it was at least fifty yards on a side and twenty feet high. The packed dirt floor supported a labyrinth of crates that was nowhere less than chest high, and in some places reached almost to the ceiling. On Earth or Venus some of the heaps would not have been stable, but in the lower gravity a somewhat more casual approach to piling things up was possible. Though Jack wouldn't have thought such sloppiness tolerable to the military men he'd known. *What sort of army is Ares running, if he doesn't give his troops the basic necessities and lets them run their camps any way they please?* A lousy one, but Jack already knew that from Anya and other sources.

Jack wandered around the warehouse, poking here and there at the crates. They were made of the same kind of metal as the warehouse walls, something light and cheap, wood being incredibly scarce and expensive on Mars. Jack opened them at random. At first he found goods you'd expect on a military base anywhere, anywhen; assorted uniforms, mismatched boots, rifles in various states of disassembly, uncomfortable looking bedding and the like. Toward the far corner of the warehouse, though, things started to get weird. More and more cases were locked, and those that weren't contained objects of no immediately obvious use: strange and ugly statuettes, half-masks that would cover the face down to the nose, and one case full of what looked like kitchen knives until he accidentally pressed his thumb against a blade and pulled back, cursing and bleeding.

What are they planning to do, fight a war on steaks? Metal banged at the far end of the warehouse and Jack ducked behind the crates. There was a burst of orange sunlight and two soldiers sauntered in. They started heading straight for his hiding place, and he scooted back towards the hole through which he had entered. *Damn!* Moishe had already driven away and sunlight was streaming in through the gap. Cursing under his breath, he scuttled along crabwise until he found a niche surrounded on three sides by towers of crates, with the open side facing away from his unwanted visitors. His Marpolski wasn't that good, and he'd missed the beginning of the conversation. Something about an officers' dance next week.

"Those are some hot chicks. Didja see Lieutenant Vranikovich's girl? Oo-ee."

"You mean the tall redhead?"

"That's the one."

"Yeah, she's hot all right. Mia is her name. Looks like the Princess Pretender Va-va-voom Anya. I hear Vranikovich likes to take her to executions."

Executions? As a date? Jack grimaced.

The first soldier said, "Eww. You mean watching guys get shot turns her on?"

"Worse than that. She gets real excited by all the blood at these new throat-cutting ceremonies the brass want."

"Yikes. Say, hand me that knife, willya, Ted? No, no, the other one. No, the *other* one. The one with the mother-of-pearl handle and the long blade. Yeah, that one. The guy we're offing tomorrow morning is a swamp-rat. Hear they have tough necks."

Jack froze.

"A swamp-rat? Really? I thought they all graduated from spy school and went back to Venus."

"Yeah, they all did almost three years ago, except for some guy named Jim Flash. Poor slob fought everything his whole life here. His back and butt are all covered with scars from the beatings he got." Something clattered. Jack toyed with Annabelle's safety.

"Oh yeah, I know who you're talking about now. Me and some of the other guys used to beat him up every day after cadet training. Once I held his head in a toilet bowl till he almost drowned."

They're making it awful easy for me. Jack flicked the safety off and stood up, blood roaring in his ears. He padded across the dirt, a lifetime of jungle tracking standing him in good stead. Ted and his pal were both bent over a crate with their butts in the air, and Jack was sorely tempted to just vaporize them in this inglorious position. Instead he got their attention by vaporizing the knife with the mother-of-pearl handle, which they'd put on the floor.

"Straighten up and turn around real slow," Jack snarled.

"Flash?" squeaked Ted. "How did you get out? I mean, I mean, look, I'm really sorry about that toilet thing and the fact they're gonna cut your head off at dawn and all, but.... Hey, you ain't Flash!"

"Worse luck for you, I'm his brother. It's a fine planet you've got here where turds try to flush men down the toilet!"

Ted let out a high-pitched giggle that ended in a squeak as Jack gave him a quick flash-gun haircut.

"Now, I'm only gonna ask once. Where is my brother?"

"In the base prison, of course, but you'll never—Ow! OUCH! Okay, just go out the way we came in, walk past five rows of barracks, make a left at the bulletin board, then a right at the dump, and there you are."

"You ain't never gonna survive to spring your brother, friend swamp-rat," the other guy cut in. "The place is guarded by MPs from my unit."

"What, the dastardly desert dumpsters? Thanks for your concern, friend dust-mite." Annabelle spoke twice, and the Martian soldiers fell, giant holes in their chests. "But I think I can manage," Jack said, waving aside the smoke as he reholstered his gun. He dragged the bodies into a corner and piled up some crates in front of them, then returned to his hiding place to wait.

Gradually the afternoon light faded and the warehouse was plunged into darkness. It might not have been the best strategy to actually blast those two dirtbags, but no one showed up to look for them. He waited some more, trying not to think about the torment Jim had been undergoing all these years while he was busy gallivanting all around the Venusian jungles and the Solar System. But every time he closed his eyes, he saw Jim holding his hands up to protect his face while a gang of jeering Martians stomped and kicked him, Jim being whipped by a drill sergeant wielding a Martian thwack-rod, Jim sitting in a cell crying from hunger, fear, and loneliness. Jack's eyes filled with large, silent tears that splashed in the hard Martian dirt and were absorbed by the thirsty ground. At first they were tears of rage, but as the hours passed Jack wept for all the years that could never be recovered.

Eventually it grew dark. *I'd better get moving before someone does come looking for Ted and his pal.* Patting Annabelle for reassurance, he edged his way to the hole where he'd entered in a crouch. Outside it was a moonless, starless night, the volcanic ash overhead so thick Jack was sure he could feel it stinging his throat. He swallowed twice and took a swig from his nearly empty canteen. Nobody seemed to be around, so he made his way slowly to the real door to the warehouse, to get his bearings. Sure enough, there were some rows of barracks, with a latrine that announced itself by its stink right in front of them. He scooted along, keeping to the shadows, as he counted off five rows, praying all the while that nobody would get up to take a piss while he was passing by. Jack hated to shoot a man in that condition; it seemed unsporting.

Now where's that bulletin board—oh, there it is. It was so big he'd almost overlooked it, a giant billboard looming over the camp, floodlights illuminating the grimly frowning, black-mustachioed face of Lord Ares III. Jack looked closely. *Katie might be on to something.* Ares' wasn't the typically Martian face, long and melancholy-looking. Instead, it was all hard lines and a permanent sunburn that looked too fierce to have been incurred on Mars. But could he really be from Earth? Jack shook his head.

But this was no time to ponder the imponderable. He had to find that dump that was his next landmark. Now where—ah, the smell could be his guide. It was pretty ripe, all right. At least he could breathe more easily there than in front of barracks full of sleeping Martian soldiers, although doing so made him want to retch. What did these people eat? *Kruckle* beans didn't smell that much, at least not going down. The powers that be had thoughtfully built the base prison right next to this dump, which seemed as much a punishment for the guards as for the prisoners. Jack scratched his chin. The poor MPs stuck with guard duty would probably welcome any excuse to get away, even for a minute. So he retraced his steps, aimed his gun right between Ares' giant eyes, fired, and hid. It took less than a minute for a very satisfactory fire to get going, eating away at Ares' face, producing gray smoke that swirled spectacularly under the floodlights. But no one was coming to look! Didn't they even patrol here at night, or were they too weak from hunger? Jack tsk-tsked to himself and, thanking his lucky stars for the hours he'd spent as a boy learning to throw his voice as a means of generating fun chaos at school, he shouted, "Fire!" making it sound as if he was standing right outside the barracks. Then he settled back on his haunches to enjoy the show. At first only a few sleepy-eyed soldiers came staggering out in their underwear, rubbing their eyes and yawning, but they woke up quickly and started yelling. In an instant dozens more men poured out into the space before the billboard, but none of them seemed to have a means or even any very clear idea of how to put out the blaze. Jack kept a careful eye to his right, where the prison was. Sure enough, three helmeted MPs came running past, their guns drawn, as if they could shoot the fire to death. Jack darted past the way they had come.

The prison loomed before him. Or maybe squatted was a better word. It was only two stories high, but solidly built of Martian *pukkstone*, a lot harder than sandstone. Annabelle wouldn't even be able to scratch it, Jack knew. Better just to walk in the front door, which was gaping wide open. He entered, his gun drawn, looking for any MPs who might have stayed behind, but he saw no one. Two tiers of cells ranged before him, totaling a couple dozen, but the number of prisoners was much larger, judging by the hubbub of voices; Jack guessed there must be at least five or six men per cell. He had to do something to get their attention, so he shot out a light bulb far overhead. Instantly there was dead quiet, except for the tinkle of shattered glass.

"I'm looking for prisoner Jim Flash," he said in Marpolski, then repeated himself in Solar.

A voice replied, "Jack? Is that you?"

Jack whipped around. *Where's that voice coming from?* The second tier. He bolted up the stairs.

"Jim? Jim, where are you?" he hollered as he ran.

"In the death cell, with the other traitors!" someone shouted. The stone walls seemed to vibrate with the cacophony that started up, voices jeering, fists and feet banging on metal cell doors. Jack ignored the curses and globules of spit hurled his way. It wasn't hard to find the right cell, as it was the only quiet one, and the face he saw framed by bars was the same as the one he saw in the mirror every morning—if he'd grown up on a starvation diet. Annabelle had the honor of melting the lock on the door, which swung open, impossibly open. And then Jim was in Jack's arms.

I can't cry now, but when we're out of here there'll be enough tears shed to start replenishing the Martian seas.

Jim thrust his chin out slightly, and Jack could now see that he was dealing with a grown man and not a lost little boy. Looking at Jim was *not* like looking in a mirror, not anymore; a lifetime of harsh experience had eroded away every soft line of his features.

"We all have to get out of here. I'm one of six men sentenced to die at dawn," Jim said. Five silent Martians clustered around them. Like Jim but unlike the other prisoners Jack had glimpsed, they had been stripped of their uniforms and now stood in ragged discards that let their underwear show through. They smelled as if they hadn't had a chance to wash in weeks, and most had at least starter beards.

"Why do they call you traitors?" Jack asked.

"We're Wandanians," a tall, skinny kid with a face composed of acne and freckles said solemnly. "Or that's what they call us. We call ourselves God-fearers. The Prophet Wanda would never have wanted her followers to use her name in place of His."

So Wanda's a prophet now. That's going to make things even harder on Anya if she ever does ascend to the throne. "So that's why they sentenced you to death?"

"Yes," said a shorter, angrier looking Martian. "That's all. To refuse to follow the pretender Ares' disgusting paganism and child sacrifice is to forfeit your life." He spat on the floor, then shook his fist at the jeering human zoo outside the cell. "Not that any decent person wants to live on this planet anymore, anyway."

"Yeah, well, much as I sympathize, I think we'd better save the religious disputes for later," Jack said. "Follow me!" And he charged out the cell door and down the stairs, followed closely by the others. The other prisoners made even more noise as the escapees ran past. *Those damned "patriotic" Martians are actually hoping to attract the guards' attention so we get caught!* Sure enough, here came the MPs, charging through the door with their guns drawn. Jack shot one, while his companions tackled the other two and quickly subdued them. They braced themselves for more MPs or regular soldiers to come pouring in, but no one else followed, and Jack gestured everyone out the door.

"I think you'd better let me lead the way, big brother," Jim said as they emerged into the night. "I spent years figuring out how to sneak off base without getting caught, along with all my other loser friends. If I'd had any money I would've been on the first rocketship back home. But I barely had enough pocket change to get drunk with my buddies." His mouth twisted. "Of course, THEY just got kicked out of the army. I'm the only one who's been sentenced to die just for being a screw-up."

"You're not a screw-up," Jack said grimly, handing him a flashlight, "and you're not going to die if I have anything to say about it. Just make sure you get us out on the northern side of the camp, I've got a friend waiting there."

They dodged up alleyways and down disused dirt tracks. A lot of the base seemed to be neglected, if not abandoned, and as the escapees ran the hullaballoo faded behind them. They slowed because the lights in this part of the base were so few and far between, but already Jack felt a lot safer.

"We used to sneak under the barbed wire back here where the ground dips," Jim said. "I'm just not sure—okay, here it is." He bent down and played the beam of the flashlight back and forth, stopping on a shallow depression crossed by the perimeter fence. "This way. But be careful, the fence is electrified."

"Who are they expecting to attack? Thistlecats? Hasids?"

"I think it's more to keep miscreants like me *in* than to keep anyone *out*," Jim responded. "In the army they like to say that electrified barbed wire is the one really useful Earth invention. But us delinquents can be pretty clever." He pushed some dried brush out of the way, revealing a ditch that ran under the fence.

"I think we better let our Wandanian friends go through first," Jack said. "It's going to be a tight fit for me."

Jim nodded. The tall Martian who had first spoken to Jack went through first, quickly wriggling under the fence and out of sight. The others followed quickly, but they seemed to take forever. *Four little, three little, two little Martians. One little Martian boy.* Then it was just the Flash brothers.

"You go first," Jim said.

"Are you nuts? I didn't come all this way to—" They were blinded by white light blazing all around them.

"The game's up, Jackflash!" an amplified voice boomed. "And all you traitors, too!"

Jack shoved Jim so hard he fell in the dirt. "Go! Get along with you!"

Jim's face suddenly turned little-boy soft and started to crumple. "But—"

"No buts! Have you forgotten your head is scheduled to be cut off in an hour? I'll keep 'em busy! Tell Anya I went down fighting!" And turning, not waiting to see if Jim obeyed, Jack fired wildly into the light.

26

Is it really true that happy families are all alike? Katie finished drying and putting away the last of the lunch dishes. *Maybe that old Russian Count, Tolstoy, was just full of it.* It was getting on toward dinnertime, and she was helping her parents get the meal on the table. Betty had run out half an hour before, saying she wanted to buy something special for dessert. Dad was hauling water from the town pump while Mom bustled around in the courtyard, corralling some squawking hens—it wasn't just the Hasidim who found the earthly birds so useful and tasty; they'd been adopted wholeheartedly by the Martian natives too. Dad came in through the back gate, quietly put down the two brimming buckets he'd been carrying, sneaked up on Mom, and smacked her on the behind.

"You no-good scamp! I'll get you for that," Mom giggled, then started chasing Dad around the courtyard amid a chaos of squawks and drifting feathers. Dad roared with laughter, then turned around suddenly and caught Mom in his arms, swinging her high above the swirling dust.

Maybe it's the unhappy families that are all alike. Betty had smiled sadly at a similar scene. With her gone, the house was pretty quiet except for the racket Katie's parents were making. Anya had stayed all day in what Katie was starting to think of as the Mourning Room, following a whispered predawn embrace with Jack, who left immediately without even eating breakfast. Maria and Kristina were on their way back from school, Katie guessed, and Pete had acted weird all day, snapping at her and treating her like a stupid kid until Katie felt like knocking his block off. Right now he was sitting in a chair in the courtyard dozing, his mouth open wide enough to catch Phobos-flies.

Betty had been behaving strangely too, shying away from everyone when she'd been so bubbly the night before. Even a back-country Panhandle girl didn't need a map. It was obvious Pete and Betty had something going on. How it was Andrzej hadn't noticed anything Katie couldn't imagine, except that he'd had to leave for work not long after Jack set out. She wished she could discuss it with Gun, but she and Eddie, perhaps sensing the change in the domestic weather, had vanished together somewhere. Katie scuffed at the dirt. If her parents weren't here she'd run off too, but despite their glee, or maybe because of it, she felt like she'd better stay and keep an eye on them.

Really, it seemed indecent for Mom and Dad to be having so much fun. Her parents hardly ever laughed or joked around. Scraping a living off the dry Panhandle land was such hard work it seemed to drain all the joy out of you. Katie had always been sure in her secret heart that she would get away from all that, but her plans had been pretty vague. Could it be that she'd never have made her escape without Rachel's miraculous intervention? She was pretty sure she could have kept fending off Johnny Marshall and his gang, but what if one of the Montoya boys, Juan or cross-eyed Freddy, maybe, had made a move on her and Mom and Dad had pressured her to marry him?

Katie shivered at the thought and went looking for Rachel. She found her in the room with Anya and Sonya, who was dozing in Rachel's lap. The two older girls looked like they hadn't moved, slept, or eaten anything since the night before. When Katie walked in, Thumper jumped off Anya's lap, as if grateful for the distraction, and twined himself around Katie's legs. *At least someone around here is acting normal.*

"I think y'all could use some air," Katie declared, yanking Rachel to her feet, dumping Sonya on the floor. The kid didn't even complain.

"I can't leave," Anya said hoarsely, "I can't let people see my face."

"Oh yeah. Well, you two Polocks, come on and let's get outdoors. It's nice outside." Actually it was filthy hot, with an overcast of volcanic ash, but there was something unhealthy about sitting in one place for all those hours. Maybe Betty had felt it too and decided she had to get away from her own home, unless what she really wanted to get away from was whatever was going on between her and Pete.

Anyway, Katie thought her friends could use a change of scenery, too. True, her parents had actually been saved, so she couldn't imagine what Rachel and Sonya were going through, but at least they were still alive themselves, weren't they? Maybe strolling around a real Martian town would take their mind off things for a while.

So she hustled them outdoors, but the village square looked deserted. There weren't even any kids around. School must have ended hours ago. Katie scratched her head as she looked around at the adobe buildings, so low and lumpy they looked like something wasps might have built. There should be people around at such an hour, walking back and forth to the well, bringing groceries home, whatever. Instead the place was as deserted as the center of Abilene on a Sunday morning, when everyone was in church. Where had Eddie and Gun gotten off to, and *what* were they getting up to?

It's not fair. How could I be so stupid as to think Pete was actually interested in me, that any *guy could ever be interested in me? As soon as Betty Bombshell appeared on the scene he started treating me like wallpaper. Gun's no great looker, but Eddie's interested in her. Jack has Anya, my parents have each other, but no one's ever gonna look twice at an ugly old tomboy like me.*

Rachel and that little girl must be getting her down. Katie turned and opened her mouth. She left it open, admitting a mouthful of dust, and swallowed frantically to avoid coughing, because at least a dozen cops were creeping toward the house with guns drawn. They *had* to be cops. Their uniforms were ragged and dirty, but they had that swaggering cop look, like Johnny Marshall and his pals. And Betty was leading them. Fortunately they hadn't glanced in the direction of the square. Rachel and Sonya stood petrified. Katie shoved them hard. "Come on! Run!" she whispered fiercely.

Rachel stared at her, stricken. "What about you?"

"My parents are back there. I'm not gonna leave them. Now go."

Rachel started to say something, but settled for gripping Katie's arm and giving her a fierce green-eyed gaze.

A lump rose in Katie's throat. *Rachel really is as beautiful as Anya, no matter how much she puts herself down.*

Then Rachel grabbed Sonya's hand and they fled across the square, while Katie ran into the house.

Katie burst in and the cops swung around, their guns drawn.

Betty pointed at her and said something in Marpolski to a short, fat, middle-aged man. The man nodded once. He had a gray-tinged reddish mustache curled up at the ends.

"Where are others?" he demanded in passable English. Or Solar.

She decided to go for the dumb country yokel act. "Huh?"

"I said, where are other spies, Earthling?" He raised his gun. Katie fought against the impulse to shut her eyes. Instead she raised her chin defiantly.

"Hey," Pete said, striding into the room. The cops swiveled and turned their guns in his direction. He smiled and said something in Marpolski to the fat cop, who glanced down at his gut, then looked back up with a snarl on his face.

"Oh, Betty," Pete said, adding something in Marpolski. The Martian lady flushed crimson.

There was a noise behind Katie. She didn't dare turn around, but the cops swiveled yet again. It was quite funny really. Katie felt an almost irrepressible urge to laugh. Well, why not, if they were going to die anyway? So she started giggling. Everybody stared at her, then at Andrzej, who brushed past Katie and confronted his wife. Betty tossed her hair and spat something back at him about not wanting traitors in her home. Andrzej shouted at her, and a fierce argument ensued.

That's a little too fierce to be just about politics. Maybe it has something to do with the goo-goo eyes Pete and Betty were making at each other.

Not that it mattered now. Katie hoped all the shouting would distract the cops long enough for Daddy and Mom and Anya to get away. But her heart sank. *I'll never see Rachel again. I'm going to die here with Pete, and we've never even kissed!* She saw her own dismay reflected in Pete's face. He closed his eyes and shook his head slightly.

"I'm sorry, Katie, really I am," he whispered in English. "Now duck."

Katie dropped to the floor. The cops spun around in confusion. Pete looked Betty straight in the eyes and smiled. There was a zap-gun in his hand. He fired first, and the cop who had spoken to Katie screamed and clutched his right arm. The other policemen cut Pete down before he could aim his weapon again. His body hit the floor with a thump. Suddenly, all the blood in her veins changed to fire, and she lunged for the nearest cop, shouting. A white-hot pain cut across her side and the world went dark.

27

When Rachel and Sonya stopped running long enough to catch their breath, they stood on a dry reddish hillside overlooking Lvovinsk. A distant fusillade of zap-guns no louder than the whine of summer mosquitoes drew their gaze back to the village. More policemen ran into Andrzej and Betty's house, but it was impossible to tell what was happening there. The sound of running footsteps made Rachel gasp.

"What's going on?" Gun asked, Eddie behind her.

Rachel shook her head, still too out of breath to speak. Sonya spoke quickly, and Gun and Eddie stared at her blankly.

"The police," Rachel began, and Eddie took off running down the hill.

"Eddie! Eddie, get back here, you fool!" Gun shouted. "You can't just go charging into a situation without...."

Gun and the two girls watched wide-eyed as two policemen emerged carrying a body.

"No," whispered Rachel. "Not Pete."

Katie came next, wriggling in the grasp of a big policeman. Another one cracked her on the head with his nightstick and she went limp.

A howl like a wolf's sounded nearby. The cops stopped, and one of them pointed up the hillside. Rachel, Gun, and Sonya ducked behind a rock. The noise stopped as suddenly as it had started.

Eddie charged into the town, whooping as if he were a whole platoon. He fired and the head of the policeman manhandling Katie disappeared in a cloud of red droplets. Rachel clapped her hand over Sonya's eyes. Then three cops tackled Eddie while another lifted Katie's limp form. A police van pulled up to the house and Eddie and Katie were loaded in, along with Pete's corpse and that of the luckless policeman. Then the van pulled away, turning left on the highway toward the distant looming mass of Olympus Mons, still trailing smoke into a cloudless sky.

Rachel slumped to the ground and wept. Her tears were interrupted by wracking coughs that left her feeling as if her insides had been scraped out. This had to be a nightmare, and then she would wake into the deeper nightmare of the ghetto and her parents' deportation. She curled up and rolled over on her side, ignoring the sharp rocks. Then strong hands gripped her, pulled her up, tugged her hand away from her eyes. She squinted up into the daytime sky. The shrunken sun's glow haloed a familiar head, a familiar face surrounded by a corona of red hair.

"Anya!" cried Rachel, jumping to her feet and wrapping the princess in a bear hug.

"Come on, there's no time to waste," Anya said, pulling away after a moment. "We've got to get word to Jack so he doesn't walk straight into a trap, and then we've got to find a way to save Katie and Eddie."

"What about Katie's parents?"

"Right here," Mary Webb said. Everyone turned and saw her half-dragging her husband into the clearing. He was holding his right hand against the side of his head and moaning softly. Thumper trotted briskly along beside them.

"Those lousy Martian cops!" Gun helped him sit and gently probed a nasty bruise above his temple. It oozed blood and was already starting to swell.

"Wasn't the cops, it was me," Mary said tartly. "I had to stop my Boo here 'fore he did the same fool thing as Eddie. Plus, he was yelling fit to bring all the police on the planet down on us." She looked a bit embarrassed. "Unfortunately, there wasn't nothin' to hit him with but a rock."

"I expect he'll live." Gun improvised a bandage and even a cold compress of sorts from the little first-aid kit she always carried. "Mr. Webb. Mike. Can you walk? I expect we'll have to move soon." Her patient nodded, then moaned. Thumper jumped in his lap and started licking the side of his head just below the bruise. Gun turned to Anya. "You're the boss, princess. Where do we go?"

Anya bit her lip. "I know who the loyalists are in Krakowicz. But out here I'm not sure.... I've never been to this village before."

Rachel snapped her fingers. "Hold on. Didn't Mrs. Walenska say something about a family that got in trouble when their son messed up a picture of Ares?"

"Agnieszka Gdanska's children, she said." Anya nodded. "Good thinking, Ray. But how do we find them? It's not as if we can stroll back down to the village and ask around."

"Not a problem, if we find you first," a new voice said. Everyone turned, including Katie's father, who cried out in pain. Mary cradled his head in her lap and whispered to him soothingly.

A sturdy-looking woman with a round, open face and a brood of three equally sturdy-looking boys stood in the path.

"Agnieszka Gdanska, I presume," Anya said.

"Princess Anya!" the woman gasped. "You are the very image of your murdered mother!" She clutched the sides of her baggy work trousers and started to curtsey, caught herself, grinned sheepishly and turned it into a bow. The boys just stood there staring until their mother clouted the oldest on the side of his head and they made their own awkward bows.

Rachel looked at them curiously. The youngest was about six or seven in Earth years and had a mischievous look, which meant he must be the "stinker" Teddy who had defaced Ares' picture. His older brothers looked about the same age as Sonya and Rachel herself, but their expressions were wary rather than playful.

"It looks like your friend there is hurt," Agnieszka said briskly. "Let's get him back to the house. I'll make a healing herb compress."

"Mrs. Gdanska, I must warn you that Ares' police are after us. If you help us, it could spell big trouble for your family," Anya said.

Agnieszka drew herself up. "The Gdanskis fear nothing. It is an honor to help the heir of Wanda the Great regain the throne that is rightly hers."

"Father would do the same," Teddy blurted out. In the ensuing silence, Anya and Agnieszka looked meaningfully at each other. The princess raised an eyebrow, but the older woman shook her head slightly.

He must be in jail, or worse. This planet felt more and more like the real Poland. Except that in the real world, at least before the Nazis invaded, you could still find some people who believed in democracy and socialism. Here if you were a decent person you had to throw in your lot with a hereditary monarch, of all things. Rachel looked at Anya. *But she's a better version of me. It's all so confusing.*

"We have to get you out of sight, now. Luckily our house is somewhat isolated. But we'll still have to go the long way around. Tomasz, you help Mr. Webb."

"Yes, Mother," the oldest boy said promptly.

And these were what Mrs. Walenska called wild boys!

As he knelt and gently draped Mike's left arm around his shoulders, Tomasz looked up and gave Rachel a wink.

"You can call me Tommy," he whispered.

The Red Planet couldn't have been any redder than Rachel was at that moment.

28

They bound Katie's hands and feet so tightly she had to be carried.

"Where are you taking me, dogface?"

The guard manhandling her sweated and wheezed, but he was twice as tall as her and weighed maybe four times as much. Also he stank like rotting garlic and didn't seem to speak any English, not that that stopped Katie.

"When I get these stupid ropes off me, I am going to rip your guts out and make you eat them," she said sweetly.

He smiled at her. His teeth were a dreadful sight, like a bombed-out cityscape.

"Yeah, you better smile now, you scumbag, because you'll be laughing out the other side of your face when I shove you out an airlock and you die, choking and freezing." A part of her, the part crouched in the darkness in sorrow and fear, was amazed, but it felt good, as did the blood roaring through her veins.

He carried her up several flights of stairs and then down a moving walkway crowded with men and women. Their neatly pressed togas in bright colors reached to their ankles and left their arms free. Everybody pointed and stared, but the guard ignored them and strode briskly along. The corridor stretched on and on. Dim fluorescents supplemented the natural light from narrow windows high in the walls. But the light that came through them was a dull gray shot through with strange colors.

We must have covered over a mile already. "I hope you get married to a really sexy girl," Katie said, "and on your wedding night, you come into the bedroom and find her with your best friend, your father, and the entire Mormon Tabernacle Choir. Then I hope she divorces you and leaves you in your underwear, on Pluto! But you ain't gonna die then, oh no, because some aliens are gonna come along and freeze-dry you for experiments. You're gonna wake up in your skivvies, but you won't be able to scream because your stuck-out tongue will have frozen onto the wall, and—"

Without warning the guard stepped off the moving walkway and walked through a vestibule decorated with an elaborate mosaic. It depicted Martians triumphantly standing astride a shattered Earth. At a set of brass doors twenty feet tall, he stopped and conferred briefly with a pair of guards even more enormous than he was, giants who belonged back in the Book of Genesis before the Flood. Each one carried a mace the size of a two-by-four topped with fist-sized diamonds. They thumped these on the floor in unison three times and the doors swung slowly open. The guard carrying Katie grabbed her by the neck so she swung with her feet just barely missing the floor. As she started to choke he strode into an enormous chamber, and deposited her on her knees, facing a golden throne large enough to seat a dozen of his fellow giants.

Occupying the throne, however, was an ordinary sized man. His lumpy face was dominated by a bushy black mustache that drooped at both ends.

"Why, if ain't Johnny Marshall, the biggest dirtbag for one hundred miles around Abilene," Katie greeted him. "Guess this proves you can read, after all—and here I thought you just liked *Lost Classics of Science Fiction* for its shiny gold title. Where's your crown, 'Lord Ares?' Too heavy to fit on your fat head?"

The royal figure laughed and shook his head. "Kaitlyn Webb, as I live and breathe. The only girl in Texas so ugly not even me and my buds ever wanted you."

"It was a black day for Texas when the Rangers took on a skunk like you. How much did your daddy pay them to get your worthless butt off his farm?"

Johnny rose and strode to where Katie knelt. He slapped her face hard enough that the crack echoed around the room and she fell over, her ears ringing.

"You know, the problem with you and the rest of you Webbs, and for that matter with my buds back home, is that y'all think too small. *Lost Classics* helped me learn to think bigger." He jerked her upright before turning away.

Blood trickled into her mouth, and she spat, hitting Johnny Marshall square in the back as he returned to the throne.

He sat with a satisfied sigh, and made a sweeping gesture with his right hand. "This," he said, "is the scale a man like me needs to operate on."

Katie craned her neck. The place reminded her of pictures she'd seen in some book of the inside of Notre Dame de Paris. There were even stained glass windows, though instead of Jesus and the blessed saints they depicted Martians conquering the Solar System and kneeling in humble obeisance to their liege lord, the former cat-torturer of Abilene.

"I see you're admiring my artwork, not that a hick like you has a lick of artistic appreciation." Johnny gestured behind his throne. "Take a look at my beautiful statues."

Unwillingly, Katie gazed upward. Behind the throne two large niches had been carved into the massive granite walls of the chamber about six feet above floor level. The statues in them were really lifelike. *Really* lifelike. Katie peered at them and gasped. Instead of statues, the niches were occupied on the left by Eagle-Eye Eddie, and on the right by Jack, both of whom, like Katie, had their hands tied behind their backs. A phalanx of sharpshooters crouched along the walls, their guns leveled at the two captives. Johnny Marshall evidently didn't believe in taking any chances.

"Hey kiddo," Jack croaked.

Eddie winked at her, a horrifying sight under the circumstances. "Don't worry, we'll have you out of here in no time."

Katie's eyes watered. *No crying! Not in front of Johnny Marshall!*

Johnny sighed in irritation, and without turning around said, "Mr. Jack-Ass, I warned you and your sidekick to keep absolutely quiet and absolutely still. Since I am a merciful ruler, you may consider this your final warning. If you make another sound, you'll get to witness your buddy's very flashy death. That goes for you too, Katie. Understood? Now," he said, standing up and looking toward a small side door, "that's enough chatter. Let's get to it. Nadia?"

The door opened, and a stunning strawberry blonde in a skirt shorter than a seven-hour Phobian orbit stepped through, pushing something on a cart. Livid bruises were scattered over her face, neck and arms.

Katie looked at the cart, and screamed.

On it sat an old manual typewriter just like the one Rachel had smashed.

"Well, I suppose it's fair," Johnny said crossly, "to give you a second chance like Jack had. All right, I admit it, I'm a softie. Plus, I *do* like an audience when I use the Corrector. Come on Nadia, you lazy girl, roll that thing over here. You *did* remember to check the ribbon this time, didn't you? We wouldn't want a repeat of what happened last Deimosday, now would we dear?"

"No, Lord Dzhonnymarshall," she replied in faltering Solar.

"Ah, there we go. Everything's ready. You have your little reading-cushion, hon? Good." She settled herself onto a plush cushion at the foot of the throne.

Johnny took a pair of reading glasses from a case hidden in his royal robes, rolled a fresh sheet of paper into the typewriter and sat for a moment, tapping his chin. Then he started typing, slowly and painfully, with his two index fingers. The tinkle of the bell that signaled the end of a line echoed around the chamber.

Katie prayed, her lips moving silently. She'd never been much of a believer and hoped God didn't hold it against her for being bored out of her skull in church. *I mean, what kind of a Supreme Being would He be to make Anya and Jack die horrible deaths just because I liked to daydream in the pews?*

"So that's a Corrector, huh? Me and my friends like to play with them things at parties. They're great for breaking the ice!" Eddie said. His voice cracked on the word "ice."

The bell dinged three or four more times before Johnny grunted, rolled the paper out of the typewriter, and handed it to Nadia. She cleared her throat and read haltingly:

```
The gunslinger Eddie's famous eagle
eyes glazed over for a moment. Then
they cleared, and he smiled a smile of
purest joy. "My sovereign," he rasped,
looking across the room to the throne,
where Lord Ares crouched, regional and
alone. "I cannot wait to put my skills
at your service!"
```

Katie burst out laughing. "You mean 'regal and alone,' you horse's ass!" she yelled. "'Regional' means 'local to the area.' That's you all over—a local bully who thinks he's made it big."

"Thanks for the correction, you ugly sow," Johnny drawled. "But it don't much matter, does it?" He pointed at Eddie. Katie gasped again. The gunslinger's eyes bugged out, then glazed over, and he fell from the niche. Two sharpshooters caught him and propped him against the wall, his long legs sticking out at awkward angles.

"Eddie? Eddie? Are you all right?" Katie cried. "Johnny, you killed him! You've murdered him!"

"I shall avenge your death, Eddie!" Jack cried.

Johnny's chuckle turned into a guffaw as Eddie blinked and slowly stood, sliding up the wall for support since his hands were still tied. Katie and Jack stared at him, mesmerized. His muddy brown eyes were unnaturally bright. Johnny stood and ambled over to Eddie, clapping him on the shoulder.

"How do you feel, my friend?"

"Why, I—just fine." Eddie sounded normal. Jack and Katie stared at him, but he only had eyes for Johnny.

"Well, good. Great," Johnny said. "Now, there's just one little test I have to put you through and then you can go sign up for my army. Ready?"

"Of course, sir. I am eager to put my skills in the service of my Sovereign."

"You're just faking Eddie, right? Right?" Katie said.

"Yeah, he's a big joker, our Eddie!" Jack's laugh sounded forced.

Johnny ignored them and signaled to Nadia, who nodded and pushed a button in the wall. A moment later a hidden door opened and a fortyish blond woman clattered in on high heels.

"Eddie!" She rushed forward, tripped and fell over Eddie, clutching him tightly.

"Lila, my love!" Eddie cried out, or at least that's what it sounded like from under the kisses she was bestowing.

"Your ex-wife?" Jack said in disbelief.

"Oh, Eddie, when they told me you were here I just had to come see you. I'm sorry I sent all those process servers after you! I just couldn't bear the thought of losing you and all we meant to each other!" Lila gasped.

"Oh, Lila! Lila, if only I could hold you!"

Katie squeezed her eyes shut. She really wanted to throw up. But nothing happened except for a lot of disgusting wet kissy noises.

"All right, you two," Johnny said. "Far be it from me to get in the way of true love. Or your desire to serve me."

"This is just a nightmare," she whispered. "It's only a dream. I got to wake up now. Those pigs need feeding. Those pigs need feeding...."

"So my friend, all you need to do is go out that door, take a left at the second corridor, go up three flights of stairs, turn right, and you'll find the Martian Space Force recruitment office," Johnny said. "I've taken the liberty of having all your paperwork sent up there in advance. All you have to do is sign."

"I can't wait to start serving Lord Ares in the vasty deeps of space," Eddie said.

Katie opened her eyes and let out a wordless scream.

Jack outyelled her. "You can't talk like that! It used to drive you crazy when I talked that way!"

Eddie shot his old friend a look of contempt.

"Don't be too disappointed, Mr. Flash, but I've decided not to Correct you," Johnny said. "It's no reflection on your skills, but merely my desire to watch you suffer as your friends betray you one by one. Including, of course—" He paused and licked his lips. "Princess Anya. My servants are bringing her here now so I can Correct her."

Jack yelled again and leapt from the niche, the rope falling from his wrists in shreds. Johnny motioned the sharpshooters back and watched as Eddie calmly stepped in the path of his rampaging friend, drew back his fist, and punched him squarely in the face. Blood spewed from Jack's nose, and he fell back against the wall with a thump, then slid to the floor unconscious.

"Eddie honey, are you all right?" Lila cried. "Let me kissy your poor fistie for you!"

Katie turned her head, bile rising in her throat.

"I'm perfectly fine, m'dear," Eddie said. "Now, if you'd care to accompany me, I have some enlistment papers to fill out. Then you can come along on the conquest of Earth I'm going to help lead. Maybe you can be embedded as a war reporter with my unit."

"I'd love to be embedded with you," Lila cooed as they disappeared through the door where she had entered. When they were gone, Johnny strode over to Katie and yanked her to her feet, then cut loose the ropes tying her wrists. She stifled a yelp as the knife nicked her.

"Don't get any funny ideas, you," he snapped, "I'm only untying you so you can clean yerself up and help make your unconscious friend over there presentable."

"Presentable for what?" Katie asked.

Johnny Marshall leered. "For the cameras, of course. You and Jack-Ass are gonna be on live TV!" She stared straight into Johnny Marshall's eyes, putting all her hatred into that one look. By rights it should have set him on fire.

29

Rachel, Anya, and Gun set out long before dawn for Krakowicz, with Tomasz leading the way. Instead of a flashlight, he had a pair of captive Phobos-flies on strings. Like a jar full of Earthly fireflies, their mellow orange glow regularly brightened and faded, but they were out of sync so that the way ahead was always lit, although the light varied in intensity. The effect was hypnotic.

Rachel caught up to Tomasz, who had been leading the way mostly in silence up and down the dry hills and valleys, skirting the occasional canal or farm.

"Tommy, I...." she began, and bit her lip.

He looked at her neutrally. "Yes?"

"I wanted to ask you something, but it's all right if you don't want to talk about it." His silence encouraged her to take a breath and say all in a rush, "What happened to your father?"

♂

When they had arrived at the Gdanskis' house the night before, two things had quickly become obvious: Mr. Gdanski had been gone for quite a while, and the subject was a painful one. Rachel could sense it in the way Agnieszka fussed over Mike Webb, putting him in her own bed and helping Mary spoon-feed him broth. With the three boys plus Sonya, the little house should have been a bedlam, but everyone walked around on tiptoe and talked in whispers. Tucked away in a remote little valley, the Gdanskis' place was much more modest than the Walenskis'. It was built of the ubiquitous shale-like Martian rock, which left a reddish powder on your skin when you brushed against it. There were only two bedrooms, which must have meant that Tomasz, Teddy, and Jerzy shared a room.

If they sometimes *were* a little wild, who could blame them. Rachel remembered her fights with Sonya and Shoshi back in the ghetto. But there was little sign of that now, and Tomasz quickly prepared and served the guests a cold *kruckle* bean stew. The meal provided the only light-hearted moment when the beans made themselves known in sound and smell, leading to a round of giggling finger-pointing until Mrs. Gdanska stormed out of her room, distributing swats to all three boys with a fine indifference to "who started it." She took the opportunity to announce the sleeping arrangements in a tone that brooked no disagreement—the Webbs would take her bed, while Rachel, Anya, Gun, and Sonya would sleep in the boys' room. Tomasz, Teddy, and Jerzy found themselves corners of the combined living room/kitchen to stretch out in, while Mrs. Gdanska slept in an easy chair that didn't look all that easy to Rachel. Thumper, of course, made himself at home wherever he pleased.

Rachel ended up sharing a bed with Anya. In repose, with the mask of self-confidence Anya wore all day lowered, the princess's face looked more than ever like the one Rachel saw in the mirror.

Does that mean that if I could feel about myself the way she does about herself, I could be like her? It seemed an impossible dream. She turned away from her near-twin and looked at a blurry family picture on the wall. The faces were difficult to make out in the flickering candle-light, but she studied Mr. Gdanski—she had heard Mrs. Gdanska refer to him as Thad. He had a tentative smile and sad eyes, eyes that reminded Rachel of her own father. The portrait blurred as tears wet her pillow.

♂

As they made their way over a low ridge with the lights of Krako-wicz glowing softly on the horizon, Tomasz took his time answering Rachel's question. "He was arrested for sedition under the old Ares," he said shortly. "This was years ago. I was still little, Jerzy was a toddler, and Teddy was a baby. Mom never would tell me exactly what 'sedition' was, but he kept a portrait of Prince Witold, Anya's father, in the grain silo he used to run. Well, lots of people have pictures of the prince, but they're too cowardly to put them on public display like Dad did." He sighed. "Or maybe too smart, depending on how you look at it. They sentenced him to five years at hard labor, so he should have been getting out around now. But then the new Ares overthrew the old one. And one of his first laws was to double the sentences of all 'traitors.' Then he confiscated their property, so we lost the silo. Then last year he, well, he, they, they...."

Rachel could hardly speak around the lump in her throat. "They killed him, didn't they?"

Tomasz nodded and jerked at the Phobos-flies' leashes. They buzzed angrily. "We were luckier than some. At least they notified us. And let us have his body. Though we had to pay first. Plus a special fee for the bullets they used. It took most of our savings. I had to drop out of school and go to work at the silo we used to own so we could make ends meet."

They walked in silence for a long time after that. Rachel's head was spinning. Thad Gdanski didn't deserve what had happened to him, and neither did his family. But at least he had had a choice. He didn't have to put that picture of Prince Witold up in his grain silo. If he'd kept it in a drawer at home and kept his mouth shut, Ares' men would have left him alone. Back on Earth, the Nazis didn't care that Dad hadn't bothered anybody as a university professor, much less Mr. Goldberg when he was selling insurance. They were Jews, and that was enough. You couldn't get away from that. *Not even on Mars.* Rachel shivered, remembering the soldiers laughing as they tossed around Moishe's hat.

"How do you stand it? How do you go on?" she said suddenly. Tomasz was perhaps the only person who could answer the question for her, even though she'd just met him.

He stopped walking, turned, and put his hands on Rachel's shoulders.

Coming up behind them, Gun and Anya also stopped walking, and Anya called out, "Hey, is anything wrong?"

"Nothing. We just need to stop for a second, Your Majesty," Tomasz said.

She and Gun took the hint and walked a little further off. Rachel looked up into Tomasz's eyes—somehow being able to look up to him was reassuring, even though he wasn't that much taller than her, and even though the glow of dawn on the eastern horizon behind him cast his face into shadow.

"I don't have any choice, Miss Rachel," he said gravely. "I'm the man of the house, now. My mom needs me, and so do Jerzy and Teddy. I can't let myself think about the fact that I'll never see Dad again—that I'll never...." He paused, blinked and continued, "I just can't. Maybe when this is all over, when that bastard Ares, begging your pardon miss, has gotten what he deserves and Princess Anya rules over this planet, maybe then I'll have time to mourn. Right now I *just don't have the time.*"

It was hard to tell what color his eyes were in the uncertain light. Some dark color, but they also glittered. Rachel wished she could drink in his strength from those wide, deep pools. He seemed to be physically about her age, yet he was a man, and what a man! A man everyone could depend on. She wondered if she could ever be as strong as that. Maybe not, but maybe she could comfort the fatherless boy he'd hidden deep within himself. She reached up, but he suddenly spun away from her and bounded off almost noiselessly, back the way they had come. Her mouth fell open.

She heard a yelp, then a familiar voice. A familiar, annoying voice saying, "Ow! Let go of me!" Gun and Anya hurried over to join Rachel just as Tomasz came back, his arm wrapped firmly around a small figure.

Rachel groaned. "Sonya, I told you to stay put with the Gdanskis and help them take care of Mr. Webb!"

"But that's *bor*-ing," Sonya whined as she wriggled free of Tomasz's grip. "You guys are going to kill that bad old Ares and take over the kingdom, right? I want to help!" She stuck out her chest. "I may be only a girl, but I can fight!"

Especially if you're up against your little sister. She wanted to laugh and smack Sonya's face, at the same time. But another thought brought her up short. *Sonya's no different from Tomasz or me. She also lost her parents. And her sister!* Rachel stared at her. *No, she's not like me. Like Tomasz, she's not letting it stop her. Not letting it crush her.*

But hugging *Sonya* would just be going too far. "Well, now that the brat's come all this way, I suppose she'd better stay with us," Rachel said.

"There's not much choice," Anya agreed, and wagged her finger under Sonya's nose. "But you'd better do what we tell you, and no more talk about what we're going to do to Ares! This isn't some fairy tale!"

"Yes, Princess," Sonya said.

30

Afternoon shadows climbed the sandstone buildings as Rachel and the others stumbled into a neighborhood of Krakowicz that reminded her a little of the Warsaw Ghetto. That is, it was the sleaziest, most run-down part of town, heavy with the stink of untreated sewage. Worse, the presence of armed soldiers made people scuttle around in fear, although here unlike in Warsaw nobody seemed to be starving, patched and threadbare as their "exotic" tunics might be. But the sight of all those rusty-red uniforms obliged the hungry and thirsty travelers to dodge down alleyways and flatten themselves into neglected corners, sometimes more than once in the same block. Rachel stifled a sneeze as she waited for a pair of soldiers to pass by and asked Tomasz in a whisper how much further they had to go.

"My aunt and uncle live in the next street," he whispered back.

"Are you sure they'll be home?"

He shrugged. "Uncle Kris—he's Dad's little brother—has been out of work for more than a year. There's just no call for canal engineers anymore, with all the war talk. He used to go out drinking but Margo won't let him anymore, not with money as tight as it is and the baby to feed."

Sounds like a fun family. Would the parents of a little baby want to chance having the most famous fugitive on the planet stay with them? At least on the surface, though, it seemed she needn't have been concerned. Kris, who turned out to be a tall, broadly built man with a bushy beard, welcomed "my little man Tommy!" with a slap on the back that would have sent anyone else sprawling, and followed it up with a bone-crushing hug. "You look just like Thad did when we was kids," he drawled.

It must have been tough for Tomasz to hear that, but he merely nodded seriously. "They're big shoes to fill, Uncle Kris."

"You've certainly got big enough feet! Just look how you've grown!" exclaimed Margo, a short, round-faced woman, who was visibly pregnant. In the crook of her right arm was the baby, who looked at the guests silently with huge dark eyes. When Anya walked in the couple grew as round-eyed as their son. Kris bowed low, while Margo dipped in an awkward curtsey.

"Please don't," Anya said with a sad little smile. "I'm a wanted criminal, not anyone's ruler."

"Not to us, you're not," Kris said firmly. "Please, consider whatever is best in our poor home your own."

The home really was poor, two little rooms crowded with bedding, pots and pans, and what must have been Kris' work tools—a battered tripod, various measuring implements, and a sturdy-looking pick and shovel.

Anya shook her head. "I wouldn't have thought anyone could neglect the canals worse than the previous Ares, but the so-called world-conqueror actually has him beat. What does he plan to do, transport all of Earth's water to Mars after he conquers it?"

Kris laughed uneasily. "Don't make jokes like that, Your Highness. You're liable to give the maniac ideas."

"You're right, of course," she sighed, clearing a stack of clean diapers off a chair so she could sit down. "Well, we'd better figure out what we're doing here, so we don't have to impose on your hospitality for too long."

"I agree, but I think we may need to have a rest before anything else," Gun said, looking at Sonya, who was snoring on a sofa cushion that was leaking stuffing.

"Not for my sake," Rachel said. *I'm not just a useless whiny Earth girl!* "I'm not tired at all."

She blinked. The far wall of the room sped away.

♂

Everything had gone dark, and there was a heavy weight on her chest. She pushed it off but it rolled onto her ribs, making her gasp. She struggled with the weight, which finally slid off her and landed, gently snoring, on the floor. *Gently snoring?* Sonya's head had been crushing her chest, but she hadn't even woken up. Rachel staggered to her feet. In the corners and on the battered sofas lay various still dark forms. Her stomach rumbled. *I must have missed supper. Maybe they left me something.*

A slight noise outside made her freeze in place. *Someone's out there.* She scrabbled for anything that could be used as a weapon. The frying pan still had some greasy scraps of bean stew left in it. She grabbed it and inched toward the door, shoving food in her mouth. The door was slightly open, bumping softly against its frame in a gentle night breeze. Rachel eased it open, praying that it wouldn't squeak. A dark figure stood on the left. Rachel raised the frying pan high.

The figure turned and Tomasz eyed her in surprise.

"Rachel, what are you doing up?" he whispered, laying his hand on her arm. The frying pan slid out of her grasp, but Tomasz grabbed it before it could clatter on the cobblestones.

"I, um, I heard a noise." *Stupid, stupid, stupid. Tomasz is going to laugh at me.*

But he nodded gravely. "Gun, Princess Anya, and I are taking turns standing watch."

Rachel bowed her head. *Of course they didn't give me a shift, they think I'm too useless to do anything but scream.*

Well, she'd show them. "Why don't you get some sleep? I'll take the rest of your shift."

He nodded gratefully.

"I can't keep my eyes open." He yawned. "We would've given you a shift, but you were already asleep. Come to think of it, you didn't have supper. I can bring you some leftover *kruckle* bean stew."

Rachel sat on a little bench outside the front door, and Tomasz brought her a bowl of stew and sat beside her. As soon as she had finished wolfing down the beans, her stomach voiced its displeasure. "Don't you Martians get tired of beans all the time?"

"It *does* get a little boring," he admitted, "but ordinary people can't afford much else, and since the rationing started it's hard to get enough food even if you have the money. Even thescnuts are hard to get, unless you're willing to pay a lot on the black market." He stopped and blinked. "But you're not Martian? I never met an offworlder who could speak Marpolski so well. Not that I've met many offworlders!"

"I'm from Poland, on Earth. Our language is kind of similar.... But it's a wonder the Martian atmosphere isn't half bean farts." Rachel clapped both hands over her mouth.

Tomasz chuckled, then yawned again. "Thanks for taking my shift. Really. But leave the frying pan. Just raise the alarm quietly if you see the police or anything." He stood, stifling another yawn, and Rachel stood with him. "Good night," he mumbled, turning his head toward her. Something soft brushed her forehead.

Was it his lips? Had he kissed her? Had she, Rachel, just been kissed? Hot and cold waves chased across her skin. She wanted to run back into the house and ask Tomasz if he'd just kissed her. But what if he hadn't? He'd laugh. And if he *had*, and she was so naïve that she had to ask, wouldn't he be insulted? Her mind tumbled around and around this question just as she had tumbled around and around Eddie's rocket on the perilous journey from Ganymede. Soon she felt almost as dizzy as she had then. Maybe it hadn't been such a great idea to volunteer to stand watch. After all, she was still tired and weak from the long walk.... Maybe it wouldn't hurt if she closed her eyes just for a second....

She lifted her head and crossed her arms. NO! She was responsible for everyone's safety now, not just her own! She stood straight and stared at the dark street, the slummy buildings, thinking again how drearily familiar they looked even though they were on an alien world. Gray predawn light began to seep into the alleys. Back in Warsaw, before the Nazis came, the day would just be beginning at this hour. The milkman would come around clinking his bottles. There would be trash pickup. Sometimes a ragman would drive by in a cart just like the one rounding the corner down the street. The cart would be pulled by a lame old horse or sometimes by mules, just like the pair pulling the cart toward her now. And the ragman would call out his wares, sometimes in Yiddish just like this one was doing: *Al-tee zochen, al-tee zochen....*

She shook her head. Had she fallen asleep again? Rachel pinched her left arm savagely. *Ow!* But the mule-drawn cart was still there. And the driver was indeed chanting *al-tee zochen, al-tee zochen.* She peered up at his face. "Moishe!" She darted forward.

"Interested in some gently used clothing, miss?" he said loudly in Marpolski, "Be quiet, you silly girl, we don't know who's watching!" he hissed in Yiddish.

"Oh! Sorry," she whispered back. Then, louder, "Yes, I sure could use a new dress. Please come inside and show us what you've got!"

She turned to open the door and was almost knocked over by Anya.

"Jack! Where's Jack!" Anya breathed. "Oh! My darling...."

Rachel dodged Moishe and the man behind him. Jack? She looked again. He looked a lot like Jack, but wasn't. He was too skinny and sad to be Jack.

"Hello, Jack's princess. I'm Jim," the man said heavily. "I'm afraid I have some bad news."

♂

Anya hustled Jim and Moishe into the house, where everyone was wide awake. Kris and Margo offered them two battered chairs. Jim accepted a bowl of *kruckle* bean stew, while Moishe took a glass of tea.

Rachel stared at Moishe. He explained that he'd hidden in his cart outside the Martian army base for hours. He didn't have to add that he would have been shot out of hand if he'd been caught. When Jim and the other condemned men arrived, he hid them under the same tarpaulins Rachel and the others had used, and drove away as fast as Azri and Shimmie could go.

Anya added that if he was caught *now* he would be tortured before they killed him, and much worse, everyone in his village would be in danger. But he'd done the right thing anyway.

"What happened to Jack?" she asked, turning to Jim. Rachel admired her poise.

"He saved us, princess. He stormed the prison all by himself, and broke us out of the death cell. I led him and the others to a hole under the perimeter fence, but he insisted all the Martian prisoners go out first—and then me, when the MPs were about to catch us."

"My hero," Anya murmured.

"Moishe rode hell-for-leather across the desert. Who would've thought you could *make* mules go that fast? They still would have caught us for sure, only he seemed to know every gulch and canyon between the base and the outskirts of Krakowicz. Once we got there, most of the guys wanted to split up right away, but Leszek thought it would be better to stick together until we got to his folks' house—they own a flower shop in the Bazaar and it's way easier to avoid the cops in there. Leszek's dad told us that he'd heard through the underground that Kris and Margo had taken in some fugitives from Lvovinsk, and here we are."

"That sounds really efficient," Rachel said, "but weren't you afraid that someone might betray you to the police?"

"We didn't have any choice," Moishe said.

"If we don't trust each other, we're just as bad as our enemies," Anya said, folding her arms and eyeing Rachel as if she'd insulted the planet Mars.

That's very noble, but awfully naïve. Rachel had been naïve, until she'd learned the hard lessons of the intrigue and vicious anti-Semitism her father had had to deal with at the university. Her parents always tried to protect her from it, but she'd always taken their closed bedroom door and hushed voices as a positive commandment to eavesdrop. Once the Nazis occupied Warsaw, they started rounding up Jews. A former student of Dad's was supposed to hide them, but he'd been mysteriously unavailable at the critical moment. And that was why they ended up crammed into the slummy apartment with the Goldbergs.

Someone pounded on the door and Rachel jumped. *It's Lvovinsk all over again.* Her stomach turned over.

Margo stood and motioned everyone into the bedroom. Kris frowned, but she whispered in his ear and he nodded. Rachel's hands shook. Tomasz squeezed her shoulder and gave her a reassuring smile. She smiled back. *I can be brave for him, at least.*

In the bedroom, Rachel started counting heads. "Where's Moishe?" she whispered to Tomasz, who shrugged and pointed to the door to the front room.

Rachel held her breath as she heard the outer door open. "I hope you get good use out of the pans, missus," Moishe said loudly. "Excuse me, Your Excellency."

"No, you better stay and listen to this too, Jew," a high-pitched, nasal voice said. The baby started to cry.

"Shut that brat up! This is important!" the stranger said. He lowered his voice and Rachel strained to hear. "Lord Ares…important announcement…entire block."

As soon as the door slammed, everyone crowded out of the bedroom.

"What did he want?" asked Anya.

Kris looked tired and irritated. "We have to watch whatever the 'important announcement' is on the telescreen at the Thescnut Tree Café down the block. But damn that Leo anyway. Other block captains aren't so strict about keeping attendance."

Margo glanced around the room. "I should start breakfast so we'll be finished by the time we have to go."

"I'll take your place," Rachel said. "It might be interesting."

"Trust me, it won't be," said Kris. "It's usually some garbage about the latest super-weapon that's sure to conquer the entire Solar System for the Martian Master Race. And you have to look enthusiastic, too, because these damn telescreens watch *you* while you're watching *them*."

"Sounds awful," Rachel said, but she looked forward to escaping from the crowded little house, with its smells of sour milk, dirty diapers, and the sweat of so many frightened people.

"I'll come too." Tomasz winked at Rachel and her face grew warm.

"Suit yourselves," said Kris, and a few minutes later the three of them set off. The narrow avenue filled with shabbily dressed, grumpy-looking men and women, some of whom greeted Kris. He introduced Tomasz as his nephew and Rachel as "Tommy's girlfriend." Her heart tried to jump out of her throat at that, so she just nodded. Tomasz smiled a little and gently squeezed her hand. Suddenly she didn't care what a bunch of strangers thought. She squeezed his hand back, and they walked in silence to the Café. A hand-lettered sign on its door said it was closed until further notice due to rationing. A small crowd was already gathered around a spindly thescnut tree. No leaves adorned its branches, and a small gully filled with trash circled its thin trunk. The tree itself was barely over seven feet, and it looked too frail to support the weight of the boxy device dangling from one of its branches. It was made of metal and had what looked like a dull mirror on one side. It suddenly lit up, and a picture of the modified Texian flag Mars was now using fluttered in a breeze.

A bright and brassy trumpet sounded over the suddenly silent crowd.

"Attention! Your attention! Our Royal Majesty, Lord Ares, has an important announcement to make!"

Rachel stared mesmerized at the screen.

The fluttering flag dissolved and was replaced by a large, elaborate room. Ares—Johnny Marshall, Katie had called him—sat smirking on a huge throne, his hands casually draped over the arms. Rachel snorted. He was no more Martian than she was! His mustache reminded her of the Soviet dictator Stalin. Marshall had grayish blue eyes and, again like Stalin, pockmarked skin. How could the Martians have accepted him as their leader for one minute? Two niches with statues were on the wall behind him. One of the statues moved, and Rachel gasped. Katie and Jack, bound and gagged! Tomasz squeezed her hand hard. Rachel nodded slightly, and turned her attention back to the telescreen, where Marshall was drawling away in very ungrammatical Marpolski.

"My fellow Martians, good morning. As y'all know, 'cause I told you so many times, there's sinister forces working against our destiny as the Master Race. They know we will conquest the Solar System, and they doesn't like it!"

Rachel wanted to laugh in Johnny Marshall's face. But the fact that he could talk like that and nobody *dared* laugh at him—that was terrifying.

He stood up and gestured grandly at his two captives. "Behold, behind my royal self y'all see two spies captured by our loyal hardworkin' Martian Rangers. Spies for Earth! They will meet the end of all traitors, o'course, but I got somethin' special planned for them!" He paused dramatically. "They shall be sacrificed atop Olympus Mons! Thrown alive into the crater, that's what I means to say! A real auto-daffy!"

Katie twisted her head, freeing her mouth from the gag, and hollered in English, "That's auto-da-fé, you ignorant pig Johnny Marshall! Fé! It rhymes with pay, which is what you're gonna do for this stunt—"

A guard slammed the butt of his rifle into her chest, and she toppled out of the niche. The guard kicked her, joined by several others.

A bellow seemed to shake the telescreen. The picture swung wildly. Jack had somehow gotten free of *his* bonds, and threw himself on the guards, shouting, "Unhand her, you brutes!"

But they're not even using their hands, A dozen more guards came running and threw themselves on Jack. *At least they've messed up Marshall's little propaganda show.*

But the fake Ares seemed unruffled. The picture steadied and caught him beckoning imperiously. "My fellow Martians, y'all can see plain as days how dangerous these-here spies are. The auto-daffy shall take place tomorrow at dawn, soon as my priests can arrange for the god Moloch to be present so their souls can feed his hunger. Thus shall the war god be with we in our war of conquest. Gods bless you, and gods bless the United Empire of Mars. And a good mornin' to y'all."

♂

Katie awoke lying on her back in darkness. Had she gone blind? Nope. There was a little light. Hard to breathe, though. Her chest felt like it was on fire. She tried to sit up, but a hand pushed her gently back down.

"Better not move, Kaitlyn," Jack's voice said out of the darkness.

Why was he being so formal?

"I think the bastards broke your ribs. If you turn the wrong way you could puncture a lung, and I can't help you. I've been yelling for a doctor, but the guards just laugh. Uh, sorry for the bad language."

Katie chuckled, then gasped at the pain. "It's all right, Jack. You can call them bastards." She shut her eyes, and red dots danced around the edges of her field of vision. "I wouldn't worry about no doctor, anyhow, Jack. Not after what Johnny Marshall said, may he roast in hell."

"You understood him? How?"

"Anya taught me a little Marpolski."

"Wow. Even with her help, I never got much beyond 'hello' and 'put your hands up, foul villain!' myself."

"Yeah. Anyway, that sumbitch said he's gonna throw us into Olympus Mons to appease the god Moloch."

Jack Flash said a word Rachel had probably never written for him.

"It's a funny thing, isn't it, Jack?" Katie said after a moment. The red dots were growing larger. She opened her eyes. They were still there.

"What is, Kaitlyn?"

"All these guys. These world conquering types. Alexander, Julius Caesar, Genghis Khan, Napoleon, Hitler, Stalin…and their two-bit imitator, Johnny Marshall. They want to rule over everything and everyone, don't they? Like God Himself, for the people that believe in Him. But God is the creator, they say. He makes life. All these guys know how to do is kill, and kill, and kill some more."

"I don't understand it any more than you do, Kaitlyn," Jack said.

Katie stared at the ceiling. The dots grew into red blotches that pulsed against the blackness. The pain grew with them, until it threatened to drown her. "Something else real funny, Jack." She had to focus to say each word.

"What is it, Kaitlyn?"

"H-hero."

"What?"

"I never thought I'd die 'longside a real, gen-you-wine hero."

A drop of something cool fell on her burning face. She licked her lips and tasted salt.

Jack's voice came from far, far away. "Me neither, Kaitlyn Webb."

31

Rachel buried her head in her hands. Everyone had been arguing for hours, ever since she, Tomasz, and Kris had returned with their devastating news. Hours ticking toward the moment when Katie and Jack would be thrown alive into the crater atop Olympus Mons, the tallest mountain in the Solar System. In her own world, Olympus was a dead volcano, extinct for millions of years. So why did it have to be furiously alive here? The erupting volcano and Johnny Marshall's villainy were so gaudy and over-the-top. This was the sort of thing that gave science fiction a bad name. She should have listened to her mother and never started writing "such trash." *But then I'd probably have been rounded up with the Goldbergs and shipped to a labor camp. Or killed. But Katie would have been safe! Or at least her parents would have been there with her in that prison camp. It's my fault she's in danger!*

Gun, Sonya and Tomasz had brainstormed one hare-brained rescue scheme after another. Gun's sounded the least improbable, but it would require them to build a glider in the next few hours and somehow haul it up Olympus Mons without attracting attention. Once there, she explained, she'd be able to take advantage of the thermal updrafts created by the roaring heat of the magma in the crater to soar high above the procession and drop improvised bombs on it.

"Those jerks will panic at the first explosion and go running in all directions, and it'll be a cinch for Jack and Katie to escape."

"But where would you get the materials to build one?" Kris demanded.

Gun turned on him. "I thought you were an engineer?"

He flushed. "I'm a canal engineer, dammit. And I can't get at any of my old tools and materials, except the few things I've crammed in here."

"What about a Martian Space Force base?"

"You've got to be kidding. They're better guarded than the Imperial Palace. You'd have a better chance trying to storm *that* to rescue your friends."

"Well, have you got any better ideas?" Gun demanded. Kris looked at the floor. "Does anybody?" Sonya opened her mouth and Gun said, "I'm sorry, Sonya, but 'building a big enough gun to shoot Ares right in his fat face' isn't going to work in the time we've got."

"If we had more time I could talk to some of my old colleagues and see what materials we could cobble together for a glider," Kris said in a pleading tone. "But I can't do it in the next couple of hours!"

Moishe suddenly said, "Forgive me for making this suggestion, but my people have long experience with tyrants such as Lord Ares. One thing we know: they are always greedy. Perhaps you could offer a ransom."

This produced a thoughtful silence, but finally Kris shook his head and said, "No offense, rabbi, but you don't understand just how evil Ares is. He won't want money for his captives. He wants them to suffer and die in front of the whole planet so that everyone can see how powerful he is."

Moishe mumbled, "I'm not a rabbi. My uncle is. I wish he was here."

But what possible solution could he have to offer? Then Kris's words struck home and her eyes filled with tears. He was right, Johnny Marshall was in another league altogether—a league of sadists who enjoyed inflicting pain. Katie had told her as much.

Anya had been quiet, so when she spoke she instantly had everyone's full attention. "There's only one way to save them," she said. "I'll marry Ares, if he agrees to let Jack and Katie go." Everyone started shouting, and she held up her hand. "No, it's the only way. And once I'm married to him, I can try to be a good influence. It's my duty, not just to Jack and Katie, but to my whole kingdom."

My duty to my kingdom. Suddenly the helplessness that had gripped Rachel from the moment she had seen Katie and Jack tied up and beaten, if not from the moment she had stepped onto Martian soil, fell away as she realized what she had to do. She stood slowly. "No, princess," she said quietly. "You can't do that. It would destroy the hopes of all the good people on this planet." She raised her chin. "I'll go in your place."

The room was silent. Even the baby, who had been wriggling and squalling in Margo's arms, stilled.

"This isn't what I meant! It is forbidden to ransom one human being with another! The Torah forbids it!" said Moishe.

"Then why didn't you speak up when the princess offered herself?" Rachel spoke Yiddish so only Moishe would understand.

He had the decency to blush. "That's not the point, *maidele!* This isn't some fairy tale here! You're not from Mars, you don't know what Ares is capable of!"

But you, my friend, have never heard of the Nazis.

"I do know, Moishe. But I'm surprised at you. Remember Esther, in the Bible? If she could marry King Ahash'verush of Persia, why can't I marry the king of Mars?"

"Ares is not Ahash'verush, *maidele*," Moishe said, matching her confidential tone. "He's Haman." The villain of the Book of Esther, the one who had plotted to kill all the Jews.

"That may be, but I've still got to try."

"You can't do it, Ray." Tomasz stood and put his hand on her arm, a now-familiar gesture.

She raised a defiant eyebrow. "Why not, Tommy?"

"Because you don't look like..." His voice trailed off as he darted a glance at Anya.

"But I do. I look just like her, and the resemblance will be even closer with a change of clothes and a, hmm, a somewhat more delicate way of walking."

"By God and the burning thistlecat, she *does* look like the princess," Kris said in a half-whisper.

"I don't know why I never noticed it before, but there *is* an amazing resemblance," Gun said softly. Then she shook herself. "But that's beside the point. Nobody is sacrificing themselves to Ares! Not you, Ray, and not you, Your Highness."

Rachel pulled away from Tomasz. "No, it has to be me. We can't risk losing Anya. She's too important to the future of Mars. Hell, she's too important to the whole Solar System. I'm just a stranger. Someone who doesn't even belong here. And I—I have my reasons." *Ones that Katie would understand, if she were here. Though by God she'd give me a harder fight than any of you are doing!* Rachel turned to Anya. "I'm right, princess. Aren't I right?"

"No, Ray, it's *my* duty...."

"To stay in hiding and lead your people," Rachel said firmly. "It's settled, then. Anya, you'll lend me some of your good clothes and I'll be on my way. Tomasz, you can escort me to the Imperial Palace." *So I don't lose my nerve.*

No one said a word. Rachel glanced at Anya and her heart skipped a beat.

"I don't have any good clothes left," Anya said, but she looked relieved.

Anya and Margo took her into the bedroom to prepare. After she had changed into Margo's wedding dress, long and pale pink, with a relatively restrained complement of ruffles, and Anya had piled her hair high in formal Martian style, Rachel took a deep breath and asked, "How do I look?"

"You are the sister I always wanted," Anya whispered, taking her hand.

Rachel squeezed Anya's fingers and smiled around the lump in her throat.

When she stepped into the front room, all heads turned in her direction, and several people gasped. Tomasz's wide-eyed, admiring gaze warmed her face and stiffened her spine. She could do this.

Gun gave an awkward half-curtsey. "If Ares doesn't fall in love with you, immediately and completely, he's as blind and stupid as he's vicious and cruel," she said. There was a murmur of agreement.

Sonya—sullen, complaining Sonya—just stood and stared at her, mouth open and eyes alight with wonder.

"Close your mouth, Sonya, you'll catch Phobos-flies," Rachel said. "And those things can really choke you." Sonya shut her mouth with an audible snap.

Kris handed her a dust-storm poncho, and Rachel put it on. She would go incognito until she reached the plaza in front of the Imperial Palace. Otherwise, she might be recognized and arrested, and then quietly *disappeared*. Her only chance was to make her proposition in full public view.

Tomasz silently slipped his arm through hers and they walked outside.

Moishe murmured a few words. She hoped it was a prayer.

Tomasz was silent as they walked from the winding, stinking alleys of the slums through a crowded marketplace with foods and spices of unearthly shades and odors so pungent they could stop your breath. *Must be the bazaar Jim mentioned.* Then they found themselves in a well-to-do neighborhood. The homes were built of that hard Martian *pukkstone*, cut and polished to a roseate shine. Fountains played in the gardens of some of the fancier places, amid the red-tinted, fleshy-looking leaves of exotic plants.

"This is where all of Ares' hangers-on live," Tomasz said quietly. His frown deepened. "In Lvovinsk they keep cutting the water ration. You need to present a ration coupon just to use that dirty old well in the plaza. Mom makes us eat in the dark so we don't have to see how dirty the plates are—she's ashamed she doesn't have the water to clean them properly—and sometimes the food ain't fit for looking at, either. As for our clothes, well," he smiled in embarrassment, "I hope the smell hasn't been bothering you too much, Ray. But here! They spit water up into the sky, just to taunt us!" He clenched his fist, but Rachel worked her fingers into his until he relaxed.

"We're going to change all that for the better," she said softly. "It *has* to change." She put one foot in front of the other and kept her gaze on the ground. She would *not* think of everything that could go wrong, not just with their plan but with any attempt to "make things better." She half-hid her face with a fold of the cloak to avoid attracting attention. It was strange and exhilarating, this walk through an alien city. The Martians used rounded corners, as she'd already noticed in Lvovinsk, although the rough-hewn stone they used there obscured the builders' intentions. Here, though, grand mansions were giving way to looming government buildings with massive porticos and fifty-foot-tall columns, all with gracefully flowing lines, as if in building them the Martians had put all their yearning for water into stone. You could almost forget that this place had been ruled by tyrants for generations. Almost, that is, until you saw the police who swarmed down the broad boulevards, their faces hidden behind mirrored sun-shields.

Rachel squeezed Tomasz's hand, and he squeezed back. "Courage," he whispered.

She nodded slightly. She had *not* created this world, because it was more wonderful and more terrible than she could have imagined. And there were too many unexpected details, like those fountains, beautiful despite—or maybe because of—the injustice they represented, and the slightly sweaty warmth of Tomasz's hand and the way he rubbed the ball of his thumb against her palm.

"Tommy," she whispered. "I—why have we stopped walking?"

He drew her into a building's shadow. "See that open space there at the end of the boulevard?" he said. "That's Imperial Palace Plaza. You're going to have to walk the rest of the way alone." He looked a little pale. "Unless you want to forget this whole crazy idea. It's not your job to save the world, Rachel. Not *this* world. You're not even a Martian!"

She smiled sadly. "Actually, I'm afraid it *is* my job, Tommy. But—"

He leaned over and kissed her softly. His lips were warm and dry. She blinked, then put her arms around his shoulders and held him close.

"I've never kissed a princess before." He pulled away. Her gaze followed him as he disappeared around a column as thick as a small house. Disappeared, without a backward glance.

Because if he looked back, he wouldn't be able to let me go. Before she could change her mind, she set off down the boulevard, taking one ordinary step after another. *Look at your feet. Concentrate.*

One step. Her parents.

Another step. The typewriter on which she'd first dreamed of Mars, of Princess Anya and Jack Flash.

Another step. The living, breathing reality of Jack and Anya, so much stronger and sweeter and more annoying than she'd ever imagined.

Another step. Katie, who had become her best friend.

Step, step, step. Wanda and the burning thistlecat, instead of Moses and the burning bush. Queen Esther and Princess Anya. The Hasidim of the Martian canyons.... And suddenly, she was there. The plaza stretched all around her, a mile wide, with a fountain whose spray seemed almost to touch the feathery mare's tail clouds in the thin blue sky. There were soldiers everywhere. One noticed her and pointed, sauntering off in her direction with two of his fellows. When they were close enough for her to see their faces (the soldier who had pointed had a crooked nose, as if he'd broken it in a fight), she threw off her cloak. All three men staggered back as if struck.

"I am the Princess Anya Olympulska," Rachel said, loud and clear. "And I demand that Lord Ares come and parley with me." *Parley, that's a good touch. Just the kind of word a princess would use.*

"We'll take you to him." One man took a tentative step and stretched out his hand.

She stepped back and said louder still, "No! I demand Lord Ares come out here, where the people can see and hear us."

Among the soldiers were ordinary sightseers, and they were already pointing and whispering among themselves.

The soldier retreated and huddled with his fellows. After a moment one of the others darted off in the direction of the palace. An interminable time passed, during which no one came close to her. As if by unspoken agreement, a crowd quickly gathered but left her standing in an empty circle of crimson flagstones some fifty feet across. Rachel kept her chin up. *I am the Princess Anya Olympulska.* She repeated it over and over, crowding out all other thoughts. *I am the Princess Anya Olympulska. I am the Princess Anya Olympulska. ...*

Suddenly a commotion broke out in front of her, and the crowd parted to let a lone figure stride forward. The mustachioed man she'd seen on the telescreen. Lord Ares. Katie's Johnny Marshall. In person, he was not very impressive. He had at most an inch or two on her, and under his purple toga he looked as if he was running to fat.

Rachel looked him slowly up and down. She wanted to laugh. This was the man who terrified millions of people?

"Well?" he barked suddenly. "They say you will ask—did asked—*asking* to speak with me. Why should I speaking with you, and not cutting off your head here and now for the traitor you are?"

"Do not dare speak to the heir of the House of Olympulska in this manner!" *In this manner! Nice one, Rachel!* "I am here to demand the freedom of the two hostages you are threatening to murder like a pagan barbarian!"

"Demand?" Marshall said. He muttered the word in English, as if to confirm what he had heard. "Demand?" Suddenly he began to laugh. He laughed so hard he doubled over and tears came to his eyes. For a moment the crowd stayed deathly quiet, but people began to elbow each other and a roar of forced laughter went up.

It was the most horrible sound Rachel had ever heard. But eventually Ares straightened up and glared at her, and the crowd stopped laughing as abruptly as it had started, leaving no sound but the wind blowing through the vast plaza.

"You demand—" he started to say, but Rachel cut him off.

"And in exchange, I will agree to marry you, to bring peace to our world."

A gasp echoed in the Plaza. Ares stared at her, and Rachel stared right back.

"Very well," he said slowly, "it would be as you saying. Free spies," he said with a touch of exasperation. "Spies be free. I oath."

Rachel shook her head slowly. "Oh no, you don't. Your word is worth less than what comes out a thistlecat's rear end." Someone let out a hysterical giggle. "You let them go right here, right now. I see them walk away. Then I agree to marry you."

Lord Ares flushed. But his beady little eyes darted back and forth, seemingly taking the temper of the crowd. "Yes. It be as you saying. Spies free, *now*."

The soldiers stirred behind him. Rachel waited, eyeball-to-eyeball with the ugly little toad who planned to conquer the Solar System.

I am the Princess Anya Olympulska. I am the Princess Anya Olympulska! Never had a lie held so much power.

Eventually a commotion broke out in front of her. A man staggered out of the crowd, holding something in his arms. No, it was some*one* he was holding.

Rachel swallowed a scream.

Jack's bruised and swollen face looked equally shocked. "Anya, what—"

"She me marry, save your sorry ass!" Ares jeered.

Before Jack could react, Rachel ran to him. "Jack!" she whispered. "It's me, Rachel!"

His mouth fell open.

Rachel's gaze fell on the motionless body he carried. "Katie! Is she—"

"Alive, barely, I think," Jack whispered. "Rachel, you can't—"

She's alive. She's alive.

Rachel turned away and moved to Ares' side. He leered at her. His breath stank so much Rachel almost gagged.

"Very well," she said, "let me see them walk away, and then I'll go with you."

"LEAVE, TRAITOR!" Ares barked at Jack. "And be grateful for my mercy!"

Several soldiers aimed their guns at Jack. He opened his mouth, but no sound came out. Then he began to back slowly away. The crowd moved aside to let him go, and her gaze followed him until he had backed all the way down the grand boulevard Rachel had walked up an eternity ago, turned a corner and vanished.

32

"If you're just returning from your officially approved three-minute bathroom break, there are two minutes and fifty seconds left in the second quarter of this very exciting game pitting the West Tharsis Thistlecats against the Elysium Mons Mountainbats. Zbig, you wanna sum up what's happened so far?"

"Love to, Gusav," beamed Zbig. "The Thistles came on strong in the first quarter, but then their star quarterback Wojciech Jaruzelski missed that field goal, and under Lord Ares' rules was impaled and burned to death on the fifty-yard line. That did not make the West Tharsis fans happy, and it took the entire 91st Army Battalion to put down the riot. Police haven't yet released casualty figures, but what *is* certain is that the Mountainbats came squeaking back strongly once order was restored, even though *their* star linebacker, Wladyslaw Gomulka, had been impaled himself just last week for failing to stop that seventy-yard pass by East Tharsis in last Saturday's game."

"Yes, some very sad events," agreed Gusav. "So now Elysium is ahead 14-13—would be a tie, but for Jaruzelski's missed field goal, and he certainly paid for that in blood, ha ha! The countdown now at one minute, thirty-four seconds, but the Thistlecats' coach, Lech Pawel, has just called a time-out. He'll want to keep it short with this crowd though—they can't wait for the halftime show!"

"And on top of those scantily clad cheerleaders—well, in *addition* to those scantily clad cheerleaders," Zbig chuckled boozily, "and let's face it, it's thanks to them that football became as popular as it is, as fast as it did here on Mars—though no question, anything that Lord Ares loves would've caught on real fast anyway—anyway—what was I saying, Gusav?"

"Looks like you took a few too many tackles head-on, ol' buddy," Gusav said. "*After* the scantily clad cheerleaders, of course, we've got the royal wedding coming up!"

"Oh yes, the royal wedding," Zbig burped. "And that Princess Anya, she's one hot little number herself! Though unhappily for us viewers, she gets to wear something more than pasties and a g-string."

"Hey, a little less *lèse majesté*, buddy ol' pal!"

"Les Majorski? Who said anything about him? He was burned at the stake last year for failure to inner-cept!"

"Just have a little more respect, that's all I'm saying, Zbiggie. Or a little more beer. Or a lot more beer! What the hey, I'm gonna have one too."

♂

Trash still smoldered high in the stands where Jack crouched, sighting along the barrel of the zap-gun he'd taken from a soldier who had been trampled by enraged West Tharsis fans in the first-quarter riots. Too bad about the poor guy, but he was already dead, and his weapon was a lot better than the one Jack had been carrying (though not as good as Annabelle; he'd vowed revenge for her loss). The whole riot had been a godsend, actually, making it a lot easier for him, Gun, and Anya to get into position, as those fans who had not become casualties or fled had moved into the lower tiers, leaving lots of room for maneuver. Not that Anya should have been there at all, of course. But she had quietly insisted, and Gun said she'd better come along too "to watch both your fool backs."

At least he didn't have to worry about Tomasz, Sonya, or Jim. He'd sent the three of them back to Agnieszka Gdanska's home in Moishe's mule cart, giving Tommy and Jim both strict instructions to watch the Earth girl every minute to make sure she didn't sneak back to Krakowicz. Tommy had been reluctant to go, insisting that he had to help save Rachel. They'd probably been hiding in dark corners to hold hands and kiss. Well, good for them, but Jack didn't need any more lives on his conscience.

"Your mom needs you," Jack told Tommy, and when he bristled, Jack put his hand on his shoulder and said, "*I* need you, to protect not only Sonya, but Katie." Jack and Gun had decided that Katie, who had not woken up since Jack had carried her away from the palace, should also be taken to Agnieszka Gdanska's home, where a loyalist doctor had agreed to care for her. That far away from the city, it would be hard to get the equipment the doctor might need, but also hard for the secret police to sneak up on them. And besides, Thumper was there; if she woke up (*when* she woke up) she'd need his furry comfort. Tommy nodded reluctantly at this logic.

"And when she does wake up," Jack said, squeezing the boy's upper arm, "you have to make sure she stays in bed and doesn't try to go rescuing Rachel when she needs to rest and recover. All right? You have a big responsibility, son. And you too, little brother," he added, turning to Jim, who eyed him resentfully. "What? Don't tell me you want to come along on this suicide mission."

"What if I did?" Jim snapped. "You're still the big brother, the one who gets to make all the decisions."

Jack glared. *Is this the thanks I get for saving your life?* All he said was, "You know that if you stay here in Krakowicz, much less go out in public at the stadium, you'll be caught and killed quicker than you can say, 'Jack Flash to the rescue!'"

"Oh yeah, I know that. Wouldn't want you to have to save the day yet again, Jackie my boy," Jim said.

Jack blinked, shook his head, and walked away. *People. I'll never understand them.*

The night before they'd embraced and cried for a long time after Jack told Jim what had happened to their parents. Dad had died in a rocket crash eight Venusian years before, and Mom took her own life less than a year later. *Too much sorrow*, she wrote in the note she left behind for Jack to find when he returned from fighting the Pyromaniacal Pirates of Pluto (whose hideout was actually on Charon, but they liked the alliteration). He remembered standing there holding the three-word note in her darkened apartment. *Too much sorrow.* Her younger son, and now her husband. But she'd thoughtfully avoided leaving a mess for Jack to clean up, by booking passage on the same line her husband had died on, and walking out of the airlock somewhere between Venus and Luna. *Too much sorrow.*

Feeling it together for the first time—Jack had never let himself cry about Dad or Mom, not even with Anya—had seemed to erase the different lives he and Jim had led, to make them twins once again. But now came this anger and resentment, these hurts from a childhood vanished and forgotten. What could he say to Jim now? *I'm sorry for saving your life?* Maybe it was better for them to be apart.

Moishe's mule cart had clattered down the street with Tomasz, Sonya, Jim, and Katie aboard. Now Jack could throw himself into his desperate plan to rescue Rachel by assassinating Lord Ares. It would have been a lot easier if he hadn't had to make allowances to protect Anya and Gun, but they both insisted on coming along. *Everyone had to be a hero.* Anya had to assuage her guilt at letting Rachel take her place, and apparently Gun felt all protective of the princess's strange double, too. He gave them both short-range radios and told them to pretend to be part of the cleaning crew. Anya had disguised herself in some of Margo's old clothes, smudging her face with charcoal and tying her hair up in a bandanna. Jack tried to keep her out of trouble by telling her he needed her to observe from as far up as possible on the northern side of stadium, high above the Thistlecats' goalposts, while he and Gun would get as close as possible to opposite ends of the fifty-yard line, he on the western side and she on the eastern side. The riot had forced them both to climb much further up, almost as high as (he hoped) Anya was standing. But this meant he and Gun were pushing the limits of a zap-gun's effective range. *Well, the limit of an* ordinary *zap-gun's effective range,* Jack sighed to himself. *Annabelle would've been a different story. Although not having to push through a crowd and worry about stray beams hitting innocent bystanders is certainly a good thing.*

Darkness had long since fallen. High up in the sky, Deimos cast a cold light bright enough to be seen from the stadium despite the overpowering glare of the enormous klieg lights mounted around the field. *Deimos, god of panic. Let's hope Ares feels a moment of that, before I fry him.*

A shrill whistle stopped the action on the field, and the two opposing teams separated and trotted daintily off. The score was still stuck at 14-13 in Elysium's favor. Jack tensed. Any second now, Ares was going to emerge on the field with Rachel at his side. They would be a good couple hundred yards away, and surrounded by other people. The shot was going to take all of Jack's skill.

There was a stir down below Jack's position. He steadied his right hand, which held the zap-gun's grip, with his left. Through the gunsight he saw the top of a red head, a tiny mass of copper curls.

Don't worry, Rachel, in a few seconds you'll be free. But then he saw another red head. And a third. Then two blond heads…four brunettes…there must have been two dozen young women…and their hair was almost all the covering they had. Quickly and efficiently, the Royal Martian Cheerleading Squad formed a pyramid.

Jack knew the statistics. At sixteen miles in height, Olympus Mons is far and away the tallest volcano in the Solar System. It has a diameter of 374 miles. The caldera, or crater, at its top measures fifty miles from side to side, and when a major eruption is brewing, as was the case now, reddish-orange magma boils up out of its depths. It is one of the wonders of the known universe, and Jack had been looking forward to seeing it, albeit without the threat of his friends being thrown into it. Now he knew the effect would be spoiled for him. The zap-gun slipped from his hand and clattered to the metal floor as he stood staring at the pyramid of nearly naked Martian cheerleaders, an even greater wonder of the known universe.

Jack's radio gave out with a loud burst of static. He jumped so high he almost fell into the next tier. "What! What is it?" he yelled frantically.

"Jack, stop watching the cheerleaders and concentrate!" Anya demanded.

♂

In a basement chamber twenty stories below the stadium, Rachel shifted uncomfortably in her chair. Her nose itched, but she couldn't scratch it, as her hands were tied behind her back. Rachel wasn't one of those girls who spends every free moment daydreaming about her wedding, but being bound with tough *kruckle* bean stalks in a reeking locker room painted fifty shades of gray wouldn't have been any part of her fantasy. She had been left here all alone for what she guessed was the better part of two hours, but all her struggles against the vinelike cords had been in vain. When all else failed she'd taken to comforting herself by thinking up every Yiddish curse she could remember to dump on Johnny Marshall's head.

"He should marry the daughter of the Angel of Death instead of me! All his teeth should fall out, except one to make him suffer! He should end up like a chandelier—hang all day and burn all night! He should...." There was a loud clang as a door opened behind her. There were voices, too low to make out what they were saying. Rachel stiffened, wondering if she dared to hope....

There was the sound of something heavy being dragged along the cement floor. A strawberry blonde in a very short red skirt appeared, her face red with effort as she dragged a heavy table with something bulky under a dust cloth.

"What is this? Who are you?" Rachel demanded. "When is somebody going to untie me? I demand to be untied! I am the princess, and..."

"Patience, patience," Johnny Marshall chuckled as he strode up beside his panting servant. He winked at Rachel. Her stomach twisted. "'Scuse me one second, my bride." He wrapped his arms around the blond woman's waist and bent her over backwards as he kissed her hard on the mouth.

"Getting in one last fling before we are married, oh Great Ares?"

"Hmm?" he said absently, standing back up and patting his greased-down black hair while the woman adjusted her skirt. "One last fling? Of course not, m'dear, I will intended—did intention—*intending* to keep having flings, every single day! Especially with my tasty little Nadia, ain't that right, sugarpie?"

"Yes, my lord," she mumbled, her eyes fixed on the table. Rachel couldn't help staring at it too.

Ares caught her gaze and chuckled. "Wondering what that is, my sweet? Surely you hear of the Corrector!"

The Corrector? That Martian agent on Venus had mentioned something about it. Some sort of torture device. Was this creep really going to torture her just before he forced her to marry him?

Ares whipped away the cover with a flourish. Rachel gasped. On the table sat a typewriter, just like the one she had smashed in the desert.

"I see you do knowing," Ares gloated. "I do you favor, you know. Right now you hate me, but in a minute you eating out of my hand."

Rachel closed her eyes. She wished she could tell Johnny Marshall to just speak in English, except that his English was probably almost as bad as his Polish. Now he was going to use that typewriter to make her do whatever he wanted, or so he thought. It wouldn't work, or at least she *hoped* it wouldn't, but she was going to have to pretend it *was* working, that she was completely under his control, at least until she could figure out a plan. But what if he wanted her to do something really gross?

"You going to want to open you eyes for this, princess," Ares cooed. "Nadia, you got that paper in there good?"

"Yes, my master."

"Good. I want you type—" He switched to English and Nadia pecked haltingly at the keyboard:

```
When she felt the ropes come off
Anya slowly stood up from the chair.
It was a relief to be able to move
freely again, a relief that she owed,
as she did all the good things to
come, to one man: Lord Ares. A light
came on in her eyes and she walked
slowly, gracefully toward him, her
arms outstretched. "My master," she
whispered throatily. She kissed him
slowly, deeply, took his hand and
said, "Come, my love. Let's get
married, so I can be your slave
forever."
```

Rachel's eyes were still closed when the ropes loosened. Okay, I don't really want to be his slave. So I'm still me. And it's not so bad, what he just said, is it? I can pretend I'm kissing Tommy. But how in heaven's name do you make "a light come on in your eyes?" Well, first you open them. She did so and smiled up at Ares, staring hard enough that his face blurred and she could replace it with Tommy's in her mind. "My master," she said, and coughed. That made it throaty, didn't it? Come on, it's just one little kiss, she told herself. And a few stupid words to say after that.

I'll go through with the ceremony and escape from his horrible palace tonight, or die trying.

Rachel stood up and Ares lunged at her. Startled, she stumbled backward over the chair, which fell over with a crash. Quickly, before he could try to kiss her again, she gasped, "Come, my slave. I'd love to get married so you can, uh, be mine forever."

Ares and Nadia both stared at her.

I messed up my lines somehow, and now he's going to kill me.

He barked out a laugh and clapped his hands together. Turning to Nadia, he said, "Amazing how well it works, ain't it?" Then he clasped his arm around Rachel's waist—she willed herself not to shudder—and continued, "Come, all Mars will wait—did have waited—*waiting* for our wedding."

He deserves to die for his grammar, if nothing else. They started for the door, Nadia meekly following behind.

♂

Twenty stories up, Jack fixed his gaze rigidly on the northern end of the stadium, where Anya was, so he could only see the field out of the right corner of his eye. The pyramid had been dismantled but had been followed by potentially even more distracting gymnastics involving pom-poms and other props, and he was in a cold sweat waiting for the cheerleaders to finish. At last, his peripheral vision told him the field was clear, and he turned. A troop of gaudily togaed individuals emerged in single file from a door on the opposite side of the fifty-yard line. Had he made the wrong choice of where to stand after all? He whipped out the little pair of binoculars he'd brought, regretting for a fraction of a second that he'd forgotten all about them during the assembly of the pyramid. *Concentrate!* A quick sweep was enough to reassure him that neither Ares nor Rachel were among the marchers, who were taking up positions in a loose circle around the center of the field. Three plainly dressed men were carrying large metal panels, which they quickly assembled into a small podium. A short, balding man in a scarlet tunic climbed this and stood facing Jack. Jack studied him through the binoculars. He was wearing an oddly-shaped orange cloth cap and holding a book in his right hand.

The preacher. A minute passed, then another. The crowd began to get louder. All at once a great cheer went up. Jack tensed and turned the binoculars toward the western end of the fifty-yard line, the side closest to where he was standing. There was definitely movement down there. He saw a woman's blond head emerge.

Blond? That can't be right. And she's wearing a red miniskirt. What woman wears red to her wedding, even on Mars? Then he spotted the back of Rachel's head, alive with coppery curls. She marched woodenly behind the other woman. Nadia, that was her name! Ares' much abused secretary. *What's he doing, marrying both of them at once?* Jack's finger tightened on the trigger as he saw the slicked-back black hair on the back of Ares' head. *C'mon you bastard...step away from Rachel just a little bit....*

Suddenly the crowd roared. Ares, Rachel, Nadia, and the men in togas all turned to the left, toward the northern end of the stadium. Jack swung his binoculars in that direction.

Anya walked with slow, measured paces toward the center of the field.

No! She took off her bandanna and shook out her long red hair.

He grabbed his radio. "ANYA! What are you doing?"

She flinched and tossed her radio to the ground.

Whatever else was happening, he still had a job to do. Jack swung his zap-gun around and trained it on Ares' forehead. "Lights out, Lord Ares," he whispered.

Abruptly the gun was wrenched away him and something cold pressed behind his ear.

"Don't move, Jack," Eddie said.

♂

On the field, the wedding party watched Anya's approach in stunned silence. Ares' gaze moved between her and Rachel. He opened his mouth, but the only sound that emerged was a gurgle.

Anya stood before Ares. "My master," she whispered throatily. "Come, my love. Let's get married, so I can be your slave forever." Her jade-green eyes were unfocused and unnaturally bright, and she wobbled as she walked.

Ares turned to Rachel, grabbed her arm and spun her around. "What this mean?" he demanded.

Rachel shook him off. "You got me, Johnny Marshall," she said in English. He staggered back. "I am not Princess Anya Olympulska. My name is Rachel Zilber, I'm the author of 'Zap-Gun Jack Flash and the Dame-Eating Monsters of Venus,' and I do *not* like what you've done to my story!"

She had to hand it to him, he recovered quickly. As Anya wobbled her way into his arms and the guards grabbed Rachel and forced her to her knees, Ares sneered and said, "Oh yeah? Well, who cares what *you* think? It ain't your story anymore, it's mine. Just watch," and he turned to Anya and bent her over backwards in a kiss, just as he had done with Nadia.

Rachel wanted to throw up. Anya trembled violently, but there was nothing she could do to help her. *If only I could get to the typewriter.* But the guards had tied her arms behind her again.

Ares straightened. "See? She's my obedient slave, just like I wrote her."

"Oh darling," Anya said.

"Yeah, what is it?" Ares stared at Rachel. "I'm just gonna kill this-here worthless imposter, then you and I—"

He crumpled to the ground. Anya lowered the zap gun she'd hit Ares with, and pointed it right at him. Blood streamed from her ears, down her neck, soaking her shirt. She swayed on her feet, but the gun didn't waver. There was a light in her eyes, all right, but it wasn't a light of love.

"I shall be revenged," she said.

33

To Rachel, trussed like the chicken her mom used to serve for Passover every year, the crowd noise was just a physical presence, as easily pushed aside as the spreading numbness in her arms and legs. It was the following night—they'd been spared for twenty-four hours so that the growing eruption would have time to build to a point sufficiently dramatic for their immolation, hers and Anya's. They were tied to the same upright post in a cart that could only be described as a tumbrel, both wearing dresses that could only be described as scarlet parodies of wedding gowns, "the better to please Moloch," as a leering guard told them. Rachel knew the word *tumbrel* from reading about the French Revolution, and a fat lot of good the knowledge was doing her now. It didn't much matter whether you were sacrificed to Moloch or to liberty, equality, and fraternity. Dead was dead.

That wasn't Anya's view, of course. Rachel wished she could share Anya's seeming dreamy serenity in the face of death.

"We all have to die sometime, Rachel," she'd said as they were being tied up. "The main thing is to die well."

"I'd rather not die at all," Rachel had responded, provoking a snort from the bruiser who was manhandling her.

"Me either," Anya had whispered. She moaned quietly as they bound her to the post.

Her wrist. The guards had broken it wrestling the zap-gun away from her. The bleeding from her ears had stopped, but her speech was still slightly slurred.

Anya continued. "But the people will remember how we go to our deaths. Not all of them are with Ares, whatever you see and hear out there now. Our martyrdom will be the match that kindles the flame of resistance. Lord Ares cannot kill the legend that will grow in their hearts.

"As for me, I'll be seeing Wanda soon, and I'll have to apologize for failing where she succeeded."

I wish I could share her faith. But it was miracle enough that Anya had been able to resist Johnny Marshall's attempt to rewrite her personality, wasn't it? It was just a pity that she'd felt compelled to make that little speech before shooting him. Wasn't it the bad guys who were supposed to make that mistake?

Now the procession was moving again. Rachel swam in and out of blackness, from the pain in her shoulders and the constant roar of filthy abuse. *It isn't about me, these people hate everyone who isn't a Martian, everyone who isn't* their kind *of Martian*. But the thought didn't help much, and her soul ached as much as her body.

"Rachel," Anya whispered, "let's sing."

"Sing? But Anya, nobody can hear us in all this racket."

"Doesn't matter. We're not singing for them." And she began to chant that marching song she had sung aboard the *Komodo Dragon*:

> *When Wanda sat upon the throne—Hurrah! Hurrah!*
> *No Martian had to fight alone—Hurrah! Hurrah!*
> *All Red Men joined the common cause*
> *To green the desert with God's laws...*

Anya's voice cut off with a grunt.

"Quiet back there," a deep voice growled, "you'll be singing soon enough, when the magma reaches you."

There was a squeal of feedback as Ares' loudspeaker came on in the royal "carriage" that drove slowly along in front of the tumbrel. This was a sleek red sports car modeled on a Lamborghini Johnny had once seen in a museum in Dallas. He started to chant, and the crowd joined in: *"Blood and fire! Blood and fire! We shall redeem you, holy Mars, in blood and fire!"*

Rachel wished she could cover her ears.

♂

Johnny smiled in the back seat of the carriage and waved languidly at the crowd with his right hand, holding Nadia tight with his left. She shivered. "See how the people love me," he said dreamily.

"Yes, master."

Not that they could see him returning their love, since the car had no sunroof. Johnny had paid a visit to the museum at Dealey Plaza just after his visit to the Museum of Automotive History. No way was he going to give some Martian Lee Harvey Oswald a chance to get off a shot at him. Not that Nadia was likely to weep over him, and he gave her a playful punch on the arm. She jerked, hit her head on the car door, and lay stunned on the real thistlecat-leather seat. Johnny pressed the intercom button and told the driver to stop, then pushed the loudspeaker button again. "People of Mars!" he boomed in his most impressive voice. Even through the soundproofing he could hear the tidal roar of the crowd rise in volume and pitch. Pretty girls pushed their way through to where the cops stood with linked arms. The police had standing orders to let them through. Ares examined them and licked his lips. He was getting tired of Nadia and her disgusting bruises anyway; when the day's work was done, he'd have the hangman dispose of her and select one of these love-lies to be chief concubine in her place. But there'd be plenty of time for all that later. He thumbed the megaphone button again.

"People of Mars! The master race of the Solar System! The day of destiny has arrived!" The noise out there must be deafening. Suddenly the car shook. There were screams in the crowd. Nadia moaned and rubbed at her fresh bruises. Johnny sat up straight and tapped the driver on the shoulder. "What was that?" he asked, in English.

The driver was listening intently to his earpiece. "Nothing to worry about, my lord. It's just a marsquake, because of the eruption."

Johnny smiled and leaned back. "Thanks, Eddie." *What a great special effect for my speech!* He thumbed the button yet again. "The gods are with us!" he shouted. The crowd was going into a frenzy. "To keep their favor, the Princess Pretender Anya and an alien girl spy shall be sacrificed to the god Moloch, he who lives deep within Olympus Mons!"

He grinned again, then signaled Eddie to open a secret panel that gave a view of the trunk, in the front of the car. Jack lay there helplessly, his arms and legs tied with *kruckle* bean stalks and a thick strip of electrical tape plastered over his mouth. Johnny leaned forward. "Sorry, friend, but the folks don't get so excited about seeing a guy thrown into a live volcano, know what I mean? But you've got a front-row seat, and after-wards, my professional hangman will give you his personal attention. Do I know how to take care of my friends or what?"

Jack didn't even try to reply, so Johnny used Annabelle to give him a nasty burn on the back of his right hand.

♂

Rachel was glad Anya couldn't see the flash of the zap-gun inside the carriage, nor Jack's involuntary flinch. She longed with all her heart to shout abuse back at the crowd, and wouldn't have minded if someone had thrown something hard at her and knocked her cold, but she didn't want them hurting Anya or denying her the martyr's death she desired. It was no good wishing for absolute freedom to do as you pleased. To the last moment of your life, you had responsibilities to other people, as her parents had taught her. If you didn't believe that, you ended up like Johnny Marshall, a black hole in the shape of a human being. So maybe there was something she could take with her to her death, after all. She closed her eyes and felt the tumbrel tilt as it reached the edge of town and started climbing the mountain.

♂

On the other side of Olympus Mons, Moishe's mule cart bumped along a neglected track. He had made a lengthy detour around the western side of the mountain, and Gun had spent the extra hours working feverishly to put together a glider from the pieces she'd assembled after the disaster at the stadium. When she'd stumbled back to Kris and Margo's home the night before, the only mercy was that she hadn't had to tell them anything—they had watched the proceedings live on the telescreen at the Thescnut Tree Café. Waking out of a dead sleep in a panic hours later, she found Moishe, Jim, Tomasz, and Sonya all gathered around her. As soon as Agnieszka had come running back from the Lvovinsk town square with the terrible news, all four had set out for Krakowicz in Moishe's cart.

"Fantastic," Gun rasped. "This isn't a rescue mission, it's an ethnic joke. A Belter, two Jews, a Martian, and a Venusian set out in a mule cart...."

Without Jim, she could never have built the glider. His army buddy Adam, who lived just a few blocks from the Gdanskis and was home on leave, donated tools and even aluminum struts for the frame. Moishe drove his cart to an army surplus store and traded what was left of his wares for several yards of polyester cloth for the wings. Tomasz and Sonya collected the other odds and ends Gun needed. By the time they finished, it was after lunch and Moishe declared that they had to leave right away to have any chance of reaching the mountain by sundown, when the "auto-daffy" was supposed to begin.

Although the others had done a great job of getting her the materials she needed, their attempts to help with the assembly drove Gun into yelling at them to let her do it herself.

Jim had no problem with sitting back and watching—"I'm sure a big part of the reason they sentenced me to death was that Sarge couldn't watch me try to assemble a rifle even once more," Jim said—but Tommy looked hurt and Sonya started to cry.

Gun just shrugged. "You can both be big babies and distract me, or you can let me try to rescue our friends!" she snapped.

Sonya shut up. Jim opened his mouth, then closed it.

Gun grunted and tugged at the straps and struts, making sure everything was nice and tight—it would be embarrassing to have a wing fall off a few hundred feet above a seething cauldron of magma. Then she checked that her blasting caps hung loosely around her tool-belt, where she could easily reach them. No self-respecting Belter went *anywhere* without a supply of high explosives sufficient to tunnel her way out of a massive cave-in.

She sat back on her heels. *I'm as ready as I'm ever going to be.* "How we doin' there, Moishe?"

He pointed at a plume of steam shooting up from what looked like a massive rockfall, though it was difficult to get a sense of scale in this rubbled landscape. "That looks like the sort of geyser you told me to search for, does it not, Miss Gunnarson?"

"Looks okay," she grunted. "And you should be able to hide the cart behind those rocks. Find a nice cave and makes yourselves comfortable until I get back. Here," she said, handing him a bag of oats Margo had given her, "that ought to keep your poor beasties happy." As the cart approached the geyser, Gun turned to Tomasz and Sonya with an imitation of her stepmom Barb's most fearsome scowl, the one she used when she caught young Sherilynn messing around with her miner's rig. "You two squirts are gonna stay here and keep Moishe and Jim company till I get back, you got that? Kids like you have no business playing hero. If you let this annoying little brat come to harm, Tommy, you'll have me to answer to. Is that clear?"

"Yes ma'am," Tomasz said.

Sonya piped up, "If we both get killed, how's Tommy gonna answer to you?"

Gun put her face up to the little girl's and snarled, "I'll tear his ghost limb from limb! Yours too! Now be good!" She hopped out of the cart and climbed to the top of a pile of rocks overlooking the geyser, dragging the makeshift glider behind her.

♂

On the top of the rocks, she adjusted her straps, stuck her finger out to test the air currents, then leapt lightly off the precipice. At first she plummeted, causing Jim, Tomasz, and Sonya to gasp while Moishe mumbled a Hebrew prayer. But then the wings caught a powerful thermal updraft and Gun began to ascend in a slow, wide spiral that tightened as the glider soared farther and farther aloft.

When she was just a speck in the sky Tomasz turned to Sonya and said, "Ready?" She nodded and he offered her his hand. Together they jumped off the cart and ran upslope, dodging the geyser and rubble piles.

"Hey!" Moishe shouted after them. He shook his fist. "Come back here you *vilde chayes*, you wild animals! Get back here this instant!"

Sonya turned and thumbed her nose at him and Jim, who merely sighed and rolled his eyes.

Moishe plopped down in his seat with an undignified grunt. "Well, at least someone listens to me, right, Shimmie and Azri?" he said to the mules, who turned and looked at him with their large dark eyes. "Snack?" he said, offering the bag of oats. Azri practically took his arm off lunging for it.

♂

High overhead, Gun whooped and hollered. The last time she'd felt this exhilarated was when she owned her own sleek little prospecting ship and spent all her time dodging the tiny, dangerous little space rocks that were her home and her living.

With a joyous shout she christened the glider *Deadman's Bluff II*. The landscape below her was a vision of the end of the end of the world, all geysers, fumaroles and rubble. Clearly the enormous volcano was waking up, and it was in a lively mood. The heat from a miniature caldera sent her soaring higher, ever higher. *Don't get carried away*. The Martian atmosphere was famously thin, even at canal level, and she wouldn't do Rachel, Anya, and Jack much good if she blacked out for want of oxygen. But it wouldn't harm them any if she did a few fancy aviators' tricks on the way to save their asses, would it? No, it wouldn't, and she executed a figure eight, a loop-the-loop, and a dizzying dive to within yards of the ground, followed by a swooping ascent that took her higher than the mountain's peak, now just a few miles away.

"I'll get there in plenty of time to save the day!" she giggled, wondering if the lack of oxygen was getting to her. It was certainly making her see things, because down below, picking their way daintily through the rubble, was what looked like an enormous herd of orange-and-white-striped tigers the size of the woolly mammoths she'd once seen a drawing of, with dandelions gone to seed where their heads should have been. "Ha ha, what a ridiculous hallucination! That's just perfect! And what makes it even better, oh my gosh, that looks like Tomasz and Sonya walking right up to them! Author! Author!"

♂

Tomasz stopped abruptly and stood very still when he spotted the herd of wild thistlecats. He knew all about them, because Dad had been an amateur zoologist and used to take him camping in search of the beasts, which were growing rarer and rarer outside of zoos and government-controlled farms. They weren't naturally hostile to people, but they'd learned to be wary, and if you got too close and sparked a stampede, you could get trampled.

"What are those?" Sonya asked, pointing.

"Shh! Keep your voice down. Thistlecats don't like loud noises!" He'd forgotten that Sonya was from Earth. He looked wildly around for a rock to hide behind, but they were standing on a field of black ash. To his horror, Sonya marched straight up to the nearest of the thistlecats, a calf judging by its size, and stood there staring up at it. He wanted to pull her to safety, but his feet wouldn't move. "Sonya! Get back here!" he hissed.

"Shh, stop talking! I can't hear what Jummela is saying!" she replied, her gaze fixed on the huge animal.

"What are you talking about? Who's Jummela?" He gulped as two adult thistlecats wandered over. They looked big enough to use his old school for a litterbox. Not that that would be any great loss, but....

"Now you really have to be quiet, her parents are both talking and I can't listen to so many people at once," Sonya said in a tone that reminded him of his Mom when she was annoyed.

Tomasz swallowed again, his throat dry. Could Sonya actually be communicating somehow with the thistlecats? There was no record of anybody being able to do that. Well, no *scientific* record, anyway. Tomasz's parents were good Wandanians and had taught him all the legends, but Dad had made it clear that they were just that, legends meant to help you learn the difference between right and wrong. That's what the story of Wanda and the thistlecat that had its claws caught in the cleft of the rock was all about, wasn't it? There hadn't really been a thistlecat that called out to Lady Wanda in a voice like a scared small child, "Please save me, oh great lady!" Had there?

Now Sonya turned around and looked at him so seriously he knew she couldn't possibly be pulling his leg. Her eyes flashed blue in the evening sun. "They will help us, they say, to repay us for what Wanda did for their ancestor. Even though the rest of you are deaf to their plain thoughts. But we have to hurry. Ares has led the procession almost to the top of the mountain, which is getting ready to blow! We'll never get there in time if we try to walk. So the thistlecats have offered to...."

♂

High above, Gun broke into uncontrollable laughter. "Oh, that's too much!" she chortled. "Now them kiddos are actually riding on the backs of them Martian super-tigers! Wheeeeeeeeeeeee! If this is oxygen deprivation, I have to try it more often!" And she soared aloft on a thermal updraft, higher and higher, heading for the yawning red mouth of the main caldera directly ahead.

♂

Rachel struggled to stay conscious as the procession ascended the mountain. Only Johnny's praetorian guard and the hardiest members of the huge jeering crowd that had lined the streets of Krakowicz had followed them. Why was the sun setting, but the day growing hotter? The mountain rumbled. Oh.

The procession rounded a rocky promontory as tall as a five-story building and a reddish-orange lake stretched to either side as far as the eye could see.

A sea of lava. Waves sloshed and sent sprays of molten rock leaping dozens of feet into the air. The Lamborghini spun around, coming to rest with its front bumper inches from the tumbrel. Gravel hit Rachel in the face and she cried out.

"What's happening?" Anya murmured.

Rachel's terror was so all-encompassing that suddenly she seemed not to feel any fear at all, as if she'd been running through a pelting rainstorm for so long she'd stopped noticing she was wet. Her mouth felt dry and yet sticky, like a bottle of glue that has been left open overnight.

"We're here," she managed to say at last. "The crater. We've stopped moving." The heat was all around her, overwhelming, reminding her stupidly of going to the baker with Mom on a Friday morning. But she forgot all about her discomfort when the hood of the car flew up and she saw Jack lying in the trunk, looking up at her helplessly. She wanted to cry. Then she saw Johnny's shiny leather boots.

"How y'all doing?" he said jovially. "This is some eruption, ain't it? Hot enough for ya? 'Course, back in the Texas Panhandle, we call this a mild spring day."

Rachel tried to create some spit. Anya seemed to be murmuring a prayer.

"Nobody feels like laughin'? That's okay, you'll be screaming soon enough," Johnny said, and, reaching into the trunk with both hands, dragged Jack out, propped him up against the left front wheel. "Got a decent view of the lava, Jack-Ass?" Ares asked. "I do want you to see everything. And I mean everything."

Rachel finally found enough spit to hit Ares, narrowly missing his eye.

He chuckled. "Now sweetiepie, I wouldn't do that if I was you," he said, reaching into his pocket and flicking open a huge knife. Jack threw himself around, straining against his bonds, but Johnny only cut Rachel and Anya free. They both slumped to the ground, moaning at the agony of returning blood flow.

Bubbling magma drowned out most other noise, but Rachel thought she heard the crowd of soldiers and gawkers who had followed them give out with a cheer.

Johnny bowed deeply. "Come on, girls," he said, yanking Rachel and Anya to their feet. "Moloch's gettin' hungry." He smiled broadly. "Can you believe these saps believe that horseshit? Still and all, it *is* gonna be fun shovin' you two stuck-up dollies into the drink. Looks like the magma's on the boil, running high, all ready for you. In you go, then." He started to drag them toward the edge. Something exploded behind him.

♂

"Ha ha! Take that, you sumbitch!" Gun chortled as she soared and dipped on the powerful currents of hot air churned up by the lava lake far below her. She had watched Ares' sports car do its dramatic fishtail at the edge of the caldera, but had held back from dropping her little asteroid-mining bombs in case the thing was armor plated. Which was just as well, when Johnny dragged Jack out of the trunk. As Jack had found back at the stadium, it was virtually impossible to get a clear shot at Johnny that would not endanger his hostages, so she settled for keeping him from the edge of the caldera. The two mining charges Gun threw served this purpose admirably, if temporarily, and she had the satisfaction of watching him reel back in surprise. He kept his grip on both Rachel and Anya, however, and his chauffeur got out of the car and joined the mob of bodyguards and onlookers who surged forward.

Time for some more bombs. One landed at the chauffeur's feet and several others exploded in a neat little row before the leading edge of the mob. It was like kicking over an anthill, the one activity she'd really enjoyed on her one and only to visit to Earth, when she was twelve.

"Scurry, scurry, you red cowards!" she shouted with glee. Someone fired a zap-gun at her, but the normally invisible beam was an easy-to-see bright orange slash in the ash-filled air and she dodged it easily. "Missed me!" Another beam flashed nearby, and another. Time to offload the rest of her bombs and hope the confusion she caused would give her friends enough time to escape. She started to take aim, but jerked in surprise when a herd of those Martian tigers appeared around an outcropping of rock and began to charge toward the mob, which broke and started running away, back down the mountain. Were those two tiny human figures mounted on the backs of the two lead animals, right behind their bizarre thistlelike heads? Was it actually possible that she *hadn't* hallucinated what she'd seen earlier?

Then something enormous grabbed her right wing, and she spiraled downward, out of control.

♂

The first explosion took Johnny Marshall completely by surprise, but he tightened his grip on his two captives and looked wildly around for its source. He finally looked up, and gasped. What was a large bat doing here, silhouetted against the burning sky? He heard a car door slam and Eagle-Eye Eddie came running around the car.

"Shoot that thing while I get rid of these two!" Johnny yelled.

Eddie nodded and unsheathed his zap-gun. But he'd only got off a single wild shot before someone hit him from behind and he crashed into the gravel. Jack had wriggled free and was now wrestling with his erstwhile friend.

Johnny raised his clenched fists in frustration and shouted. *Wait! I'm no longer holding anybody's hands!* Then two red-haired hellcats attacked him, trying to push him into the crater. He threw a punch and one of them toppled over. The other one threw herself on him, shouting about revenge, but a fist in the gut sent her reeling back.

He staggered, panting. Suddenly a vision stood before him, a vision in a red miniskirt. "Nadia," he gasped. She looked as if she had just stepped out of the shower, all damp and sweaty. *Maybe I won't have her whacked, after all.* "Thank G—thank Moloch!" Johnny exclaimed. "Git that typewriter out of the car. We got some serious rewritin' to do."

She just stood there, looking casually at her clothes.

"C'mon, you silly b—I mean, Nadia, this ain't no time to worry 'bout your outfit!" *What's she so interested in her stockings for anyhow…wait a sec, that's where I ripped them when I was smackin' her around a bit.…*

She looked up and smiled, and Johnny let out a gasp of relief. "Anything you say, Dzhonny Marshall," she lisped. Then she thrust out her open right hand, and shoved him over the rim into the sea of magma.

♂

Jack stood over the unconscious Eddie, who was bleeding from the temples. *Hope I didn't kill him, but there's another guy who most certainly* does *need killing.…* Turning, he was just in time to see Nadia push Ares into the caldera. A soft *gloop*, a muffled scream, and he was gone, just like that. Jack stared, then staggered away. Where were Rachel and Anya? They hadn't gone over the edge.… No, that was Rachel on the ground—at least, he thought it was Rachel—it had to be Rachel, now sitting up slowly and holding her hand to her head, because the other red-haired beauty had thrown herself into his arms with a cry and was kissing him manically.

The blood pounded louder and louder in Jack's ears as Anya settled in for a really long, deep kiss. But it wasn't his heart, or even the erupting volcano. Something roared, something as loud as a rocket coming in for a landing. It actually *was* a rocket coming in for a landing. Anya broke off the kiss and together they stared as it touched down, its hatch opened, and Karolla and a dozen other stout, furry N'Bialy bounded out onto the peak of Olympus Mons.

"Where is Ares, tell us right away! We have come to spoil his day!" they chorused in unison.

$$\male$$

When Gun, Tomasz, and Sonya walked to the landing site a few moments later—the Belter leaning on the two "kids" for support, having twisted her ankle when two thistlecats caught her falling glider—they were amazed to find Jack, Anya, and Rachel, all with various wounds that needed immediate attention, rolling around on the cinder-strewn rocky ground laughing their heads off.

34

"I don't think I can do this," Anya kept saying. "How can I do this? I'm still a kid. I don't know anything about running a planet!"

"You can't possibly do worse than Johnny Marshall," Katie said dryly from her wheelchair. Thumper purred in her lap, and she scratched him behind the ears.

Lady Diana, Anya's long-lost aunt, sighed. "Shut up and get that coronation dress on. If it doesn't fit, we'll have to take it to a tailor in the Bazaar I know."

Rachel wished they would *all* shut up. Only three days had passed since her close encounter of the igneous kind, and she was still feeling a bit rocky. And everybody kept yapping! While they were still within spitting distance of the caldera, Karolla had felt compelled to explain in heroic couplets how the N'Bialy had gotten hold of a rocket. ("It's thanks to Afro-Port's corruption foul / That we could fly to make the tyrant howl." Somebody with a better grasp of English verse than Rachel would have to judge whether "boxing in" was really an acceptable rhyme for "oxygen.") Sonya and Tomasz felt compelled to explain to Gun, who was threatening to magmify them for disobeying her even though she couldn't even stand up without assistance, that they hadn't been taking an insane risk because the thistlecats were telepaths. Eddie was explaining to everybody at the top of his lungs that he had no memory whatsoever of the past week, but everybody was avoiding him because his eyes were still too bright and Lila the Intrepid Interplanetary Interviewer had attached herself to his hip and was trying to "smooch away your widdle boo-boos." Probably the thistlecats, which were still milling around, were trying to explain something to somebody, but luckily nobody except Sonya could "hear" them.

Rachel looked forward to the ambulance ride for the peace and quiet, but the hubbub only grew when they reached the hospital and were instantly mobbed by a million Martians who had been secret Loyalists all along. *Sure you were.* They pushed up against her gurney and even tore little pieces off her sacrifice-to-Moloch outfit for souvenirs until the nurses finally chased them away. Even losing consciousness didn't give her much relief from all the voices, because they pursued her into her dreams.

Everyone kept coming in and talking, talking, talking while Rachel and Anya tried to rest and recuperate in a private hospital ward—the princess had insisted that "my most loyal friend" be allowed to stay with her, which brought tears to Rachel's eyes. But they never had a moment of peace. First thing the next morning, Gun shouldered her way in, elbowing aside an officious Martian Secret Service guy, to give them her best regards and tell them she was getting the hell out of Dodge.

"But I was planning to ennoble you," Anya said.

Gun rolled her eyes. "Lady Gun? Don't be ridiculous."

"Won't you even stay for my coronation?"

"Meaning no disrespect, Your Highness, but I've already booked passage on the first flight for Ceres from Olympus Spaceport. It's in two hours, which is one hundred twenty minutes too long for me. I'd rather work as an indentured rockhound for twenty years than put up with one more day of being treated like a hero on Mars."

"I can see you've made up your mind. I admire that. I kind of wish I were going with you," Anya half-whispered. "You'll be so free out there."

"That's the idea, Highness, yes." As soon as Gun limped off to catch her flight, Anya called over the nearest flunky and ordered him to have a brand-new top-of-the-line asteroid mining ship waiting for Lady Sherilynn Gunnarson as soon as she stepped onto Ceres, all paid for by the Royal Exchequer.

"It's good to be the queen," Rachel murmured.

Anya raised a half-burnt eyebrow. "Given the history of the world, it's kind of hard to say that. Helping other people is the only pleasure I'm going to get out of this job, I can tell you."

As if to confirm this prediction, a portly individual wearing a purple-edged toga bustled into the room. "Forgive me, Your Highness, but I must inform you that you are not permitted to disburse funds from the Exchequer, nor indeed to issue any other orders, until you are crowned queen."

"Well then, crown me now," Anya said, sitting up in bed and attempting to straighten her hospital gown. "Let's get it over with."

"Ah, you see, Your Highness, I'm afraid it's not as simple as that. There's the matter of your age…a regent will have to be appointed.…"

Anya directed a ferocious frown at him. "And this regent would, of course, be yourself, Senator Syzygy."

"Well, myself and the other eight members of the Privy Council.…"

"Who meet in the outhouse?" Rachel said. If nobody was going to let her get any sleep, she could at least ruin their day right back.

Senator Syzygy jerked as if someone had goosed him and glared at Rachel, but the effect was more ridiculous than intimidating. The senator's colleagues piled into the wardroom after him, and the air was soon thick with obscure lawyer talk, which grew louder and louder until they were interrupted by a loud clang. Anya had thrown her bedpan against the wall, splashing Senator Syzygy and two or three others.

"Shut up! Shut up, all of you!" she yelled, clapping her hands over her ears. "If you all want to be a Regency Council that badly, you can do it! And you can throw me straight into the boiling heart of Olympus Mons while you're at it!"

Wow, and I thought only we Jews used that kind of guilt trip to get our way!

"I'll happily abdicate, you hear me!" Anya shouted.

"'*Abdication*, noun. An act whereby a sovereign attests his sense of the high temperature of the throne.' Ambrose Bierce, *The Devil's Dictionary*," a familiar voice drawled from somewhere around waist level.

Senator Syzygy stopped swiping at his toga and yelped as Katie ran over his foot with her wheelchair. His cry of pain mingled with Rachel and Anya's shouts of joy, and the princess ordered the scandalized senators out of the room in a tone that threatened decapitation as the price of non-compliance. When the three of them were alone, Katie said, "I had a feeling you two redheads were gonna need my help. It ain't goin' well, is it, Anya?"

"It sure don't...*doesn't*...feel like it," the princess groaned. "These senators are trying to keep me from becoming queen on the grounds that I'm too young!"

"And your scatological argument didn't do the trick, I take it," Katie said. She'd finally hit on a word Rachel didn't know, and when Katie saw her puzzled expression she smiled and said, "*Reductio ad poop*, that's what I mean."

"Ah."

"Who does the actual crowning?" Katie asked, turning back to Anya.

"Hmm? Oh, it has to be a member of the royal family. But my parents are dead, and there's no one else...."

"Your Aunt Diana," Rachel reminded her. Anya looked at her with such round eyes it was hard not to laugh. Finding Diana took both Flash brothers two full days, and when she did show up, carrying a tarnished silver coronet that looked suspiciously as if it had come from a pawn shop and a pink "coronation gown" that gave Rachel the willies, it looked so much like Margo's wedding dress, Anya had an attack of nerves at the very idea of being queen.

"I should let Syzygy and the others be regents!" Anya moaned. "They at least have experience in government..."

"...having licked all three Ares' boots, some of them..." Katie said.

"...and the problems they left behind are too big to solve!" Anya waved some papers around with her good hand. "Three-quarters of our farmland is a dustbowl because the canal system is a ruin. Three or four thousand offworld mercenaries—no one knows how many there are, exactly—are running around loose because Ares wanted the baddest criminals in the Solar System to train his army of conquest. I can send all the draftees home, but there are no jobs for them. Then there's all the no-good sons and grandsons and third-cousins-twice-removed of Ares I and II, who'll be just waiting for me to screw up so they can have themselves proclaimed king. Not to mention those damned senators! I can't trust anyone!"

"You can trust us, Anya," Rachel said shyly, reaching out to touch her hand.

Anya smiled through tears. "I know that. But we're not enough all by ourselves to fix a whole planet! It's hopeless!"

Katie cleared her throat. "There's no one else who can even try to solve all those problems, Anya."

"I know," Anya said, looking at the floor.

"It's your duty, Anya," Diana said.

"I know!"

Then Rachel had a brainstorm. "I read a story by Mark Twain once," she said. "It was called 'The Prince and the Pauper.'"

Katie snapped her fingers "Of course!"

"And if we just...."

"Yes, yes, YES!"

Anya looked from Katie to Rachel and back again, her eyes narrowing. "This doesn't involve any 'interdimensional dynamicalizers' or Correctors, does it?"

"Nope, nothin' like that," Katie said. "It's real simple, Your Highness—sorry, I mean Anya. What if you could take a day or a week off from bein' queen, every now and then, and live as an ordinary Martian? Rachel could take your place, *and no one would know the difference.*"

Anya swiveled her head and looked at Rachel, whose face had more or less resumed its normal shape now that the swelling was down. She jumped up and took her double's hands, pulling her to her feet. "Thank you! Thank you, Rachel," she cried, kissing her on both cheeks.

Don't blush. No more blushing, ever. Queens don't blush.

There was the sound of a throat being discreetly cleared. All four women turned and saw Jack standing in the doorway, looking slightly embarrassed. "Ladies, I'm sorry to interrupt," he said, "but I need a moment alone with Anya."

"Can't it wait till after I'm crowned, Jack? Sir Jack, I mean," Anya said with a sly smile. But his expression was somber.

"I'm afraid not, princess. Rachel, I hope you're all right to—"

"I'm dying to get out of this room, actually," Rachel said quickly. Katie and Diana followed her out into the hallway, scattering a knot of nurses who straightened up and tried to look busy.

"How's your father?" Rachel asked Katie after a pause.

"Hmm? Oh, Dad's much better, thanks. He and Mom seem to be pretty serious about homesteading here on Mars. I made 'em a deal—I'll help out on the farm soon as I'm better, till I'm ready to go to college."

"That's good," Rachel said. "Yeah, real good." She was starting to pick up Katie's bad speech habits. Dad would've killed her if he heard her abusing "Shakespeare's language" like that. *Oh, well.* "Oh, there's one more thing I wanted to ask you. How's what's-his-name doing?"

"Who, Teddy or Jerzy?" A gleam came into Katie's eye. "They're both good. By which I mean, really bad, of course. And I think Sonya's giving them even more ideas about tricks to pull. Why, just yesterday Mrs. Gdanska came back in from shopping and they had a whole bucket full of that nasty red desert dust propped up over the door. You should've seen the look of relief on her face when my parents said they'd take Sonya in, which is one reason *I* plan to spend as little time at home as—"

"I don't care about Sonya!!"

"Oh, you're asking about *what's* his name. I guess you mean *Tommy.* Tommy's well. Fit as a fiddle."

Damn you, Katie. "I'm sure he's got lots to do helping out his mother...with all those wild little kids running around...."

"He sure is busy. Yep." Pause. "Real busy. What with chasing after them kids, helping his mom, and asking every two seconds, 'How's Rachel? Is she all right? When am I gonna see her again?'"

"Kaitlyn Webb, I don't know whether to slug you or hug you!"

"Neither, please, Rachel. My ribs...."

At that moment the door of the wardroom swung open, hitting the wall with a gentle bump, and Jack strode out, his expression a blank.

"Jack, what? Wait a minute...." said Rachel.

"Hey, stop a second...." Katie wheeled around.

At the end of the corridor, he half turned and waved, grinning his crooked grin. He waved a zap-gun around and mouthed, "I got back Annabelle!" Then he was gone. Rachel hurried back into the wardroom, closely followed by Katie and Diane.

Anya stood beside the bed in her coronation gown, picking lint off the sleeves. When she looked up, her eyes were dry. "We'd better get started," she said briskly. "Rachel, you and Katie are witnesses.... Diana, you have the crown?"

Five minutes later Senator Syzygy bustled into the room, looking more pompous than ever. "Your Highness, I have news that will please you. The Regency Council has decided that you may ascend to the throne on your next birthday, instead of—"

"It's Your Majesty, now."

"I beg your pardon?"

"I am your queen, now."

"But that's impossible—the Wandanian Charter is quite clear that if no members of the royal family survive, the Regency Council—"

Diana cleared her throat. Syzygy glanced at her without interest, then did a double take.

"It's good that you are here, Senator," Anya said. "As representative of the Council, you can take down my first orders as queen."

"I've got a pencil and paper for you, Senator, if you need 'em," Katie said, handing the dazed Syzygy the items in question.

"Excellent!" said Anya. "Item the first. The so-called 'Master Race University' in Krakowicz is to be restored to its proper name, Wandanian University. Item the second, for services rendered the crown, full royal scholarships are awarded to Lady Rachel Zilber and Lady Kaitlyn Webb—"

"Webb has two b's in it," said Katie, who was peering over Syzygy's shoulder.

"Item the third, Kaitlyn's parents, Michael and Mary Webb, are hereby awarded a land grant of prime canal-front, volcanic soil property north of Krakowicz. Item the fourth, all political prisoners are to be released immediately, and the Valles Marineris 'concentration camps' are to be dissolved effective today...."

There was a long list of other items that required immediate attention, and Rachel's mind wandered. She thought about her parents, and how they had planned to move to Palestine and "make the desert bloom" to build a Jewish state. Well, Mars had plenty of deserts that could use irrigation, and it even had a few Jews. She doubted Mom and Dad would have approved of her consorting with royalty, much less accepting a title, but nothing was perfect.

"...and that's all, I think, for now," Anya was saying. "Did I leave out anything? Lady Kaitlyn?"

Katie whispered something in Anya's ear. "Oh, of course! Item the twenty-fifth, a draft is to be drawn on the Royal Exchequer in the amount of 432 Solar zlotys and 65 Solar groszys, payable to one Adrian Josephus, a barkeep in Aphrodite Port, Venus."

♂

A Martian year later, Rachel bent over a detailed map of the West Tharsis canal system, conferring with Kris Gdanski and four other engineers about the most urgent repairs to be made, when Katie burst into the room. Her breath came in gasps and sweat streamed down her face, as if she'd raced her wheelchair at top speed, all the way from her parents' farm.

"I have to talk to you *right now*," Katie said, and only then seemed to notice that she and Rachel weren't alone in the room. "Your Majesty," she added, with only the faintest trace of sarcasm.

Rachel and Kris exchanged a quick glance. He was the only other person in the room who was in on the secret: that Lady Rachel, not Queen Anya, was giving her official counsel about the repair of the canal system. She was well qualified for it, seeing that she was majoring in canal engineering at Wandanian University. Anya had been delighted at her choice. "I haven't got a head for science, Rachel," she confessed.

"That's all right, you're royalty. You're supposed to be useless," Rachel said, narrowly dodging the ornate cushion the princess threw at her. Not that she really minded studying canal engineering instead of physics as she'd once dreamed of doing. It actually involved a lot of physics, she told herself. And when she needed a break from her studies, Tomasz could usually take a break from *his* studies to take her out for frozen luftberries, the Martian equivalent of ice cream.

Rachel looked at Kris, Kris looked at Rachel, and she said in her best imperial tone, "Would everyone please leave except Mr. Gdanski and Lady Kaitlyn." The other engineers quickly complied, although not without several curious glances at Katie, who was clutching her chest while Rachel looked on with concern.

"Katie, what the hell!" Rachel said, as soon as the door closed. "You shouldn't have raced down here like that. You know Dr. Kaczynski said if you injure your ribs again, you can forget about ever walking!...."

"Don't worry about me. I'm fine," Katie gasped. "It's Sonya! She's been kidnapped."

ABOUT THE AUTHOR

Martin Berman-Gorvine is the author of two previous science fiction novels: *36* (Livingston Press, 2012), and, as Martin Gidron, of *The Severed Wing* (Livingston Press, 2002), which received the 2002 Sidewise Award for Alternate History (Long Form) at the International Science Fiction Convention in Toronto in 2003. His short story "Palestina," set in an alternate history in which Israel lost its war of independence, was published in Interzone magazine's May/June 2006 issue, and was a finalist for the Sidewise Award (Short Form), and his short story "The Tallis" appeared in Jewish Currents magazine, May 2002. He is a professional journalist, currently serving as a reporter for the Bureau of National Affairs newsletter *Human Resources Report*. His website is www.martinbermangorvine.com, his Facebook page is www.facebook.com/martingorvine, and his musings on politics and life can be found at http://rebmordechaiofchelm.blogspot.com. He lives in the suburbs of Washington, D.C. with his wife, two children, two orange tabby cats, two shy kittens, and a sort of Muppet dog.

www.ingramcontent.com/pod-product-compliance
Lightning Source LLC
Chambersburg PA
CBHW020802250626
47155CB00003B/1171